The Art of the Turkish Tale

The Art of the Turkish Tale

Volume One

Barbara K. Walker

Illustrated by Helen Siegl

Texas Tech University Press
1990

Volume One

Printed in the United States of America

This book was set in Berkeley Old Style Book and printed on acid-free paper
that meets the guidelines for permanence and durability of the Committee on
Production Guidelines for Book Longevity of the Council on Library Resources.∞

Cover and jacket art by Helen Siegl
Design by Cameron Poulter

Library of Congress Cataloging-in-Publication Data

Walker, Barbara K.
      The art of the Turkish tale / Barbara K. Walker ; illustrations by
   Helen Siegl.
         p.   cm.
      ISBN 0-89672-228-7 + (v1)
      1. Folk literature, Turkish.   I. Siegl, Helen.   II. Title.
   PL246.W35   1990
   398.2'09561—dc20   90-39477
                                                                      CIP

90 91 92 93 94 95 96 97 98 99 / 9 8 7 6 5 4 3 2 1

Texas Tech University Press
Lubbock, Texas 79409-1037 USA

In memory of Neriman Hızır,
our beloved Ayşe Abla,
radio storyteller to the Turkish nation

Contents

Foreword

Turkish Tales
Fun and Fantasy for All Ages

In Anatolia's culture, oral literature has played a vivid role since the earliest times. Aesop came from Phrygia, whose capital, Gordium, stood on a site not far from Ankara, the capital of modern Turkey. Homer was probably born and reared near present-day İzmir and wandered up and down the Aegean coast amassing the tales and legends that came to be enshrined in his *Iliad* and *Odyssey*.

Several millennia of the narrative arts have bequeathed to Asia Minor a dazzling treasury—creation myths, Babylonian stories, the Epic of Gilgamesh, Hittite tales, Biblical lore, Greek and Roman myths, Armenian and Byzantine anecdotes. The peninsula's mythical and historical ages nurtured dramatic accounts of deities, kings, heroes, and lovers. Pagan cults, ancient faiths, the Greek pantheon, Judaism, Roman religion, Christianity, Islam, mystical sects, and diverse spiritual movements left behind an inexhaustible body of legends and moralistic stories that survived throughout the centuries in their original forms or in many modified versions.

Anatolia witnessed—and took delight in narrating—the episodes of Zeus, the wealth of Croesus, Alexander's cutting the Gordian knot, Darius's building a bridge of rafts across the Bosphorus, and Leonardo da Vinci's contemplating a bridge linking Asia and Europe. It reveled in the escapades of the Argonauts in quest of the Golden Fleece, the dramas of the Trojan War, the touch of Midas, the adventures of the Amazons, Leander's swimming the Hellespont toward Hero, and Medea's murderous vengeance as well as the fertility rites of Cybele and the dithyrambic rituals of Dionysus.

If Carl Jung's "collective unconscious" has any validity, the memories of Byzas's founding Byzantium across the "land of the blind," Xenophon's marching with the Ten Thousand, Belisarius's fighting an ancient Moby Dick, Noah's Ark on Mt. Ararat, Nemesis's wreaking her vengeful havoc, Endymion in his eternal sleep, Xerxes' relentlessly pressing forward, Anacreon's turning out his lovely lyrics, Achilles and Agamemnon in their heroics, Julius Caesar's emerging victorious to return to Rome with the triumphant slogan "*Veni, vidi, vici,*" and so many other recollections and legends must still be alive in the Anatolian mind. That mind recalls and reveres the names of Virgin Mary, St. Paul, St. Peter, and St. Nicholas (later Santa Claus). It evokes Pericles, Hannibal, Hadrian, Augustus, Brutus—and Antony and Cleopatra.

The history of Asia Minor reverberates with countless vivid accounts left on monuments, temples, stelae, walls, and rocks, and also in the vivid books written by Herodotus, Strabo, Thucydides, Pausanius, Procopius, and a distinguished array of other historians. The Anatolian gallery is also peopled by Constantine, Justinian, and Theodora, who stand out as the most dramatic figures of Byzantine history, and whose episodes challenge the frontiers of the imagination. In the mnemonics of the region, the tales of the Crusaders still echo, as do their sabre rattlings.

The Turks stormed into Asia Minor in an exodus from Central Asia, wave upon wave, bringing on horseback their autochthonous culture rich in tales and legends, music and dances, poems, elegies, lullabies. Since their emergence "in time immemorial" (as official textbooks often boast) and certainly no later than the sixth century A.D., when Chinese sources started to mention their "powerful state" in Inner Asia, they had created a vibrant and rich literature, the written specimens of which date from the early eighth century, the earliest being the Orkhon inscriptions about the victories and defeats of the Göktürks. Although many Turkic communities were sedentary, the majority probably led a nomadic life. In fact, the Göktürk state, which is often referred to as an empire, was a mobile confederacy of nomadic tribes.

Oral literature—a hallmark of nomad culture—flourished among the Turks in their early centuries. An extensive repertoire of creation stories, myths and legends, narratives of their communal emergence and struggle for survival, shamanic tales, accounts of pagan and totemic beliefs, descriptions of heroic deeds, love stories, and satirical and amusing anecdotes evolved along with a large body of verse. Examples of this heritage may be found in an impressive study (Nora K. Chadwick and Victor Zhirmunsky: *Oral Epics of Central Asia*, Cambridge University Press, 1969). Central Asia, the mother soil of the Turkic epic tradition, produced not only an immense corpus of short tales but also many major epics including the *Manas* epic, a heroic cycle and one of the world's longest and most encompassing epics. This Kirghiz masterwork continues to compel public interest in Central Asia as part of Turkic oral culture, which has helped keep nationalism alive in resistance to Soviet rule.

The Turkish migration into Asia Minor from the ninth century onward brought with it not only the Central Asian oral tradition but also innumerable tales, stories, and legends from the legacy of China and India. Some of the arriving Turkish communities had already been exposed to the proselytizing efforts of Muslim missionaries, evangelists, and mystics. In their doxologies and homiletics, they recounted the stories of early Islam, of the events in the life of the Prophet Muhammad, of the legends of the saints and revered religious leaders. Typically these missionaries went by the name of *rawi* (storyteller) or *meddah* (encomiast). Among the Ottomans, the *meddah* was to become an entertainer (the sit-down version of the American stand-up comic) whose stories, although occasionally they would have a moralistic message, served no religious function.

The penchant of the Turks for narrative literature had spanned the millennium of their presence in Anatolia. They brought to it the sprawling geography of the tales from their own creative tradition or borrowed from other cultures. The greatest epic achievement of their own was "The Book of Dede Korkut," twelve interrelated stories of nomadic tribes. Twice translated into English (*The Book of Dede Korkut: A Turkish Epic*, translated by Faruk Sümer, Ahmet E. Uysal, and Warren S. Walker, University of Texas Press, 1972, and *The Book of Dede Korkut*, translated by Geoffrey Lewis, Penguin Books, 1974), this national epic, which evolved through several centuries, is a vibrant account of Turkish tribal life before conversion to Islam, but exhibits early

Islamic orientation as well. Its narrative art is a testament to the Turkish predilection for stories about heroism, love, and honor.

As the Turks embraced Islam and its civilization and founded the Seljuk State (mid-eleventh century to the late thirteenth century) and then the Ottoman State (in the closing years of the thirteenth century), they developed a passion for the rich written and oral literature of the Arabs and Persians. Having brought their indigenous narratives in their horizontal move from Central Asia to Asia Minor, they were now acquiring the vertical heritage of the earlier millennia of Anatolian cultures, cults, and epic imagination as well as the Islamic narrative tradition in its Arabo-Persian context. The resulting synthesis was to yield a vast reservoir of stories. It would also give impetus to the creation of countless new tales down the ages, for all ages.

The synthesis was significantly enriched by the lore of Islamic mysticism. Romantic and didactic *mesnevi*s (long narratives composed in rhymed couplets) compelled the attention of the elite poets. Perhaps the most profoundly influential masterpiece of the genre was the *Mathnawi*, written in Persian by the prominent thirteenth-century Sufi thinker Mevlana Celaluddin Rumi, the patron saint of the Whirling Dervishes, who lived in the ancient Anatolian city of Konya. Referred to as The Koran of Mysticism and The Inner Truth of the Koran, this massive work of close to 26,000 couplets comprises a wealth of mystico-moralistic tales, fables, and stories of wisdom.

Ottoman elite poets produced—often with the inspiration or story lines they took from *Thousand and One Nights, Kalila wa Dimna,* Firdausi's *Shahnamah,* Attar's *Mantiq at-Tayr,* Nizami's *Khamsa* (Five Narratives), and many others—impressive *mesnevi*s ranging from *Leyla and Mecnun* by Fuzuli (d. 1556) and *Hüsn ü Aşk* by Şeyh Galib (d. 1799), both allegories of mystical love, to *Harname* by Şeyhi (d. 1431), a socioeconomic satire, *Hikayat-i Deli Birader* (Mad Brother's Anecdotes), a garland of humorous and salacious stories, by Gazali (d. 1534), and *Şevk-engiz,* a funny debate between a ladies' man and a pederast, by Vehbi (d. 1809).

From the urban-establishment writers came some remarkable works that incorporate stories from the oral tradition, principally the *Seyahatname*, the massive travelogue and cultural commentary, by Evliya Chelebi (d. 1682) and the fascinating *Muhayyelat* (Imaginary Lives) by Aziz Efendi (d. 1798), a collection of three unrelated novellas that amalgamate fantastic tales, novelistic depictions of İstanbul life, preternatural occurrences, mystical components, and selections from the repertoires of Ottoman professional storytellers.

Ottoman oral creativity flourished less in written works than on its own terra firma. In the rural areas, it was, along with poetry, music, and dance, a focal performing art. It enchanted everyone from seven to seventy, as the saying goes, at home or at gatherings in villages and small towns. In İstanbul and other major cities, particularly after the mid-sixteenth century, it held audiences captive in coffeehouses. A testament to the popularity of storytelling is the crowded vocabulary identifying the various genres within oral narrative (*kıssa, hikâye, rivayet, masal, fıkra, letaif, destan, efsane, esatir, menkıbe, mesel,* and so forth).

The art of the tale was predominantly a continuation of the tradition that the Turkish communities had brought with them from their Asian centuries. It was not so much an elite phenomenon in Ottoman society, but rather a natural expression of the common people, of the man in the street, of the *lumpenproletariat* who had little else for diversion or entertainment, of the men and women who kept their cultural norms and values alive in giving free rein to their imaginative resources. In the high drama of Ottoman life, their authentic tales vied for public attention rivaling accounts of the sultans' deeds, of viziers and commanders, of feudal lords, of real heroes and villains. The leading figures of Ottoman history never ceased to fire the people's imagination. Mehmed the Conqueror, Prince Jem, Selim the Grim, Süleyman the Magnificent, Selim the Sot, İbrahim the Mad, Hürrem Sultan (née Roxelana), and Empresses Kösem and Nakşidil (née Aimé) became mythic names, synonymous with the Empire's triumphs and defeats, glories and treacheries.

Storytelling was nurtured also by children's tales told by mothers. Turkey's influential cultural analyst Ziya Gökalp (d. 1924) observed, "Popular poetry goes down from father to son, storytelling from mother to daughter. There are, to be sure, male storytellers, but most storytellers belong to the feminine gender." Gökalp's hyperbole distorts the facts: The tradition was always alive and well among both sexes.

In coffeehouses, where the art of storytelling flourished alongside *Karagöz* (shadow theater), the *meddah*s were male professional comics. Their performances offered humorous stories and a broad range of imitations and impersonations. Significantly, whereas the Karagöz repertoire (notwithstanding its colorful comedic representations of the life of the common people in an urban setting) was relatively fixed in its content, the *meddah* stories held infinite possibilities of improvisation and originality.

The supreme figure of Turkish tales was, and remains, Nasreddin Hoca, a wit and raconteur who lived presumably in the thirteenth century. A culmination of the earlier tradition, he became the wellspring of the succeeding centuries of folk humor and satire. Popular all over the Middle East, the Balkans, North Africa, and many parts of Asia, he disproves the assumption that one nation's laughter is often another nation's bafflement or boredom. He is Aesop, the Shakespearean clown, Till Eulenspiegel, Mark Twain, and Will Rogers all rolled into one. His humor incorporates subtle irony and black comedy, whimsical observations about human foibles and outrageous pranks, self-satire and bantering with God, twists of practical logic, and the outlandishly absurd. But his universal appeal is based always on *ridentem dicere verum*.

In the art of Turkish tales, Nasreddin Hoca looms large. There are of course other figures of comic wisdom: The Ottoman centuries reveled in the humor of Bekri Mustafa, İncili Çavuş, and a host of other funny characters including those from the Ottoman minorities. With their irreverence and nonchalance, the Bektashi dervishes generated a huge number of quips and anecdotes that have come down the ages. But Nasreddin Hoca is the humorist par excellence. His universality has been recognized in Europe and America as well. Since the nineteenth century, the Hoca tales have been translated into the world's major languages.

Among dozens of Hoca books in English, the works of Barbara K. Walker and Warren S. Walker stand out for their reliability and charm. In a sense, they have been for Nasreddin Hoca in English what Phaedrus, Babrius, and Planudes Maximus had been for Aesop. It is a tribute to the Walkers' consummate artistry as well as to the fundamental transcultural appeal of these tales and many other types of Turkish oral narrative to say that the humor and folktales of other nations can and do travel well. Wisdom always does. Warren S. Walker's *Tales Alive in Turkey* (a collaboration with the Turkish scholar-translator Ahmet Uysal) and now the volume that you hold in your hands prove that there is no validity to the much-bandied-about theory that humor cannot crisscross cultural boundaries.

Perhaps Nasreddin Hoca's most telling sight gag is the best metaphor for the openness, the accessibility, of national humor, although initially it might seem forbidding: His tomb in the Central Anatolian town of Akşehir originally had walls surrounding it and an iron gate with a huge padlock. In time, the walls came down, but the iron gate with the huge padlock still stands.

It is said that President Woodrow Wilson told, at least on one public occasion, a Nasreddin Hoca story. Today, conversations and some types of popular writing in Turkey (and elsewhere) sparkle with Hoca gags or punch lines. Remarkably, the lore has grown by leaps and bounds through the centuries, because much new material has been ascribed or adapted to him by the public imagination.

Since the middle of the nineteenth century, Western narrative traditions have penetrated Turkey at an ever-quickening pace. LaFontaine is a prime example: Şinasi (d. 1871), a poet-playwright and a pioneer of Ottoman enlightenment, adapted some of LaFontaine's fables into Turkish verse and composed a few of his own in a similar vein. A century later, two great figures, Orhan Veli and Sabahattin Eyuboğlu, offered their splendid translations of the Fables in separate books. Likewise, feverish translation activity has contributed to the Turkish synthesis the best of the narrative literature of Europe and America: the Brothers Grimm, Hans Christian Andersen, Perrault, and others, in the field of children's tales and Boccaccio, Chaucer, Rabelais, and others, for adults. The list is long, and the influences run deep.

More recently, the premier satirist Aziz Nesin has become a culture hero. His immensely popular short stories have inspired people to coin such expressions as "straight out of Nesin" and "almost as funny as a Nesin story." The most popular anecdotes of the last decades of the twentieth century are Laz jokes. Comparable to Polish jokes and in some cases identical, these ethnic jokes, told in the accent of a minority from Turkey's Northeastern region near the Black Sea coast, pepper social gatherings, newspaper columns, and radio-TV shows. A new craze has developed in "Prime Minister jokes." Early 1990 witnessed the eruption of hundreds of stories ridiculing the ineptness of a new Prime Minister—many adapted from a variety of sources, some truly original. No political figure had been the butt of so many humorous stories. Within a few months, several collections of these jokes were published in book form, and a major İstanbul daily held a Best PM Jokes contest for which it received several thousand entries.

The tales in this volume and its forthcoming sequel are a wondrous selection from the best of the repertoire, traditional and contemporary. They range from simple parables to elaborate stories of quest, from spare narratives to the *tekerleme*s (imaginative verbal devices that go beyond jingles), from the heroic deeds of a Turkish Robin Hood to the bizarre doings of jinns and fairies. Here are drolleries, cock-and-bull stories, old wives' tales, but also artful stories of psychological insight and spiritual profundity. The versatility is striking: picaresque, picturesque, humoresque, burlesque.

Virtually all of the tales provide their stimulation through two functions, moral and morale. In this sense, they constitute a strategy for living. For common people oppressed by poverty and other deprivations, they are a diversion, an entertainment, to be sure. Many of them, with their leaps of the imagination, transport the listener to idealized realms or into worse-than-real-life situations. In both, there is some measure of comfort for the suffering. The moral of each story, even if elusive, provides equipment for survival in a harsh world. The *Keloğlan* tales are compelling examples: The everyboy, who will grow up to be everyman, proves time and again that the meek—although they might not soon inherit the earth—will endure, sometimes prevail, and at times triumph. *Keloğlan* and other protagonists who are presented as underdogs offer hope and optimism to the listeners. The assurance, ritually repeated, is vicarious but not precarious. The tales are sources of solace, but also a strong boost to the people's morale.

Folktales in the Turkish experience, as elsewhere, are notable not only for their ways of overcoming a weakness or frustration, bringing about the fulfillment of dreams and wishes, and even achieving the impossible, but also for serving as a continuing critique of and a challenge to entrenched authority, especially against unjust rule. They are not merely a type of *refoulement,* but a form of resistance against tyranny, inequality, or any iniquity. Because most of them possess freedom from time and place, they function in terms of eternal and universal validity. But because they are narrated at a specific moment and locale and couched in the vocabulary of a particular culture, they have as their targets the symbols of an identifiable society (sultan or vizier, religious judge or feudal lord).

Barbara and Warren Walker collected these tales during numerous tours through the Turkish countryside. As a result, they have been able to create an archive on a scale greater than what any other person or institution has been capable of. Folktales hold a special place in Turkey's culture and mass communication. Their transcription came much later than comparable work in the West, and took place on a much more limited basis. Consequently, the oral tradition has continued well into our times without freezing on the printed page: it remains alive with new versions and adaptations as well as completely new oral narratives. Even today, despite the intrusions of radio and television, storytelling is alive in many parts of rural Turkey. How long it can survive is a matter of conjecture. The art might be crushed under urbanization or television. We have, however, the wonderful solace of knowing that, thanks to decades of assiduous and expert work by the Walkers, the Archive of Turkish Oral Narrative in Lubbock, Texas, has preserved for posterity several thousand tales recorded in Turkey.

Fıkra malum is a two-word sentence that people use in introducing a tale or anecdote: "The story is familiar." Whether or not it is, the teller goes ahead and gives his or her version of it anyway. Barbara Walker's collection, in two volumes, contains dozens of familiar and unfamiliar, and many surprising, tales. In them, the reader will find a panorama of Turkish life and legend. Certainly many archetypal figures populate them—folk heroes, innocent girls, wise men, cruel rulers, clever young-sters, greedy rich people, avenging angels, gullible youths, loyal friends. The tales celebrate ultimately the triumph of the good.

In her enlightening introduction, Barbara Walker provides an excellent analysis of the functions, the narrative element, and the performance element of the tales. This will stand as a fine, quintessential contribution to Turkish folk literature for a long time. Her elucidation of the performance element is especially welcome in dem-onstrating that the tradition retains its inner dynamism, that each teller reinterprets or even recreates the story.

The versions herein are not adaptations. They are faithful translations of the stories as recorded by the tellers. She has wisely stressed the authenticity of the tales and of the telling. For her, the storyteller is no less a hero than the hero of a story. Her respect for the teller as a creative artist shines through, and one hears the whis-pers of the original voices in these versions, all of which are in idiomatic English, artful, recast in colloquial rhythms, and couched in a style that conveys the sub-stance, the shape, the spirit, and the sumptuousness or the simplicity of each tale without compromising modern English usage. As a result, *The Art of the Turkish Tale* finds its best expression in English although it is a radically different language from Turkish in structure, vocabulary, and sound.

"Three apples fell from the sky," says a storyteller at the end of a tale, "the first for the teller of this tale, the second for the listener, and the third for the one who says, 'I'll tell it, too.'" Thank you for all these delicious apples, dear storytellers and dear Barbara Walker—and may the listeners and those who also tell these tales have all the luscious apples of the world.

Talat Sait Halman

Acknowledgments

N o presentation of field-collected Turkish tales is possible without the assistance, cooperation, and moral support of colleagues dedicated to recording and preserving those tales. Drs. Ahmet Edip Uysal, Warren S. Walker, Ahmet Ali Arslan, Tüncer Gülensoy, and Saim Sakaoğlu and the late Bn. Neriman Hızır (Ayşe Abla) have contributed immeasurably to the range and validity of these tales. To their efforts I am heavily indebted.

Furthermore, no field collection can be achieved without the willingness of Turkish storytellers to share via tape recordings the narrative treasures they have accumulated and preserved. Their delight in sharing these treasures with those both within and outside their own communities is evident in the spirited tellings to be found in this volume. I wish to acknowledge here, by name, Turkish province, year of recording, and title(s) of tale(s) told, all those generous tradition bearers whose narratives are included in this volume.

Medet Acar, Afyon, 1974: "The End of the Tyrant Bolu Bey"
Mustafa Akdağ, Ankara, 1985: "A Tale of Prayers Answered"
Duralı Akkaya, Muğla, 1976: "*Tekerleme*"
Osman Akyel, Ankara, 1961: "The Shoemaker and the Snake"
Gülfiye Aydın, Kars, 1975: "How the Siege of Van Was Lifted"
Salık Aydın, Bilecik, 1976: "The Defendant Who Won through Discretion"
Zehra Bakır, Erzurum, 1972: "Four Purchased Pieces of Advice"
Mehmet Balcı, Bilecik, 1979: "The Pilgrim Pays His Debt"
Havva Balkan, Konya, 1989: "The Cock and the Prince"
Nebiye Birkan, Kastamonu, 1964: "Sheepskin Girl and the Promise"
Ayşe Bostancı, Bolu, 1970: "The Two Stepdaughters"
Hicriye Ceren, İçel, 1974: "Community Mourning for Brother Louse"
Rıfat Cüre, Kastamonu, 1964: "Akıllı, Taşkafalı, and the Three Gifts"
Ali Çiftçi, Yozgat, 1964: "Camesap and Şahmeran" and (from Yozgat in 1981) "Cihanşah and Şemsi Bâni"
Mehmet Doğan, Konya, 1962: "The Quest for a Nightingale"
Altın Erol, İstanbul, 1966: "Cengidilaver"
Filiz Erol, Ankara, 1962: "The Careful Servant and the Curious One"
Hasan Erol, Yozgat, 1974: "Okra for Dinner"
Hatice Gölcük, Konya, 1989: "The Fisherman and the Jinn"
Ayşe Güldemir, Tokat, 1961: "The Patience Stone," "The Stepdaughter

and the Black Serpent," and "The Stepdaughter and the Forty Thieves"

Dikmen Gürün, Hatay, 1974: "The Hoca and the Drought"

Bozkurt Güvenç, Ankara, 1966: "Nasreddin Hoca as Preacher"

Neriman Hızır, Ankara, 1961: "The Cutworm and the Mouse," "The Hoca and the New Barber," and "'If Allah Wills'" and (from Ankara in 1962) "'A Bouquet of Roses for an Eye!'" and "The Prince, the Parrot, and the Beautiful Mute"

Hasan Işık, Bolu, 1969: "The Farmer and the Padishah of Fairies"

Selahattın Kalman, İstanbul, 1964: "The Woodcutter's Heroic Wife"

Fadime Kayacan, Bilecik, 1976: "The Frog Wife" and "The *Hoca,* the Witch, the Captain, and the *Hacı*'s Daughter"

Cemşit Kayalar, Trabzon, 1984: "The Wordless Letter"

Hülya Kırkıcı, Denizli, 1985: "'Who's Selling These Pomegranates?'"

Suzan Koraltürk, Trabzon, 1961: "The Princess and the Red Horse Husband" and "The Shepherd and His Secret" and (from Trabzon in 1962) "All for a Wrinkled Little Pomegranate"

Mehmet Kara Koruk, Eskişehir, 1975: "Backward on the Donkey"

Şükrü Koş, Manisa, 1964: "The *Köse* and the Three Swindlers"

Behçet Mahir, Erzurum, 1964: "The Stonecutter"

Mehmet Ali and Makbule Ögülen, Erzurum, 1968: "The Donkey That Climbed the Minaret"

Rıfat Önen, Erzurum, 1979: "The Uncontrollable Desire and the Irresistible Urge"

Türköz Özdemir, Ankara, 1962: "Pears and Pears"

"Büyük Anne" Sümer, Konya, 1966: "The Unfaithful Wife Detected"

Hâlil Şengül, Bolu, 1970: "Good to the Good and Damnation to the Evil"

Hediye Temiz, Erzurum, 1973: "The Faithful Son of the *Lâla*"

Haydar Tufan, Amasya, 1973: "The Authority of a Host"

Metin Yıldız, Diyarbakır, 1962: "The Two Brothers and the Magic Hen"

Osman Yılmaz, Yozgat, 1966: "Charity above All"

By no means to be overlooked is the work of many who have prepared literal English translations of the tape-recorded Turkish tales. Of these, the most outstanding contributors are Dr. Ahmet Edip Uysal, the late Bn. Neriman Hızır, the late Bn. Zafer Çetinkaya, Dr. Dikmen Gürün, and Bn. Necibe Ertaş. Without their intensive efforts, preparing this volume would have been far less pleasurable.

The loving and painstaking skill expended by Helen Siegl in her drypoint etchings and collagraphs to bring both color and visual support to tales from a culture too little known and appreciated has provided an indispensable artistic dimension to this communal project.

To all these contributors I extend my thanks and my congratulations for work well done indeed. Together, *İnşallah,* we have been able to open at least a small window on the art of the Turkish tale.

The Art of the Turkish Tale

Introduction

This volume first introduces the oral tale as a form and then examines the Turkish tale by the same standards. Representing the Turkish tale are fifty-one previously unpublished samples deriving from the Archive of Turkish Oral Narrative and requiring no annotation for their understanding and appreciation. Readers who are unfamiliar with Turkish culture will find helpful the Guide to Pronunciation and the Glossary of Turkish Terms and Folk Elements.

The Turkish narratives selected offer only a taste of more than three thousand field-collected tales presently in the archive, which is housed at Texas Tech University in Lubbock. Still, these few provide a tempting variety: anecdotes, fables, wonder tales, a *tekerleme,* a cumulative tale, a legend, and an episode from the adventures of the Turkish Robin Hood, Köroğlu.

The Art of the Turkish Tale is intended as an appetizer to encourage further reading of Turkish tales.

The Oral Tale

In essence, a tale is a *folk*tale only if it has a teller and at least one listener. It serves as an intimate act of communication in which the teller shares one of his treasured narratives with a listener eager to receive that treasure. This eagerness prompts the teller to stretch tradition and talents to their outermost limits. The tale depends for its effectiveness on committed oral-aural interaction.

The Functional Element

There are three distinctive yet interlocking elements in the art of a living tale: the functional element, the narrative element, and the performance element. Of these three, the functional element is primary. In fact, it underlies the whole development of storytelling, a uniquely human achievement almost as old as language. Initially, the sharing of news or information was the basic function of the tale.

As clans developed, the tale gained a significant additional function: it carried ground rules for peaceable coexistence, a system of values making individual and communal living feasible and attractive. Tales were told by adults to adults to interpret, reinforce, and perpetuate these values. Listening also were the children, for no censor determined what was suitable for their hearing. The storyteller may well have been the first teacher and the only moral monitor in the early community, as he continues to be in unlettered settlements around the world today. And what was told was committed to memory by the listeners, to be applied to everyday living and to be passed on orally to successive generations.

In time, adaptations were made in the tales to accommodate changed living conditions and expanded outside contacts. Still, the heart of a given tale—plot structure, character contrasts, traditional beginnings and endings, and the imperative feature of repetition—remained the same.

But the tales served as more than precept vehicles, moral guides. They carried details familiar and dear to the listeners: settings, forms of work, customs, dress, traditional greetings, housing, conflicts between those holding power and those subject to that power, festivals, and rites of passage. All these and many other homely details provided the ambience for the action. Each time a given tale was told, this cultural baggage was transmitted with it. Thus much can be learned about the everyday lives, as well as the values, of any group of people through tales kept alive in the oral tradition.

Furthermore, in any given culture the personal and sociological needs of the members were and still are served by tales told within the community. Among these are the need to laugh, to see those in power reduced through some failing or another, to enjoy wish fulfillment, to share heroic adventures, and to be entertained and refreshed by a break in the ordinariness of their own days. All these needs and many more are met through listening to tales derived from one's own cultural background. In short, the well-told tale functions as minister/rabbi/priest/imam, historian, extended family, museum docent, entertainer, and psychiatrist.

The Narrative Element

What determines whether or not a tale which meets one or more of the functional criteria will be retained in the oral tradition? Both of the remaining interlocking elements, narrative and performance, figure strongly in the longevity of any given tale. Of these two, the narrative element carries the greater weight.

The narrative element involves the actual plot construction: the beginning, the introduction of simply but clearly defined characters who will interact to produce a plot, the steps in the plot itself, a satisfactorily resolved conflict, and an ending. Although the term *oral narrative* is broad enough to include all stories passed along by word of mouth, such forms as the fable, anecdote, cumulative tale, legend, and heroic romance each have characteristics peculiar to themselves. Too, each differs in one way or another from what is loosely called the fairy tale. All of these forms, however, have one or more of the following earmarks: beginning and ending formulas, restriction to a single plot, simplicity of characterization, the presence of two strongly contrasted major characters, persistent use of repetition, and ultimate success of the character initially considered weakest or youngest or most despised.

The formulaic nature of beginnings and endings is immediately obvious. "Once upon a time" and "they were married and lived happily ever after" are signals widely recognized throughout the English-speaking world, and they have their equivalents in all languages in which storytelling has been studied. Such signals allow the teller to remove his listeners from their familiar surroundings and everyday concerns to a setting in which wishes are fulfilled, ambitions are realized, love finds a way, courage matters, and action is plentiful. Likewise, once the action is completed, the conflict resolved, the storyteller moves his listeners back to their familiar surroundings and everyday concerns but with a heartening sense that all's well with the world.

Also apparent is the use of a single plot; once the action begins, the narrative moves without distracting subplots to its foreordained and well-justified conclusion. The demand for a single plot does not obviate complications in that plot, but whatever complications occur are directly and intimately related to the plot. They serve both to heighten suspense and to increase satisfaction with the plot's resolution.

Simplicity of characterization is clearly recognizable in the well-constructed oral tale. Only those character traits that function within the action are supplied. Less important traits, though still occasionally operative, are more often revealed through behavior or through dialogue than through outright declaration. One character may be lazy but clever; another may be abused but resourceful; still another may be small but courageous; yet another may be beautiful but deceitful. For both teller and listener such simplification assists in recollection and clarifies the characters' functions in the plot.

Among the characters, no matter how simply described, there tend to be two that are sharply contrasted with one another. Opposed to the hero is a villain, to a clever one a fool, to a beautiful stepdaughter a woman plotting evil, to a faithful son a faithless one. Between each of these paired characters there is conflict that is central to the plot. In the majority of tales that are still being told today and that can be recorded on tape (ones that might be termed living or surviving tales), the plot resolution brings the victory of good over evil, interlocking the narrative element with the functional one and enabling perpetuation of values held within the culture from which the tales derive.

The use of repetition—of words, of phrases, of episodes—is a strong and recognizable feature of the living tale, and it is likewise a requirement of a tale well told. Cumulative tales are relished by listeners for precisely this feature of repetition, which pleases the ears of hearers as it carries the action forward. But quite apart from cumulative tales, repetition is both functional and appreciated. In a tale in which the conflict has been satisfactorily resolved, the hero is often asked to recount his adventures and so he does, giving both teller and audience occasion to enjoy the action all over again. Likewise, in a tale in which the hero is given instructions about how to succeed in his perilous venture, the listeners first hear the instructions as the hero hears them and then relish the working out of those instructions through the action.

There is a final earmark of the well-constructed tale: the ultimate victor in the action is the character who initially seemed least likely to achieve that distinction. Many a youngest child immersed in fairy tales draws comfort from the certainty that finally he will have his reward. But it is not only children who benefit from that assurance; so do the peasant abused by an overlord, a small man considered a weakling, a woman overworked and underappreciated. This feature is tonic also to one presently in a post of authority who might abuse that position: there is the possibility, borne out by tradition, that a seemingly unlikely contender will topple him.

The Performance Element

The third element, that of performance, includes the devices used by the storyteller to capture and convey the full flavor of the tale. Such devices include extended formulaic beginnings and endings, alliteration, metaphors and similes, exclamations and other expressions particular to that culture, and the use of numbers such as three, five, and seven that hold symbolic meanings. Further devices are markedly increased use of repetition, songs or poems traditionally associated with the tale being told, appropriate proverbs, transitional expressions introducing changes in scene, and lively conversation.

These devices are not part of the structure of the narrative; they may differ widely from one narrator to another, even for the same basic tale. They are personal marks of delivery, of the *manner* of sharing the *matter* of the tale. The more eagerly the listeners respond to such devices, the more motivated the teller becomes to enrich the telling. But the wise storyteller never forgets that the tale is more important than the teller. His performance devices do not alter the narrative itself or overlook the function of the tale or introduce elements alien to the shared culture.

Inapplicable in most traditional storytelling situations is "performance" as it applies to theatrical productions. If gestures are used by the storyteller, they arise from the demands of plot or of characterization. To draw attention to the teller himself as a performer is to distance both teller and listener from the tale being told. Central to both storyteller and audience is the tale itself.

From Oral Tale to Turkish Oral Tale

Suppose, then, that an English-speaking teller wishes to capture and convey the flavor and worth of a tale derived from a culture not his own. How does he handle the challenge posed by such an undertaking? I do not know what techniques are used by others, but I do know the method that has worked best for me in communicating Turkish field-collected tales to an English-speaking audience.

Throughout twenty-nine years of field collecting via tape recorder in Turkey, observing closely both tellers and listeners in varied storytelling settings, I have come to recognize the importance of voice in tale-telling. By *voice* I mean much more than sound produced from the vocal cords; I mean the total communication impression created by a given teller. *Voice* in this sense includes attitude toward his own culture, concern about sharing a portion of that culture, evidence of commitment to the tale being told, and awareness of audience reaction. It includes, as well, such devices as intonation, gestures and other body language, use of conversation and proverbs and onomatopoeia, use or omission of traditional narrative formulas, and incorporation of traditional expressions.

Because voice can make or break even the best-constructed tale, I find use of the field recordings indispensable in communicating the full flavor of the telling of a given narrative. A surprising amount of the ambience of the storytelling is also revealed through the tape recording, providing a bonus in the effort to recapture the excitement of the telling. And since the recordings are in Turkish, I can catch the internal rhyming that characterizes Turkish storytelling.

But because my first language is English, I need also a literal translation of the content of the tale, a translation done by someone who shares my concern for authentic preservation of oral narrative. Thus I can be certain that I have missed neither the function of the tale in the culture nor any of the details of plot or character. Since no literal translation into English can capture the flavor of the Turkish telling because of the flexibility, economy, and euphony of Turkish, the voice is silenced in the translation. Therefore, I use translation and recording together, with repeated readings and listenings, until I am satisfied that I can convey the English version in the voice of that particular narrator. Ideally, American listeners and readers will feel the same stirring of delight in the English-language version that I continue to feel as I listen to the Turkish telling.

My concern for communicating both content and voice has overridden the impulse to make these tales fit a literary Procrustean bed. As a consequence, information so familiar to Turkish listeners that the narrator did not need to provide it may well prompt questions among readers. An excellent example of omitted information occurs in the heroic romance "The End of the Tyrant Bolu Bey." To those unfamiliar with the Köroğlu cycle of heroic tales, Demircioğlu's failure to come to the rescue of his wounded comrade in the deadly battle between Köroğlu and Bolu Bey would be puzzling. But both Demircioğlu and Turkish listeners knew that heroic convention demanded a duel, a one-on-one battle, between Köroğlu and the cruel bey who had blinded the hero's father; interference in that duel would have constituted a breach of honor, an unforgivable offense. On the other hand, the adopted son of Köroğlu, Ayvaz, would be allowed, *if asked*, to replace his adoptive father in the effort to avenge the blinding. My introduction of the above information in purporting to present the content and voice of "The End of the Tyrant Bolu Bey" would constitute an infringement on the narrator's right to have the tale recreated as he had told it. Respect for these narrators and their tales demands that I let *them* tell the tales without intrusion.

The Turkish Tale

The Turkish tale reaches back into antiquity. Evidences of its longevity can be found today in episodes we have collected from the Gilgamesh Epic, from Biblical times, and from the times of the conquerors Alexander, Attila, and Tamerlane. There are traces, too, of the earliest contacts of the Turkic peoples with the multiethnic, multicultural residents of eleventh-century Asia Minor.

During the period of the long-lived Ottoman Empire, tales provided both entertainment and information in settings as varied as the sultan's court, the harem, the Turkish baths, the coffeehouses, the marketplace, and rural social gatherings. Also, life during that period gave rise to a great number of new tales to fit the multifaceted empire's leading figures and events. Many of the tales in today's Turkish oral tradition derive from these roots. A number of those tales, too, are available on tape.

More recently, the War of Independence produced a flood of tales, both legends and personal experience accounts incorporating episodes from folktales afloat orally. These tales still circulate today.

Updated variants of much older tales with universal interest and appeal continue to find a place in Turkish storytellers' repertories. These new turns on old tales thrive alongside the time-honored versions of those same tales. And evidence of these strands, too, is held today on tape.

As varied as the tales themselves are the voices of the tellers. Each narrator's voice has been preserved for you in the tales included in this collection. The narrators chosen, divided equally between males and females, ranged in age from nine to ninety, came from many different walks of life, were recorded over a twenty-nine-year period, and represent twenty of Turkey's sixty-eight provinces. (The geographical range, incidentally, reached from

xxvi

Muğla in southwestern Turkey to Kars in northeastern Turkey and from İstanbul in northwestern Turkey to Diyarbakır in southeastern Turkey.) Therefore, you will find here almost as many voices as there are tales.

Some of these voices may not appear to you as art at all. For example, the teller of "Okra for Dinner" was far more interested in making his point about a clever villager's adjustment to city living than he was in telling an imperishable tale. The telling thus seems quite prosaic, as entertaining as a laundry list. But it is entirely in keeping with his own need and with the needs of his fellow exvillagers, so often the butt of humor in other anecdotes. It is an honest tale, forthrightly told, genuinely *folk*, and it will last and spread because others just like him are eager to hear it and to pass it along.

Another voice, that of Behçet Mahir in "The Stonecutter," reveals almost a lifetime of commitment to tale-telling as a means of preserving the Turkish value system. Necessary to his purpose are the moralistic passages often found in the minstrel tradition, a tradition for which Behçet Bey underwent extensive apprenticeship. Such passages are not likely to be found in retellings done by those unfamiliar with Turkish culture and unaware of the importance of *function* in the telling of tales. They are, however, very much a part of the voice of the teller.

Since as far as possible I have included tales which I myself collected, I recall vividly the circumstances under which they were recorded and the responses of the various audiences to their telling. Most memorable of all is Altın Erol's recounting of "Cengidilaver," a tale passed down in his family since well before the end of the Ottoman Empire. During Altın's lifetime, this was considered "his" story because he told it best. Midway through the telling, we were interrupted by a visitor, also a storyteller, but one given to altering the endings of tales to teach moral lessons to young readers. "Turn off the tape recorder!" said Altın Bey. "I don't want him to spoil *my* story!" And the recorder was immediately turned off. Two hours later, following the visitor's departure, we replayed the entire first half of the recording. Caught up once more in his love of the tale, Altın completed the telling to his satisfaction and ours. Altın Bey has gone now, but "Cengidilaver" will endure in Altın's voice.

The Functional Element

Two basic functions are apparent in most of the tales in this volume: the need to interpret, reinforce, and perpetuate the strong value system and the hunger to preserve familiar elements of Turkish culture. In addition, various tales support pride in the Turkish past; ventilate resentment concerning all-too-fallible judges, rulers, and religious leaders; provide reprisal against city-bred people who mock village folk; provoke laughter; and offer refreshment from the tedium of everyday life.

To the telling of a tale, both narrator and listener bring the value system common to the culture. The narrator can exercise one of two options in prompting concern for a given value implicit in the tale. He can demonstrate the value by having the protagonist exemplify it and thus persuade the listener of its worth. Or he can involve the listener even more deeply by choosing an antagonist who lacks that value. The listener may not comment on the missing value, but his mental and emotional response to its absence will reinforce his own commitment to that value. Both of these approaches to the value system are used effectively in various narratives in the present collection.

The first option is clearly chosen in "The Quest for a Nightingale" and "Cengidilaver," where the value of persistence is inherent in the respective protagonists. This same value marks Perihan in "Sheepskin Girl and the Promise" and Prince Hasan in "All for a Wrinkled Little Pomegranate." On the other hand, the most striking use of the second option occurs in "The Frog Wife": absence of the love of family in the antagonist (the father) prompts him initially to humiliate his youngest son and subsequently to attempt thrice to cause that son's death. Other instances of choice of the second option are evidenced in "'A Bouquet of Roses for an Eye!'" and "The Stepdaughter and the Forty Thieves," in which the antagonists' lack of love for family members prompts both physical and emotional abuse of the protagonists. Neither tellers nor listeners can be oblivious to the presence or the absence of the values identified through the characters and their actions.

What, then, are the values that are emphasized in these particular tales? In descending order of frequency, the following values are stressed in at least a dozen of the narratives: persistence (37), soundness of character (26), curiosity (26), love of family (22), compassion (20), concern for those outside family (20), hospitality (19), respect for elders (19), trust in Allah (18), obedience (14), helpfulness (14), charity (13), friendship (12), gratitude (12), and cleverness (12). Among other values represented, though in fewer tales, are chastity, childbearing, community concern, courage, industriousness, justice, loyalty, marital fidelity, mercy, reliability, respect for advice, and self-respect. Clearly, these values are not peculiar to the Turks. They are indeed universal values, recognized worldwide although honored more strongly through practice in some cultures than in others.

From this list of values, I have chosen curiosity as a subject for special comment. What has been termed *curiosity* is a reflection of Turks' genuine interest in others and in the affairs of others. They are also inquisitive about what lies beyond their own borders. Curiosity prompts Cihanşah, in "Cihanşah and Şemsi Bâni," to "travel around the entire world to see what is there." This curiosity therefore sets in motion the whole plot; it also leads him to open the forbidden door; it tempts him as well to discount the warning given to him by Murguşah and thus to forfeit temporarily his beloved Şemsi Bâni.

Curiosity urges the former shepherd's wife to hazard her husband's life in "The Shepherd and His Secret." Curiosity moves the two dervishes in "The Stonecutter" to examine the valuable stones; from that point on, the plot is irreversible. Curiosity motivates the grand vizier to appropriate the letter and at length proves the wisdom of the saying "Good to the good and damnation to the evil" in the tale by that name. Curiosity about the woodcutter's refusal to obey the padishah's order in "The Woodcutter's Heroic Wife" leads to the tale-within-a-tale that enriches the structure of that narrative. In short, curiosity as a value is highly functional not only in these and other tales in the present collection but also in hundreds of others in the archive. Still, curiosity is not in the long run a value to deride; without it, modern science and technology would be in sorry state. Isn't one of man's most basic drives the need to *know*?

Curiosity and the rest of the values listed as emphasized in this collection can be perpetuated most readily through the art of the Turkish tale. The tale is engendered out of these concerns, is polished through frequent retellings, and reaffirms and reinforces those values that have marked Turks both as a people and as a part of the human community throughout the many centuries of their history.

But the tales also serve as preservers of Turkish social practices and material culture. The customs attached to hospitality provide a sound example. Travelers, whether beggars or beys, can be certain of a warm welcome as "guests of Allah" when they arrive in a village or at a shepherd's fire at nightfall. The disguised sultan and his grand vizier are housed and fed by a shepherd in "The Authority of a Host," and they learn something valuable about the responsibility of a guest in the process. The excessive hospitality shown to the laborer in "Four Purchased Pieces of Advice" had held a strong lesson indeed for those visitors who had preceded him. The younger brother in "The Two Brothers and the Magic Hen" is taken in as a son by a poor woman. The youngest brother in "The Quest for a Nightingale" is made welcome by the nine-headed female giant and her nine nine-headed sons after he has nursed at her breast and has thus become a milk son (a custom followed to this day among many Turkish women to foster ties between families, but, alas, without the giants!). The shah and his wife in "The Pilgrim Pays His Debt" host a lost pilgrim for the traditional three days and three nights—a hospitality violated—before restoring him to his fellow pilgrims en route to Mecca; the mercy shown by the shah is later amply compensated. In "Sheepskin Girl and the Promise," Perihan is warmly welcomed by the wealthy widow; this hospitality, too, has its reward. Şahmeran, the padishah of snakes, hosts Camesap for seven years in "Camesap and Şahmeran." In "Cengidilaver," two abandoned infants are taken in and reared for sixteen years by a childless widowed miller; subsequently, the two are adopted, though this second time perhaps for gain, by a childless widowed jeweler. In "'A Bouquet of

Roses for an Eye!'" an old shepherd and his wife take in a girl blinded by her evil aunt; again, that hospitality is well rewarded. In all of the instances of genuine hospitality, and in dozens more besides, the offer of hospitality is made with no thought whatsoever of gain. The principle used is that any stranger is "the guest of Allah." The reward that often follows—whatever it may be—serves, however, to reinforce in the minds of the listeners the worth of that value and the customs attending it.

The precepts of Islam continue to influence customs and practices in Turkey despite the fact that Turkey is by law a secular state. Turks share, therefore, with other Muslims throughout the world the reverence for Allah and respect for the Prophet appropriate to that faith. Observance of the annual fasting period called in Turkish "Ramazan," the five daily prayer times, the Friday noon service (considered the most important of the services held all week), the giving of alms, and the pilgrimage to Mecca persist among many Turks and in their tales. The pilgrimage is a plot factor not only in "The Pilgrim Pays His Debt" but also in "The *Hoca*, the Witch, the Captain, and the *Hacı*'s Daughter." The Friday service figures not only in "Nasreddin Hoca as Preacher" but also in "The Defendant Who Won through Discretion"; in the latter tale is a *hacı*, one who has completed the pilgrimage.

The padishah of India, in "The Faithful Son of the *Lâla*," goes out to the marketplace himself on the last day of Ramazan to seek special *bayram* treats for his arrogant daughter. That daughter, contrary to Muslim custom, refuses to pay her respects to her father during the *bayram,* but insists he come instead to her, a detail serving to emphasize the arrogance of the princess. In "Charity above All," following the three repentant brigands' proper observance of mosque attendance and prayers, both Allah's mercy and His judgment are clearly shown. (Curiously, Allah uses as His agent Hızır, a saint firmly espoused by the folk but not recognized by the religious establishment.) Although the anecdote "Nasreddin Hoca as Preacher" takes the Friday sermon as a subject for humor, the humor is not at the expense of religion. Instead, it provides one more instance of the cleverness of the traditional and beloved folk figure Nasreddin Hoca. And the vow made to Allah by the childless father in "The Donkey That Climbed the Minaret" is taken seriously indeed.

The use of Allah's name is common in such expressions as *"Bismillâh!"* ("in the name of Allah!"), *"İnşallah!"* ("if Allah wills!"), and "Allah *göstermesin!*" ("Allah forbid!"); these terms are common, too, in the Turkish tale. The Nasreddin Hoca anecdote "'If Allah Wills'" turns on the Hoca's refusal, despite his wife's repeated entreaties, to say "if Allah wills" as he is announcing his plans for the following day. In the tale "The Stonecutter" the two old dervishes are assumed to be pious because of their prayer beads and their *Bismillâhs*. Throughout the tales in this volume are many other uses of the term "Allah," among them "May Allah be with you," "As Allah would have it," "For the love of Allah," "By the grace of Allah," "Praise Allah!" and "Go with Allah." The name of Allah is also invoked in one version or another of the formal proposal of marriage: "In the name of Allah and with the consent of the Prophet, I ask for the hand of your daughter Ayşe in marriage."

Proper Islamic burial practices are reflected in the tales as well as in everyday life: the ritual washing, the shrouding, the carrying to the graveyard in the community coffin, and the lowering of the body into the grave wrapped only in the shroud. In "The Stepdaughter and the Forty Thieves" the prince's mother is horrified, upon secretly unlocking his room, to find there a girl, apparently dead, and moreover "without a proper burial!" The action taken immediately to remedy this latter situation contributes directly to the development of the plot. The former shepherd in "The Shepherd and His Secret" makes the preparations for his own proper burial. Curiously, although customarily Muslims are buried without material goods, the young husband in "The Frog Wife" is sent to the underworld to recover the ring from his dead grandfather's finger. Plot requirement here takes precedence over Muslim practice.

The influence of Islam on the lives of women in these tales is far less evident than is the inheritance of the pre-Islamic tradition, in which women enjoyed equality with men. (Interestingly, of the tales giving strong or heroic roles to women, roughly half were told by males and half by females.) In "The Hoca, the Witch, the Captain, and the Hacı's Daughter," Gülistan's parents and brother have gone on the pilgrimage to Mecca. Gülistan, also a Muslim, uses ritual ablution as a ruse to effect her escape from the lecherous captain, an escape requiring the raw courage dealt evenly to males and females in the Turkic tradition. The petulant padishah determined to drown all the women of his region because, he says, "all women have long hair and short brains" more than meets his match in the woodcutter's heroic wife in the tale bearing that title. Gülsün, in "All for a Wrinkled Little Pomegranate," obeys her husband not because of Muslim suppression but because she loves him and wants to please him. Yes, in "The Frog Wife," the bride does go in her frog form to "the women's quarters," but this "retreat" serves as a narrative device. It removes her from the scene while her jealous father-in-law sets successive impossible tasks for her husband in order to possess her himself; through her efforts, his plotting reaps the result it deserves. In short, the women in these tales are ones to reckon with; they demonstrate both the will and the ability to take matters into their own hands.

The tales carry many reflections of Turkish material culture: housing, dress, foods. But since Turks do not need to tell each other what Turks eat, foods are mentioned by name only if they figure in the plot: garlic and onions in "Good to the Good and Damnation to the Evil," milk in "The Stepdaughter and the Black Serpent" and "Camesap and Şahmeran," a cucumber in "The Frog Wife," okra in "Okra for Dinner," helva in "The Hoca, the

Witch, the Captain, and the *Hacı's* Daughter," pomegranates in "'Who's Selling These Pomegranates?'" and "All for a Wrinkled Little Pomegranate," and yogurt in "How the Siege of Van Was Lifted," for example. All of these reflections function in the plots.

Likewise, the mention of a tiled roof in "The Two Brothers and the Magic Hen" is functional rather than descriptive. The magic stick's beating on the tiled roof prompts the beautiful girl to throw the stick's owner into a well, thus advancing the plot considerably. Too, in "Sheepskin Girl and the Promise," the housing of Perihan in a little room "next to the stable" both reflects the two-story structure of many Turkish houses and gives the girl the privacy she needs to maintain her disguise. The detail is thus functional rather than decorative.

The centrality of the mosque, the fountain, and the coffeehouse in Turkish communal living is amply reflected in the tales. Of these three, the fountain proves most functional in the present collection. In "The Quest for a Nightingale," the hero's praise for the muddy water flowing from a fountain proves a saving factor in his success. Breaking the pitcher of a woman fetching water at a fountain brings a curse on the prince in "The Faithful Son of the *Lâla*." At another fountain in the same tale, the wakeful son of the *lâla* receives instructions that ensure the safety and success of the quest for the prince's bride. Ablutions to be taken at a fountain allow the escape of the abused young wife in "The *Hoca,* the Witch, the Captain, and the *Hacı's* Daughter." At another fountain in this tale, the *hacı's* daughter had earlier won the affection of the Syrian prince. At a fountain, Beyoğlu in "Sheepskin Girl and the Promise" discovers the identity of the mysterious stranger he desires to marry. A fountain with curative waters is functional in "Cihanşah and Şemsi Bâni." In these and in a number of other instances in the present tales, the fountain—significant in Turkish everyday culture—provides both the scene and the stimulus for dramatic advancement of the action.

Since agriculture has for many centuries been the means of livelihood for rural Turks, the tales also show various aspects of farm life: actual farming (in "The Farmer and the Padishah of Fairies," "*Tekerleme,*" "The *Köse* and the Three Swindlers," and "Charity above All"), fruit growing (in "Pears and Pears," "'If Allah Wills,'" and "'Who's Selling These Pomegranates?'"), horse herding (in "The End of the Tyrant Bolu Bey"), sheepherding (in more than half a dozen tales), and goose herding (in "All for a Wrinkled Little Pomegranate"). Also reflected are two of the problems that attend agriculture, drought (in "The Hoca and the Drought") and the pest called the cutworm, which undoes much of the farmers' hard work. (For this reason, "The Cutworm and the Mouse" enjoys tremendous popularity: rural folk take understandable satisfaction in having that thankless cutworm *stamped down* into the mud. This tale thus provides welcome release for feelings of resentment and frustration.) In each tale except "The Cutworm and the Mouse," the agricultural activity serves to move the action forward; it is functional in the structure of the tale.

Likewise functional in the plots of these tales are such elements of Turkish culture as apprenticeship (in "A Tale of Prayers Answered"), wedding feasts and festivals (in many tales), use of the *hamam* (in "The Patience Stone," "All for a Wrinkled Little Pomegranate," and "The *Hoca,* the Witch, the Captain, and the *Hacı*'s Daughter"), management of household servants (in "The Careful Servant and the Curious One"), the sending out of town criers (in many tales), and dozens of other elements of Turkish life, including the various roles of women, that will be apparent to those who read the tales. Suffice it to say that the Turkish tale carries sufficient cultural baggage to satisfy the most curious inquirers and it uses that cultural baggage as an integral part of the action.

The Narrative Element

Among the tales in this collection, sixteen have narrative structures dictated by their distinctive forms: the anecdote, the fable, the *tekerleme,* the legend, the heroic romance, and the cumulative tale. These sixteen evidence only a few of the six features expected in the so-called fairy tale.

Six of the sixteen are Nasreddin Hoca anecdotes: "'If Allah Wills,'" "The Hoca and the Drought," "Backward on the Donkey," "'Who's Selling These Pomegranates?'" "Nasreddin Hoca as Preacher," and "The Hoca and the New Barber." Of all Turkish folk characters, English-speaking readers are most likely to be familiar with Nasreddin Hoca, sometimes wise, sometimes foolish, but always thoroughly human. Hoca anecdotes are the ones most likely to be told when Turks are asked for tales.

Three of the sixteen are fables: "The Uncontrollable Desire and the Irresistible Urge," "The Shoemaker and the Snake," and "The Fisherman and the Jinn." The third is familiar from other cultures; the other two seem sprouted directly from Turkey's soil.

Three of the sixteen are anecdotes reflecting everyday Turkish concerns: "The Wordless Letter," "The Careful Servant and the Curious One," and "Okra for Dinner." Mandatory military service, difficulties with household servants, and the ongoing battle of wits between rural and urban dwellers have given rise to many such anecdotes, and they are very much alive in the oral tradition today.

The legend "How the Siege of Van Was Lifted," the heroic romance "The End of the Tyrant Bolu Bey," "*Tekerleme,*" and the cumulative tale "Community Mourning for Brother Louse" complete the sixteen not requiring special analysis. "*Tekerleme,*" told here by the teller as a separate tale, appears far more often as an extended beginning formula for a far different tale; there it serves to remove the listeners from their everyday concerns and to prepare them to hear a story.

In most of these sixteen tales, beginning and ending formulas are absent. Action is limited to a single plot; characterization is simple and clear, whatever conflict develops is resolved, and there is ample use of repetition.

The structural element most frequently found in the remaining tales is the use of beginning and ending formulas, formulas that give a distinctively Turkish stamp to the tales. Only four of the tales lack some kind of formulaic beginning, and only seven lack a formulaic ending of some sort. The nonsense beginning characteristic of most Turkish tales is quite brief: "Once there was and once there wasn't" or "Once there was and twice there wasn't." Extensions and elaborations of these basic introductions are performance characteristics and will be presented later. Among the formulaic endings, there is much greater variety than exists among the beginnings. Curiously, only two in this collection use the formula found in many of the other archive tales: "Three apples fell from the sky, one for the teller of this tale, one for the listener, and one for whoever will pass this tale along." Apart from this formula, the most common ones are some version or another of "May we all share in his (their) good fortune," "May we share in his (their) happiness," and "They had their wish(es) fulfilled. Let's go up and sit in their seats." (The last one refers to the rural custom of providing the best seat [the one opposite the door] to the guest being honored.) All the rest of the tales have highly individual touches that are performance rather than narrative devices; samples of those endings will be provided later.

Each of the tales in this collection has a single plot, one of the marks of a well-constructed tale. Several of the longer tales include plot complications, but in each instance those complications serve to heighten suspense, to advance the plot, or to provide occasions for repetition. In "The Woodcutter's Heroic Wife," the angry padishah's plan to destroy all the women of his region, complicated by the woodcutter's refusal to surrender his wife, prompts a tale within the tale that alters the outcome of the basic plot; the complication is therefore functional. The complication of Şemsi Bâni's retransformation in "Cihanşah and Şemsi Bâni" prompts Cihanşah's quest for her in a complete repetition of his initial adventure. "The Stonecutter" includes as a result of a plot complication a second tale within the tale that functions in bringing the plot to its appropriate close.

All of the tales meet the test of simplicity of characterization. In none of the tales, either, is there any real doubt about which character is the hero and which the villain, or which is the clever one and which the fool, or which is the deserving stepdaughter and which the undeserving one. Both the requirement of simplicity of characterization and that of strongly contrasted characters are clearly met in these tales.

As for the use of repetition, twenty-nine of the tales (except the sixteen initially discussed) are rich in the repetition of episodes. Also, almost all of the narratives in the present collection include at least some repetition of words and phrases. Still other tales, instead of actual repetition of episodes or, indeed, of entire adventures, use a summary such as "When it was his turn, the boy told his own story from first to last, leaving out not a single detail" (in "The Two Brothers and the Magic Hen") or (as in "Cengidilaver") "And he told the sultan what had happened at their birth, and how they had fared since the evil woman had set them adrift on the river." The completeness of the repetition is a matter of performance rather than of narrative, and it, too, will be considered later.

Among the tales provided here, a number include characters despised or considered unlikely to succeed; a sampling of these will suffice to demonstrate that point. Taşkafalı, the stupid brother in "Akıllı, Taşkafalı, and the Three Gifts," in the end proves superior to clever Akıllı, who had cheated him out of his fair share of their inheritance. The youngest princess in "The Princess and the Red Horse Husband" is finally victorious over her envious, scheming elder sisters. In "The Frog Wife," the young husband at last defeats his jealous father in repeated attempts to acquire the frog wife for himself. It is a mild but resourceful old woman who saves the Turks in "How the Siege of Van Was Lifted." And in two tales, "The Stepdaughter and the Black Serpent" and "The Two Stepdaughters," the girl despised and rejected by the stepmother proves the winner.

The Performance Element

The voice of the teller, as described above, is most evident in his performance, and in the performance details also lies the most distinctive mark of the Turkish oral narrative. Extended formulaic beginnings and endings differ markedly from one teller to another. In the tellings of many are found formulaic descriptions of weddings and their festivities, of the beauty of girls, the handsomeness of men, and comparisons of relative beauty or size, and of the use of "three or five" to indicate quantity of items or length of time. Less frequently found in this collection are traditional patterns for the traveling of distance, a formula found here in only a handful of tales. Onomatopoeia enriches almost every teller's performance, as do alliteration and metaphor and simile. Poems and songs are provided by several of the tellers where such devices serve the narrative. Internal rhyme, difficult to reproduce in English without loss of flavor, is everywhere present. And rhetorical questions spark the listener's attention, while transitional expressions carry the listener readily from one scene to another related but quite different one. Too, the use of such symbolic numbers as three, seven, and forty occurs in the majority of tellers' tales. The performance element in the Turkish narrative is rich indeed.

Extending the traditional "once (twice) there wasn't" opening are such details as "when the flea was a porter and the camel a barber" (nine instances), "when Allah's creatures were many, and to talk too much was a sin" (six), and "when I was rocking my father's (mother's) cradle *tıngır mıngır*" (four). Ending the tale may tie the tale to the audience: "And for us, may we have mates who are faithful," "As for me, I came here to tell you this tale. May it bring you joy," "May there continue to be such noble women in our land," and "And may we put such good advice in our own pockets!" Three other distinctly different closings are these: "The matter had ended, just as our story has ended," "And if you have not been as fortunate as they, I can at least wish health to the ears of those who heard this tale and health to the tongue of him who told it," and "I and many others have seen that tomb ourselves. And it is said that the account of Cihanşah and Şemsi Bâni was told by Şahmeran, padishah of snakes, to Camesap during those seven long years that Camesap spent in the otherworld. May it live long!" (This last example, closing a tale told by Ali Çiftçi in 1981, ties that tale to one told by the same narrator in 1964!)

In Turkish tales, most weddings are celebrated for forty days and forty nights; in several of the tales, the husband and wife, separated by one difficulty or another for a long period of time, "for pure joy were married all over again, with a wedding that lasted for forty days and forty nights." In "All for a Wrinkled Little Pomegranate," the two principals celebrate *three* weddings, the first and the third for the forty-day period and the middle one performed simply by a village *hoca*. There are almost as many variations in the treatment of weddings as there are tellers.

Descriptions of beauty or handsomeness and comparisons of relative beauty or size are frequent elements in performance. Since the moon is considered exceptionally beautiful, the beauty of girls and the handsomeness of men are often described in such terms as "as beautiful as the fourteenth of the moon" (the moon at its fullest) or "so handsome he could say to the moon, 'Either you or I shall rise tonight.'" For girls compared for beauty, "each one was more beautiful than all the others." And as for the nine nine-headed giant sons, "each one was slightly larger than all the others."

Onomatopoeia, a device used by most of the tellers, includes "*Tak! Tak! Tak!*" (for the knocking at a door), "*mışıl mışıl*" (for soft snoring), "*Çüş!*" (the Turkish equivalent of "Whoa!"), "*Tup!*" and "*Put!*" (for the fitting of eyeballs into their respective sockets), and countless others that appear in the tales. Likewise, metaphor and simile are frequent: "with scarcely wit enough to salt one dolma," "with his heart more and more on fire," "his blood froze in his veins," "still, Rüstem Pasha felt the small bird of hope alive in his breast," "you all have got me wall-flat," and "you would not put my words in your pocket" (that is, remember them). Further, a sampling of similes includes these: "as like as two halves of the same apple," "shining like tinned kettles," "a horse as thin as a needle," "as different from one another as oranges are from pomegranates," "with his eyes flowing like two fountains," "chattering like a nightingale," and "began to see as clear as a mirror."

Among the many versions of the formula used to describe time consumed or distance traveled, these will serve as samples: The father in "The Two Brothers and the Magic Hen" "went a little; he went far. He traveled straight over hills and over dales. He traveled six months and a summer, and when he turned back to look, he found that he had gone no farther than a grain of barley on his journey." The princess in "The Princess and the Red Horse Husband" "went and went, six months and a summer, straight over rivers and over dales; when she turned back, she saw that she had gone only the length of a grain of barley in her journey. She went for months and years, and she became very tired." And later in the same tale, the princess and her beloved "went a little; they went far. They went six months and a summer. They went straight over hills and over dales, but when they turned to look, they had gone no farther than the length of a grain of barley in their journey." Quite clearly, this formula is common property in the Turkish oral tradition, to be used in performance as the teller and the audience choose.

The completeness of a repetition depends partly on the teller's own preference, partly on the audience's receptiveness to repetition—and the teller does "read" the audience's reactions—and partly on the time available for the telling. If the hour is late (as it was for the completion of Altın Erol's "Cengidilaver") or some other business is pressing, repetition, despite the delight of both teller and listeners in it, is the element most readily reduced in performance without damage to plot and characterization and without loss of the functional element of the tale.

A performance device used effectively in the present tales is that of the rhetorical question, one present in a number of the tales. Consider these, for example: (in "The Prince, the Parrot, and the Beautiful Mute") "How can a table talk?" and later "How can a chair talk?"; (in "The *Köse* and the Three Swindlers") "Of course, he was just running away, but how could the swindlers know that?" and "After all, wasn't the whole town talking about those three clever fellows?" and "How could he hope to escape?" and "How could he know that the first one was not indeed saying 'Forty!' but was gurgling as he drowned?"; (in "The Two Brothers and the Magic Hen") "How could she know that the gold had appeared only because the boy had eaten the neck of the hen?" This last example has an added feature: it enabled the storyteller to supply a fact about the magic hen that had been overlooked when the cook had told the brothers the benefits of swallowing the hen's head and neck.

With this instance of performance skill, I rest my case.

Cengidilaver

O nce there was and once there wasn't, when the flea was a porter and the camel a barber, when I was rocking my father's cradle *tıngır mıngır*—well, in those times, there was a powerful sultan. The sultan had all the good things of this earth. But above them all, he prized his wife, a woman as patient and good as she was beautiful. If only they could have a child!

Now, at this time in the palace there was a clever woman, beautiful but mean and envious, who wished above all else to bring ruin to the lovely sultana and to marry the sultan herself. Learning that the sultana would soon bear a child, this evil woman arranged to be appointed midwife. In a little while, not one but two children were born, a boy and a girl, as like as two halves of the same apple, and beautiful, besides. As soon as the mother had fallen asleep, the midwife wrapped the two babies in a blanket and hid them in her own room. In the mother's bed, she put two puppies in place of the babies. Then she sent word to the sultan that he might come in to see his children.

Eagerly, the sultan bent to look at the babies. But what was this? Puppies in the bed? He turned to question the midwife.

"Sire, these are the babes your wife bore. But, alas, they are not what you expected. How strange that a woman should bear puppies." And she was pleased as the sultan's horror and anger grew.

"This woman!" he exclaimed at last. "*Aman, aman!* My wife is a monstrous, unnatural mother. But what to do about it?"

"Sire," suggested the woman, "surely such an unnatural woman should be exposed to shame. Perhaps she could be buried alive."

"But that is not enough," said the sultan. "I shall have her buried in earth up to her neck, and require all who pass by to spit upon her face."

Roughly awakening his wife, the sultan had her carried away and buried up to the neck in a place just outside the palace gate. And to make certain she would live to endure her shame, he ordered that food be provided to her four times a day. As for the puppies, they were given into the care of the midwife.

Meanwhile, the evil-minded woman had put the two babies into a basket and set them adrift on the river which flowed past the palace. Time came, time went, and the river carried them at last to a mill.

The next morning the miller was puzzled to find that his mill wheel was

1

still. "Perhaps some branch has caught in the stream," he thought, and he hurried out to look. To his surprise, he found a basket washed up against the weir. He pulled out the basket and looked inside, and, "Allah be praised!" he exclaimed. "Here are two babies for my very own!" Carefully he took the basket to his little hut behind the mill. Since he had no wife anymore, he tended the children himself, and no woman could have cared for them better than he. His two goats were milked to feed the babies, and they grew strong on the simple fare.

Sixteen years passed, with the children happy and contented in the only home they knew. Then one day the miller called the boy and the girl to his bedside. "I am old and ill," he said, "and it is the will of Allah that I shall soon die. My death I regret not for myself but for you, my children. Who will look after you when I am gone? I have nothing but the mill to leave you—ah, the mill and these three magic feathers." And he took from beneath his pillow three silver-gray feathers, each more beautiful than the others. Handing them to the boy, he said, "When you are in danger or distress, burn one of these feathers. Allah willing, you will receive aid. But do not burn a single feather until you have need of it. And now, may Allah preserve you both." With these words, the miller stretched out a hand to each child. Sighing deeply, he breathed his last breath and was gone.

After the miller's death and a proper burial, the boy and the girl agreed between themselves to leave the mill and seek shelter in the town at the far edge of the forest. "Come, my sister," said the boy. "If we walk quickly, Allah willing, we can have a roof over our heads before nightfall." And the two began walking along the worn path through the forest, with the girl weeping as they went.

Suddenly through her tears she saw a stone sparkling at the edge of the path. "Ah, look, my brother, at this diamond," said the girl, and she bent to pick it up.

"Diamond!" the boy scoffed. "It is only a stone, my sister. Come along. We must hurry, for it will soon be dark."

But as the girl picked up the stone, she saw others even more beautiful, and she turned aside and gathered them into her sash. "Come, my brother. You have room in your sash, too. Who knows? Perhaps these stones will buy bread for our mouths." And she and the boy gathered all the shining stones they saw. Then they went on their way again, and came at last to the town.

Hungry from their long walk, the children went first to a bakery. "Sire," the boy said, holding out one of the shining stones to the baker, "is this stone of any worth? If it is, we should like to buy some bread with it."

Shaking his head from side to side, the baker said, "I don't know, my boy. I think Hasan Bey the jeweler is still in his shop. Go next door and ask him. He will know."

The children hurried to the jeweler's shop. "Sire," said the boy, laying

2

one of the stones on the counter, "is this stone of any worth? We would like to trade it for a bit of bread and a night's shelter."

The jeweler stared at the stone, amazed. Then he looked curiously at the children. "Tell me where you found this precious stone. And tell me, too, why you are in need of bread and shelter. Where are your mother and your father?"

From first to last, the boy told the jeweler their story, beginning with the miller's finding them and ending with their arrival at the jeweler's shop.

"And you have no parents?" the jeweler asked.

"None, sire, that we know of," answered the girl.

"Then you shall be my children," decided the jeweler. And he took them home to his own little house. "My wife died many years ago," he said, "but you will be comfortable here."

Little by little, the stones were exchanged for money, and the jeweler and his children began to live even more comfortably in a house as fine as a palace. But such news does not take long to travel, and soon the evil woman, now the sultan's wife, learned that there were twin children, as like as two halves of the same apple, living in the fine house. Curious to learn more about them, she went *patur kitur* to the house while the jeweler and the boy were away. *Tak! Tak! Tak!* She knocked at the door.

The girl answered the door, and, as was the custom, she invited the woman in. "Welcome," she said, as she led the woman inside.

And, "I feel welcome, my dear neighbor," the woman replied, looking about in amazement at the fine furnishings. "Now, tell me about yourself, child." As she sat listening and sipping the cup of good Turkish coffee that

the girl had prepared, the woman realized that this girl was none other than the sultan's own daughter. Fearing that the sultan would someday discover the truth, she determined to destroy the children.

Slyly she said, "My dear, you have a lovely home. If I were living here, I would yearn for only one thing more." She paused.

"Yes? And what is that?" asked the girl eagerly.

"Ah," sighed the woman, "if you had but one rosebush from the garden of Cengidilaver, your garden would be complete. Such beautiful roses! Such a wonderful scent!" And she looked about her as if suddenly the house had lost its charm because it lacked the rosebush.

"A rosebush from the garden of Cengidilaver," murmured the girl. "Yes, perhaps you are right. I shall ask my brother about it when he comes home this evening."

Soon after that, the visitor left, and the girl began to look here and there about her. Soon, wanting the rosebush had become needing the rosebush, and the girl began to weep. By the time of her brother's return, the girl could think of nothing else. "We *must* have a rosebush from the garden of Cengidilaver," she insisted, with her eyes flowing like two fountains.

"Oh, but my sister," the boy answered, "surely we have all that we need here to make us comfortable and happy. What is one rosebush more or less?"

"Indeed," she cried, "if I cannot have a rosebush from the garden of Cengidilaver, I shall die of grief." And it seemed as if she might.

"Hush, sister; tush, sister," the boy said at last. "If your heart is set upon the rosebush, then I must try to get it for you." And carefully removing from his sash one of the three magic feathers, he went out into the garden to burn it.

No sooner had the smoke begun to curl from the feather than there came a gash of lightning and a crash of thunder sufficient to shake the boy to the soles of his sandals. Suddenly there stood before him an enormous jinn, with his toes touching the earth and his turban scraping the sky.

"Ask whatever you will. Your wish I must fulfill," said the jinn, his eyes fixed upon the boy.

For all his fright, the boy somehow found his tongue. "Sire," he began, "my sister longs for a rosebush from the garden of Cengidilaver."

"No!" roared the jinn. "It is impossible. Cengidilaver is a monster. He would tear you apart, piece by piece."

The boy was resolute. "Whatever Cengidilaver may do to me, I must try to get the rosebush. Tell me what I must do."

"If you must, then you will," grumbled the jinn. "But listen carefully, and do exactly as I say. Tomorrow at the first silver streak of dawn, you will find a white horse standing in front of your door. That horse will take you with the speed of the wind to the garden of Cengidilaver, but you must at no time look behind you. When you come to the garden gate, you will find a wolf and a sheep. Before the wolf there lies some grass; before the sheep

4

there lies a piece of meat. Give the meat to the wolf and the grass to the sheep. You can then pass through the gate. Inside the garden you will find two doors, one closed and the other open. Open the closed door and close the open door. Beyond the doors, at the center of the garden, Cengidilaver will be seated at the foot of a great tree. If his eyes are closed, he is awake. If his eyes are open, he is asleep. If his eyes are open, run and pull up a rosebush, thorns and all, and then leave the garden as fast as you can. Remember, you must never look behind you, no matter what happens. Once you pass through the garden gate again, you will be safe."

Just as the jinn had said, the next morning in the silver dawn there was a white horse standing before the house. The boy rode the horse—*Prrrt!*— and in the winking of an eye he came to the gate of Cengidilaver's garden. As the jinn had directed him, he gave the meat to the wolf and the grass to the sheep, and so he was able to pass through the gate into the garden. As the jinn had directed him, he opened the closed door and closed the open door, and then he found himself at the center of the garden. There sat Cengidilaver, horrid monster that he was, with his eyes wide open. "Ah, praise be to Allah, Cengidilaver is asleep," thought the boy, and he went straight to a rosebush and tugged and tugged until he had pulled it up, thorns and all.

At the moment the roots left the earth, all the other rosebushes began to cry, "Awake, awake, Cengidilaver! Cengidilaver, awake! Your rosebush has been stolen."

Instantly, Cengidilaver blinked his eyes and was awake. Seeing the boy running toward the doors, he shouted, "Closed door, closed door! Catch the thief who took my rosebush."

But the closed door answered, "*I* will not help you. You have kept me closed for forty years, but today the boy opened me. I will not catch him."

Then, "Open door, open door!" shouted Cengidilaver. "Catch the thief who took my rosebush."

The open door called, "I will not help you, Cengidilaver. You have left me open for forty years, and today the boy was kind enough to close me. I will not catch him at all."

Seeing that the boy had safely passed the doors, Cengidilaver called out, "Wolf, catch him! He has taken my rosebush."

"Indeed, I will not," answered the wolf. "For forty years you have given me nothing but grass to eat. Today the boy came along and gave me meat. I will not catch him."

"Then, sheep, *you* catch him!" shouted Cengidilaver.

But the sheep said, "I will not catch him, either. For forty years you have given me nothing but meat to eat. Today the boy came along and gave me grass. *I* will not catch him."

The boy ran safely through the gate, leapt on the white horse, and with the speed of the wind came home to his own house. He and his sister planted Cengidilaver's rosebush in their garden, and the wonderful scent of the roses reached every corner of the house.

Not many days after that, the evil woman happened to pass that way, and she smelled the roses in the jeweler's garden. *Tak! Tak! Tak!* She knocked at the door, and the girl came at once to answer it.

"Welcome," said the girl, and led the woman inside.

"I feel welcome, my dear neighbor," answered the woman. "I see that you have one of the rosebushes from Cengidilaver's garden. How happy you must be!"

"Ah, yes," said the girl. "I had no idea how much our garden needed a rosebush just like that." And she prepared a cup of fine Turkish coffee for her visitor.

"My dear," said the woman slyly, "it is true that your house is very lovely. But I miss the song of a nightingale. If I lived here, I could not bear to be without a nightingale from Cengidilaver's garden. But then, I suppose you scarcely miss it."

"A nightingale?" the girl asked. "I had never thought of a nightingale. Yes, a nightingale would please me very much."

Not long afterward, the woman left, and the girl began thinking about a nightingale. Thinking led to yearning, and soon she was weeping. Her brother was troubled to see her in tears, and it was not long before she told him, "Oh, my brother, I cannot live without one of the nightingales from Cengidilaver's garden."

6

"My sister, do not weep about a nightingale," he said. "After all, one bird is as good as another. Our garden is full of birds already."

"But there are no nightingales," she sobbed. "How I long for just one nightingale from the garden of Cengidilaver!" And she cried and would not be comforted.

At last her brother removed from his sash the second magic feather and went into the garden to burn it. No sooner had the smoke begun to curl from the feather than there came a gash of lightning and a crash of thunder that shook the boy to the soles of his sandals. Suddenly that enormous jinn appeared, with his toes touching the earth and his turban scraping the sky.

"Ask whatever you will. Your wish I must fulfill," rumbled the jinn, gazing straight at the boy.

Frightened as he was, somehow the boy found his tongue. "Sire," he said, "my sister longs for a nightingale from the garden of Cengidilaver."

"No! It is impossible!" roared the jinn. "Cengidilaver is a monster. He would tear you apart, piece by piece."

But the boy was resolute. "I do not care what Cengidilaver may do to me. I must have a nightingale for my sister, for she is most unhappy without it."

"If you must, then you will," grumbled the jinn. "But listen carefully, and do exactly as I say. In that way, you may still escape from Cengidilaver." And the jinn told the boy, as he had done before, to ride the white horse as far as the garden gate, to place the meat before the wolf and the grass before the sheep, to open the closed door and close the open door, and to beware, above all, of looking behind him. As for the nightingale, he warned, "Be sure that Cengidilaver's eyes are open before you try to take the nightingale. Take only one, and then run as fast as you can. If you can pass through the garden gate, you will be safe."

Just as the jinn had said, the next morning in the silver dawn there stood the white horse. The boy rode—*Prrrt!*—and in the winking of an eye he came to the gate of Cengidilaver's garden. He did exactly as he had been told, placing the meat before the wolf and the grass before the sheep, and thus he was able to enter the gate safely. Coming to the doors, he opened the closed door and closed the open one. Finding himself at the center of the garden, he stood quietly and watched Cengidilaver. The monster's glowing eyes were open, so the boy tiptoed to the corner of the garden where the nightingales perched. Gently he picked up the nearest one and turned to leave the garden. But the moment the bird's feet left the branch, all the other nightingales began to sing, "Awake, awake, Cengidilaver! Cengidilaver, awake! Your nightingale has been stolen."

Instantly, Cengidilaver blinked his eyes and was awake. Seeing the boy running toward the doors, he called, "Closed door, closed door! Catch the thief who stole my nightingale!"

Again, the door replied, "Indeed, I will not catch him."

7

And the open door also refused to catch the boy, so he ran and ran toward the gate.

Angrily, Cengidilaver called, "Wolf, wolf! Catch the thief who stole my nightingale."

Again, the wolf replied, "No, indeed, I will *not* catch him, for today he gave me meat."

As the sheep also refused to catch the boy, he ran out safely through the gate. Leaping upon the white horse, with the speed of the wind the boy came home to his own house. He and his sister found a fine place for the nightingale in a corner of the garden, and its songs brought new joy to their lives.

One evening not many days after that, the evil woman happened to pass that way and she heard the glorious song of the nightingale in the garden. The next morning—*Tak! Tak! Tak!*—she knocked at the door, just after the boy had gone to the shop with the jeweler.

Answering the door, the girl cried, "Welcome," and she led the visitor at once to their garden. "See," she said, "over in that corner we have the nightingale. How right you were! We needed that lovely song in our garden."

Biting her lip, the woman tried to think of some way in which she might truly be rid of the two children. At last she had arrived at a plan. "My dear," she said slyly, "you have a beautiful garden, but it would be even lovelier if you could have Cengidilaver himself as your gardener. Those roses need pruning, and the walks should be trimmed and weeded. No one in all the world is as fine a gardener as Cengidilaver."

After a cup of good Turkish coffee and talk of this and that, the woman left, and the girl went back to look more closely at the garden. Yes, the visitor was right. Near the fountain, there were spots of mildew. The rhododendron looked straggly, and the whole garden had an untidy air about it. The longer she looked, the more dissatisfied and disappointed she became, until she fell to weeping. By the time her brother came home for dinner, she was truly miserable.

The boy, surprised to find his sister weeping again, asked her what could be troubling her now that she had the lovely rosebush and the sweet-voiced nightingale.

"Alas, my brother," she cried, "what good are rosebushes and nightingales in an untidy garden? I want a good gardener to care for our garden. I want Cengidilaver himself to come and be our gardener." And from yearning for that gardener, the girl wept afresh.

"Cengidilaver!" the boy exclaimed, his heart suddenly chilled. "My sister, you do not know what you are asking."

But the girl cried and cried, and would not be comforted. At last the boy sighed and carefully took from his sash the last of the magic feathers. Putting one foot before the other, he went into the garden to burn the feather. No sooner had the smoke begun to curl upward than there came a gash of lightning and a crash of thunder that shook the boy to the soles of his sandals.

8

Suddenly that enormous jinn appeared, with his toes touching the earth and his turban scraping the sky.

"Ask whatever you will. Your wish I must fulfill," rumbled the jinn, staring straight at the boy.

Though the boy trembled with fright, he somehow found his tongue. "Sire," said he, "my sister wishes to have Cengidilaver as her gardener."

"No, no, no!" shouted the jinn, and every leaf in the garden quivered with the force of his voice. "You know well that Cengidilaver is a monster. Allah alone has spared you, or Cengidilaver would have torn you apart, piece by piece."

Pale but determined, the boy said, "No matter what happens to me, I must seek Cengidilaver himself."

"If you must, then you will," groaned the jinn. "But listen very carefully, and do exactly as I say. In that way you may yet escape with your life. And certainly your courage will stand you in good stead." And the jinn told the boy, as he had done before, to ride the white horse as far as the garden gate, to place the meat before the wolf and the grass before the sheep, to open the closed door and close the open door, and, above all, to beware of looking a single time behind him. "As for Cengidilaver himself," continued the jinn, "there is something very strange about him. I have heard it said that Cengidilaver has been placed under a spell, and he remains a monster as long as he stays in the garden. But if someone is brave enough to lift him and strong enough to carry him beyond the garden gate, he will become harmless. He will lose his monster form and will be no more dangerous than any other man—indeed, he will become a man himself. The danger lies within the garden. Go, my boy, and may your way be open."

Just as the jinn had said, in the silver dawn the white horse stood again before the house. Murmuring, "*Bismillâh!*" the boy mounted the horse, and—*Prrrt!*—in the winking of an eye he came to the gate of Cengidilaver's garden. Once again he placed the meat before the wolf and the grass before the sheep, and entered the garden. Once again he opened the closed door and closed the open door, and came to the center of the garden.

There sat Cengidilaver beneath the tree, his glowing eyes wide open and his great arms folded across his chest in sleep. Tense and watchful, the boy stood for a moment, gathering all his strength for what he must do. Then, striding forward, he grasped the monster firmly and flung him over his shoulder. As fast as he could, he hurried toward the garden gate. This way and that, Cengidilaver struggled, and the two were locked together in deadly combat. But the boy's determination gave him greater strength, and at last he was able to carry the monster beyond the gate.

At that very moment, Cengidilaver lost his monster shape and became a gentle, grave man. "You have great courage, my boy. Again you have finished what you set out to do. As for me, the spell that made me a monster and put me in that garden is now broken, and in gratitude I shall serve you all my

9

life. Take me where you will." The boy and Cengidilaver mounted the white horse and in scarcely more than a thought's worth of time they arrived at the boy's home.

That evening in the garden Cengidilaver drew the boy aside and gave him a small gold ring. "This ring," he said, "belongs to your mother. Your mother was once the wife of your father, the sultan, but through the deceit of an evil woman she was buried in earth up to her neck. She still lives, Allah be praised! But your father does not know that you are his children, for at your birth that evil woman stole you and your sister out of your mother's bed and put two puppies there instead. She set you adrift in a basket, and you were saved by the miller, who brought you up as his own children."

The boy was surprised indeed to learn these things about himself and his family, and he grieved for the injustice done to his mother. "If I could save her . . .," he said.

"This is what you can do," said Cengidilaver. "Invite the sultan here for dinner. Among the other foods, serve *pilav*, and in the *pilav* you serve to the sultan, hide the gold ring I gave you. When the sultan sees the ring, he will recognize it, and then you can tell him what I have told you."

After a few days, the boy sent a messenger to the palace to invite the sultan to honor their home by coming to dinner. Now, the sultan had noticed the jeweler's house, as beautiful as a palace, and he was curious to see who lived inside it. So he came at the boy's invitation. For dinner, many fine dishes were served, among them an elegant platter of *pilav*. As the sultan was eating his portion of *pilav*, he bit down on something hard, and, surprised, he removed a small object from his mouth. He stared at it, and then he exclaimed, "This is my first wife's ring! Where did you get it?"

"It is the ring which belonged to my mother," cried the girl, running to put her arms around the sultan's neck.

"We are your children," said the boy. And he told the sultan what had happened at their birth, and how they had fared since the evil woman had set them adrift on the river.

"Ah!" exclaimed the sultan. "There is only one woman who could have done that evil thing, and she is now my wife. Tomorrow she will pay with her life for the harm that she has done to you and to your beautiful mother."

That very evening, the sultan and his children went to the palace together. At once the sultan ordered his first wife removed from the earth and bathed and dressed and brought to them. In almost the same breath, he sent his men to take the life of the evil woman.

The sultan and his beautiful wife were married all over again, with a celebration lasting forty days and forty nights, and the two dwelt with their children in happiness all the rest of their lives.

They had their wish fulfilled. Let's go up and sit in their seats!

10

Tekerleme

T ime within time, when the sieve was just a hoop, and when I was rocking my mother's and father's cradles, I was then a *keloğlan*. One day my father became ill, and I carried him to a doctor. He suggested this cure and that cure. He gave me an egg to break over my father, but I dropped the egg and a rooster came out of it.

I put a harness on that rooster and made him carry heavy loads. The harness rubbed the rooster's back and made it sore. I broke an egg over the sore place and wrapped it with a pecan leaf. Soon a pecan tree grew from that leaf, and after a while there were many pecans on the tree. People passing by threw dirt clods and stones at the pecans to knock them down. First there was a heap of dirt clods and stones around the pecan tree, and after a while this heap grew into a large field.

I planted wheat in that field. Soon it had grown to the height of an ant's knee. When harvest time came, I took a sickle and went to the field. As I got there, I saw a boar running about in the wheat field. I threw my sickle at that boar, and the handle of the sickle stuck in the boar's rectum. This frightened the boar, and he began running around the field even faster than he had been running before. As he ran here and there and everywhere, the sickle kept cutting the wheat. In this way, the entire field was harvested in a very short time.

The Princess and
the Red Horse Husband

Once there was and once there wasn't, long ago, when the camel was a barber and the flea was a porter—well, in those times there was a padishah who had three daughters. Time passed, and the padishah still did not have them married.

"*Aman!*" the three daughters said. "This won't do." So they called their servant and they said, "Please bring us three watermelons, one overripe, one ripe, and one underripe."

"All right," said the servant and brought the watermelons.

The oldest daughter said, "Now, take these to our father."

The watermelons were taken to the padishah. "What is this?" he asked.

"Open them up and see," said the servant.

They cut the watermelons, one by one. When they cut the first one, they saw that it was overripe. When they cut the second one, they found that it was just right. Then they cut the third one, and it was underripe. "What does all this mean?" said the padishah. "I don't understand what this means."

"Would you permit me to explain?" said the servant. "They want to get married."

"All right," said the padishah. "If it's husbands they want, we'll send criers out to tell everyone, rich or poor, noble or not, to come and pass in front of my balcony. I'll give a golden ball to each of my daughters, and they may choose whichever one they want and throw the ball at him. I'll marry them to the men they want."

The next morning, he had three golden balls made for them. The criers went out calling, and everybody, rich or poor, noble or not, high officials and low officials—everyone got dressed up and started parading in front of the palace. The oldest princess threw her ball at the son of the vizier. The middle one threw hers at the son of the imam. But the ball of the little one rolled and hit a red horse.

"Oh, look! It didn't work!" they cried. They brought it back and she threw it again. It hit the horse again.

She tried the third time, and again she hit the red horse.

"Oh, what a pity for my youngest!" said the padishah.

He got everything ready for his other daughters' weddings. When it came to the youngest, he got everything ready, but there wasn't any bridegroom except the red horse. In the evening when they were shown into the bridal chamber, it was arranged as a stable. "What else for a horse?" said the padishah.

12

"Ha, ha, ha!" laughed her sisters. "Your husband is a horse, and ours come like lions in the evening."

Home in the evening came the horse, *tukkır, tukkır*. He came into the room and closed the door. He shook himself, got out of his horse's skin, and he was as handsome a man as could be. He took off his coat and he sat down, and they were happy. He said to his young wife, "Now, look. You are not to say anything about me to your sisters. If you do, that will spoil the magic, and you'll lose me. Let me stay as a horse in the daytime, or you'll lose me." You see, he was the fairy giant king's son.

Time passed, and her sisters kept on making fun of her. "What happened when you got married? All you got was a horse. We are having wonderful lives with our husbands. But all you have is a horse who comes *tukkır, tukkır* home in the evening." And the time came when she couldn't bear their teasing any more.

"What makes you think he's a horse?" she said. "Some night you come and watch us through a hole in the door. He's such a youth that he would buy fifteen of yours."

And the sisters came in the evening, after the horse had gone in and locked the door, and what they saw was a very handsome man, so handsome that he could say to the rising moon, "Either you or I may rise tonight."

"*Aman!*" they said. "We thought that he was just a horse, but he is a very prince of men!" And they resolved to trick their sister out of her husband.

13

In the morning, after the handsome man had become a horse again and had gone away, the sisters said, "You are right. He is very handsome. But you have no wisdom; you have no brains. Someday you must burn that horse skin. Why have him a horse?"

"Oh, no, I can't," said the girl. "No, I can't throw it into the fire, because that would spoil the magic." But they talked and talked about it, and finally they convinced her.

One night, when he was out of his horse skin and had gone to bed, she got up and grabbed the skin and threw it into the fire.

"What have you done?" shouted her husband. "You have spoiled everything. You can't have me any more." And he became a bird and flew away.

The girl cried and cried, and beat her knees in grief. "What shall I do? Where will I find him again?" And she could talk of nothing else.

Finally she went to her father, for her father had heard about it, and she said, "If you love me, Father, get me a pair of iron shoes and an iron staff, and I'll go and look for my husband. I'll walk until I find him."

"You must be crazy, my daughter," said the padishah. "You say he became a bird and flew away. Then he must be the son of the fairy giant king."

"Yes, he is," said the girl. "I was happy with my husband, and I'll look for him until I find him or until I die."

They could not make her listen to reason, so they gave her a pair of iron shoes and an iron staff and a bag full of gold. The padishah said, "All right. May your way be open." She kissed her parents' hands, and then she started to walk.

She went and went, six months and a summer, straight over rivers and over dales; when she turned back, she saw that she had gone only the length of a grain of barley in her journey. She went for months and years, and she became very tired. One day as she sat by a fountain to rest, she lifted the sole of her iron shoe and saw that there was a hole in it. "Just think!" said she. "Iron shoes so worn as to have holes in them!"

While she was looking at her shoes, *prrrrt* came a bird and shook itself, and there was her husband.

"Oh, you came!" said the girl. "You don't *know* what I've suffered and how I've walked, and I can't bear it any longer."

"Yes," said her husband, "but how can I take you home to my country?" For it seems that his mother had engaged him to his cousin. But he prayed and then blew on the girl and turned her into an apple and he put her in his pocket to take her home, because his mother and father were giants.

When he got into the house, his mother said, "Shah Selim, I can smell human flesh on you."

"No, Mother, no." And he prayed and blew on the apple, and hid the girl in a corner of the cupboard.

Then came his father. He sniffed and sniffed. He said, "Woman, I smell

14

human flesh in this house."

"No, no," she said. "There is no human flesh here. It must be something between your teeth. Pick it out and eat it." And he picked it out and ate it. Then they sat down and ate and drank.

For a while he hid the girl. But he was engaged to his cousin and was soon to marry her. One day he said to the girl, "When my mother is kneading dough, she throws her breasts behind her over her shoulders. While she is kneading dough, you must go behind her and nurse from her breasts. Then she won't kill you."

So one day when the giant mother was kneading dough, with her breasts thrown back over her shoulders, the girl went up behind her and nursed from her breasts. The woman turned around and saw a girl as beautiful as the fourteenth of the moon. And the woman said, "Oh, Shah Selim, this is your doing! Where did you find her?"

And Shah Selim told his mother everything.

"But," said the woman, "you are going to marry your cousin."

"All right," said the young man. "We'll get married, and this one will be around to serve us."

"What will your father say?"

"Don't worry. I'll hide her when Father comes."

The girl worked in the house for a while. She washed and swept and

cooked, and when the father came they turned her into an apple or a pear and put her away.

When the prince was to be married, his mattresses had to be filled with feathers. The giant mother gave the mattress covers to the girl and said, "Now, you take these and fill them with birds' feathers to the very brim, and bring them back."

After the giant mother had left, the girl began to cry. "Where can I find so many feathers in a strange land?" While she was crying, Shah Selim came, and she said, "Why shouldn't I cry? Your mother has told me to fill two mattresses with birds' feathers, and how can I do it?"

"Oh, what's easier?" he said. "Stop worrying. Just go to the top of that hill and cry out three times, 'Shah Selim is dead!' When you say that, all the birds in the world will come and shed their feathers in sorrow. Then you'll fill the mattresses, and what's easier than that? Fill them and carry them down." Shah Selim knew that his mother planned to kill the girl if she could not fill the mattresses, and so he helped the girl.

She went to the top of the hill and cried out, "Shah Selim is dead! Shah Selim is dead! Shah Selim is dead!" Just as Shah Selim had said, all the birds in the world came *prrrt, prrrt, prrrt* flying there, beating their feathers and shedding them for sorrow. She gathered the feathers up and filled the mattress covers, tied them up, and took them down the hill.

The giant mother said, "Hmmmm, she did it. It's Shah Selim's doing again." Then she said to the girl, "Go and bring the bread griddle from the aunt's house. We are going to make bread."

As soon as the girl had gone outside the house, she began to cry, and with good reason, for she had been told that there were fierce animals and magic doors on the way there. She was still crying when Shah Selim came and said, "What's wrong, my princess?"

"Your mother told me to bring the bread griddle from the aunt's house. How can I? I am afraid, and that's why I'm crying."

"Oh, it's easy," he said. "You don't need to cry. This is what you have to do. You close the open door and open the closed door. There is a dog with grass in front of him, and there is a horse with meat in front of him. Take the grass from the dog and give it to the horse, and take the meat from the horse and give it to the dog. Then run and get the griddle from behind the door and come back without being seen by anyone."

"All right," she said, and she went. She closed the open door and opened the closed door. There was a heap of grass in front of the dog and a heap of meat in front of the horse. She gave the meat to the dog and the grass to the horse. Then she grabbed the griddle from behind the door. But when she was running away, the aunt saw her and shouted, "Catch her, you dog!"

But the dog said, "Why should I? All this time I had the heap of grass before me. Does a dog eat grass? I'll not catch her."

"You, horse, catch her!" shouted the aunt.

"No, I won't. Does a horse eat meat? Only she gave me grass."

"Door, you catch her!" shouted the aunt.

The door said, "No. All my life I lived closed, and she opened me. I'll not catch her."

"You other door, you catch her!" the aunt shouted.

And the other door said, "No. Why should I catch her? All the while, I stood open, and she closed me. I won't catch her."

So the girl brought the griddle home. "Oh," Shah Selim's mother said. "You got through that, too. It's Shah Selim's doing again."

Now it was time for the wedding of Shah Selim and his cousin. The girl was very sad, but what could she do? She loved her husband, and she kept quiet. She never said anything, and the wedding was finished and the bride was brought. The padishah's daughter was watching the bride from behind the door when the giant mother said, "Come out here." And she took ten candles and stuck them on all ten of the princess's fingers, and she said, "You're going to hold these for the bride all night. You'll hold these until the morning."

The girl said, "Yes," but she cried and cried, with her two eyes like two fountains. "What will happen to me? When the wax melts, my fingers will burn, and then the fire will consume me."

"There's no need to cry, my princess," said Shah Selim. "Let the candles stand on your fingers until the wax melts and your fingers become hot. Then press your hands on the bride's face and smear the wax on her. I'll be behind the door, and the horses will be waiting to carry us away. We'll run away together. Did you think I would really take her as my wife? I promised because I feared my mother, that's all."

Finally they brought the bride in, and they lighted the candles on the princess's fingers. The wax began to melt and to burn her fingers. She pressed her fingers down on the bride's face. And there was Shah Selim behind the door. They got on their horses and rode away. They went a little; they went far. They went six months and a summer. They went straight over hills and over dales, but when they turned to look, they had gone no farther than the length of a grain of barley in their journey. Now let's come back to the giants' house.

In the morning, the father came and wanted to see the son and the bride. As to the girl, they were certain that she must be dead. When they came to the chamber, what did they find? The bride had fainted, with wax all over her face, and the padishah's daughter was nowhere to be found. They looked for Shah Selim, and he was gone. "*Aman!*" said the father. And he dug himself into the clouds and followed after the boy with a sound as loud as thunder.

"*Aman!*" said Shah Selim. "My father is coming. What shall I do?"

17

"Do what you can," said the princess.

"This is what I'm going to do," said Shah Selim. "I'll make you a deaf gardener, and I'll make myself a vegetable garden. He'll come and look around. And you won't say anything except that you'll ask him what vegetables he wants." And he prayed and blew on the girl and she became a deaf gardener, and he turned into a vegetable garden.

The father came, and he understood, of course. Wasn't he the fairy giant king? "What shall I do now?" he said. "If I pick one vegetable, it may be Shah Selim. If I take something else, it will be Shah Selim. How can I touch anything? Oh, you—the son of the unbeliever!" "What do you sell?" he said to the gardener.

And the gardener said, "Hnnh? What do you want? Do you want cabbages or tomatoes or lettuce?"

"This isn't what I said," said the father. "I didn't say that. Did a boy and a girl pass this way?"

The gardener said, "I don't know."

And the father turned back.

The son prayed and blew, and they became boy and girl again, and they started on their way. As they went, they heard another noise, *gurul, gurul, gurul, gurul,* like a black cloud coming after them. "That's my mother," said Shah Selim. "She's worse than my father. What shall I do?"

"Do whatever you can," said the girl.

"Here's what I'll do," said the prince. "I'll make you a stick, and I'll be a serpent wound around the stick. We shall lie down on this road." He prayed and blew on the girl, and she became a stick on the road, and he became a serpent and wound himself around and around the stick.

When the mother saw them, of course, being a fairy she knew what they were. She had a big knife in her hand, and she wanted to break the stick. "But if I strike here, it's Shah Selim. If I strike there, it's Shah Selim. Oh, you—daughter of the unbeliever! No part of her is out in the open so I can cut her." And the mother went back, crying.

They became boy and girl again, and they ran and ran until they came to the padishah's daughter's country. They found that her father had become blind from grief over his daughter. They went and told him that his youngest daughter and his son-in-law were back. He was so happy to have them back that he prepared a new wedding for them that lasted forty days and forty nights. The son-in-law made a magic medicine for the padishah's eyes, so he could see again. And they all lived happily until they died.

May we, too, have a share of their happiness!

The Cutworm and the Mouse

Once there was and once there wasn't a cutworm. One day the cutworm was roaming around and she met a shepherd. The shepherd said,

"Coral Lady with long hair,
Coral Lady tall and fair,
Where are you going?"

The cutworm answered, "I am trying to find a home for myself."
"Won't you come and live with me?" asked the shepherd.
And the cutworm said, "Well, what are you going to hit me with when you're angry with me?"
The shepherd said, "With this stick."
Coral Lady said, "Let's try if it hurts."
When the shepherd hit her with the stick, it *hurt,* and she said, "Oh, no! I'm not going to marry you!" So the shepherd left her.
She went on and on. Then she met a rooster, and the rooster said,

"Coral Lady with long hair,
Coral Lady tall and fair,
Where are you going?"

The cutworm answered, "I am trying to find a home for myself."
"Won't you come and live with me?" asked the rooster.
And the cutworm said, "Well, what are you going to beat me with when you're angry with me?"
"With my beak I'll beat you," said the rooster.
"Let's try if it hurts," said the cutworm.
The rooster pecked her on the back, and her back got full of holes. So she said, "No! Stop it! I'm not going to marry you."
So she started on her way again, and when she had gone a little distance farther she met a mouse. The mouse asked,

"Coral Lady with long hair,
Coral Lady tall and fair,
Where are you going?"

The cutworm answered, "I am trying to find a home for myself."
"Won't you come and live with me?" said the mouse.

And the cutworm said, "Well, what are you going to beat me with when you are angry with me?"

"With my tail I'll beat you," said the mouse.

"Let's try if it hurts," said the cutworm.

The mouse hit her with his tail again and again, and it didn't hurt. So Coral Lady decided to marry the mouse, and they got married.

A few days later the mouse said,

"Coral Lady with long hair,
Coral Lady tall and fair,
There's a wedding feast, and I must go.
Do you mind if it is so?"

Coral Lady said, "All right. Go along. And while you are there, I'll gather up what's here to be washed and go to the brook to wash it."

So Coral Lady with long hair, Coral Lady tall and fair, put whatever there was to be washed into a bundle and tied it to her leg and dragged it along to the brook. By the side of the brook there was the hoofprint of a horse which had filled up with water. While she was doing her laundry in this little washbasin, nobody knew how it happened, but she fell into the water. While she was struggling to get out of the mud, she heard some horsemen passing by and she called out,

"Oh, you horsemen, you horsemen, with footsteps sounding sweet,
May you arrive at the bridegroom's house, honey with cream to eat;
May you tell my Mr. Mouse
To hurry to his little house,
For Coral Lady with long hair,
Coral Lady tall and fair,
Has fallen into the mud and cannot get out of there."

True enough, they went to the bridegroom's house and there was a feast, with much to be eaten. Everybody was eating and having fun, and while they were feasting, one of the horsemen said, "Will you hear this? While we were coming, we heard a sound, and there was a cutworm deep in a puddle. This is what she was singing:

"'Oh, you horsemen, you horsemen, with footsteps sounding sweet,
May you arrive at the bridegroom's house, honey with cream to eat;
May you tell my Mr. Mouse
To hurry to his little house,
For Coral Lady with long hair,
Coral Lady tall and fair,
Has fallen into the mud and cannot get out of there.'"

21

As soon as Mr. Mouse heard this, he hopped up from his place, and he dug into this plate and dug into that plate. Then he left the feast and ran to the brook. Sure enough, Coral Lady with long hair, Coral Lady tall and fair, was lying on her back, struggling in the mud.

Mr. Mouse said, "Give me your hand and I'll pull you out."

And the other one answered, "And me being angry with you."

Mr. Mouse repeated, "Give me your hand. Let me be pulling you!"

And his wife said again, "And me being angry with you!"

So Mr. Mouse became very angry himself, and he said, "And me *stamping* on you like this, and *stamping* on you like this! Let me be stamping on you! Let me be stamping on you!" He stamped and stamped and stamped on Coral Lady, until he had stamped his ungrateful wife all down into the mud.

Nasreddin Hoca as Preacher

Once Nasreddin Hoca was assigned as religious leader in a village. Taking over the duties of the former preacher, Nasreddin Hoca appeared at the mosque for the Friday noon service. But he had just moved to that village, and he had not had time to prepare a sermon. From the *mimber*, he addressed the congregation in the mosque: "O people, do you know what I shall talk to you about today?"

Hesitating for only a moment, the congregation answered, "No, we don't."

"Well, neither do I," said the Hoca, and he climbed back down the steps of the *mimber* and went along home.

On the next Friday, Nasreddin Hoca went to the mosque again and, having ascended the *mimber*, he asked the congregation the same question: "O people, do you know what I shall talk to you about today?"

"Yes, we do," was their reply.

"In that case," said the Hoca, "it will be unnecessary for me to repeat it." And he climbed down the steps of the *mimber* and went along home.

On the third Friday, the people gathered ahead of time in order to decide what to say when the Hoca asked them his difficult question. They decided that half of them would say that they knew what he was going to talk about and the other half would say that they did not know.

When Nasreddin Hoca arrived at the mosque and had mounted the *mimber*, he addressed the congregation: "O my good people, do you know what I am going to talk to you about today?"

Some said, "Yes, we do."

Others said, "No, we don't."

Upon hearing this, the Hoca replied, "If that is the way it is, then let those who know tell those who do not know." And, descending the steps of the *mimber*, he went along home.

On the following week, the people again gathered before the Friday noon service. One of them said, "This new man is so quick at repartee that no matter what we might say, he would find a reason for not preaching a sermon. Therefore, this week let us not give any answer at all to whatever question he may ask us." Everyone agreed with that suggestion.

Shortly the Hoca entered the mosque, ascended the *mimber*, and asked, "O people, do you know what I shall talk to you about today?"

No one answered a single word. He asked the same question a second time and then a third time. Still no one uttered a sound.

"Ah!" said Nasreddin Hoca. "It seems that no one has come to the mosque today to hear my sermon!" With that, the Hoca walked down the steps of the *mimber* and went along home without having delivered a sermon.

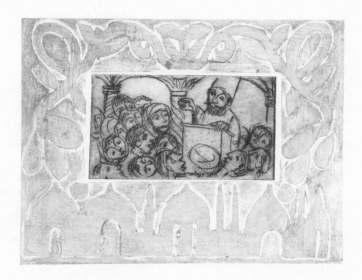

The Hoca, *the Witch, the Captain, and the* Hacı's *Daughter*

Once there was and once there wasn't a group of men who decided to make a pilgrimage to Mecca before they grew too old to travel. In that same town there lived a wealthy couple who had a son and a daughter. When this family heard about the group that was forming for a pilgrimage, they decided that three of them—the father, the mother, and the son—would join the pilgrims. They had just one problem, however. Who would take care of their daughter, Gülistan, while they were away?

"I know!" said the father. "We'll put her in the care of the *hoca*, for he is the most trustworthy person in town." They all agreed upon this, so they called the *hoca*.

"*Hoca* Effendi," they said, "we are going on a pilgrimage to Mecca, and we want our daughter, Gülistan, to be safe while we are gone. May we entrust the care of our daughter to you while we are away?"

"Of course," the *hoca* said. "You can travel without any worry about your daughter. I shall protect her during your absence."

The family locked the girl in a room and said to her, "You are never to go outside this room. Whatever you need will be brought to you by the *hoca* and passed in to you through that window." Then, having made sure that Gülistan would be safe, they turned away and joined the group of pilgrims.

For a few days, the *hoca* went to the window and asked, "My girl, do you need anything? If you do, I shall buy it at the marketplace for you." But the girl asked for nothing at all.

Then one day she asked, "*Hoca* Effendi, I should like some pomegranates. Would you please buy three or five for me at the marketplace?"

"Certainly, my girl," said the *hoca*, and he hurried to the market to buy the pomegranates. But when he saw how beautiful the hand was that reached out through the window for the fruit, the blood rushed to his head. "*Aman!*" he said to himself. "If that hand is so beautiful, how much more beautiful is the girl herself! I must possess that girl. But how can I do it?"

He thought about the matter for several days, with his heart more and more on fire. Then he remembered a witch who lived not far from the mosque. Perhaps she could get the girl for him. So he went to the witch and said, "There is a girl living in such and such a house. If you can manage to get that girl into my hands, I shall give you much gold."

After the *hoca* and the witch had agreed upon the amount to be paid, the witch said, "All right. If you will pay me half of that amount now, I shall

24

undertake the task at once." The *hoca* gave her that half, and the witch set out about a business she knew very well.

She went to the house where the girl lived, and—*Tak! Tak! Tak!*—she knocked at the door. "My girl! My girl!" she called.

"What are you asking, old lady?" asked Gülistan. "Do you need food? Do you need money? If so, I can give you some, and then you can go away in comfort."

"No, I do not need anything like that," said the old woman. "I heard that your family had gone on a pilgrimage, and I thought you might be lonely, so I came to talk with you for a while. I want, too, to pray for your family's safety on the pilgrimage."

"How kind of you!" said the girl. And she hurried to unlock the door for the old woman. "If you know my family, it must surely be all right for me to let you come in."

Gülistan served the old woman coffee, and they talked about this and that. Finally the old woman looked sad. "I feel so sorry for you, my girl, locked up in the house alone this way and with no young faces at all around you. Let me take you to a public bath where you can have some company and enjoy yourself. I'll come tomorrow and get you. I'll have my daughters there, too, and we'll all have a nice day."

"No. I cannot go," said the girl. "My father ordered me not to leave this house."

"Oh, for the love of Allah, let us go to the bath anyway. What can harm you to be among women?" Finally, she persuaded the girl to go with her to the bath on the following morning. "Now I must go along home, but I'll be back to get you tomorrow!" And the old woman went out the door and on her way.

Hurrying to the *hoca*, the witch said, "*Hoca! Hoca!* Give me the other half of my money. I have tricked the girl into going to such and such a bath tomorrow. Go now and rent the bathhouse for the entire day. And you be sure to be there!"

The *hoca* paid the witch the rest of her fee, and then he rushed to the bathhouse owner to rent the bath for the following day. *Tip tap! Tip tap!* His heart pounded as he waited for the hours to pass.

On the following day, the witch took Gülistan to the bath and left her there. "I'm going now to fetch my daughters, my dear. You will surely have a lovely day!" And she went out.

Inside the bathhouse there was no one but the *hoca*, and as soon as Gülistan had entered, he locked the door. Then he said, "Because of you I have gone mad! I have fallen in love with you, and today, here and now, you will be mine. No one except Allah will see us in here. Whether you are willing or unwilling, you will be mine."

Realizing that there was no way in which she could immediately escape, the girl answered, "Very well. I have been interested in you myself. But let us first bathe and get ourselves thoroughly clean, and then we shall do whatever you want. First you sit down, and I shall scrub you."

Because the *hoca* had a long beard and a lot of hair, the girl used two bars of soap to make a high pile of suds on top of his head. There was so much soap flowing down that the *hoca* could not open his eyes. The girl then took off her wooden bath clogs and began beating him over the head with them. She beat so hard and so long that the *hoca* finally fell unconscious to the floor. She then found the key in his clothes, dressed herself, unlocked the door, and escaped. She ran straight to her own house, entered it, and locked the door behind her.

When the *hoca* finally awoke, he was greatly worried about what had happened. He thought, "If the girl tells her father about this when he returns, I shall no longer be able to live in this town, for he is the most powerful man here." After thinking about this for a while, he decided to write a letter to her father. Taking pen and paper, he wrote, "*Hacı* Fadıl, since your departure, your daughter has been with Ahmet and Mehmet and only Allah knows how many others! Men keep coming and going, and the talk is growing. Come back and do something to restore your honor. Otherwise your pilgrimage may be of no use to you!"

In five or ten days the letter reached Gülistan's father, who was by then starting on his way home. After reading the bad news from the *hoca*, the father called his son and said, "Mount your horse and ride home at once, arriving there before we do. Cut your sister into pieces and bring me back as evidence her bloody clothes. Otherwise, I can never return to that town again."

The boy mounted his horse and hurried homeward. Along the way, however, he kept wondering if the evil news about his sister was really true. In order to find out for himself, he decided to hide somewhere outside his family's house and watch it day and night. "Also," he said to himself, "I shall go to the door and tell her that I am young, handsome, and rich. If she opens the door, then I will cut her up. Otherwise, I shall not harm her."

Day after day the boy went to the house and knocked on the door. He went there in the morning. He went there at noon. He went there at night. At no time was the door ever opened. "All that was said about her must have been a lie. If it were true, then she would open the door to me too." He went again to the house, knocked—*Tak! Tak! Tak!*—on the door, and called, "Sister, Sister, this is your brother, Ali." When she opened the door for her brother, he said, "My sister, I have orders from our father to cut you to pieces. If I do not do as he ordered, he will never forgive me."

"Very well, Ali. You are my older brother, and you can kill me if you wish."

"It is our father's order. I have no choice."

He took her to the top of a mountain to kill her, but when the time came, he said, "Oh, Gülistan, why should I sacrifice you when you have committed no sin? I shall kill a wild animal instead. Then I shall smear its blood on your shirt and take that to our father as evidence of your death. May Allah guard you! What can I do? This is your fate."

Ali killed a wild animal on the mountain and smeared its blood on his sister's shirt. Then, leaving his sister there on the mountain, he rode to meet his father. He said, "Father, here is my sister's shirt soaked in her blood. I killed her and have brought her shirt to you."

"Thank you, Son. You have done your duty well."

In the meantime, the girl wandered about on the mountain looking for a place to spend the night that would be safe from the wild animals that lived there. At last she found a huge tree growing alongside a fountain. Climbing into that tree, she slept there.

The fountain beneath the tree was the place where the Syrian padishah's son always watered his horse when he was hunting on that mountain. In the morning the son of the padishah came along with his hunting companions to water their horses there. But when the prince's horse saw the image of the girl on the surface of the water, it refused to drink from the fountain. The prince asked his horse, "What is the matter with you? You have always drunk from this fountain before. Why don't you drink from it now?" He pushed the animal's head into the water, but as he did so, he too saw on the surface of the water the image of a girl as beautiful as the moon. The prince said, "Are

27

28

you a human being or are you a jinn?"

"I am a human being," the girl answered as she climbed down from the tree.

Turning to his companions, the prince said, "Friends, I have completed my hunting for this day. Farewell to all of you!" Then, placing the girl behind him on his horse, he rode with her to Syria. When they arrived at the palace, he went to his father and said, "Father, I found this girl on a mountain where I went hunting. She is very beautiful, and I intend to marry her."

"I found you several fine girls, but you didn't want them. Now you have found this girl on a mountain. I am afraid that she will not be suitable for you."

"Well, I shall marry her anyway." Soon after, they were married, following a wedding ceremony that lasted for forty days and forty nights. But then, little by little, something strange happened to the girl. She grew mute and seemed unable to utter a word. Five years passed, and she still remained mute. No matter what they did, they could not get a word from her mouth.

As time passed, she had children—one, two, three. Women sing lullabies to children sleeping in their cradles, and one day the padishah heard the sound of a woman's voice singing in the next room, singing with so sweet a sound that it cut clear to the heart. "Where is that voice coming from?" he wondered. "It seems to be coming from my son's room, but his wife is mute." Opening the door and entering the room, he saw the woman singing and crying by the cradle. "My girl, do you really have a tongue? Let ten camels and a hundred sheep be slain as a sacrifice of thanks for the fact that my son's wife can now speak!"

After Gülistan had stopped singing, the padishah asked her, "My girl, do you have a mother and father?"

"Of course I do! Did you think that I sprang forth from a rock?"

"Where are you from?"

"I am the daughter of a man who lives at Antakya in Hatay."

"Would you like to visit your father?"

"Of course I should, if you will send me there. It has been a long time since I have seen my own country, and I should like to talk with my mother, father, and brother."

"We shall not accompany you, for I shall not go to a place I know nothing about. Nor shall I permit my son to go, either. But I shall give you a squadron of soldiers led by a captain to accompany you."

"All right," she said.

A squadron of troops was prepared and provided with arms, food, and other supplies. A captain was then appointed to lead this squadron. To this captain the padishah said, "You are to take her to her own country where she will visit her mother and father. Afterwards you are to bring her back safely. Let us see whether or not she really has a mother and father." He did not

29

permit his son to go, but he said to Gülistan, "Take the children along with you. You would miss them too much if you left them here."

Packing many things that were light in weight but heavy in value, Gülistan and her children mounted their mules and began their journey. After they had gone quite a distance, they came to a mountaintop, and there the captain ordered that the tents be pitched. "There is water here, and it looks like a good place to camp. Pitch the tents, and we shall stay here for the night." He had the girl's tent pitched apart from the others, for he thought—evil man that he was!—"When night falls, I shall go to her tent and be with her."

When it was fully dark, he took his sword, went to her tent, and opened the flap. The noise he made was slight, but she heard it. "Why are you here?" she asked.

He said, "My girl, why should you sleep only with your husband? You will be my wife on this journey, and I shall deliver you to your real husband when we return."

"I shall never do such a thing!" she replied.

"Either do it, or I shall kill one of your children."

"Better that loss than to be unfaithful to my husband!"

Slaying one of her children, he said, "Now you can see that I mean what I say. Either sleep with me or lose another child."

"Better that loss than to be unfaithful to my husband!"

Slaying a second child, he said, "Now you will accept me or I shall destroy your last child."

"Better that loss than to be unfaithful to my husband!"

After he had slain the smallest child, he said, "Now it is your turn. Either you will lie with me or I shall slay you."

Gülistan looked at her three children and she shuddered. What good could she be to her husband that way? Still, there might be another choice . . . "Very well," she said. "I must accept you, but first allow me to go to the fountain and take my ablutions and pray. After that, I shall do as you wish."

"All right, but I shall tie a rope around your waist so that you cannot escape."

The woman went outside and walked a short distance away. Then she slipped the rope from her waist, tied it to a large tree, and ran off into the forest.

After a short while, the captain pulled on the rope but was unable to draw the woman toward him. "*Aman, aman*, Allah!" he said. "Has she been staked to the ground? If not, what has happened to her?" Taking his sword in hand, he went outside and found that the other end of the rope had been tied to a tree. There was no sign of the woman anywhere.

To avoid arousing any suspicion about his action, the captain then returned to his tent for the rest of the night. In the morning, he ordered the tents to be struck and packed for traveling. "Be sure to pack up the lady's tent, too," he said.

When the soldiers went to that tent, however, they could not see any activity there. Looking inside, they discovered that the three children had been slain and that the woman was gone. "Captain, the lady is not here!" they called.

"*Aman!*" he said. "One who comes from the mountains will go back to the mountains again! The padishah's son found her on a mountaintop, a wild woman. Now she has killed her children and run away into the mountains again! What can I do about it? Let us pack up all of our equipment and supplies and return."

Returning to the padishah, the captain said, "What else can be expected from a girl who was found in the mountains, my padishah? When she saw her former surroundings, she killed her children during the night and fled into the mountains. The soldiers were all there, and so all this is no fault of mine."

"Didn't I say so?" asked the padishah. "One who comes from the mountains will return to the mountains! We never knew for certain whether she was fairy, human being, or demon. Didn't I say that she would never be a suitable wife for my son?"

While everyone was in mourning, the girl's husband wondered what had really happened to his wife. In the meantime, let us see what the girl was doing. After she had escaped from the camp, she ran from this place to that place until it was morning. Seeing a flock of sheep in a field at dawn, she went to the shepherd and said, "Good morning, shepherd."

"And good morning to you, my lady," he answered.

"If I give you some gold and this dress of mine, will you give me your outer clothing?"

"Of course! Why shouldn't I?"

"Also, I must buy a sheep from you. The meat will be yours, but the stomach will be mine."

"All right."

They slaughtered a sheep. The girl cleaned out its stomach and then put the skin covering of the stomach over her head like a hat. With the aid of that skin on her head and the shepherd's shabby clothes covering the rest of her body, she looked very much like a *keloğlan*. "Keloğlan, come!" "Keloğlan, go!" She must now expect to do the lowliest of chores, but work she must.

The girl was unacquainted with any country except her own, but she had come close to her own country by the time all these evil things had happened to her. She finally came to the town where her father lived, but where was she to stay, and what was she to say? As she was sitting and resting at a corner, she saw an old man who was a *helva* maker. He made good *helva*. But flies covered one half of it and worms ate the other half, and so nobody bought his *helva*. When the girl arrived there, the old man was again making

31

helva. He said, "Keloğlan, get away from here! There were already too many flies here before you came, but now there are even more because of your bald head!"

"My master, please don't send me away," said the girl. "I'll not do any harm here, but instead I'll clean away the dirt and wash your shop."

"All right, then. Wash it, and I shall watch you work. I am an old man anyway, with no one to look after me. I have barely enough strength to leave my chair and stand up."

Keloğlan cleaned the shop and washed all of the equipment so that everything looked much more attractive. On the following day he found some paint and painted the place. Then Keloğlan said, "Uncle, I shall make a batch of *helva* for you, and then we shall sell it." She made such a delicious batch of *helva* that even those who did not usually eat *helva* enjoyed it.

When the old man first saw the huge amount of *helva* she had made, he said, "What have you done, Keloğlan? We cannot possibly sell this much *helva*."

"Don't worry, uncle. You will see that we can sell it all." And she was right. The *helva* sold so fast that it was all gone before noon. The following day, they made four times that amount of *helva*, and it lasted only until the early evening.

The old man was greatly pleased. He said, "Oh, there is something special about you! Everyone is talking about the delicious *helva* that you make!" Well, let them make *helva* for a while as we take a look at what the padishah's son was doing.

The son of the padishah of Syria said, "I am going to find my wife. Wherever she went, I shall find her."

"I shall go with you," said the padishah.

Accompanied by the same squad of soldiers and the same captain, they began to search for the lady. The soldiers showed them where they had pitched their tents on the mountaintop and the place from which the lady had fled. They searched here and there along the way for her, and they finally reached the woman's town. There they asked, "Who is the wealthiest man here?"

"*Hacı* Fadıl is the wealthiest man in this town," they were told. "He has a mansion. You should stay with him while you are here."

They went to *Hacı* Fadıl's home and stayed there. Thus the padishah, his son, and the captain all stayed at the home of Gülistan's father. That evening after dinner, *Hacı* Fadıl said, "Call the young *helva* maker and we shall have him make *helva* here to serve to our guests."

When Keloğlan received the summons from *Hacı* Fadıl, she went to her father's house. As soon as she entered the house she saw her husband among those present, and she wanted to rush to him and embrace him, but she did not do so. She next recognized that another of the guests was her father-in-law. Then she saw that a third guest was the villainous captain who had slain her children and tried to dishonor her. Gülistan was amazed to encounter all of these people in the same house.

Then Keloğlan made the *helva* and placed it in the midst of the people gathered there. As they were eating this, the padishah asked, "Doesn't anyone here know any stories of past events in this town which he could tell to entertain us tonight?" He was seeking clues about his son's lost wife.

"We do not know any such stories," the other guests replied.

"Doesn't *anyone* know any old stories?" he asked again.

Keloğlan then spoke up and said, "I do, sir. I know some good stories."

"Come, then, and entertain us this evening," said *Hacı* Fadıl.

"Sir, I shall tell you a story, but I should like to ask that you first have the *hoca* brought here, too."

"All right," they said, and they sent a man to fetch the *hoca*.

After the *hoca* had arrived, Keloğlan said, "Sir, there is also a woman who lives in such and such a house whom you should bring here, if you please."

"All right," they said again, and they then brought the witch to the gathering.

Keloğlan then started his story. He told everything that had happened to Gülistan since the time that her parents and her brother had left home to go to Mecca. He told everything that the *hoca* had done to Gülistan, and the part that the witch had played in deceiving her, and everything that the captain had done to her. As the story went on, the captain asked, "May I have permission to leave? I must go to the toilet."

"Ask Keloğlan," they said.

"No!" said the *keloğlan*.

Then others wanted to leave, too. The *hoca* said, "I must go to pray."

"I need to leave in order to do something," said the witch.

"No. No one may leave the room!" said the *keloğlan*.

At the end of the story, Keloğlan said, "I am not really a *keloğlan*, or a boy at all. I am Gülistan." Taking the sheep's stomach off her head, she embraced her husband. Then she said, "Two of these men, the *hoca* and the captain, tried to dishonor me, and the second, the captain, killed my children."

The padishah summoned his executioners and ordered that the *hoca*, the witch, and the captain be beheaded. The three were executed right there and then. The padishah then took his son and daughter-in-law and returned with them to his own country. There they ate and drank and had all of their wishes fulfilled.

And if you have not been as fortunate as they, I can at least wish health to the ears of those who heard this tale and health to the tongue of him who told it.

The Prince, the Parrot, and the Beautiful Mute

Once there was and once there wasn't, long ago, when I was rocking my mother's cradle *tıngır mıngır*—well, in those times there was a padishah who had one son. The son grew tired of sitting by himself. "I'll buy a parrot to talk to me," he decided, so he went to the bazaar and bought a parrot. Home he came with the parrot and put it in a cage next to his window. He waited and waited for the parrot to speak, but it said not a single word.

One day a swallow came and perched on the windowsill. When the parrot saw the swallow, it said, "Swallow, oh, swallow, pray weep for me, for I have lost my mate."

Now, the padishah's son was there, and when he heard the parrot speak, he said, "You have never talked before. Why haven't you talked to me?"

"Well," answered the parrot, "some time ago, I lost my mate, and I have been too sorrowful to speak."

"At least you have *had* a mate," said the prince. "The girl I long to marry is mute. Unless I can cause her to speak, I cannot make her my bride. Come, now. Help me to win the girl I love, and may Allah Himself cure your grief."

"Tell me of this girl," said the parrot. "Perhaps I can help you."

"She is the most beautiful girl in the world," sighed the prince. "But she is also the cleverest. She will not speak until she has found a man more clever than she is. She has never spoken to any man. Whoever wishes to marry her must cause her to speak to him three times. Princes from around the world have tried, but none has been able to make her speak even once."

The parrot considered the matter. "Yes," he decided, "I shall help you. Let us go to see her tomorrow."

The next day the prince arose early and dressed with great care. Gently he tucked the parrot into the folds of his silk-embroidered sash, and they started on their way. The beautiful girl saw the prince coming.

"Ah, ah, ah!" she said to her maidservants. "Here comes another fool to try to make me speak. Call him in!"

When the prince entered, he saw a lamp table in one corner of the room. Taking off his silk-embroidered slippers, he put them under the lamp table. Inside one slipper he carefully tucked the parrot. All this time, the girl sat behind a heavy satin curtain, concealed from the prince but able to hear him.

"Greetings to you, lamp table!" called the prince.

And, "Greetings to *you!*" answered the parrot, from beneath the table. "May you come a hundred times, my prince."

They sat silent for a moment or two. Then the prince said, "Silence is tiresome. Either you talk while I listen, or I'll talk while you listen. Suppose *you* talk first."

"Very well," answered the parrot. And he began to tell a story. "Once there were three friends, and all three of them wished to marry the same girl. The girl said to them, 'Go out into the world and work. Work hard, and learn some special skill. Come back at the end of a year's time. I shall marry the one of you who has learned the most unusual skill.'

"The three men journeyed afar, and they worked hard. Each one was determined to gain a special skill for himself. At the end of the year, they all started home. They met at an inn not far from their own country.

"One of them said, 'Listen, my friends. We all wish to marry the same girl. But how do we know even whether she is still *alive?*'

"The second one said, 'I have learned the art of hearing from a great distance. Let me listen and find out how she is.' He put his ear to the ground and listened carefully. 'Oh!' he said. 'She is very ill. Doctors have come from here and there, but they are unable to cure her.'

"'Have no fear,' said the third man. 'I have learned the art of going great distances by merely wishing myself there. Hold tightly to my hands and come with me.' He closed his eyes and opened them three times, and suddenly the three men found themselves outside the house where their sweet-heart lived.

"'Come inside with me,' said the first man, 'for I have learned the art of healing every illness in the world.' They went inside. The first man laid his right hand on the girl's forehead, and in an instant she was well again.

"Now," said the parrot, "which one of the three should marry the girl?"

The prince said, "Well, if you ask me, I should say the first man should have her, because he was able to make her well again."

"As for me," said the parrot, "I should say the third man should marry her, because he was able to go quickly to her side."

The beautiful girl all this while was listening from behind the curtain. She clapped her hands suddenly and said, "No, no. You are *both* wrong! She should marry the second man, because he was the one who discovered that she was ill. If he had not discovered that in time to help her, neither of the others could have done anything for her at all."

The padishah's son smiled. At least the beautiful girl had spoken *once*. He felt certain that he could make her talk again. "Well, I must be leaving now, lamp table," he said. "But I shall come back again tomorrow." Quietly he picked up the parrot and tucked it into his sash. Then he put on his silk-embroidered slippers and left the room.

As soon as he had gone, the beautiful girl came out from behind the curtain. "Oh, girls!" she said. "This man was clever enough to make me speak. He can make even a *table* talk!" She walked over to the lamp table. "Greetings, lamp table!" she said. "Talk to me a bit."

But the lamp table did not answer her. How can a table talk?

The girl became very angry. "Oh, you lamp table!" she exclaimed. "You talked to him. Why won't you talk to me? Do you talk only to *princes?*" Then to her servants she said, "Bring me an ax!" And when the ax was brought, the beautiful girl chopped the table to pieces. "*That* table will not talk again," she said. "Now, girls, you must be sure not to let me talk tomorrow. Stop me, even if you have to put your hands over my mouth."

As for the padishah's son, he was very happy. Before he went to bed that night, he said to the parrot, "Well, my friend, we have made a good start. Allah willing, we shall hear her voice again tomorrow."

The next morning the prince arose early and dressed with even greater care. He tucked the parrot into the folds of his silver-embroidered sash. Then he went to the beautiful girl's house. Immediately, the servants showed him inside.

The prince looked about the room. "Oh!" he said. "The lamp table is gone. Never mind. I shall talk with this chair, instead." Taking off his silver-embroidered slippers, he put them under the chair. He tucked the parrot inside one of his slippers. "Greetings to you, chair!" he said, as he seated himself on a cushion.

"Greetings to *you*, my prince!" answered the parrot, from beneath the chair. "May you come a hundred times!"

They sat silent for a moment or two. Then the prince said, "Silence is tiresome. Either you talk while I listen, or I shall talk while you listen. Suppose *you* talk first."

"Very well," answered the parrot. And he began to tell a story. "Once there were three friends who were on their way to Baghdad. They walked a little; they walked far, until one evening they found themselves at the edge of a dense forest. Afraid to go any farther, they decided to spend the night there. 'I shall watch for an hour while you sleep,' said the first friend. 'Then I shall sleep while one of you stands guard. We shall watch, turn and turn about, until the night is past.'

"The first friend chanced to be a carver. To amuse himself while he stood guard, he cut a sound piece of wood from one of the trees and began carving a beautiful doll out of the wood. By the time his hour was over, the wooden doll had been finished. He stood it against a tree and awoke the second guard. Then he himself went to sleep.

"Now, the second one was a tailor. When he awoke and saw the beautiful doll, he said, 'Ah, I shall dress this doll.' He laid in a small heap the hats of his two friends, as well as his own hat and cloak. He gathered a plentiful supply of thorns from the tall grasses near at hand. Then, pulling out his scissors, he cut the hats and the cloak into pieces and made a dress for the doll, putting it together neatly with thorns. By the time his hour was over, the doll was very well dressed, indeed. He stood the doll against a tree. Then he awoke the third guard, and he himself went to sleep.

"The third friend was a *hoca*. When he saw the well-dressed doll, he said, 'What a pity it is that this beautiful doll is not alive.' He decided to pray to Allah that the doll might be brought to life. Long and earnestly he prayed, and, behold, before he had finished his prayer, the doll was alive and breathing.

"Now," the parrot asked the prince, "if you were asked which man was fit to become the husband of the girl, which one would you say?"

The prince answered, "The *hoca*, of course, since he brought the doll to life."

"As for me," said the parrot, "I should give her to the tailor, because he dressed the doll so cleverly."

The beautiful girl heard all this from behind the curtain. "No, no. You are *both* wrong," she said. "I should give her to the carver, because he was the one who began her."

All the servants tried to keep the beautiful girl from speaking. They rushed at her, but she shook them off, saying, "No! The truth must be told. I have to say what I think is true."

The padishah's son was pleased to hear the girl speak. He took the parrot from his slipper and tucked it into his sash. After he had put on his silver-

37

embroidered slippers, he left the room.

The moment he had gone, the beautiful girl cried, "Oh, *why* did you let me talk?"

And the servants replied, "What could we do? We *tried* to stop you, but you were determined to talk."

Angrily, the girl came out from behind the curtain. "Greetings to you, chair!" she said. "Greetings!"

But of course the chair did not answer. How can a chair talk?

The girl said, "Do you, too, talk only to clever princes? Why won't you talk to me?"

Since the chair would not answer, the girl called for an ax. She chopped the chair to pieces.

As for the prince, he had gone home. His heart was singing with hope. Surely he would hear her voice a third time.

The next day, the prince arose early and dressed with the greatest of care. He tucked the parrot into the folds of his gold-embroidered sash. Then he went to the house of the beautiful girl. The servants immediately opened the door for him, and he went inside.

As he looked about the room, he discovered that the chair, too, was gone. But there was a small bench in one corner. He put his gold-embroidered slippers under the bench. Gently he tucked the parrot into one of the slippers. Then he sat down on a cushion. "Greetings to you, bench!" he said.

And, "Greetings to *you*, my prince!" answered the parrot, from beneath the bench. "May you come a hundred times!"

They sat silent for a moment or two. Then the prince said, "Silence is tiresome. Either you talk while I listen, or I shall talk while you listen. Suppose *you* talk first."

"Very well," answered the parrot. And he began to tell a story. "Once in a far country there was a girl, the daughter of a great landholder. The family had a freed slave, and the slave and the girl had become childhood friends. One day the slave, wanting to marry the girl, asked her parents to give her to him. But the father refused to marry his daughter to the slave.

"The following day, the freed slave said to the girl, 'My dear, I asked your father for your hand in marriage, but he refused me. I am going to leave your family now and work for myself. One thing I beg of you, and one thing alone: Someday you will marry someone else. On your wedding night, in all your bridal finery, please come to me wherever I am, that I may see you. I shall roast a lamb and give it to you, and you may take it back and share it with your husband.'

"When she was old enough, the girl *did* marry. On her wedding night, while she was sitting with her husband, she said, 'I should like to ask of you a favor, my husband. Our family used to have a freed slave who became my childhood friend. He was very fond of me, and one day he asked, "On your

38

39

wedding night, come to me in all your bridal finery and let me see you. I shall roast a lamb for you, and you may take it back and share it with your husband." Will you please allow me to go and see him?'

"Her husband said, 'Yes, I shall let you go. But go at once, and come back quickly.'

"So the girl, in all her finery—gold and silver and jewelry and rustling dress—ran to the freed slave, who by that time had become a shepherd.

"Now, there were forty thieves in that neighborhood. When they saw the girl coming, they said, 'Aha!' and gathered around her.

"But the girl said, 'Please do not stop me now. I shall tell you what I am doing, and afterwards you may take from me whatever you wish.' And she told them the whole story, from first to last, leaving out not a single detail.

"'Oh!' the forty thieves said when she had finished. 'What a good man your husband must be, and what a poor soul that shepherd must be! We are not going to harm you. You may consider yourself our sister. Go, now, and may your path be open. Go on and see the shepherd.'

"She left the forty thieves and went quickly to the place where the shepherd was. He was weeping and roasting a lamb. 'I have come,' she said.

"The shepherd looked at her with tears in his eyes. Then he put the lamb on a big tray, put the tray on her head, and sent her back, saying, 'Go with Allah, and may you and your husband live long and happily.'

"Now, tell me," said the parrot. "Whose bride should the girl be?"

"The shepherd's," said the prince.

"As for me," the parrot said, "I should give her to the forty thieves. They were very good to her, though they had her in their hands, with her gold and silver and jewelry, and her rustling dress."

The beautiful girl, hearing this from behind the curtain, clapped her hands and, "No, no!" she cried. "You are *both* wrong. I should give her to the hus—" While she was talking, the servants pressed in around her and tried to stop her. But there she was, chattering like a nightingale. "Truth is not dead in the world," she said. "It is meant to be spoken. I should give her to the bridegroom, because no ordinary bridegroom would let his bride go away like that. He was such a *good* man."

Then the prince said quietly, "The beautiful girl has spoken three times. She must now become my bride."

The curtain opened, and there the girl stood before him, as beautiful as the fourteenth day of the moon. She sat down on a cushion by the prince, and they talked together.

"I am the son of a padishah," said the prince, "and I have everything needful for us. Take with you only those things which you want most, things light in weight but heavy in value. Meanwhile, I shall take my slippers and go to give the news to my parents."

He went to the bench and, reaching beneath it, took out his gold-embroidered slippers. Gently slipping the parrot into his gold-embroidered sash, he put on his slippers and left the room.

Once the prince was outside, he reached into his sash for the parrot. "Go, my friend," he said. "You have truly helped me to find my mate. Fly free, and when your heart is eased for the loss of your mate, seek another that will fill your days with joy. Go, and may Allah go with you." And he watched as the parrot flew away. Then he carried the news of his marriage to his parents.

In good time, he took the girl, with her servants and with precious goods of various kinds, and they went to the padishah's palace. They had a splendid wedding lasting forty days and forty nights, and they lived in great happiness forever after. May we have a share of their good fortune!

The Authority of a Host

Once there was and twice there wasn't a sultan named Murad. Now, this Murad and his grand vizier, disguised in ordinary clothing, often went to various parts of the kingdom to see how matters were going with the people.

One day when they were about to leave on such a journey, the sultan suggested, "Let's go to Tavşan Mountain this time." This was acceptable to the grand vizier, and they were wished well on their journey by the people gathered at the palace to see them off.

After traveling for a few days, resting along the way, they came to Tavşan Mountain just as evening was approaching. "Well," said the sultan, "I see no villages. Where are we to find hospitality? Where can we even spend the night?" As he and the grand vizier both looked in vain for shelter, they saw a shepherd tending his nighttime fire. They called to him, "Oh, Shepherd *Ağa!*"

"What is it that you want of me, O you guests in this area?" asked the shepherd.

"Would you be willing to be our host for tonight?" asked the sultan.

"I should be glad to be your host, my *ağas,* but I have no beds or fine blankets. I have a small shepherd hut here in this *yayla,* and if you would be willing to sleep there on a piece of goat's-hair blanket, as I do, you would be most welcome."

"We should be willing to sleep even in a small mill shed! There is neither village nor inn here," said the sultan.

Saying, "Well, then, come along with me," he invited them to share his fire and to stay all night with him. To his son, the shepherd said, "My boy,

41

bring along a sheep or a goat, and we shall sacrifice it for our guests."

The son brought a sheep, and after it was sacrificed and cooked, they all ate plentifully of its meat. The sultan and his grand vizier slept there that night in the shepherd's hut after an evening of pleasant conversation.

The next morning, they arose and said to the shepherd, "Well, Mehmet Ağa, with your permission we shall leave now."

"Oh, you are going? Please wait for a little while, for I must prepare some food for your travel," said the shepherd. And, "Son!" he called. "Find a sheep or a goat which can be slaughtered to provide food for these men on their journey."

When Sultan Murad heard this, he said, "What are you talking about, Mehmet Ağa? We couldn't eat even one-fourth of a sheep or a goat!"

Immediately, the shepherd slapped the sultan's mouth and said, "Be quiet! You should not interfere with the head of a household about such matters!" The shepherd did not know, of course, that this was Sultan Murad, and so he asked him, "What is your name?"

"They call me 'Steward Murad with the Big Mansion of İstanbul Village,'" answered the sultan.

After his guests had departed, the shepherd committed to memory the name "Steward Murad with the Big Mansion of İstanbul Village," but he still did not know the identity of that Murad.

When the next spring arrived, the shepherd decided to pay a return visit to his guest. He selected a choice ram and cut off its wool with his heavy sheepshearing shears; the ram was to be a gift for Steward Murad. On his feet he put rawhide sandals and on his shoulder a stick to which a packet of provisions was fastened. Then he and the ram started on the long walk to İstanbul. How many days would the journey take? He did not know, for he had never been there, but he and the ram reached the city in ten or twelve days.

In İstanbul, he asked one person after another, "Point out to me the big mansion of Murad the Steward."

"I do not know where it is." "I do not know what you're talking about." "I don't know where such a mansion is." These answers gave Mehmet Ağa no help at all. Finally, someone advised him, "Enter a place which has guards around it."

After he had walked around for some time, he saw a very large mansion with guards around it, and he tried to enter this mansion. But the guards shouted at him, "Hey! Where do you think you are going? This is the palace of the sultan."

"Murad the Steward was my guest."

"No, no! You cannot enter this building!" they said, and several of them seized him.

Finally, Sultan Murad heard the noise and came out. He said to the guards, "Release him! Release him! Do not touch him! Let him come in. He is our Mehmet *Ağa*." To the grand vizier the sultan said, "Our Mehmet *Ağa* has come!"

"Let him come! Let him come! He is welcome!"

"I brought you this ram, Steward Murad," said the shepherd, after he had entered the door. And the ram was taken off to the kitchen area.

Mehmet *Ağa* looked around as he and the sultan and the grand vizier went up the stairs. "O Murad the Steward, did you have this palace built, or did you inherit it?" he asked curiously.

"I inherited it from my father," said Sultan Murad.

"Yes, that must be so, for this is something bigger than you would be able to accomplish."

"Take him to the bath," said the sultan to the servants, "and afterward get him a suit of clothes that will fit him. Then we shall drink tea and coffee."

While Mehmet was being bathed and fitted with a new suit of clothes, the sultan said to the vizier, "How shall we get even with him for slapping me?"

"That is easy, my sultan. We can have forty pots of food prepared, and we can have these foods served on golden plates and eaten with golden spoons. Every time a golden plate has been emptied or a golden spoon used, you can throw it out of an open window into the sea. Mehmet will not be able to stand this, of course, and sooner or later he will say, 'That was made of *gold!* Why did you do that?' Then you can slap him and say, 'Never interfere with the things that are the business of the head of a household!'"

"Yes, that will be good. We have found a way," said Sultan Murad.

Now let us come to Mehmet *Ağa*. He sat down with the sultan and the grand vizier and began eating. He just kept eating without saying a single word. When the *börek* dish had been emptied, the sultan threw it out the window into the sea. And after each of the dishes containing the thirty-nine other kinds of foods was emptied, he threw it out in the same way.

When Mehmet *Ağa* did not say a word when all these golden dishes, one after another, were thrown into the sea, the grand vizier became impatient and said, "Oh, Mehmet *Ağa*, why do you not speak about what you have seen? Is the sultan mad? Everything that he has been throwing into the sea has been made of gold!"

"See here, you!" said Mehmet *Ağa*. "Murad made that same kind of mistake in my home!" And he gave the vizier a slap in the mouth, too. Then he said to the vizier, "He can do anything he wishes in his own house! He can even throw both you and me out the window, too, if he wants to do so! He is the owner of this house and the head of this household!"

After Mehmet *Ağa* had said that, they stopped talking about it. The matter had ended, just as our story has ended.

The Uncontrollable Desire and the Irresistible Urge

Once there was and once there wasn't a certain camel caravan on its way from Baghdad to İstanbul. From time to time, the caravan drivers would unload the camels and let them refresh themselves and graze while the drivers slept.

While the camels were grazing one day, another caravan passed by, and a donkey belonging to the second caravan wandered away to join the grazing camels. After this donkey had eaten his fill, he said to the old camel alongside, "My, I feel good! In fact, I have an uncontrollable desire to bray!"

"Oh, do not bray!" said the camel. "We have barely begun to rest, and our drivers have fallen asleep. If you bray, you will awaken them, and they will come and load us and lead us on! Pray, let us enjoy our rest!"

"But I must bray!" insisted the donkey.

"Please do not bray. Consider a moment: if our drivers find you here, they may well load you, too."

"You heard me!" said the donkey. "When I have an uncontrollable desire to bray, I bray, and never mind the consequences. Hee har! Hee har! Hee har!"

Of course, the drivers awoke, and one said to another, "Aha! There is a stray donkey with our camels. We'll just load him, too." And so they did.

As soon as the camels had been reloaded, the caravan went on its way, with the donkey walking at the very end, behind the oldest camel.

At first, the donkey was able to keep up with the rest of the caravan, but after half a day's journey, he had fallen farther and farther behind. Noticing this, two of the drivers picked up the donkey and balanced him on the top of the oldest camel's big load.

They traveled and traveled, until they came to a narrow trail with a mountain on one side and a cliff on the other side that dropped off more than a hundred meters. The oldest camel, stepping carefully along the trail, said suddenly to the donkey he was carrying, "Brother donkey, I have an irresistible urge to dance!"

·   The donkey said, "Brother camel, this is no place to dance! If you dance here, I shall surely roll off your back. And don't you see that cliff?"

"I cannot help it, brother donkey. When I have an irresistible urge to dance, I dance, and never mind the consequences."

So saying, the camel began to dance. With the very first turn, the donkey fell off the camel's back and tumbled down the cliff, gone forever. "So much for uncontrollable desires and irresistible urges!" said the camel, and he went on, carrying no more of a load than a camel should carry.

The Two Stepdaughters

Once there was and once there wasn't a woodcutter whose wife had died and left a young daughter to care for. Lonely, and troubled by the burden of rearing a girl by himself, he soon married again. Now, the new wife was a widow with a daughter of her own, and she brought her daughter with her. But the two stepdaughters were as different from one another as oranges are from pomegranates. His daughter was very kind and very beautiful, but hers was ugly, and, what's more, she was bad tempered.

The mother and her daughter were jealous of the beautiful one—oh, how jealous they were! And they were always at the father to take her away. At last he grew tired of their talking and agreed to please them. He took his daughter out into the forest and told her, "I'll be nearby cutting wood. Wait for me here."

But what he did was to get an empty pumpkin and tie it to a pine tree so that when the wind blew, the pumpkin knocked against the tree, making a *tum tum tum* noise. Then he went along home.

When her father did not return for her, the girl began to sing,

"My daddy who makes the *tum tum tum,*
Don't go away. Please let me come."

She sang and sang, and when there was no answer, finally she started home by herself. On the way, she met a baker with a great load of fresh bread. The baker said to her, "Where are you going?"

She answered, "I'm lost, and I'm trying to find my way home. And, uncle baker, I am so *hungry*. Could I please have a loaf of your fine, fresh bread?"

The baker said, "My girl, I have some work that you can do. Just come with me to my bakery and clean my workbench. If you do that work, I'll be happy to give you a loaf of bread."

Patiently, patiently, the girl cleaned that workbench until it shone from the scrubbing. "Very well, my girl," said the baker. "Here is your loaf of bread. May you eat it with a hearty appetite."

The girl ate the loaf of bread, and her hunger was satisfied. Then she went along the road, looking, looking. As she went, she met an old man with white hair and a long white beard.

"Where are you going?" the old man asked the girl.

"Oh, grandfather, I'm lost, and I'm trying to find my way home," she answered.

46

"My child," he said, "both my hair and my beard are just *filled* with lice.
If you will take all the lice out for me, I shall pray for you that you find both
good fortune and your way home."

"To find my way home would be enough, grandfather," said the girl.
"Of course, I'll take the lice from your hair and your beard." And patiently,
patiently, she found all the lice and killed every one of them. The old man
prayed for her, and then she left him.

She went along the road, looking, looking, and suddenly she met a dog.
The dog stopped his scratching and scratching, and he asked, "Where are
you going, my girl?"

"Ah," said the girl, "I'm lost, and I'm trying to find my way home."

The dog said, "As you can see, my body is just *covered* with fleas. If you
will pick all the fleas from my body, I shall give you a fine present. Besides,
I'll show you your way home."

"To find my way home would be enough," said the girl. "Of course, I'll
be glad to pick all the fleas from your body." And patiently, patiently, she
found every flea and killed all of them.

"Now," said the dog, "here is a key. Take this key and go down the road
until you come to a small hut. Unlock the door of the hut with this key.
Inside the hut, you will find a yellow chest. Take the chest and, carrying it on
your head, go farther along the road until you come to a bend in the road.
Just around that bend, you will find your home."

The girl took the key and walked and walked until she found the hut. Unlocking the door, she went inside, and there indeed was a yellow chest. Carrying the yellow chest on her head, the girl walked along the road until she came to a bend in it, and just beyond the bend she saw her father's house. Now, the rooster saw her coming, and he called,

"*Üh-üh-üh-üh-üh-h-h!* The sister I love best
Is coming down the road with a big yellow chest!"

The girl's stepmother said, "How can she be coming, you foolish rooster? My husband left her deep in the forest! And where would she get a yellow chest?"

But still the rooster crowed the news, and the woman went to look. There, indeed, came her stepdaughter, with a yellow chest balanced on her head. Her father was there, too, and he asked, "How did you find your way home, my dear? That was a long, long walk to come alone!"

"Well, my father, when I couldn't find you, I started walking, and I met a baker. He let me do some work for him; then he gave me a fresh loaf of bread and sent me on my way. As I went along, I met an old man with white hair and a long white beard. He had me clean the lice from his hair and beard; then he prayed for me and sent me on my way. Next, I met a dog with fleas and fleas. He had me pick the fleas from his body; then he gave me a key and said, 'Along the road you will find a small hut. Unlock the door of the hut with this key and take the yellow chest you will find inside. Then go along that same road until you come to a bend in the road; just beyond the bend you will find your home.' I did as he said, and, indeed, there *was* a yellow chest. I brought it along with me, and as I came, I heard our rooster crowing."

Well, the father and the stepmother and the ugly stepdaughter said, all in one voice, "Open the chest!" When the girl opened it, they all saw that it was filled, just *filled*, with all sorts of jewels.

And oh, but the stepmother was jealous! "My own daughter should have a present like that, too," she said. "My husband, take *my* daughter out into the forest tomorrow and leave her where you left *your* daughter. She can then find the fortune that belongs to *her*."

"Of course, my wife," said the father. And the next day, he took the ugly stepdaughter to the very spot where he had left his beautiful daughter the day before.

As soon as she was alone, the girl began walking down that same road. In a little while, she met a baker with a great load of fresh bread.

The baker asked, "Where are you going?"

She answered, "I'm lost, and I'm trying to find my way home. And I'm *hungry*. Uncle, will you give me a loaf of bread?"

"My girl," he said, "first I have some work for you to do. You must clean my workbench. After that is finished, I'll give you a loaf of fine, fresh bread."

"Oh, am I supposed to clean your dirty workbench?" said the girl. "Well, I will not do it! You can *keep* your loaf of bread." And she left without getting the bread.

Going on along the road, she met an old man with white hair and a long white beard. "Where are you going?" he asked the girl.

"Grandfather," said the girl, "I'm lost, and I'm trying to find my way home."

"My girl," he said, "if you will clean the lice from my hair and my beard, I shall pray for you."

"*Aman!* Am I supposed to clean the lice from your hair and your beard? No, I cannot do it. And you can just *keep* your prayer!" And she went on along her way.

Soon she came to a dog that was scratching and scratching himself. "Where are you going, my girl?" asked the dog.

The girl answered, "I'm lost, and I'm trying to find my way home."

The dog said, "As you can see, my body is just *covered* with fleas. If you will pick all the fleas from my body, I shall give you a fine present. Besides, I shall show you your way home."

"Oh!" said the girl. "I cannot pick those dirty fleas from your body, and I *will* not! No, no! But I *will* take the present that you have for me."

"Very well," said the dog. "Take this key and go along this road until you come to a small hut. Unlock the door of the hut with this key, and go inside. There you will find a black chest. Take the chest and, carrying it on your head, go farther along the road until you come to a bend in the road. Just beyond that bend, you will find your home."

The girl took the key and walked and walked along the road until she found the hut. Unlocking the door, she went inside, and there, indeed, was a black chest. Carrying the chest on her head, the girl walked along the road until she came to a bend in the road, and just beyond the bend she saw her mother's house. Now, the rooster saw her coming, and he called,

"*Üh-üh-üh-üh-üh-h-h!* The sister I detest
Is coming down the road with a big black chest!"

The girl's mother said, "Oh, you rooster! Why do you say such nasty things about my daughter?" But she went to look, and there indeed came her daughter, with a black chest balanced on her head. "Aha!" she said. "*My* daughter is much cleverer than *your* daughter. See how quickly she returned home!"

Her stepfather was there, and so was his own daughter. "Open the chest!" they said, both in one voice.

But the stepmother said crossly, "This is my own daughter's chest, her own fortune, and you have no business seeing what is in it!" And she and her daughter took the black chest inside the house and closed the door and locked it. They pulled the curtains at the windows, too, so that no one else could see what treasure the girl had brought home. And then the stepmother and her daughter opened the chest.

Inside the chest, though, there were no sparkling jewels. Instead, there were the glittering eyes of snakes and snakes. Biting here and biting there, the snakes went about the business they knew best, and in less time than it takes to say so, both the stepmother and her ugly daughter were dead of their bites.

Hearing shouts and cries from inside the house, the father tried the door, but it was still locked. At last, he broke a window and went inside to see for himself. He could scarcely believe his eyes, for there lay his wife and his stepdaughter, lifeless, on the floor. And the chest was empty, for the snakes had scattered to all corners of the room.

He quickly unlocked the door and let his daughter in to see what he had seen. As soon as the door was opened, all the snakes slithered across the doorstep and out into the open air and away from there.

Well, the stepmother and her bad-tempered daughter had the fortunes they deserved. And the father and his beautiful daughter were left in health and happiness.

Three apples fell from the sky: one for the teller of this tale, one for the listener, and one for whoever will pass the tale along.

"If Allah Wills"

One night as he went to bed, Nasreddin Hoca said to his wife, "Tomorrow I am going to work in my vineyard."

"You mean you will work in your vineyard *if Allah wills*," said his wife, remembering that it was always wise to say "if Allah wills," no matter what was planned.

"Ah, no," said the Hoca. "I will work in my vineyard tomorrow, and that is that!"

"But, Hoca, what if it rains?"

"If it rains, I shall cut wood in the forest," said the Hoca.

"*If Allah wills*," his wife said quickly.

"Listen, my wife," said the Hoca crossly. "Tomorrow if the sun shines, I shall work in my vineyard. If it rains, I shall cut wood in the forest."

"Please, Hoca, say 'if Allah wills.' If you do not, something bad will happen to you."

The Hoca just laughed. "I am the Hoca, and you are only a woman. Let *me* worry about Allah, my dear!" And the Hoca went to sleep.

The next morning, it was raining. "Well, today I'll cut wood in the forest," said the Hoca.

"*If* Allah wills," said his wife.

"Today I shall cut wood in the forest whether or not Allah wills!" shouted the Hoca. He picked up his ax and set off for the forest with his lunch of bread and cheese tucked into his sash. All day long, he cut wood.

Just as the Hoca was ready to go home with his wood, he heard footsteps. Four of the sultan's soldiers came by. One of them saw the Hoca.

"Hey, Hoca," said the soldier. "Show us the way to the next village."

"I'm sorry," said the Hoca, "but I haven't time. I'm on my way home."

"Oh, *haven't* you time!" said the soldier scornfully. "Get on the road this minute. You will *lead* us all the way to the village. Not only that, but you will carry all our bundles!"

All four of the soldiers piled their bundles in the Hoca's arms. Then the Hoca started toward the next village. The soldiers walked behind him. "Hurry up!" said one soldier.

Another soldier poked him with his long, bony finger. "Run along," he said.

The road was wet and muddy. The rain was just *pouring* down. Three or four times, the Hoca slipped and fell in the mud. The soldiers laughed at him.

Finally they came to the next village. "Give us our bundles," said the first soldier. "*Now* you can go home."

The Hoca hurried home as fast as he could go. All the way, he said, "Why, oh, why didn't I say 'if Allah wills'? This is what happens when I do not say 'if Allah wills'!"

At last, the Hoca reached home. He was wet and cold and very tired. He turned the knob on his door, but the door was locked. *Tak! Tak! Tak!* He knocked at the door.

The Hoca's wife stuck her head out of the bedroom window. "Who is that?" she called.

"It is Nasreddin Hoca, *if Allah wills*," answered the Hoca.

Pears and Pears

Once there was and once there wasn't a farmer who lived near the edge of a market town. On his land he had a grove of pear trees which yielded the most delicious pears in all the country.

From selling these pears, he had made himself a fine fortune. "Coins as golden as Ahmet's pears," they all said. And, indeed, it was true. Only one thing gave him more pleasure than counting the golden pears in his orchard, and that was counting the golden coins he had hidden in a sack beneath his sleeping mat.

One day Ahmet loaded a handcart with several bushels of his choicest pears and trundled them along to market. Each pear was fairer than its neighbor, and they all called out to be eaten. Ahmet found for himself a good spot in the marketplace and began to cry his wares: "Pears! Pears! Fine pears! Sweet pears! Don't you wish you could sample them? They melt in your mouth like butter! Pears! Pears!"

It was not long before a large crowd had gathered before Ahmet. Everyone knew of Ahmet's pears. And everyone knew each golden pear was well worth the high price he asked for it—a handful of kuruş. One after another, the peasants reached into their wide sashes for the money he asked. One after another, they bit into the delicious fruits, and the sweet smell of ripe pears teased the noses of other buyers in the market.

Of a sudden, there appeared a ragged dervish, a wandering holy man, among the crowd. With level gaze he studied the farmer. Then hungrily he eyed the pears. "My good man," said the dervish, "please be so kind as to give me one of your beautiful pears."

Ahmet stared at the dervish. "*Give* you one of my pears, indeed!" he said indignantly. "How do you think I could manage to earn my bread and cheese if I *gave* my pears away?"

One peasant in the crowd nudged another. "He does not know Ahmet, or he would not ask him to give anything," he murmured. And the crowd watched curiously to see what the dervish would do.

But he seemed not to mind Ahmet's scorn. "I say, my good man," he said humbly. "Those are the most beautiful pears I have ever seen. Pray, let me have one."

"If I gave one to you," said Ahmet, "I would have to give one to every beggar and thief in the market. Thief! Yes, a thief is what you are, trying to get something for nothing!"

Just then a soldier walked by. "Gendarme!" called Ahmet. "Take this beggar away. He is spoiling my business."

But the soldier saw no reason to hustle the old gentleman away. He swung his stick idly, watching to see if a quarrel might be provoked. And the crowd grew, amused to see Ahmet waving his arms in anger against a harmless old man.

"Truly, my good man," said the dervish gently, "I ask for only one pear. In so many, how could one be missed? I cannot see why you are so angry that I ask."

"You heard me the first time!" shouted Ahmet. "I do not give my pears away. Now get along about your business." Ahmet's face was flushed with anger. In all this fuss with the dervish, he had not sold a single pear.

"Why don't you give him a pear, for the love of Allah?" called one of the peasants.

"Yes, Ahmet Bey. Give him one that is bruised. It will satisfy him," said another.

But Ahmet would not hear of it. And the very notion that one of his beautiful pears might be bruised made him angrier than ever.

"Here, father," said the soldier suddenly, drawing his purse from his pocket. "I shall buy you one of Ahmet's good pears, for the love of Allah. Eat it with a hearty appetite." And he gave the old man the ripe pear that Ahmet handed him in exchange for his money.

The old man murmured his thanks to the soldier, and then he held the pear up for all to see. "My friends," he said, "you know I am a poor dervish. I gave up all I had for the sake of serving Allah and His poor creatures. You have all seen how selfish Ahmet has been with his pears. But I am quite a different sort. I have a plentiful supply of beautiful pears, and I shall share them all with you."

"Where are they, then, father?" asked a peasant. "And why did you not eat your own pears instead of asking Ahmet for one of his?"

"You see," said the dervish, "first I must plant a tree and grow them."

Laughter bubbled in the crowd. Here was a curious holy man, indeed. The crowd watched as the old man ate the golden pear, leaving only a single seed. "Yes, you shall see," he said. And, taking a pick from the pack on his back, he dug a deep hole in the ground before him. Next, he carefully planted the seed and covered it with earth. "Now," he said, "I shall need some hot water."

"*Hot* water!" scoffed Ahmet. But he watched, interested in spite of himself. A tea seller was persuaded to give some of the hot water from his urn, and the seed was watered.

Then, to the surprise of those nearest the holy man, a small green shoot appeared where the seed had been planted and watered. Before their eyes, the shoot grew, and divided, and grew, and divided, until in the space of a few minutes a young tree stood, quite covered with leaves.

55

As they watched, the tree grew and grew. Pear blossoms appeared, and then young fruit, and shortly pears and pears—golden globes of pears that were no less beautiful than Ahmet's.

The dervish smiled happily. "Now, my friends," he said, "I have a fine pear for each of you." And he handed the pears around, beginning with Ahmet, until every last pear was gone. Yes, they were delicious, those pears. Even Ahmet had to agree that it was so.

Suddenly the holy man took his pick and chopped down the miraculous pear tree. Putting the tree over his shoulder, he smiled at the astonished peasants and then he walked away.

Ahmet stared dreamily for a moment at the place where the tree had been. Then, remembering his business, he turned to his handcart of pears. To his surprise, not a single pear was left in the cart. They were all gone, entirely gone. What's more, one handle of his cart was missing.

Ahmet clenched his fists in anger. "Thief! Thief!" he cried. "That thieving dervish gave every one of my pears away! And not only that—he took my cart handle!"

Leaving his empty handcart, he started running after the dervish. Around the corner of the marketplace, he lost sight of the old man. And the tree itself had turned of a sudden into his lost cart handle, lying where the dervish had dropped it. Ahmet stared wildly about him, but the dervish was nowhere to be seen. At his back there grew a great tide of laughter.

Ahmet's arms fell to his sides. Silently he returned to his empty handcart. *Tup!* The cart handle fitted back neatly into its place. Shaking his head, Ahmet trundled his handcart back home. There would be few gold coins in the sack for this day's work. A strange business indeed . . .

As for the story of the dervish's pear tree, it grew and grew. And there have never since that time been pears to match the ones the holy man gave away.

The Hoca and the New Barber

One day when Nasreddin Hoca went to the barbershop to be shaved, he found that a new barber was doing the shaving that day. The Hoca sat down good-naturedly and faced the mirror as the young man adjusted the napkin around his neck and began to work. *Aman!* The razor slipped and took a bit of the Hoca's left cheek with it.

"One moment, sir!" said the barber, and he stuck a bit of cotton on the wound. In the next pass of the razor, another bit of the Hoca's cheek went with it. "One moment, sir!" said the barber, and he stuck a bit of cotton on the second wound. With each stroke of the razor, another bit of cotton joined the crop sprouting on the Hoca's left cheek. "Now," said the barber, "I'll do the other side."

"One moment, young man!" said the Hoca as he studied the bits of cotton that dotted his left cheek. "Stop right there! I believe I'll plant *wheat* on the other side!"

Community Mourning for Brother Louse

A louse and a flea became such good friends that they were almost brothers. One morning when they woke up, they saw that the wind was blowing and the rain was coming down as if from a fountain in the sky. The louse said, "Brother Flea, you cook us some rice for breakfast, and I'll go out and cut some wood to keep us cozy on this rainy day."

The louse went out into the yard, but a snake came along and carried him away. The flea went out to call the louse to come and eat before the rice got cold, but the louse did not answer. He called again, but still there was no answer. All he saw out there was a snake disappearing around the corner. The flea suddenly realized what had happened, and he was so grief-stricken that he sat down and began pulling his hair out.

A bird came along and asked, "What happened, Brother Flea, that causes you to pull out your hair?"

"A snake has carried away Brother Louse. That is why I am pulling out my hair."

"In that case," said the bird, "I shall pull out my feathers." He flew up into a tree and began pulling out his feathers.

The tree asked, "What happened, Brother Bird? Why are you pulling out your feathers?"

"Oh, if you only knew!" said the bird. "A snake has carried away Brother Louse. We are so sad about this that Brother Flea is pulling out his hair and I am pulling out my feathers."

"Then I shall start shedding my leaves," said the tree, and its leaves began to fall to the ground.

A cow came along and saw the leaves falling. She asked, "Brother Tree, what is the matter? Why are you shedding your leaves?"

"Oh, if you only knew!" said the tree. "Sister Cow, a snake has carried off Brother Louse. We are so sad about this that Brother Flea is pulling out his hair, Brother Bird is pulling out his feathers, and I am shedding my leaves."

"Then I shall break off both my horns and wear them on my rear," said the cow. And so she did.

When the cow walked past the fountain, the fountain called out, "Sister Cow, what happened to make you break off your horns and wear them on the wrong end?"

"Oh, if you only knew!" said Sister Cow. "A snake has carried away Brother Louse. We are all so sad that Brother Flea is pulling out his hair,

Brother Bird is pulling out his feathers, Brother Tree is shedding his leaves, and I am wearing my horns on the wrong end."

"Ohhh!" said the fountain. "If that is so, then I shall stop my water from flowing." And at that moment the water stopped.

A short while later, a woman came to the fountain to draw water. When not even a drop of water came, she asked, "What has happened to you, O Fountain?"

"Alas! If you only knew!" said the fountain. "A snake has carried away Brother Louse. We are all so sad that Brother Flea is pulling out his hair, Brother Bird is pulling out his feathers, Brother Tree is shedding his leaves, Sister Cow has broken off her horns and is wearing them on the wrong end, and I have stopped my water."

"*Aman, aman*, Allah!" cried the woman. "Then I shall show my grief by breaking all my water jugs." And one by one she smashed them against the stone base of the fountain.

When the woman went home empty-handed, her husband asked her, "What has happened? Where are your jugs?"

"Oh, if you only knew!" said the woman. "A snake has carried away Brother Louse. We are all in mourning for him, and to show our grief, Brother Flea is pulling out his hair, Brother Bird is pulling out his feathers, Brother Tree is shedding his leaves, Sister Cow has broken off her horns and is wearing them on the wrong end, and the fountain has stopped its water. What could I do, then, except to break all of my water jugs?"

The man stared at his wife. Then he shouted, "And all this was because of the loss of a *louse*? Hair, feathers, leaves, horns, water, jugs—it's *fools* you are, all of you!"

And that was the end of *that* nonsense.

The Fisherman and the Jinn

One day a fisherman had been without success in his fishing the whole day long. Although he cast his net many times during the day, he was able to catch nothing but a brass jar.

Curious, the fisherman broke the seal and opened the jar to see what was in it. As soon as the jar was opened, a great cloud of smoke came out, a cloud that quickly took the shape of a jinn as large as a giant. As the fisherman was staring in amazement at the huge creature, the jinn said, "I shall eat you!"

"But why?" asked the fisherman. "I set you free. Why should you wish to eat me after I helped you so much?"

"He who sealed me inside the jar ordered me to devour the person who let me out. I have no choice but to eat you."

"All right," said the fisherman. "If you must eat me, then you must. However, I am very curious about something. How could anyone as large as you ever be put into such a small jar?"

"Oh, that is very easy," said the jinn. "Watch how I do it." Saying this, the jinn began fitting himself, little by little, into the jar again.

When the jinn was entirely back inside the jar, the fisherman said, "Ah, now I see." As he said this, he quickly pressed the cover back on the jar and resealed it. He then threw the jar back into the sea.

The Two Brothers and the Magic Hen

O nce there was and once there wasn't, when the camel was a barber and the flea was a porter—well, in those times there was a family that had never had any good luck in life. They were very poor, and the father of the family was hard put to it to find enough work to earn their bread and cheese. One day the woman asked her husband to set forth from home and find out what his kismet was to be, so off he went. He went a little; he went far. He traveled straight over hills and over dales. He traveled six months and a summer, and when he turned back to look, he found he had gone no farther than a grain of barley on his journey. Still, at last he came upon a dervish.

"And what are you looking for?" asked the dervish.

"I am seeking to know my fate."

The dervish said, "You have set your feet in the right path. Go ahead until you come to a hill. Beyond that hill is a swamp, and there you will learn your fate."

Well, the man went on until he came to the hill, and putting one foot ahead of the other he climbed on over the hill. When he came to the other side, he found a swamp in which many reeds were growing. Some of the reeds were short and some of them were tall, but all of the reeds were the fates of different people. The tallest ones were the fates of the richest, the middle-sized ones were the fortunes of ordinary people, and the very short ones were the kismets of very poor people. He looked and looked, but he was unable to decide which one was his. At last he decided to call out. "My fate, my kismet!" he shouted. "Where are you?"

Finally a voice answered him. "I am here. I am here." And it sighed.

Following the voice, he came to a spindly reed lying in the mud. Carefully he straightened it, and then he said, "Ah, please tell me my fate, for we are now very poor, and I desire to know what is to come."

The reed stood silent for a moment, and then it began to speak. "Go over on the other side of the hill. You will find a road there, the road where the caravans pass. When you get there, stop any caravans which pass along the road; tell them that it is your road, and collect toll from them. The first caravan that passes will offer you gold and then silver as toll. Take neither gold nor silver, but tell them that you want only the hen the old man at the very end of the caravan is carrying."

After straightening up his reed again in the swamp, the man went over the hill to the other side, and there was the road. He waited and waited, until at last a caravan came along. Stopping it, he said to the head of the caravan, "This road is mine, and you must pay a toll for your passage along it."

"All right," said the caravan head. "What do you wish as toll? Will you have gold?"

"No, I want no gold," said the man.

"Well, will you take silver, then?"

"No. I want neither silver nor gold."

"What, then, will you accept as the toll?"

"I ask only the hen that is carried by the old man at the end of your caravan."

"Very well, then. Go and ask him for that hen."

The man went to the very end of the caravan. There in a carriage an old man was sitting with a hen on his lap. "I must have that hen as toll for the use of my road," he said.

"With all the gold and silver that this caravan is carrying," said the old fellow, "why do you ask for this hen?"

"It is only the hen that I want. Your caravan leader has given me permission to take it." He finally got the hen he wanted, and he walked and walked and walked until he came home.

When he got home with the hen, his wife said, "You went on a journey to seek your fate, and look what you found! A hen!" she exclaimed. "What kind of fate is that?"

So he told her about the spindly reed and the advice it had given. "'Demand a toll for the use of your road,' it said. 'They will offer you gold. They will offer you silver. Accept neither of those, but ask only for the hen that the old man at the very end of the caravan is carrying.' And so I did."

"What!" exclaimed his wife. "You refused *gold*? You refused *silver*? And you asked only for this wretched hen? You are a fool, my husband. You are a *fool*. Why did you take just a *hen*, instead of the gold and silver that we need?"

"My wife," said the man, "*this* is my fortune. We must take what my kismet has sent."

They put the hen into a coop, and when they went to feed it the next morning, they found that the hen had laid a golden egg. Picking it up, they took it to a jeweler, and there they exchanged it for money. From that time on, the hen laid a golden egg every day. At last the man had so much gold that he was very rich, and he decided out of pure thankfulness to go on the holy pilgrimage to Mecca. Leaving his wife and his home and his children, he joined a caravan of pilgrims.

After her husband had gone, the woman was left much to herself, and

she became very lonely. One day she said to her two sons, "Go out into the street and see whatever people are there, and bring them in to talk with me." The boys went out, but they could find neither neighbors nor friends, no one except a stranger. When their mother had been told this, she said, "All right. Bring the stranger in, and we shall make him welcome. After all, a stranger is Allah's guest."

She and the stranger talked and talked, and they soon became friends. After they had talked for an hour or so, she told the stranger about their remarkable hen. "It is curious that you should mention a hen," said the visitor, "for I have been very hungry for chicken. It would please me very much if we could have that hen for dinner."

"Oh, no," said the woman. "I cannot serve you that hen, for it is my husband's kismet. But we have other hens in the coop. I shall have the cook prepare one of those for you."

"But it is the remarkable hen that interests me," said the visitor. "I am certain that its flavor is far superior to that of ordinary hens. *Do* prepare that one for me." And he spoke so winningly that at last the woman agreed to serve the stranger that particular hen. She ordered a servant to kill the hen and to have the cook prepare it for the evening meal.

Now, the cook knew all about that hen, and she had been listening to the conversation all this time through a knothole in the door. "If she's such a fool as to waste her husband's kismet on that stranger," said the cook to herself, "I'll just have to mend matters myself." After the servant had killed the hen, therefore, the cook set aside the head and the neck. With the rest of the chicken, she prepared a dish that fairly cried out to be eaten. Then calling the two sons, she said, "This hen is special for two other reasons besides the golden eggs she lays. Whoever eats the head of the hen will become a padishah, and whoever eats the neck of the hen will become a vizier. Your father would want you to have them, for they are his kismet. Quickly, now! Eat them." And she fed the head of the hen to the older son and the neck of the hen to the younger son. "Now you must run away quickly!" she said, and she helped them out of the window. "Go, and don't look back!"

As soon as the hen was served to the guest, he looked closely at it and asked, "Why, where are the head and the neck?"

"I do not know," the woman answered, "but I'll call the cook and ask her." And she sent a servant to fetch the cook.

When the cook hurried in, the woman said, "The chicken looks delicious, but our guest wants to know what has been done with the head and the neck of the hen. Where are they?"

"Why, surely the head and the neck were cooked inside the hen," said the cook. "Have you looked there?"

Quickly the stranger cut the hen open, but the head and the neck were not inside. Then the cook admitted, "I gave the head to the older son and the neck to the younger son to ease their hunger, and I sent them on their way. They must be quite far from here by now." And how she was punished!

Meanwhile, the boys, once through the window safely, had run and then walked and walked, until finally they came to a fork in the road. "Since our fortunes seem to be taking us apart," said the older boy, "perhaps we should each take a different road." And they agreed to travel different ways, with the older one taking the road to the left and the younger one taking the road to the right.

The older son went on and on, until at last he came to a big city. It so happened that the padishah of that city had died, and the people of the city had met to choose a new padishah. As was the custom, they released a dove belonging to the former padishah, and when the dove perched on someone's head, that person became the new padishah. Now, the moment the dove was released, it flew directly to the head of the older son and perched there.

"Unfair! Unfair!" exclaimed someone in the crowd. "The state bird has perched on the head of a stranger. We must try again."

So the people recovered the dove and released it again. At first it flew around and around. Then it flew to the head of the older son and perched there.

Still, the people were not satisfied. "The chances of a Turk are three," one said. "We must try again." The dove was recovered from the head of the older son, and then it was released for the third time.

The third time, the dove flew directly to the head of the older son and perched there. "That decides the matter," the people agreed, and thus the older son was made padishah.

On the other hand, the younger son walked and walked along his own road, and at last he came to a city. Now, this city was draped all in black, mourning the death of its padishah. The boy knocked—*Tak! Tak! Tak!*—at the door of a small house at the edge of the city, and when the lady of the house came to the door, he asked if he might spend the night in her house.

"Welcome," said the woman. "Come in, and be comfortable, for a stranger is Allah's guest." And the boy was led to a room of his own.

The next morning, when the woman went to call the boy for breakfast, she noticed beneath his bed a cup of gold coins. Quietly, quietly, she tiptoed in and slipped the cup of gold coins into her blouse. How could she know that the gold had appeared only because the boy had eaten the neck of the hen? Still, "There is something magical about this boy," she said to herself. And she awakened him. "I have been thinking about you all night," she said. "You are alone in the world, and I have no sons. Will you stay and be my son?"

The boy was pleased, and he agreed to stay there. And morning after morning, the woman took care to waken early, so that she might pick up the cup of gold before the boy stirred from his sleep. As the days went by, the woman became rich.

But after three or five weeks, the boy chanced to waken early, and to his surprise he found a cup of gold under his bed. Saying nothing about it, he tucked it in the small chest in his room. The next morning, he again found a cup of gold, and the next morning, and the next. Still, he said nothing about the gold to the woman, and she, for her part, had become so rich that she asked no questions.

In the city where the younger son was staying, there lived the most beautiful girl in the world. She was so beautiful that the kings of faraway lands would come once a year just to see her. To see this beautiful girl, one had to pay a full cup of gold, and this is how the younger son began spending his money. Day after day, he gave his cup of gold to see the girl, for she was indeed very beautiful.

When the beautiful girl realized that this same young man was coming to see her day after day, she became curious to know how he could manage to come so often. Finally she found out his secret, and she resolved to possess the neck of the hen herself. One night during the winter, when the boy was visiting her, she gave him something to eat that made him quite ill. In his nausea, he spat up the neck of the hen, which had lain all this while undigested in his stomach. When the girl had secured the neck of the hen, she had the boy thrown out into the bushes, and she quickly swallowed the neck of the hen herself.

As for the boy, when he woke up in the morning, he found himself shivering in the bushes outside the girl's house. He looked all about for his cup of gold, but there was nothing to be seen. "I have been tricked!" he said.

"And all of the good fortune which would have been mine because of the neck of the hen has been lost! What's more, I have not a single lira in my pocket."

He wandered off into the forest, thinking what he might do. While he was thinking, he saw three hunters quarreling, and he asked the cause of their quarrel. One of the men said, "The three of us have three magic articles. One is a stick which will beat anyone or anything when it is given the order, 'Beat, my stick. Beat!' The second is a cloak which makes its wearer invisible. And the third is a carpet; as soon as one steps on the carpet, he is carried anywhere he wishes to go. We cannot decide which of us should have the stick, which should have the cloak, and which should have the carpet."

"Hmnn," said the boy. "Truly, all three of the magic articles belong together. Let me help you settle your quarrel. You have a bow and some arrows. I shall take one of your arrows and shoot it far away. Whichever of you first gets the arrow and brings it back will get all three of the magic articles. What do you think of that?"

After some discussion, the three men agreed that the boy's suggestion was a wise one, and they stood by and watched while he fitted the arrow to the bowstring. As soon as he had shot the arrow, all three of them began to run off in the snow, each determined to be the first to reach the arrow and thus to own all three of the magic articles.

The men had no sooner gone out of sight when the boy snatched up the stick, the cloak, and the carpet and ran away in the other direction. After a few moments, he stopped in the shelter of a pine tree. Putting on the cloak, he picked up the stick, stepped on the carpet, and said, "Take me to the roof of the beautiful girl's house."

Almost at once, he found himself on the girl's roof. Then he ordered, "Beat, my stick. Beat!" and the stick began beating on the tiles of the roof. The girl, hearing all that noise, sent her servant up to see what was happening on the roof. Since the boy was invisible, the servant could not see anything worth seeing on the roof. "There is nothing there but snow," he reported to the girl. But the beating went on and on.

Finally the girl herself went up on the roof. When the boy saw her looking puzzled about the beating, he thought she looked so funny that he began to laugh. As soon as he had laughed, he became visible. Pretending to be glad to see him, the girl took him in, and she and her forty female attendants teased him to stay. "You must be cold!" the girl said. "Here. Have something warming to drink." And she gave him a sleepy drink. When he had finished that one, she gave him another and then another. When he had drunk so much that he had fallen sound asleep, she took the stick and the cloak and the carpet, and then she had the boy thrown into an old well.

When the boy woke up at the bottom of the well, he said, "*Aman!* I have been tricked again by that girl! Someday, I shall have my revenge against her!"

Looking about, he found that there was no way out of the well except through a small passage at the side. He walked and walked along the passage until he came to a strange new world. There were many trees there, and they were all covered with green leaves. But outside, it was still winter . . .

He walked and walked through the woodland until he came to a vineyard bearing beautiful white grapes. Feeling hungry, he ate one grape, and suddenly he became a horse. He ran here and there, and finally he came to a vineyard bearing red grapes. He ate a red grape, and this time he became a deer. Since the big horns on his head made it impossible for him to run, he sought some other fruit that might help him. "Ah," he murmured, "there are some black grapes. Let me eat one of those. I should be happy to be anything but a deer, with these huge antlers." He ate a black grape, and immediately he became a man again.

Suddenly he had a fine idea. After picking several clusters of each kind of grape, he walked back through the tunnel and finally, leg over leg, managed to climb out of the well. He put his grapes in a basket which he borrowed from a shopkeeper at the bazaar, and he started going through the streets of the city, calling, "Grapes! Fresh grapes! I sell fresh grapes!" At last he came to the beautiful girl's house.

When the girl heard the grapeman calling—and all in the middle of winter, too—she sent a servant to buy some grapes for her and her female attendants. To the servant, the boy sold several large clusters of red grapes. As soon as the girl and her forty female attendants had eaten the red grapes, they became deer, with their antlers so huge and spreading that there was scarcely space for them all in the same room. While the girls were standing there helpless, and the beautiful girl with her head outside the window, he went upstairs and gave each of them a white grape. Immediately, each of them became a horse.

"I'll use these horses as beasts of burden," he decided. Learning that a padishah in another city was having a palace built for himself, the boy took all forty-one of the horses—with one of them the beautiful girl—to help in the construction of the palace. Thus he had ample revenge on them all.

When the palace was finished, the boy went to get his money for the hire of his horses. Now, it seems that for his own entertainment, the padishah required everyone who came to get money to tell a story before he could be paid. When it was his turn, the boy told his own story, from first to last, leaving out not a single detail. As soon as the padishah had heard the story, he recognized the boy as his younger brother. They embraced one another, and then the padishah told his own story, concluding, "But, alas, I am still unmarried."

The younger brother said, "I know just the right bride for you. She is the most beautiful girl in the world, and you should marry her." Leading before the padishah the horse which was really the beautiful girl, the boy gave her a black grape to eat. As soon as she had eaten it, she became a beautiful girl again. Giving the other forty horses black grapes to eat, the boy returned them to their old forms as servants, and put them under the padishah's service.

The padishah made his younger brother his vizier, and thus their kismet was fulfilled. In good time, the beautiful girl was married to the padishah, in a wedding that lasted forty days and forty nights, and as the girl, too, was content, they all lived happily from that time on.

Great joy for them, and a story for us.

The Wordless Letter

A young man named Dursun from the town of Perşembe was far from home doing his military service. Every day, a large quantity of mail arrived at the training base, and every day the recruits gathered eagerly for letters from home. The only one who had received no letters at all was young Dursun.

Now, at that camp the base commander read all the mail before it was given to the men. Yes, it was a kind of censorship, but it helped to keep the troops together. Suppose, for example, that Mehmet received a letter saying that his cousin had died, or that his brother was in trouble, or that his wife was flirting with another man. Wouldn't Mehmet be likely to run away home to see what help he could give there? The camp could not be kept together with such comings and goings!

69

Well, one day Dursun finally received a letter from home. The base commander opened the envelope and pulled out the letter, but there was nothing at all written on that piece of paper. It was blank on the front and blank on the back. "Aha!" said the commander to himself. "There is something suspicious about this letter!" He tried in every way he knew to see what the letter said, but he could discover nothing. Finally he called Dursun to his office and said to him, "Dursun, you have a letter. Here it is. Read it." Saying this, he handed Dursun the envelope.

"A letter!" Dursun exclaimed. "It is probably from my older brother." Removing the paper from the envelope, he looked at the front of it, but it was blank. He turned it over and looked at the back side, but there was nothing written on the back side, either. Smiling to himself, he folded up the piece of paper and put it back into the envelope. "Thank you, sir!" Dursun saluted the commander and started to leave.

"Dursun, wait!" said the commander. "There is some kind of message in that letter. Is your brother trying to get you to come home? Perhaps there is some kind of signal or code for you. Anyway, read the letter aloud."

"But, sir," said Dursun, "there is nothing on the paper in that envelope—nothing on one side and nothing on the other. See!" And he removed the paper from the envelope and showed it to the commander.

But the officer was still not satisfied. "Dursun," he said, "why would your brother bother to send you nothing but a blank piece of paper? Why wouldn't he put some kind of message on it? Why? Tell me!"

"Well, sir," said Dursun, "two years ago, my brother and I had a quarrel, quite a serious quarrel, and since that time we have not spoken to each other. That's all there is to it. That's why he didn't say anything in the letter. A brother's a brother; we remember each other. But home or away, we don't speak to each other!"

"Who's Selling These Pomegranates?"

One day Nasreddin Hoca loaded a tray with his finest pomegranates, intending to sell them in the public market. Mounting his little donkey and balancing his tray carefully, the Hoca rode to what he considered the most desirable corner of the marketplace, and there began to cry his wares.

"*Nar var!*" he shouted. "*En güzel nar var!*" ["Here are pomegranates! Here are most beautiful pomegranates!"]

His little donkey took up the cry, braying "Hee har! Hee har! Hee har!"

Annoyed, the Hoca glared at his donkey, and tried once again to attract buyers for his pomegranates. "*Nar var! En güzel nar var!*"

Encouraged, the little donkey took up his own version of his master's cry: "Hee har! Hee har! Hee har!"

By this time, a small crowd had gathered around the Hoca and his assistant, eager to see how the Hoca would dispose of this problem.

For the third time, the Hoca called, "*Nar var! En güzel nar var!*" looking hopefully at the crowd.

Gleefully the little donkey echoed, "Hee har! Hee har! Hee har!"

This was too much for the Hoca. "See here!" he said crossly to the donkey. "Who's selling these pomegranates, *you* or *I*?"

Chortling with delight, the crowd pressed in to buy the Hoca's goods.

The Stonecutter

L isten, now, to my story.

In the old time, the time of happiness, a certain young man earned his bread by breaking boulders into building stones and carrying those stones to market. On one day of all days, this man, a poor stonecutter all his years, found within a boulder two strange stones the size of eggs. He marveled as they glowed, stones unlike the ones that he had cut before. What, he wondered, was their value?

He put the two shining stones inside his shirt. Then, stone by stone, he loaded the rest onto his cart and trundled his load to market. "Stones! Building stones!" At last he had sold them all.

On he went to a jewelry shop. Drawing forth one of the shining stones, he held it toward the jeweler. "Sir, will you look at this stone and tell me its worth?"

The jeweler looked at the gem, for gem it was, and at the poor young man who held it. "Where did you get this?" he asked.

Why should the stonecutter lie? He had lived honestly all his days. O heed this truth, a truth worth knowing: We must be straight. We must make ourselves and our words true above all. Men will believe the words of our mouths. Men can be misled by those words, but Allah will not. Allah will know the straight from the crooked. Allah knows the heart. Therefore, we should live as we look to others. Our tongue, our appearance, and our heart should all offer the same message.

So the stonecutter said, "It came out of a boulder I was cutting. There was another stone like it." And he showed the second stone.

The jeweler—Allah be praised!—was also honest. He said, "Young man, there is no way that I can set a value on these stones. You have shown them to me, but do not show them to anyone else here. Only the greatest padishah of our time can set a value on such stones; only he can pay you their worth. No jeweler alive will tell you their true value."

"Very well," said the stonecutter, and he put the bright stones back inside his shirt. "I shall first ask my parents' blessing and then seek the greatest ruler of our time. Thank you. And may Allah keep us all."

The greatest ruler of that time was the padishah of Yemen, so after the stonecutter had kissed his parents' hands and asked their blessings, he put on his sandals and set forth. Day after day he walked. In his walking, he overtook two white-haired, white-bearded dervishes. "*Selâmünaleyküm!*" he greeted them.

And "*Aleykümselâm!*" they returned his greeting.

"Young man," said one, "where are you going?"

These two old dervishes had reverent tongues; they carried prayer beads; they spoke gently. And they waited for his answer with fatherly concern.

"Dervish fathers, I am going to Yemen," the stonecutter replied. He had never lied before; he told the truth now.

"And why are you going to Yemen?" the other asked.

"Sirs, I have a reason: I am a poor stonecutter. I break boulders into building stones and sell them in the market. Not long ago, I found two gems in a broken boulder. The jeweler could set no value on them. 'Go to the greatest padishah of our time to seek their worth,' he said. Now I am taking them to show to the padishah of Yemen. Surely he will know their value."

"Ah! Can we see them, young man?" asked one. "Let us see the gems. We have traveled far and viewed much. We may know something of their worth."

The stonecutter took the jewels from his shirt and showed them to the dervishes so that their hearts might be content. Alas! The step from content to greed was all too short. Desire for the gems inflamed the hearts of both old men.

Still, the stonecutter was too supple and strong to be overcome by force. They must plot a safer way to make the jewels their own. So, "They have great value indeed. May they be blessed to you!" said one, and they returned the shining stones.

"Let us go with you to Yemen to assist you in your errand," the other offered. "With three of us, and two of us holy men, you may well travel more securely. And perhaps the padishah of Yemen will offer us poor dervishes some small reward for your safe conduct. Please take us as your companions."

The stonecutter, young and innocent, said, "Of course, dervish fathers, come with me. If the padishah gives you nothing, I shall give you five or ten coins for your trouble." And so the three went on together, with the dervishes all the time intent on stealing the gems as the young man slept.

Near sunset, they came to a village, and they stayed as guests at the home of a kindly man. "Welcome!" he greeted them. "You are indeed Allah's visitors!" And he gave them first a hearty meal for their hungry stomachs and then comfortable beds for their night's rest.

The stonecutter soon fell sound asleep, still fully dressed. With a full stomach and a clear conscience, why shouldn't he sleep? As for the old men, they made short work of removing the gems from the sleeping young man's shirt. "In the morning, we'll leave him and go another way," said one. And the other agreed.

The next morning, as the three took their ablutions before their morning prayers, the stonecutter discovered that his gems were gone. Young and innocent though he was, he knew the folly of charging the old men with the theft. "My true words would seem a lie, and their lies would seem the truth," he thought. And thus he gave no sign that he knew of his loss.

And indeed, who would doubt the innocence of the two old dervishes with their prayer beads and their *Bismillâh*s and their long white beards? There are such men among us even now: they look respectable on the outside, but no man knows what black thoughts live in their hearts. Yes, many try to deceive others by their outward pious appearance. Only Allah knows the hearts of such as those.

Not long after the three had left that village, one dervish said, "Young man, we cannot keep our promise to you, after all. We must take that other road instead of going on to Yemen. May Allah be with you on your journey!"

And, "Yes, young man," agreed the other one, "my brother is right. Our business does not lie in Yemen. Go with Allah!"

As for the stonecutter, he was fully determined that they would come with him. "Remember," he said, "I still have the jewels, and you have promised to be my companions on the journey, to safeguard me. Have you forgotten our agreement?" And he grasped each dervish so firmly by the collar that they had no choice but to go as he went.

At last they came to Yemen, still three companions. "Let us rest a little now," said the stonecutter. "Here is a coffeehouse. I shall go and order something to refresh you."

As the two old men sat, looking here and there for a means of escape, the stonecutter spoke secretly to the coffeehouse owner. "Please serve those two dervishes what they wish, but keep them here with you until I return. I trust them to your care." And the coffeehouse owner agreed to watch over them.

As the dervishes refreshed themselves, the stonecutter went out another way to find a petition writer. The petition writer carefully inscribed the young man's message, directed to the padishah of Yemen: "Oh, Most Excellent! I was a stonecutter. I used to sell the stones I cut. One day while I was cutting a boulder, two gems came out of it. When I showed the gems to a jeweler, he could not set a value on them. Instead, he sent me to you, who alone could know their worth. On my way to see you, I met two old dervishes. After seeing the gems, they joined me on my journey. I thought they were as honest as I am. But they stole the gems from my shirt while I slept. They look unlike thieves. No one would believe me if I accused them of the theft, because they look honest as angels. I ask you to hear my case and restore my gems to me. We are resting at Ahmet's coffeehouse. Please send your guards to take all three of us to your court."

He paid a messenger to take the petition to the padishah, and he himself returned to the coffeehouse. As he entered, he saw that the two old men were trying to leave but were being prevented by the coffeehouse owner. "Your friend entrusted you with me," the owner was saying. "I cannot let you go until he comes." And they were forced to stay. As the stonecutter came to them, the padishah's guards entered the coffeehouse and took all three to the presence of the padishah.

The three were immediately sent under guard to another room while the padishah reread the petition. "What am I to do?" the padishah said. "Suppose the old men do not have the gems? These old men look honest. But what is within their hearts? Only Allah knows!"

The ruler's young daughter was standing beside the padishah. As our fathers say, "One is as wise as one's head, not one's years."

The girl said, "Father, judge them in a different court, a court of discernment."

"A *discernment* court, my daughter? What do you mean by a discernment court?"

"Do not trouble yourself about this matter, my father," she answered. "If you will let me handle this case, I can show you clearly the characters of all three of these men."

"And how can you do this, my daughter?"

"Leave it to me, Father. I shall speak in your name, and let them reveal themselves."

"Very well. Do as you please. And may Allah help you in this discernment court of yours!"

She ordered all three brought again to the padishah's presence. As they stood before her, she said, "Oh, dervish fathers, and you, young man, welcome! My father says that we shall keep you as our guests for three days. You will have the same foods and services that we ourselves enjoy. On the fourth day, we shall show our respect and bid you farewell. It is my padishah fa-

75

ther's wish that you be accepted as the guests of Allah."

The girl then ordered servants to take each of the three guests to separate rooms. When they had left, she said, "Father, give me those three days, and in your name I shall let them reveal themselves in their true characters."

"So this is to be your discernment court, my daughter? We shall see how well justice is served by this new court!"

The daughter assigned three beautiful young ladies to serve the guests. She said to each servant, "Put on coquettish airs as you go in each time, and let's see how these men behave. Let me know about what they do and say."

When the servants went into the old men's rooms, *hink-mink*, they flirted and swished their skirts, and the old men responded eagerly. Each one winked at his servant and reached out to fondle her. The servants understood at once that beneath their pious appearances, these old men had base intentions. The girls reported to the padishah's daughter, "Our sultana, the old men are very bad inside. As we put on coquettish airs, they were ready to be with us if we should agree."

"Is that so? Then continue to do exactly as you have been doing," she said. "Let them reveal their own characters."

But when she questioned the one who served the young man, the servant was puzzled. "Oh, my sultana," she said, "the young man doesn't seem to be of this world. When I enter his room, he looks only at the floor. He will not look at my face at all, no matter how coquettishly I behave. If you called all three of us servants together and asked him to point me out, he could not do it. He would not know my face."

"Oh? Is that so? Then continue to behave just as you have been doing, and tell me how he responds."

After three days and nights of reports from the servants, the padishah's daughter understood what she had half suspected from the beginning: the old men's hearts were evil, but the heart of the young man was clean. On the fourth day, she had the three guests brought into her father's presence. She called to one of the old men, "Oh, dervish father, come forward a little. I wish to ask your advice about something."

"Very well, my girl," the dervish answered, and he stepped forward. "What do you wish to know?"

"White-bearded men have had many experiences. Only such men could be able to answer what I shall ask," she said. "At one time, a padishah's daughter, like me, had a gardener. Are you listening, father?"

"Yes, my girl. I am listening," he answered.

But not only that old man was listening. All of the thousand people in her father's presence were listening as the girl went on. "This gardener worked in the girl's garden, in the vineyard, and among the flowers with full devotion. Fifteen years went by this way. Then her destiny opened, and she was engaged to the son of a padishah. The girl called the gardener to her

76

room. 'Oh, gardener,' she said, 'my destiny has opened, and my father has engaged me to a man. When I'm wedded, they'll take me away to another country. But you have worked with devotion in my garden for fifteen years. I have been very pleased with you. Since you have worked faithfully for me for such a long time, tell me your wish, and I shall fulfill it!' Are you listening, father?"

"Yes, my girl. I'm listening." In truth, not only that old man but everyone else in the padishah's presence was listening.

"'Gardener, why don't you speak?'

"The gardener said, 'My girl, are you really going to fulfill my wish?'

"'Yes,' said the girl. She thought perhaps the gardener would ask for money.

"'Well, what I wish is not money or jewels. I wish only that you would come to the garden house at midnight tonight wearing your wedding gown and all your jewels. Do not tell anyone you are coming to me. I shall look at you for one hour. That is my wish. Then you may go. And may Allah give you to the one you love. I wish nothing more from you than that.'

"'Oh, gardener, there is to be nothing else? You will only look at me for one hour. Is that your wish?'

"'Yes, my girl. May my arm drop off if I even stretch forth my hand toward you!'

"'All right. I shall come tonight at midnight for you to look at me for an hour, since that is your wish.' And the girl, without telling anyone where she was going, wore her wedding gown and all her jewels to the garden house at midnight that night.

"On that same night, a thief was outside, intent on robbery. He appeared suddenly before the girl, with her *fışır-fışır* dress and all her jewels. 'Aha!' he said. 'I have found my prey. Give me all your jewelry and your *fışır-fışır* dress.'

"'Oh, thief, please don't stop me now. I have a wish to fulfill. I'm going to the garden house wearing my wedding dress and all my jewels. The gardener will look at me for one hour. You wait for me here. When I come back, I shall give you my jewels and my *fışır-fışır* dress. Only let me go now to keep my promise.'

"'All right. I will wait for you here,' said the thief, and the girl went on her way. Now, dervish father, I want to ask your advice about this thief. Please understand that I am not comparing you with the thief! But if you were in his place, tell me truthfully what you would do if you were that thief. When you found a girl like that, would you let her go or would you rob her?"

"That thief had no brains at all," said the old man, and he laughed. "My girl, if he has gone out to rob, why should he let such good prey go? Should he wait for the prey to come back? What if she never returns? That thief had no sense at all. Isn't that so?"

77

"Yes, father, you are right," the padishah's daughter answered. Then she called the second old man. "Come forward, father. I have asked the other father about the thief who is waiting. I will ask the rest from you. Give me a truthful answer. The girl went on to the garden house in her *fışır-fışır* dress and with all her jewels. She went inside and closed the door, and she stood before the gardener for one hour. The gardener watched her for the whole hour. At the end of that hour, the girl asked, 'Has your wish been fulfilled?'

"'Yes, it has.'

"'May I have your permission to go now?'

"'Yes, of course. Go. I have been given what I wished.'

"The girl went out of the garden house and walked along another road to her own home because the thief was waiting on the first road. Now, I'll ask you to tell me truthfully about this gardener. The other father spoke the truth from his heart. If you were in the place of that gardener and a beauty of that kind should come at midnight to your house in her *fışır-fışır* dress and with all her jewels and without telling anyone else where she was going, would you let her go away after looking at her for an hour, or wouldn't you? Tell me truthfully from your heart."

The old man laughed, and then he said, "My girl, that gardener had no brains at all! If a beauty of that kind had come, what benefit would I get from just looking at her for one hour? Dogs also look at the meat in the butcher shop, but what do they get into their mouths? If I were that gardener—death is one day, and mourning is one day. I wouldn't let the girl go as a virgin. Isn't that so?"

"Yes. You have answered correctly and from your heart. Now, young man, come forward. These two old men have spoken the truth from their hearts. Now I will ask your advice about the gardener. The second old man said, 'Death is one day, and so is mourning.' If you were in the gardener's place, what would you do to a beauty of that kind, in your house with the door shut, and no one else knowing where she is?"

The young man groaned and said, "My girl, that gardener had neither mercy nor honor."

"Why, young man, that gardener had so much mercy and so much honor that he didn't even lay a finger on her. He just watched her for one hour and then let her go."

"Still, I say it again," the stonecutter answered. "That gardener had neither mercy nor honor. If I were in the gardener's place . . . that old man is *wrong*. You said that the girl had been stopped by a thief on her way to the garden house, so she went home by another road?"

"Yes."

"If I were in the place of that gardener and a beauty of that kind, keeping her word, came to my house in the middle of the night and stood before me for one hour, I would take whatever weapons I had to protect her and lead her safely back to her house. The thief was waiting for her on the first road. What if another kind of evil had been waiting for her on the road she took home? If something bad happened to the girl, wouldn't it be the gardener's fault?"

"Yes, it would," said the padishah's daughter.

"So you can see that the gardener had neither mercy nor honor. He just said 'go' to the girl. He didn't lead her back to her door." After hearing this, not only the padishah's daughter but all those others in the padishah's presence understood that the young man's heart was as clean and straight as his outward appearance.

The padishah's daughter called the two old men forward again. She questioned the first one: "You said that if you had been in the place of that thief, you would have robbed the girl instead of letting her go. Isn't that what you said?"

"Yes."

Then, to the second old man, she said, "And you, dervish father, if you had been in the place of that gardener, you wouldn't have let her go as a virgin. Isn't that what you said?"

"Yes."

"Now think what this young man said. He said that gardener had neither mercy nor honor. As for you, dervish fathers, *you* have neither mercy nor honor. Your hearts are black. Your *Bismillâh*s are just a show for the people around you; your characters are bad. Now, take out this young man's gems and return them to him, or I'll call the executioners to cut off your heads!"

The old men valued their lives more than the stones, so they took out the gems and handed them to the stonecutter. Begging the padishah's permission to leave, they backed out of the court and hurried away, thankful to have their heads safely on their necks.

The padishah's daughter then turned to her father and said, "This is how the court of discernment works, Father. Every person eventually reveals the nature of his own heart. Allah alone can be sure of what is within any man, no matter how pure that man may appear on the outside. But what the heart feels, the mouth must speak, and thus these two old men revealed themselves as they really are. As for the stonecutter, his heart is clean. May his way be open, and may Allah preserve him as he goes."

In good time, the stonecutter accepted from the padishah of Yemen a very large sum of money in exchange for the gems, and he returned home not only richer in pocket but wiser in heart about the ways of the world. May we ourselves fare well in such a court!

The Cock and the Prince

Once there was and twice there wasn't, when the flea was a porter and the camel a barber—well, in those times, there was a cock who lived just outside the padishah's palace wall. One day he flew over the wall and began scratching in the garden looking for food. As he was scratching away, he dug up a gold coin.

When he looked up, he saw the son of the padishah watching him from a window of the palace. The cock then sang loudly, "I've found a gold coin! I've found a gold coin! I've found a gold coin!" Since the prince made no response, the cock sang, "The prince is afraid of me! The prince is afraid of me! The prince is afraid of me!"

When he heard this, the prince said to one of the palace servants, "Go down and take the gold coin away from that cock!"

After the gold coin had been taken from the cock and brought to the prince, the prince held it up and said, "Here it is! Here it is! Here it is!"

As soon as the cock heard this, he answered so loudly that everyone in the palace could hear him: "The prince is so poor that he needs my gold! The prince is so poor that he needs my gold! The prince is so poor that he needs my gold!"

At that, the prince was so angry that he said to a servant, "Go and cut the throat of that cock and bring him here!"

After his throat had been cut and he had been taken to the prince, the cock sang out, "What a sharp knife it was! What a sharp knife it was! What a sharp knife it was!"

They cleaned the cock and put it into a pot of water to be cooked. From the pot came the cock's voice, singing loudly, "What a fine bath this is! What a fine bath this is! What a fine bath this is!"

When the cock was cooked, it was placed upon the table in the great hall of the palace and served to the prince. From the platter where it lay, the cock sang out, "What a big barn this is! What a big barn this is! What a big barn this is!"

As the prince was eating the cock, the cock called out after every swallow, "What a narrow lane this is! What a narrow lane this is! What a narrow lane this is!"

After it had gone down into the stomach of the prince, the cock called out loudly, "What a nasty-smelling place this is! What a nasty-smelling place this is! What a nasty-smelling place this is!"

Upon hearing this, the prince said, "What a terrible creature this cock is! I must get rid of him!" Going to the toilet, he took with him a servant bearing a loaded gun. When the cock came out, the servant shot at it, but the cock flew away unharmed.

A *herrop!* for him and a story for us!

81

The Stepdaughter and the Forty Thieves

Once there was and once there wasn't, when Allah had many creatures, and to talk too much was a sin—well, in those times there was a beautiful girl whose own mother had died. After three or five years of loneliness, her father had married again.

But this second wife was an evil one, determined to destroy her stepdaughter. "Take her away!" the woman raged. "How can there be peace between us while that girl remains here?"

She kept *at* him and *at* him, until finally one day the father said, "My daughter, this woman is now my wife, and she insists that she cannot rest until you have gone. My heart aches for you, but I must see you on your way. Tie all your belongings in a bundle and come with me."

The girl obeyed her father—how could she do otherwise?—and, carrying her bundle on her head, she followed her father up a steep hill until they had reached the very top. "Now, my daughter, I'll take your bundle and roll it down the other side of this hill. Go wherever your bundle rolls, and where it stops, you must find a new home. May Allah be with you, my daughter."

He started the bundle rolling, and then he turned away so that she could not see his tears. As for the girl, she followed the bundle down the hill, going where it went, until it finally came to rest at the house of forty thieves. *Tak! Tak! Tak!* She knocked at the door, but there was no answer. Finding the door unlocked, she opened it and went inside. She looked here and there, and saw that there was food in abundance, but nothing had been prepared for a meal. Surely the owners would be hungry when they returned . . .

"Let me make a big kettle of good soup," she said to herself, "and then I'll cook a big kettle of macaroni. And of course I'll need to bake plenty of bread." When the girl had finished these things and had set the table nicely, she tidied the house all around. Then she slapped herself on the cheek and became a broom.

When the forty thieves came home, they found their table all set and their food all cooked. "*Aman!*" cried the eldest. "Who has done these good things for us?" But there was no sign of the girl.

After three or five days had passed over their heads, with each day bringing the same wonderful surprise, the eldest of the forty thieves said, "I'll stay at home today and find out who this good person is." He stayed and waited and waited, but at last he became so sleepy that he couldn't keep his eyes open any longer, and he fell asleep. Then the girl came out again, quietly,

quietly, and she cooked and tidied and set the table and washed herself. Then she slapped herself on the cheek and became a broom.

When the eldest thief awoke, he found that everything had been done again as before. There was a great kettle of soup prepared, and another huge kettle of macaroni, and plenty of fresh bread, and the house was tidied all around. But though he searched here and there, he could not find out who had done it.

The rest of the thieves came home and found their dinner all ready, and they asked the eldest, "What have you seen? Who was it?"

"*Aman, aman,* Allah!" said the eldest. "I fell sound asleep, and I saw no one."

"Oh!" they said. "You couldn't do it."

The next one said, "I'll try tomorrow."

The others said, "If the eldest couldn't do it, you surely cannot."

"Still, I'll try," said the second. "I'll stay awake, and I'll find out who is doing these good things for us." And the next morning, he stayed behind when the rest of the thieves left. He watched and waited and waited, but at last he, too, fell asleep. Then the girl came out, and, quietly, quietly, she cooked and cleaned and tidied all around and she washed herself. When everything was ready, she slapped herself on the cheek and became a broom.

When the second one of the forty thieves awoke, he found that everything had been done again as before. There was a great kettle of soup pre-

pared, and another huge kettle of macaroni, and plenty of fresh bread, and the house was tidied all around. "Oh, I couldn't do it, either!" he exclaimed. "*Why* did I fall asleep?" He searched here and there, but he could not find out who had done it.

The rest of the thieves came home and found their dinner all ready, and they asked the second one, "What have you seen? Who was it?"

"*Aman, aman,* Allah!" said the second one. "I fell asleep, and I saw no one."

"Well, *I'll* do it!" said the youngest of the forty thieves. The rest just laughed at him, but he was determined. "I'll watch faithfully, and I'll find out who is doing these good things for us." And, true enough, he stayed behind when everyone else went off to work.

To make certain that he would not fall asleep, the youngest thief cut his finger deeply and rubbed salt into the wound, and, oh, how it hurt! It hurt so much that he couldn't sleep; he shut his eyes, though, and snored softly, pretending that he was sound asleep. But all the time, he was really watching.

The girl came out, and, quietly, quietly, she cooked, and set the table, and tidied all about, and washed herself till she shone like a tinned kettle. When she was ready to slap herself on the cheek and become a broom again, the youngest thief jumped up and caught her. He held her hand and said, "I saw what you did. It's all right. You will become our sister, and you will live with us."

When the rest of the thieves came home, they all felt very happy, and they ate and drank, and they gave her forty strands of gold. "You will be our sister," they all said. And so she was.

Meanwhile, the evil stepmother wondered what had become of the girl, and she dressed herself as an old, old woman and searched here and there until she had found the house of the forty thieves. And there was the girl, washing and washing a window.

Tak! Tak! Tak! The old woman knocked at the door, and she said, "Open the door, my girl. I must come inside and kneel to pray. Won't you let me come in?"

"No," said the girl. "I won't let anyone in. I have forty brothers. If they come and find you here, they will make you as if you never were." And she refused to unlock the door.

The old woman begged and begged, and still the girl would not open the door. Finally the old woman said, "Your stepmother sent you a ring, and she wanted me to give it to you."

"No," said the girl. "I want nothing from my stepmother."

The old woman said, "Please. You don't need to let me in. Just stick your finger out through this knothole in the door, and I'll slip the ring on it."

Tempted despite herself, the girl stuck her finger through the knothole, and the old woman slipped the ring on it. *Eyvah!* As soon as the ring had

84

settled on the girl's finger, she fell dead. Satisfied, the wicked stepmother left.

When the forty thieves came home that day, their sister did not greet them at the door. They said, "Unlock the door and let us in, Sister." But she did not unlock the door.

They shouted, "Sister, open the door!" But nobody opened the door.

"Something is wrong here!" said the youngest thief. And he went to the window and broke the glass and climbed inside. "Ah, ah, ah!" he said sadly. "Come and see!" And he unlocked the door for the rest of the thieves.

There lay their sister on the floor, dead. Oh, they knelt by her and cried and cried.

Finally, they built a box and padded it with cotton and lined it with cloth. They laid the girl gently in the box and closed the cover. Then they tied the box securely on the back of a camel and let the camel go.

The camel went and went and went, and finally it came to a fountain in front of a palace to drink some water. While the camel was drinking and drinking at the fountain, the padishah's son saw the camel and went to see what was in the box. When he saw what was in it—a girl as beautiful as hyacinths and angels—he untied the box and took it to his own room. Then he said to his mother, "Look, Mother. There are forty keys to the forty rooms in this palace. The other thirty-nine rooms are yours, but this one—the fortieth—is mine. If you dare to come into this room, I shall put an end to my life!" And everyone else in the palace was forbidden to enter that room.

One day soon afterwards, while the son was away from home, his mother went secretly to the fortieth room. "I am curious," she said. "I must see what he has inside his room that he hides from even his own mother." Using the fortieth key, she unlocked the door and went inside. There was a box . . . She opened the cover, and when she saw a dead girl inside, was she angry! "What is this!" she exclaimed. "The girl is dead and without a proper burial!"

She called several of the palace servants, and together they washed and washed the girl to get her ready for a decent burial. While the girl's hand was being washed with soapy water, the ring slipped off her finger. As soon as the ring was off, the girl awoke, and, "Oh, how long I have slept!" she said.

Just then, the padishah's son rushed into the room. "Mother, I *told* you that if you came into my room that would be the end of me!" he shouted. He ran to the box, and there, beautiful as hyacinths and angels, was the girl, sitting up and smiling at him.

In three or five days, arrangements had been made for a grand wedding, and the padishah's son and the stepdaughter were married, with festivities that lasted for forty days and forty nights. They began to live happily together.

Within the first year, the girl gave birth to a daughter. The news of the birth traveled from mouth to ear throughout the padishah's kingdom, and of course the stepmother ground her teeth in anger. Immediately, she came to

the palace and demanded to see the girl. True enough, the new mother *was* the stepdaughter, alive in spite of the stepmother's efforts to destroy her.

"This is my husband's daughter," she said to the servants. "I must stay with her while she is in childbed." And how could they refuse her? As soon as the servants had left the room, the stepmother stuck a needle into the girl's scalp, and the girl became a bird and flew away. Immediately, the stepmother got into the bed beside the baby.

When the padishah's son came in, she said crossly, "To the other woman, you came every hour. Why do you come only once a day to me?"

The padishah's son stared at the woman. What was this nonsense she was speaking? And what had become of his beautiful wife?

Next to the palace, there was a big garden, and every morning the girl who had become a bird began to come to that garden and to call to the gardener, "Hoo, hoo, gardener!"

And, "Hoo, hoo!" the gardener would answer.

"Is my husband asleep?"

"Yes. Your husband is asleep."

"Is my little princess sleeping?"

"Yes. Your little princess is sleeping."

"Let that witch of a stepmother of mine sleep and never wake! And let the branch that I am standing on wither away." And then she would fly away.

She was a very beautiful bird, but, true enough, whatever branch she

stepped on would wither away and die. As one after another the trees in that beautiful garden had branches that withered and died, the padishah's son asked the gardener what was causing this change.

The gardener told him the story. "There is a beautiful bird that comes to our garden every morning and says, 'Hoo, hoo, gardener!' And when I answer 'Hoo, hoo!' the bird says, 'Is my husband asleep?' 'Yes. Your husband is asleep,' I answer. 'Is my little princess sleeping?' the bird asks. 'Yes. Your little princess is sleeping,' I answer. Then the bird sings, 'Let that witch of a stepmother of mine sleep and never wake! And let the branch that I am standing on wither away.' And after that, whichever branch of the tree the bird has stepped on withers and dies. You could watch with me tomorrow morning and see the bird for yourself."

That very night, the prince and the gardener slept in the garden. And, true enough, early in the morning there came that beautiful bird, and she and the gardener talked to each other in the same way they had those other mornings.

"Hoo, hoo, gardener!"

"Hoo, hoo!"

"Is my husband asleep?"

"Yes. Your husband is asleep."

"Is my little princess sleeping?"

"Yes. Your little princess is sleeping."

"Let that witch of a stepmother of mine sleep and never wake! And let the branch that I am standing on wither away." And then the bird flew away.

"I must catch that bird," said the padishah's son. "Today, smear pitch on all the branches of all the trees, so that no matter which branch the bird stands on, it will be caught." And the gardener did as the padishah's son had directed.

Early the next morning, the bird came again. "Hoo, hoo, gardener!"

"Hoo, hoo!"

"Is my husband asleep?"

"Yes. Your husband is asleep."

"Is my little princess sleeping?"

"Yes. Your little princess is sleeping."

"Let that witch of a stepmother of mine sleep and never wake! And let the branch that I am standing on wither away." But when she was ready to fly away, her wings and her claws were caught by the pitch.

The padishah's son approached the bird quietly and began to caress it. As he was stroking its feathers, he saw that a needle had been driven into the skin of the bird. He pulled the needle out, and at once the bird became human again, the beautiful wife he had lost and the mother of his child.

"That stepmother of yours is indeed a wicked woman," he said to his wife. "Should we send her beyond seven seas and beyond seven mountains? Or should we give her her choice between forty swords and forty horses?"

"No distance is too great for that witch of a stepmother to come in her effort to destroy me," said the wife.

The padishah's son then called for the stepmother. When she came, he said, "You have done nothing but evil since you first became the stepmother of my wife. Now take your choice: Will you have forty swords or forty horses?"

The stepmother's eyes flashed with hatred. "Keep the forty swords for the throat of your sweetheart," she said. "As for me, I shall take the forty horses and return to my home."

The padishah's son ordered forty horses and a large quantity of rope. With the rope, the servants tied each part of the stepmother to a different horse, and then the horses were whipped. Each horse went in a different direction from the others, and every part of the evil stepmother was left at the foot of a different mountain.

When *that* was finished, the prince's wife sent for her father, and for pure joy the padishah's son and the stepdaughter were married all over again, with a wedding that lasted forty days and forty nights.

They had their wishes fulfilled. Let's go up and sit in their seats!

The Unfaithful Wife Detected

Once there was and twice there wasn't, when camels were barbers and fleas were porters—well, in those times, there was a woman who had a fine husband. What's more, she had three lovers. Of these lovers, the husband knew nothing, though all of his neighbors had reported to him, "Your wife has lovers when you are away from home."

"No, no. Don't tell me that," said the man. "She is my wife, and I do not believe such a thing about her."

Still, one day the man harnessed his animals and said to his wife, "Woman, I am going to the mill. Will you be afraid to stay here alone while I am gone?"

"Why should I be afraid?" she asked. "This is my home, and I always have my neighbors."

In their village there was a *hoca* whose eyes were blind but whose ears were exceptionally sharp. Before leaving for the mill, the husband took this *hoca* to his home to discover what his wife did during his absence. His wife was surprised to see him back so soon, and even more surprised to see that he was bringing a guest. "Why did you bring this *hoca* here?" she asked. "We have only a small house, and he will make it crowded."

Her husband answered, "He is only a poor old *hoca* who is both blind and deaf. Let him sit here in the presence of Allah." So the woman had the *hoca* sit in the chimney corner, out of the way.

When darkness came, one of the woman's lovers came and knocked—*Tak! Tak! Tak!*—on the door. "What is it?" asked the woman. She heard no answer.

"What *is* it?" the woman asked again, more loudly this time.

"Here. I brought you a watermelon," said the lover.

"I'll just put it here in the corner," she said. Then she and the lover went into another room and enjoyed themselves. When they had finished, the lover left.

Shortly afterwards, there came another knock at the door—*Tak! Tak! Tak!* "What is it?" asked the woman.

The second lover answered, "Here. I have brought you a fine sausage."

"Let me put it in the cupboard," said the woman. Then she and the lover went into another room and enjoyed themselves. When they had finished, the man left.

Soon there came another knock at the door—*Tak! Tak! Tak!* "What is it?" the woman asked.

"I have brought some yogurt for you," said the third lover.

"I'll put it in the closet," she said. Then the two went into another room to make love, but before they had finished, there was another knock at the door—*TAK! TAK! TAK!* Recognizing the knock, the woman said, "*Aman!* My husband has returned!"

"Where shall I hide?" asked the lover.

"Crawl into the oven," she said. And after the third lover was safely inside the oven, she went and opened the door for her husband.

He said, "Come here, woman, and sit on my lap for a minute or so. I am very cold."

She went and sat on his lap and asked, "Where are your animals, and where is the flour from the mill?"

"I tied the animals in the stable. As for the flour, when I got to the mill, there were three or five people ahead of me with wheat to be ground, so I decided to come along home. Now, my dear, I am warm enough. Go to the kitchen and make me a good, hot dinner."

While the woman went to prepare something for her husband to eat, the husband spoke to the *hoca*. He asked, "Brother *hoca*, are you well?"

"I am fine. And you have returned from the mill?"

"Yes, I have returned, and I am curious to know what you have detected here since I left."

"Since I came here, different things have arrived. There were hands and feet, and something heavy came—like a watermelon—and it was put in a corner. Then there were other hands and feet, and there came a sausage,

which was put into the cupboard. More hands and feet came, and something that splashed and flowed, like yogurt, went into a closet. Now I can hear my heart beating hard, like that of the man in the oven."

The husband understood at once the whole situation. Taking a heavy rope, he tied his wife and the man from the oven to the door frame until morning should come. When morning came, he loaded them both onto the back of his faithful donkey and took them to the top of the next mountain and tied them to a large tree. "There, now, you are together. There is no room in my house for you anymore."

Then, returning to his house, he loaded his animals with the bags of wheat and set off for the mill. As for the *hoca*, he made a fine meal of the food the wife had prepared, and then he went his way. And for us, may we have mates who are faithful!

The Careful Servant and the Curious One

Once there was a man who had a rather stupid young servant. No matter how patiently he had worked to train this servant, the boy continued his foolish ways. Finally, the man decided to take the boy with him to a house where the servant was quick and clever. Perhaps he could learn by watching . . .

As Allah would have it, one Friday during Ramazan the man was invited to share the evening meal with a good friend, a man whose servant was excellent. "I'll take my servant with me," the man decided, "and let him see how a really good servant behaves." So that evening, he took the boy with him.

While the two friends were talking and waiting for the meal to be served, the host became thirsty and sent his own servant for glasses of water for the two men. This servant went out quickly to fetch the water and came back with the two glasses filled almost to the brim. Before he took the water to his master and the guest, however, the servant went over to the kerosene lamp and looked closely at the water in both glasses. Satisfied, he gave the water glasses to the men. Both men drank and were refreshed.

As the visitor watched the careful servant, he thought, "Now, *my* servant would never think to be so careful. İnşallah, he will notice what has happened here and learn from it."

The visitor's servant watched as all this business was going on, and he said to himself, "Hmmnn! I've never done such a thing for my master and his

91

guests, but if this servant does it, I can do it, too!"

Well, the meal was a fine one, and the two men enjoyed both their food and a good, long evening of conversation. At last, the visitor said, "It is late, my friend. May we have your permission to leave?"

"Of course," said his host. "I thank you for honoring me with your company." And he walked to the door with his guest and the foolish servant to wish them well on their way.

As they walked homeward, the guest remembered the careful servant's attention to the water, and he decided to test his own servant to see what he had learned from that example. Soon after they had reached home, the man said, "Suddenly I feel thirsty. Bring me a glass of water."

His servant went to fetch the water, and, as he had seen the other servant do, he examined the glass of water in the light of the kerosene lamp before he served it to his master. The master drank only a little—after all, he was just testing his servant—and then he handed the glass back to the boy.

The servant ran quickly to the kerosene lamp and looked carefully again at the water. Then, nodding and smiling, he took it out to the kitchen.

Puzzled, the man called his servant back. "My boy," he said, "I understand why you looked at the water the first time, but I don't understand why you looked at it the second time."

"Oh, it's very simple, sir," said the boy. "The first time I looked, I saw a fly in the water, and I was curious to see whether it was still there!"

The Pilgrim Pays His Debt

I n earlier times, people used to make the pilgrimage to Mecca by camel. They would travel day and night without stopping. For safety, they would travel with forty pilgrims in a group, each mounted on his own camel and with a camel driver at the head.

About halfway through a pilgrimage that had started at Konya, the rider of the last camel fell asleep, and the camel wandered away from the caravan. Since darkness was upon them, the caravan leader did not notice that the last camel was missing from the group.

The camel that had become separated from the caravan soon lost his way and wandered here and there through a forest with his rider still sound asleep. When that pilgrim awoke, he found that it was sunrise, the time for the first morning prayer, so he dismounted and took his ablutions and prayed with great earnestness. Puzzled that he had lost the caravan, the pilgrim remounted his camel and looked about him in despair.

Just then, he noticed two tents standing nearby, one of them red and the other one white. When the pilgrim rode closer to the tents, a woman came out of the red tent and a man came from the white one. The man was the shah of that region. He asked the pilgrim, "Friend, where do you come from, and where are you going?"

"I have come from Konya, and I am on my way to Mecca on a pilgrimage," answered the pilgrim. "Somehow, I fell asleep on my camel and became separated from the rest of the caravan. My camel kept on walking and brought me to this place."

The shah said, "Since you are on a pilgrimage, I shall consider you my guest. I host my guests here for three days and three nights."

"Oh, please," begged the pilgrim, "help me instead to rejoin my caravan. I must go on to Mecca with the others."

"Do not worry about that," said the shah. "After I have kept you as my guest for three days and three nights, I shall help you to catch up with your caravan." And the pilgrim agreed to stay.

The shah then said to his wife, "I must go to keep watch over my territory. While I am gone, you will take good care of our guest. I shall return in the evening." Bidding good-bye to his wife and the guest, the shah mounted his horse and left.

After the shah's wife had prepared some food, she brought it to the pilgrim. The pilgrim, upon taking one good look at the woman, desired her. He drew from his sash the one hundred liras that he was carrying. Taking out twenty liras, he dropped them into the hand of the woman as she was serving him his food. Without responding in any way, the woman took the money and returned to her own tent.

In the evening when the shah returned, the woman went to meet her husband. He asked, "How did you get along with our guest? Did you make him comfortable?"

The woman handed him the twenty liras and said, "Your guest offered me this."

When the pilgrim saw the shah and his wife talking to one another, he felt afraid. Was that woman going to tell her husband about the money she had been given? What, then, would the shah do to a guest who had thus violated his hospitality?

Meanwhile, the shah had said to his wife, "Don't be afraid. I know your virtuous character." Then, while his wife took the horse to the stable, the shah went to his guest as if nothing at all had happened and made him feel comfortable. He talked with the pilgrim most of the night and helped him feel at ease.

In the morning, the pilgrim and the shah ate breakfast together. Then the shah mounted his horse and again went out to patrol the area, saying that he would be home again in the evening. Again the pilgrim remained throughout the day with the shah's wife. Thinking that the money he had given her yesterday had not been enough to win her over, this time the pilgrim gave her thirty liras when she delivered his food to him. How he desired this woman! But the woman took the money after setting down the food, and she left without making a response of any kind.

That evening, the woman met her husband when he returned. She gave him the thirty liras and told him exactly what had happened. Again, he said, "Do not be afraid. I know what I am doing. I have never harmed anyone here, and I am sure that no one will harm us." He then joined the pilgrim again and talked with him even more cordially than he had done the previous night.

On the morning of the following day, the shah went out to patrol the area again. As before, the pilgrim remained behind with the shah's wife. This time, when the woman brought him his noon meal, the pilgrim gave her fifty liras. But just as she had done before, the woman took the money without making the slightest response or comment.

For the third time, the woman met the shah as he returned from his day's patrolling. She told him what had happened and gave him the fifty liras. Without any sign of being upset or angry, the shah again joined his guest and again talked with him throughout much of the night.

Thus the pilgrim remained there as a guest for three days and three nights. On the morning of the fourth day, the pilgrim said to himself, "Well, my money is all gone." And to the shah, he said, "Please give me permission to leave."

The shah replied, "I shall allow you to depart after we have eaten breakfast."

This worried the pilgrim so greatly that he was unable to eat more than a taste or two of the meal. Was the shah intending to kill him?

But after breakfast, the shah said, "All right; get ready now. You will ride on your camel, and I shall ride on my horse." They mounted their animals and rode steadily all that day. The shah, who knew every part of that region, took a shortcut, and by the end of the day they had overtaken the caravan. The shah pointed out the caravan to the pilgrim. "You see," he said. "Those are your friends over there, aren't they? They have only now arrived here because they took the longer route."

When the pilgrim saw the caravan, he was greatly relieved. At last, he would be freed from his fear of the shah's rightful anger at his abuse of generous hospitality. "Ah!" he exclaimed. "Let me join my friends now."

"Wait a moment," said the shah. "Let us be sure they are your friends. Can you recognize them? Count them to see how many they number. Is this perhaps some other caravan? Do not be in such haste to leave."

The pilgrim shook with fear as he examined the caravan. He counted the camels, then, and he said, "That *is* my caravan. I can tell, because there are only thirty-nine camels in it."

"Shall I accompany you until you join your friends?" asked the shah. "Or do you wish to go by yourself?"

"I shall go by myself," the pilgrim said. He then reached for the shah's hand in order to bid him good-bye.

But the shah did not give him his hand. Instead, he said, "I want to ask you a question. When my wife showed proper respect for you on the first day, did you give her twenty liras? Did you then give her thirty liras on the second day and fifty on the third day?" Holding the one hundred liras toward the pilgrim, he asked, "Is this not your money? Did you indeed do this dishonorable thing?" Shamed, the pilgrim had no answer for his host. The shah continued, "How many children do you have? I forgive you for the sake of your children. Here is your hundred liras, to which I have added another hundred for your children. Instead of going on a pilgrimage to Mecca, perhaps you ought to return to your own country and provide for your wife and children. If it had not been for the thought of your children, I'd have used my sword against your throat! Go now and join your friends. I shall not accompany you."

The pilgrim was doubly happy to join his friends. He had not only rejoined the caravan, but he had survived a very dangerous situation. Furthermore, the wronged shah had forgiven him. Thankfully, he watched as the shah returned to his home.

Within a month after that time, the shah became involved in a war with his enemies. The war went badly for him, and his forces were defeated. The shah himself barely escaped with his life, and he was forced to flee from that country. His enemies took the shah's wife captive and made a slave of her.

After a short while, the woman managed to escape, and she fled into the pilgrim's country as a refugee. There one person after another provided hospitality for her for two or three months. At the end of that time, it was announced that if no one claimed the woman as his wife within a certain number of days, she would be put up for sale on the slave market.

By that time, the caravan had returned from Mecca. The pilgrim, by the grace of Allah, just happened to walk into the marketplace on the day when the woman was scheduled to be sold. In his first look at the woman, the pilgrim recognized her as the wife of the shah who had been his host. Going to the official in charge of the market, the pilgrim said, "What is the price for this woman? Let me pay the price and take her. She is my relative."

The pilgrim paid the price that was asked and took the woman from the market. As they walked toward his home, the two talked. The pilgrim said, "Perhaps you do not remember, but I was the pilgrim who stayed as a guest with you and your husband. Where is your husband, the shah?"

"I do not know," the woman said. "Not long after you had left, my husband began fighting with his enemies. He was defeated by them, and I do not know what has become of him."

When the pilgrim arrived home with this woman, his wife asked him, "Who is this woman, and why did you bring her home? What are we going to do with her?"

He said, "She and her husband gave me hospitality on my way to Mecca. They treated me as their brother, and I shall always be grateful to them. This woman will be our sister. We have two houses. One will be ours, and the other one will be hers." So they settled the shah's wife in their second house.

Three or five weeks later, the pilgrim was again walking here and there in the city, and he happened to walk into the marketplace. There he saw a shabby, discouraged man seated at the edge of the crowd. Looking more closely, the pilgrim recognized him as the shah, the man who had had mercy on him. Going up to him, the pilgrim held out his hand and asked, "Where have you come from, and where are you going? I recognize you now as the shah who provided for me while I was on my way to Mecca. I shall forever be in your debt. Do you remember me?"

The shah arose and embraced the pilgrim. "Indeed I *do* recognize you, but I myself have fallen on hard times."

"Those hard times are now over," said the pilgrim. "Such hard times

come from the hand of Allah and are mended by those who trust in Allah."

"But I have lost my wife," said the shah. "What has become of her? Did they slaughter her?"

The pilgrim put his arm around the shah. "Come. Let me find a wife for you. You will see that she will suit you very well."

"Please do not torment me," said the shah. "I am burning with grief and anguish."

"Trust me," said the pilgrim. "Only come and see." Taking the shah by the arm, he led him to the house where the shah's wife now lived. When they arrived at that house, the pilgrim said, "My sister lives in this house. What's more, she has the title deed to it. If she suits you as your wife, may you both enjoy long life in it."

Tak! Tak! Tak! They knocked at the door, and a woman came to answer it. "My wife!" cried the shah, and he and his wife embraced one another with joy.

Let us leave them there together. And may we, too, have such a happy end to all our troubles!

Backward on the Donkey

One Friday as Nasreddin Hoca was getting ready to go to the mosque to read the lesson from the Koran to the congregation, he heard a *Tak! Tak! Tak!* at his door. As he opened the door, he found all the boys from his school standing in the courtyard. "What is this!" he exclaimed.

"Well, Hoca Effendi, we decided to go with you to the service today," said one. And the others agreed that this was so.

"I'll be happy to have you attend the service," said the Hoca, "but I'm not quite ready yet to leave. Just wait out there, and I'll be along in a minute or so."

The Hoca shut the door and quickly put on his long coat and his ample turban. Then he hurried to the door, opened it, slipped into his shoes beside the doorstep, and rushed across the courtyard to mount his little donkey. But in his haste, he mounted his donkey backward!

The boys began to grin and to nudge one another, wondering what the Hoca would find to say about his ridiculous mistake. As for the Hoca, he was wondering, too, but he kept a firm grasp on his wits as he glanced from one boy to another.

"I suppose you are all wondering," he said, "why I have seated myself backward on my donkey, but *I have my reasons.* If I were to seat myself forward on my donkey and ride ahead of you, I could not keep my eye on you.

On the other hand, if I were to sit forward on the donkey and ride behind you so that I could watch you, that would be improper, for I am your master. Therefore, I am riding ahead of you *and* keeping my eye on you!"

The End of the Tyrant Bolu Bey

In times long gone by, there was a cruel overlord called Bolu Bey. This overlord had a son of fourteen who was a very unhappy boy. He seemed to be sad all of the time, and day by day he grew paler and paler. Bolu Bey said to him, "My dear son, what is the matter with you? Tell me! What is there that would make you happy?" But the boy gave no response.

Bolu Bey then went to his son's friends and appealed to them: "Can you discover for me the cause of my son's discontent? What is it that is troubling him? If you can find the answer to that question, I shall fill your pockets with gold."

The boy's friends found the answer the next day during a conversation with Bolu Bey's son. Going to the bey immediately, they said to him, "O Bolu Bey, your son has grown ill yearning for a very special horse. That is his only problem."

"What a pity!" said Bolu Bey. "I am the overlord of all these lands, and yet I do not have a horse that will satisfy my son!" True to his word, he filled the boys' pockets with gold, and then he sent criers to all of the towns and villages in his area announcing, "Everyone must take his horse or horses to Bolu Meadow by Bolu River at such and such a time." Because Bolu Bey was known to be very cruel indeed, feared by everyone, all the people took their horses to Bolu Meadow.

At Bolu Meadow all of the horses were paraded, one by one, before the son of the bey for his inspection, but the boy did not care for any of them. The bey then sent out his criers again. This time they announced, "To anyone who can bring a horse that pleases my son I shall give a large amount of gold."

Living near Bolu, there was a poor unemployed groom named Yusuf. When Yusuf heard the message from Bolu Bey, he thought, "What have I to lose? I shall go and ask from Bolu Bey a supply of food in order to find the horse that his son wants." Going to Bolu Bey's mansion, he presented himself to the bey, saying, "*Selâmünaleyküm.*"

"*Aleykümselâm,*" answered Bolu Bey.

"My bey," said Yusuf, "I shall find the kind of horse that will please your son."

"What will you ask for doing that?" said the bey.

Yusuf answered, "I want only enough food for forty days."

The bey said to his attendants, "Give the man food—whatever he likes." They gave Yusuf both food and some money, and after receiving these, he set out in search of the special horse.

Yusuf traveled and traveled. He went for thirty-nine days without having seen any unusual horses. Finally on the fortieth day he saw a pack of wild horses grazing along the seashore. Observing these horses closely, he saw that they were all mares, with not a stallion among them that he might take to Bolu Bey. While he was gazing at these wild horses and wondering what he should do, two sea stallions came forth from the waves and joined the pack on the beach. The chestnut-colored stallion went to a chestnut-colored mare and mated with her, while the gray stallion went to a gray mare and mated with her. Yusuf tried to catch the two stallions, but both escaped him and returned to the sea. Disappointed by his failure, he decided that he would claim the two colts borne by the chestnut-colored and the gray mares. He then herded the mares together and drove them slowly to the nearest village.

The people of that village were surprised to see the pack brought to them so easily by Yusuf, for they themselves had tried in vain for many years to capture those wild horses. They asked Yusuf what his name was, and after he had told them his name, he said to them, "Hey, men, let these horses be yours. Let me tend them for you, and I shall take very good care of them."

101

The villagers, very pleased at this proposal, asked Yusuf, "What do you want for your services? What will be your price for doing this for us?"

Yusuf answered, "I want only the colts borne by these mares, if indeed they should have colts. I'll take my chances on that, and if there are no colts borne, then you will owe me nothing."

The villagers were glad to accept this offer, and Yusuf began tending the pack of wild mares, grazing them on the slopes of the nearby mountain. Each day a villager would take Yusuf a fresh supply of food and water. Time passed, and after several months had gone by, the chestnut-colored mare gave birth to a chestnut-colored colt, and the gray mare bore a gray colt. Yusuf thought, "For some time these colts will need their mothers' milk. I cannot take them to Bolu either now or in the near future. I had better herd the horses for another year while these colts grow large enough to be separated from their mothers."

After a year had passed, Yusuf took the pack back to the village. He said to the men there, "Here you are. This is your pack of horses, and these are my two colts. As we had agreed, these two colts are my pay for my many months of service. I shall leave now, and I shall take these colts with me."

The villagers had been very pleased with Yusuf's work, and they insisted for some time that he remain with them as their herdsman. "But I have my own family in my own village," he said, "and I have been away from them for a long time. I must return to them." When they realized that he was determined to leave, they gave him permission to depart and to take with him the two colts that he had earned.

Yusuf traveled to the town of Bolu. As he entered that town, he fell into conversation with a man, and after a while he said to this man, "Friend, you can tell Bolu Bey that I am bringing him two very beautiful colts." But, unfortunately, Yusuf said this to the wrong man. Back in those days, just as now, there were bad-natured people, the sowers of discord. The man with whom Yusuf had spoken was just such a person. He went immediately to Bolu Bey and said, "Oh, Bolu Bey, that man Yusuf that you have been waiting for is bringing you two donkeys instead of two horses. He is clearly mocking you."

When Bolu Bey heard this, he became very angry. Without demanding any evidence from the man, he called his executioners and ordered them to kill Yusuf at once. But his executioners thought that this punishment was too harsh. They said, "Oh, Bolu Bey, we should not kill Yusuf for such a reason. We shall blind him, instead, in order to teach him not to tell lies. His blinding will also serve as a warning to others not to lie."

"Very well, then," said Bolu Bey. "Go and blind him."

The executioners then blinded Yusuf. Poor Yusuf! He had great difficulty in reaching his home. He stumbled along clinging to the tails of his horses. Yusuf had a ten-year-old son, and when he reached home, he said to this boy, "Son, place these horses in a dark stable and keep them there for five years. Give them their food and water each day without allowing any ray of sunlight to fall upon them."

In those days, young people gave strict obedience to the commands of grown-ups. Without any hesitation or questioning, therefore, his son said to Yusuf, "Father, I shall do exactly as you say."

The boy kept the horses in the dark stable for five years, without allowing, he thought, a bit of sunlight to strike them. At the end of that period, Yusuf said to the boy, "Son, the time has now arrived to test the qualities of these two stallions. Take them out of the stable and bring them here to me."

Removing the two horses from the stable, the boy took them to his father. Yusuf felt every spot on the body of the gray horse from his head to his tail. He then said, "Son, this horse is excellent! We shall call him Kırat. Now put him back in the stable and bring me the chestnut-colored horse." After he had examined this stallion in the same way, he said, "Son, somehow some sunlight must have fallen upon the feet of this chestnut-colored horse." (There was an old expression among the Ottomans which said, "Take the gray horse without question, but ride the chestnut horse before you buy him.")

After that, Yusuf said to the boy, "Son, go now and thoroughly water the lower field. Water it continuously for ten days." The boy proceeded to follow his father's directions, and after ten days the field was very deep in mud. Yusuf then said, "Son, now take the chestnut-colored horse and ride him around in that muddy field."

Taking the chestnut-colored horse to the muddy field, the boy rode him around for a short while. But the chestnut-colored horse was able to cross that field only with great difficulty. After that, the boy reported to Yusuf, "Father, we managed to get across the lower field, but we were just barely able to do so."

Yusuf said, "All right, Son. Now take the gray horse to the lower field and ride him through the mud."

This time the boy took the gray horse to the field and rode him across the deep mud. The gray horse moved very easily and very quickly, his feet cutting through the mud to the dry ground below the mud. The boy then reported to his father exactly what had happened and how Kırat had performed.

Yusuf said, "Son, keep an eye on that gray horse, Kırat! Until now you have not known why I have been asking you to do these things with the horses, but now I shall tell you. I was not born blind, but I was blinded by the cruel Bey of Bolu. It was he who had me blinded at an early stage of my manhood. If you do not take vengeance for me against this man, then you are not worthy to be my son. You must avenge the great injury done to me by Bolu Bey!"

The boy said, "Very well, Father. I shall continue to avenge your wrongs until the very last drop of my blood is spent! Furthermore, though you gave

103

me a name at my birth, I shall with your permission take a new name: Köroğlu, the son of the blind man. In that way, not only I but others will be reminded of this great wrong done to you and of my intention to bring death to the doer of that wrong!"

Soon after that, Köroğlu took his father's bow and arrows, mounted the gray horse, and set off in the direction of the land of Bolu Bey. As he rode, he took the chestnut-colored horse behind him in tow as a spare mount. As he neared Bolu, he came to a town which had a blacksmith shop. Köroğlu asked the blacksmith, "Friend, do you have horseshoes strong enough to be suitable for my horse?"

"Yes," said the blacksmith, handing Köroğlu a set of horseshoes to examine.

Taking one of these horseshoes in his hand, Köroğlu squeezed it until the two ends began to bend in toward each other. That is how strong he was! Then he said to the blacksmith, "Ah, I knew that they were not strong enough for my horse, but I shall buy these shoes anyway." He then gave the blacksmith a gold coin.

When the blacksmith received this coin, he began to bend it. He continued to bend it back and forth till it snapped into two parts. He then said to Köroğlu, "Friend, that was not money that you gave me. It must have been just a gold-colored spangle."

Köroğlu gave him another gold coin, and by squeezing it, the blacksmith again made a gold coin look like no more than a gold-colored spangle. Köroğlu then handed him a third coin, but this time he said, "Oh, no, friend. Do not destroy the money this time!"

The blacksmith then said, "But I was only doing to your money what you did to my horseshoe. Furthermore, I know where you are going and why you are going there. It was that same cruel Bolu Bey who also killed my father. Alone before now, I have not been able to take any action against him. Take me with you now, however, and together we can take vengeance against this cruel bey more easily. I am called Demircioğlu, the son of the blacksmith."

Köroğlu agreed to this proposal and said, "All right. You may ride on the chestnut-colored horse which I have in tow." The two of them rode together, galloping their horses much of the way, straight to the town of the bey. As they came to the outskirts of the town, one of them said, "We need the services of a clever and shrewd boy. How can we find such a boy?"

They asked a shepherd that they saw, "Do you know where we can get a clever and capable boy to work for us?"

After listening to them describe the kind of boy they wanted, the shepherd said, "There is in this neighborhood one boy who has all the qualities you have described. Bolu Bey has a brother who is a butcher, and that butcher has a son who would serve you very well."

Köroğlu and Demircioğlu began to think about how they could get this boy into their service. Köroğlu said, "Let's go to his father's butcher shop and tell him that we have brought him seven flocks of sheep and that every one of those sheep has four horns. We can tell him that he can have the sheep on credit. The boy will undoubtedly be very curious about sheep with four horns, and when he follows us to get a look at such sheep, we shall be able to capture him very easily."

They then went to the shop of the bey's butcher brother. They said to the butcher, "Friend, we have just arrived here from Yemen, and we have brought with us seven flocks of sheep all of which have four horns. Because we wish to sell these sheep as soon as possible, we shall sell them to you on credit. You need not pay for them now at all."

The butcher was very pleased with the chance to buy a great number of sheep without having to pay for them immediately. He said, "All right. Under those conditions, I shall buy them."

The butcher's son was listening to their discussion, and he became very curious about the four-horned sheep from Yemen. He said to his father, "I shall go with these men in order to take a look at those sheep."

They went out of the city into the countryside. There Köroğlu and Demircioğlu pointed out several flocks which did not, of course, belong to them at all. They then said to the boy, "All those sheep are your father's flocks, but Ayvaz is ours."

Taking Ayvaz up behind him on his horse, Köroğlu galloped away accompanied by Demircioğlu. They continued riding hard for four hours, going a considerable distance during this time, but they were pursued.

The butcher sent in pursuit of the fugitives a very powerful wrestler named Kenan. He was not only very strong but very quick, also. Riding after the fugitives, he caught up with them after five hours. But this powerful wrestler intended them no harm whatever, for he was as angry about the cruelty of Bolu Bey as they were. He said to them, "Friends, tie me up very tightly. Then take the boy and go!" When Köroğlu and Demircioğlu objected to tying up this good man, he said to them, "Do as I told you! It is for your own safety."

They then proceeded to tie up Kenan very tightly and left him there. After a while the bey's soldiers caught up with him, and they were amazed to see Kenan bound hand and foot and lying on the ground. They asked, "Kenan *Ağa*, what happened? You are the strongest of men and the one on whom we rely most heavily. What happened to you?"

Kenan said to them, "The men we are pursuing are unbelievably strong! Those two men are equivalent in strength to a hundred men like you. My advice to you is that you should turn around at once and return to the town." Frightened by this warning from Kenan, the troops gave up their pursuit of the fugitives and returned to Bolu.

In the meantime, Köroğlu, Ayvaz, and Demircioğlu continued on their way. They entered the Bolu mountains, where they camped for a while. The day after they arrived there, the three of them passed some time by wrestling with each other. Much to the surprise of Köroğlu and Demircioğlu, Ayvaz defeated both of them at wrestling. They said, "If we had not lost to him, we should never have known of his great strength." Ayvaz was truly a very strong boy.

After they had pitched their tents securely, Köroğlu took up his *saz* and began to play and sing. Let us listen to what he sang:

Hey, hey! Hey, hey! Carry my greetings to Bolu Bey!
Let him seek the mountains to try his strength today.
Crossing Sırat causes brave men's shields to sound.
Let him prompt such echoes in these mountains 'round.

When the people heard these words of Köroğlu, they immediately reported them to Bolu Bey. They said to him, "O Bolu Bey, there is a new outlaw in the mountains who now challenges you! He speaks openly against you!"

Bolu Bey realized that he was faced with a very powerful outlaw. Gathering together all of his troops, he led them to the mountain where Köroğlu was now living. When Köroğlu saw them approaching, he sang to his two companions the following words:

Aha! Make ready, for the enemy draws nigh.
Black destiny is written on their foreheads high.
Has true bravery been lost to the guns they trust?
Should a well-curved sword in its sheath now rust?

When Bolu Bey heard these words sung by Köroğlu, he suddenly felt contempt for the outlaw. He said to his men, "This one is nothing but a weakling of a bandit. You might as well return home, for I can handle him all by myself." After that, he gave formal orders for his troops to return to Bolu.

Bolu Bey went riding on his horse up the mountain the rest of the way to the place where Köroğlu awaited him. As the two came closer, each called to the other to surrender, but neither of them was willing to do so.

Hey, hey! Hey, hey! Köroğlu now fights with Bolu Bey!
Both of them from Holy Allah draw their aid today.
They clash and clash in combat, one times seven;
The seven wounds of Köroğlu could take him straight to heaven.

Köroğlu slipped from his horse, but Bolu Bey did not kill him, for in those days there was a code of honor. He walked around and around Köroğlu, leading his horse and awaiting his challenger's last words. Köroğlu crawled to his couch only with the greatest of difficulty. He then called out to Ayvaz:

Oh, Ayvaz, Ayvaz, come and help your father. Hear!
My blood is flowing freely like the Suna River clear.
My life has fallen victim to our villain's great hurrah!
Come quickly now, my Ayvaz—my lion—my shah!

But Ayvaz did not appear upon the scene. Because he was sleeping at the time of the encounter between Köroğlu and Bolu Bey, he knew nothing of what was happening, and he heard nothing that Köroğlu sang to him. Köroğlu therefore called to him again:

Come help me now, my Ayvaz, for my back is bent.
My sword is lying broken, and my strength is spent.
My life, bold name for courage, ebbs with blood from wounds so raw.
Come quickly now, my Ayvaz—my lion—my shah!

This time, Ayvaz heard Köroğlu's call, and he went to him at once.

Ayvaz came right speedily and gazed into his eyes.
"May you recover quickly; may your strength anew arise!"
Then Ayvaz challenged Bolu Bey with youth's own great hurrah!
Strike hard now, golden Ayvaz—my lion—my shah!

Now it was Bolu Bey who expressed himself. Let us hear what he had to say:

> Gaze not with yearning, Ayvaz, into eyes now going blind.
> The recovery that you wish him he will never ever find.
> Risk not your precious life against the victor, Bolu Bey.
> You're still a child. Lay down your arms, and fight another day.

When Ayvaz heard these words of Bolu Bey, he became very angry. He said to himself, "I am not a child but a young man!" But to his opponent he sang quite different words:

> The brave man takes the battlefield, no matter what the cost.
> He howls from the stream bed like a gray wolf lost.
> The brave look not for shelter; on the battlefield they stay.
> To save their timid, worthless lives, the evil slink away.

Having sung this, Ayvaz rode forth on Kırat to clash with Bolu Bey in battle:

> Now astride the strong gray horse rides Ayvaz to the fray.
> The blood he draws from stirrups gold flows freely on the way.
> And with his one gigantic blow unhorsed is Bolu Bey.
> Now prance, my gray horse! Prance, Kırat! The field is yours
>   today!

Kırat, the gray horse that had cost Yusuf his eyes, now began to walk around the fallen Bolu Bey where he lay on the ground mortally wounded. When Kırat looked upon Bolu Bey lying there, it began to rear up on its hind legs. Ayvaz then began to praise the horse:

He twists, my gray horse, twisting like a rabbit in the chase;
And like the wily partridge, up the hillside he can race;
And like the gray wolf glaring, he intimidates our foes;
Kırat, my horse, my lion horse—just see how bold he grows!

Since Kırat was of Arabian breed, it was not surprising that he reared up
in excitement. This frightened Bolu Bey, however, and he thought to himself,
"This horse could kill me whether or not Ayvaz is on his back. I'll try plead-
ing with Ayvaz."

Now let us listen to what Bolu Bey said to Ayvaz:

Oh, Ayvaz, fire and smoke came here from some ferocious land,
Reducing me to this sad state from my position grand.
Oh, come, Ayvaz, my brother's son; be reconciled with me.
Together let us ride, companions, back to life that's free.

Be reconciled, my Ayvaz bold, and come where you belong.
Together let us ride our mounts, as kinfolk brave and strong.
Five thousand golden coins are yours if you will only say
That young Ayvaz and Bolu Bey are reconciled today.

Ayvaz answered him in this way:

Five thousand coins might tempt the weak, but they hold naught
     for me.
They couldn't even buy one shoe for the prancing steed you see.
Ten thousand coins would not suffice to buy an extra breath.
For all the lives that you have crushed, prepare now for your
     death.

Dismounting, Ayvaz went to Bolu Bey and cut off his head. Then he
went to Köroğlu and dressed his seven wounds. "Sleep well, my father, hero
bold, that you regain your strength," he said. "I shall await your recovery,
here with Demircioğlu."

Seeing a bottle of *rakı* in Bolu Bey's saddlebag, Ayvaz offered it first to
Demircioğlu and then drank the rest himself, saying,

Now, Bolu Bey, as you lie dead, I take this single prize.
Your whole long life you've hurt the poor; let them your pay
     devise.
This *rakı* runs along my throat as smooth as the Suna flows,
And—*İnşallah!*—wakes Köroğlu to fight against our foes.

110

The Patience Stone

Once there was and once there wasn't a dwarf. If you ask what his mother's name was, it was Nebiye. I flew across and looked at his roof, with its one side of straw and its other side of smoke and dust. The blacksmith beats the iron with skill, and the painters paint with many colors. Here and there they fight with cannons and guns. "What is this? What is it?" you ask. Listen! This is a lie, and that is a lie. So? A snake swallowed an elephant. And there went someone riding a donkey across a river with a camel on his lap. That is a lie, too. Well, now, we get to the story:

Once there was a girl, the only child of her father and mother. To the girl's windowsill one day came a bird. The bird perched on the windowsill and sang, "Oh, you poor girl. Oh, you poor girl. You will watch by the bed of a dead man for forty days, and then you will marry that dead man."

The girl gave food and water to this bird, and then she sat by the window and embroidered. But still the bird came the next morning and perched on the windowsill and sang, "Oh, you poor girl. Oh, you poor girl. You will watch by the bed of a dead man for forty days, and then you will marry that dead man." This time, the mother heard the bird singing, and she felt very sad.

One day soon after that, the girl and her mother went walking. They walked a little, they walked far, and suddenly they came to an enormous house, surrounded by a high wall. There was a big iron gate in the wall, and this gate was neither closed nor open. It just swung back and forth, swung back and forth, and each time it swung, it hit the frame of the gate, *rık, rık, rık.*

"I wonder who lives there?" said the mother. "Go, my girl, and see if there is someone behind the wall next to the gate who is opening it and closing it."

The girl went inside to see who was swinging the gate, and—*Glak!*—it swung shut and it would not open again. The mother and the girl could see each other through the bars of the gate, but the mother could not get in, and the daughter could not get out. They cried and they cried, with their eyes flowing like fountains, but what could crying do? The gate wouldn't open, and at last the mother went along home alone.

After her mother had gone, the girl felt hungry. "This will not do," she

111

said. "I will look around and see what there is to see." So she went inside the enormous house and opened the door of the first room. Inside that room, there were piles and piles of gold coins and heaps and heaps of jewels—diamonds and pearls and rubies, all glowing in the sunlight. "Well, there's *that* room," she said.

She went and opened the second door, and that room was filled, just *filled*, with carpets, each one more beautiful than the next. And, "Well, there's *that* room," she said.

She went and opened the third door, and that room was filled with delicious foods and drinks. And the girl *was* hungry. She ate and drank, and after she was satisfied, she went to the fourth door and opened it.

In that room, she found a handsome young man, a man so handsome that he could say to the moon, "Either you or I shall rise tonight." But the young man was lying on a bed. He was not dead, if you say "dead"; he was not alive, if you say "alive." He was just lying there as if he were *stuck* to the bed.

"What is this?" cried the girl, but the young man did not stir at all. At last the girl understood that this was the fate that the bird had foretold: she would marry a dead man.

"I'll watch by his bedside, then," she said to herself. "I'll watch and I'll wait, watch and wait." So she brought a chair and she sat by the young man's bedside, watching and waiting. When she was hungry, she hurried to the third room and ate and drank until she was satisfied, and then she hurried back to the young man's bedside to watch and to wait. But she did not sleep. She just watched, day after day after day after day, until she had lost count of the days.

Then one day she heard a Gypsy caravan coming along the path. She ran to the window to look, and there among the Gypsies was a girl of about her own age. "Oh!" she said. "How I would like a companion!" And she called from the window, "Please let that young girl stay with me and be my companion! If you will leave her here, I shall give you a belt full of gold."

The Gypsies tried the gate, but it would not open. And on the other side of the gate, the first girl held out a belt full of gold that she had gathered from the first room . . . So all the men in the caravan pulled and tugged at the bars until they had made an opening just wide enough for the Gypsy girl to slip through. As soon as the Gypsy girl was inside, the first girl handed the Gypsies the belt full of gold, and they went along on their way.

As for the two girls, they ate and drank and talked and watched and waited at the bedside of this young man who was neither dead nor alive. Of course, the first girl told her new companion about the bird's song and about her finding the enormous house and about her watching and waiting for days and days and days—so many that she had lost count of them. "But on the fortieth day," she said, "he will wake up—*İnşallah!*—and then the watching

112

and waiting will have been worthwhile." And the Gypsy girl agreed that that was so.

Now, the first girl had not had any sleep in all those days of watching and waiting, and she was tired, *so* tired. Finally, she said to the Gypsy girl, "Oh, I am so tired and so sleepy. I do so want to go to sleep. Will you please sit down here and let me put my head on your knees and sleep a little? While I sleep, you can keep watch over him." And the Gypsy girl sat down, and the first girl put her head on the Gypsy's knees. She was so tired that she just *dropped* off to sleep.

As it happened, thirty-nine days of the forty had already come and gone, and the time for the young man's release from the spell was very close. Three or five hours after the first girl had fallen asleep, the young man yawned and then he woke up. When he saw two girls at his bedside, he asked, "Which of you is the servant and which one is the lady?"

The Gypsy said, "Why, I am the lady, and she is my servant."

"All right," said the man. "Put her down, and stand up." So the Gypsy girl moved the first girl very carefully from her knees to the floor, with the first girl so deeply asleep that she felt nothing at all. While the first girl slept on and on, the young man found some beautiful clothes for the Gypsy girl, and while she was dressing nicely, he fetched a *hoca*, and the young man and the Gypsy girl were married.

113

When the first girl finally awoke, she found that the young man was already awake and had married the Gypsy girl. She was very unhappy about it, but she never said a word about it. She was treated exactly like a servant. "Wash the dishes and make the fire!" "Cook the meals and do the laundry." She was doing all this all day long. She was a very patient girl, and she never said anything.

Now, the young man was a wealthy merchant, and he was to go to İstanbul to buy goods to sell. Because his wife was going to have a baby, he asked her what she would like from İstanbul. She ordered many things for the child and many things for herself. When he came to the first girl, the one who was now the servant, he asked her what she wanted, and she said, "If you will, please bring me a sharp knife and a patience stone."

"A patience stone? What is that?" asked the young man.

"Oh, you wouldn't care about one," she said, "but I want one. You can ask for it in the market. And if you do *not* bring those two things to me, may storms block your way."

He bought what he needed for his business, and he bought what he had to buy for the baby and for his wife, but he forgot to buy the knife and the patience stone. On his way back, a great storm began, and his caravan could go no farther. "Oh, now I remember. I was asked to buy two more things, and I shall go and buy the patience stone and the knife."

He went back to the market and bought those two things, but the man who sold them to him said, "You must be careful not to leave alone the person who is going to get these things. Do not let him be by himself."

When the young man returned to the caravan, the storm had gone and the road was open. As soon as he reached home, he gave to his wife what he had brought for her and for the child. To the servant he gave the knife and the patience stone, and the girl took them to her room at once.

Several days later, the Gypsy girl said, "Get the towels and clean clothes ready. We are going to the *hamam*." So the two girls got everything ready, and they went to the bathhouse. But when they got there, the servant said, "Oh, I forgot to bring along my *peştamal*. I left it at home. Please let me go quickly and get it."

The Gypsy girl said, "All right, but go quickly and return quickly."

So the servant ran home, and the young man was there. She hurried to her room and locked the door from the inside. The young man, remembering the shopkeeper's warning, came to her door to listen, and he also looked through the keyhole.

The girl took the patience stone in one hand and the sharp knife in the other hand, and she began to talk. "Oh, patience stone, I used to be my mother's and father's only child. There used to be a little bird who came to my window and sang, 'Oh, you poor girl. Oh, you poor girl. You will watch by the bed of a dead man for forty days, and then you will marry that dead

114

man.' One day my mother and I went for a walk, and we came to an enormous house. The gate in the wall kept on swinging and knocking itself against its frame. And Mother wanted to know why the door kept on swinging like that. I went in to see if there was anyone behind the wall who was swinging the door. But—*Glak!*—it closed shut, and I was left inside and Mother was outside. I could not come out, and I cried and she cried for a long time. Then she went, and I went into the house. I found jewelry in one room, and rugs and carpets in the second room, and lots of food in the third room, and in the fourth room there was a handsome young man sleeping. I kept watch over him night and day. Oh, stone of patience, what would you do if you were in my place?" And all the time she had the stone in one hand and the knife in the other.

And then she went on talking again. "As I was watching from the window, I saw some Gypsies pass by, and I asked for a girl of my age to come and be my companion. I gave money, and I took her for a companion. I was very tired, and as I went to sleep on her knees, he woke up and he got married to the Gypsy girl. Oh, stone of patience, what would you do if you were in my place?" As soon as she said that, the patience stone broke into two with a big *KRIK-KRAK*. When the stone broke into two, saying that *he* could not bear it, the girl said, "All right. Neither can I bear it." And she grasped the knife firmly and aimed it at her breast.

Suddenly the young man broke the door open and dashed into her room. "Why, *why* did you not tell me about all this?" he said.

The girl said, "What did you expect me to say? Did you ever ask me questions? You made a servant out of me. And you all have got me wall-flat."

"Oh, is that so?" said the man. "All right," he said, and he decided to marry that girl.

The Gypsy girl, who was still at the *hamam*, became angrier and angrier. Finally she rushed home. When she came home, she found her husband was married to the lady she had made a servant of. She said, "Oh, it is all right to get married, but why did you keep me waiting at the *hamam?*"

The young man was very angry, and he said, "You come here. You were the Gypsy. You knew that you were the servant and she was the lady. Why did you not tell me so?"

"Why should I?" said the Gypsy. "Allah's hand was on me. That is why you took me. Why should I tell you?"

"All right," said the man, "I am asking you. Do you want a horse, or do you want a sharp saber?"

"What should I do with a sharp saber?" said the Gypsy. "Let it be used on your sweetheart's neck. I want a horse so that I can ride and go to my parents."

"You have asked for a horse, and a horse you shall have," said the young man. And he ordered a horse brought from the stable. He had the groom tie

115

the Gypsy girl to the horse's hind hoofs, and then he whipped the horse so that it reared and ran, knocking the Gypsy girl against the rocks and the trees until she was left in pieces here and there.

Then he and the first girl had a long, long wedding, and they lived happily ever after.

A Tale of Prayers Answered

Once there was and once there wasn't a widow who had an only child, a son. She wished to place this boy in a trade so that he could earn a living. One day she went to the owner of a shoe store and greeted him. "Abdullah Effendi," she said, "I should like to have my son, Ahmet, learn your trade. Would you accept him as an apprentice?"

"It would be my pleasure to do that, Aunt Hatice," he answered.

"As you know," she went on, "his father died just a short time ago, and my son needs to provide for himself now. I am entrusting Ahmet first to Allah and then to you. His bones are mine, but his flesh is yours. I do not want any money for his services. Instead, you can just send our daily bread home with him each day. Let my son be trained to be a shoe merchant like you. That is all I ask."

"I shall see that he is well trained," said Abdullah Effendi. "Send him to me tomorrow morning."

Ahmet began to work in the large shoe shop, but he was quite different from the other apprentices who worked there. He had a lively wit, and he took every opportunity to make people laugh. He was such an entertaining fellow that the other employees would say, "Let's listen to him and see what in the world he will think of next." They enjoyed his humor so much that they often neglected their work just to listen to him.

But every up has its down. One day someone in the town died, and all of the other workers in the shoe shop were silent with sadness. Ahmet, thinking to tease them out of their silence, told them such a funny story that he had them all laughing again. But this was not an appropriate time for laughter, since it was the mother of one of the other apprentices who had died. The oldest of the apprentices complained to Abdullah Effendi, "We like Ahmet's jokes, but today was not a day for joking. We were grieving for Celâl's mother's death, and Ahmet had us all laughing. We were ashamed of ourselves for laughing in the presence of Celâl."

When Abdullah Effendi heard this complaint, he felt greatly annoyed at Ahmet, and he slapped him hard in an effort to teach him better manners.

"Your mother entrusted your training to me," he said. "You behaved shamefully today. You should have respected Celâl's feelings and shared the grief of your fellow workers."

Now, Ahmet was greatly upset by Abdullah Effendi's action and his words. "I did not know that Celâl's mother had died," he said. "I never ask my fellow workers about such things, and I never ask anything from them. When I ask for something, I always ask it of Allah. For example, I prayed to Allah, 'My dear Allah, please give me a beautiful girl with blue-gray eyes, and give me also a sack of gold.' Having prayed that way, I never give up hope of receiving what I asked for."

Abdullah Effendi was shocked at the boy's response. He slapped Ahmet again, even harder, for his presuming to ask Allah for such things.

Ahmet was so troubled by this treatment that he decided to run away. He walked and walked, over mountains and through valleys, until at last he reached İstanbul. Because he had come from a rather small town, he was amazed at many of the things that he saw in the city. As he stared curiously all around, an old man noticed his confusion and called to him, "Son, come over here. Where do you come from? What kind of work are you able to do?"

Ahmet said, "Oh, father, I can do anything that you ask of me. I came here from a small town in Anatolia."

The old man thought to himself, "The Anatolians are usually plain, honest people. I shall try to help this young man." Then to Ahmet he said, "Son, you will work at my house for one hour each day, and for that hour's work I shall pay you a lira. But you must not tell anyone about what you have seen in my house. You must hold your tongue about that."

In those days, a lira was worth a great amount, and Ahmet was pleased. "Sir," he said, "I shall be happy to work for you. And of course I shall never tell anyone else about that work or about your house. Besides, I am a stranger in this city, and there is no one to whom I would tell anything anyway."

The old man then took Ahmet to his home. After they had entered the house and the old man had locked the door, he blew out all the lanterns and lighted a small candle. "Now, son," he said, "take off all of your outer clothing."

Ahmet was amazed by this order. He thought, "This old man! What does he want, anyway? Why should he want me to take off my outer clothing?" And he just stood there in the flickering candlelight.

The old man repeated, "Son, remove all your outer clothing, keeping only your underwear." Ahmet did as he was told.

Then the old man led him to a dark and somewhat musty-smelling room with not a single window in it. At first, by the dim candlelight Ahmet could not see what was in that room, but when he became accustomed to the near-darkness, he saw that the room was full of gold coins. His job was to shovel up the gold and put it into bags so that it would not be tarnished by the dampness in the room. "Ah!" thought Ahmet. "Now I see why I had to

117

118

remove my outer garments. This old man wanted to be sure I would not hide any of this gold in my pockets."

Ahmet shoveled gold and shoveled gold for a whole hour. The old man then called, "Son, your time is up. You may come out of that room now." After the boy came out and had dressed again, the old man paid him the lira he had promised. Then he said, "Son, now you have learned the secret of my house. Look here through this window. You can see that there is a mosque behind this house, and in the courtyard of that mosque there is a fountain. Come to that fountain every day, and I shall call for you to work for an hour each day for a lira. Is that agreeable to you?"

"Of course it is!" said the boy eagerly. "I shall come every day."

The old man then unlocked the door, and Ahmet left the house and went to a nearby inn. There he rented a room for a very small part of his lira. "My daily meals here will cost me very little, so I shall be able to save most of my earnings," he said to himself.

The days passed quickly. Three days, one week, ten days passed, and every day he worked and received his one lira. Then one day while he was working his hour in the gold room, he noticed sunlight coming through a small hole where a brick in the outer wall was broken. After a few minutes he saw a little cat squeeze into the room through that small hole. Around the cat's neck was a sack of small stones that some mischievous boys had tied on the poor cat's neck before they turned the cat loose. Ahmet thought, "Why don't I take out those stones and fill that cat's sack with gold? Perhaps some poor person will find the cat and be saved from poverty." Replacing the stones with gold, he tied the sack around the cat's neck again and forced the cat to leave through the hole in the wall.

The following day, Ahmet went, as usual, to the mosque courtyard to await the old man's call, but the old man did not appear or send any messages. He went there for several more days, and still no one called him to work in the old man's house. Ahmet thought, "*Aman, aman*, Allah! I should not have put gold in the sack of that cat. The old man must somehow understand what happened. He may even be a saint and thus be able to know without seeing. I shouldn't have done that. Now I may again become poor and hungry. My savings will not last very long."

While he was walking about, sad and discouraged, he saw the little cat with that same small sack tied around its neck. Catching the cat, he removed the sack and looked inside. Praise Allah! The gold was still there! He went to a money-changer and had one gold coin exchanged for many, many liras.

With his new wealth, Ahmet went to a clothing store and bought a fine new suit and new shoes. On his way back to the inn, he saw a sign announcing that there was an old house on a large lot for sale at such and such a place. When he went to that place, he discovered that it was the house of the old man for whom he had worked. It seems that the old man had died and that his daughter had put the house up for sale. At the auction, everyone was bidding and bidding and thus driving up the price of the house. Ahmet asked, "May I enter the bidding?"

"Of course," they said. "If you have enough money to compete with the other bidders, you have as much right to bid on the house as they do."

As soon as he entered the bidding, Ahmet said, "I shall pay eleven thousand liras for the house."

The other people interested in the house were astonished. They had been raising the bidding price at the rate of fifty or one hundred liras at a time, and here was a buyer who had raised the bid by one thousand liras. They said to each other, "Don't bother to offer any further bids. He wants the house, and he will get it."

Thus the house was sold to Ahmet. He was very happy to make this purchase, for he knew well what he was getting. He was getting much more than an old house.

One day while he was having some repairs made on the house, he found a beautiful girl sitting on his doorstep and crying. Looking more closely at her, he discovered that she had blue-gray eyes. This, then, might well be the girl he had asked from Allah. "What about this girl?" he asked some people nearby. "Who is she? And why is she crying?"

They said, "Her father died very recently, not long after her mother's death, and she is now an orphan. The man sitting over there on that bench is her uncle. If you want to know more, you should ask him about the girl."

Going to the uncle, Ahmet said, "Sir, what plans do you have for that girl? Is she married?"

"No," said the uncle, "and I scarcely know what to do about her. I have

120

four daughters of my own already."

"Would you consider letting me marry the girl?" asked Ahmet. "I own that house over there. I could provide well for her."

The uncle was greatly surprised by this question. He thought, "This young man seems to be both respectable and quite rich. If he married my niece, I should not have to worry my head about her." But to Ahmet he said, "Son, let me talk this matter over with my family and with the girl. Come here again a week from today, and I shall give you my answer."

The following week, the uncle agreed when Ahmet said, "By the will of Allah and in the name of the Prophet, I ask for the hand of your niece in marriage." A simple wedding ceremony was arranged, and the two were married. They then moved into the house he had bought. Little by little, Ahmet had the house improved until it was almost as fine as a palace. At the same time, he opened an elegant, large shoe store where only the most expensive shoes were sold. Knowing the secret of the room full of gold, he was able to accomplish all this with no difficulty.

Meanwhile, what had become of Ahmet's mother? The evening of the day when Abdullah Effendi had slapped him, Ahmet had not gone home to his mother's house. The following day, his mother went to Abdullah Effendi's shoe store and said to him, "Oh, Abdullah Bey, my son did not come home last night. Where is my son? Tell me! I want my son back, dead or alive."

"He is not here, Aunt Hatice," said Abdullah Effendi. "He left my shop yesterday and did not return. But I am responsible for him, and—*İnşallah!*— I shall find him." He posted notices throughout the town offering a reward for information about a shoe seller's apprentice named Ahmet, but no one came to claim the reward. Ahmet had simply vanished, and no matter how long he looked, Abdullah Effendi could not find the boy. He spent so much time and so much money seeking the lost apprentice that he lost everything, even the shoe store he had owned. After the store had been closed, he went out along the roads, wandering far and wide in search of the boy.

After traveling to many different places in the country, he came at last to İstanbul. There he asked everyone he met about a shoe seller's apprentice named Ahmet. No one had heard of such a person, but several people said to him, "The only Ahmet we know who has anything to do with selling shoes is Ahmet Bey, the owner of a very large shoe store. He came from somewhere in Anatolia, but he was a very rich man and not an apprentice. He bought an old house and rebuilt it so well that it is now fine enough even for a padishah."

After he had heard these things, Abdullah Effendi became curious about this wealthy Ahmet Bey. He went to Ahmet's store and walked about, amazed at the elegant shoes sold there. As he was doing this, he was seen by Ahmet from his large, comfortable office. Ahmet called out, "Abdullah Effendi! Abdullah Effendi!"

Abdullah Effendi was astounded to hear someone in İstanbul calling his

121

name. He looked to his left, he looked to his right, and then he saw the young man gesturing at him, calling him. He did not at first recognize this tall, handsome, well-dressed man as his former apprentice. When he finally realized who the young man was, he said, "Ahmet, how you have changed!"

"Please sit down, Abdullah Effendi; sit down. I recognized you at once." He offered Abdullah Effendi coffee and tea, and then he sent a message to his wife, saying, "I shall bring a guest home with me. Do get everything ready for our guest."

Then he took Abdullah Effendi to his home. After they had eaten their dinner, they went into the sitting room to drink their coffee. Ahmet said to a maid, "Ask my wife to serve us the coffee." When his wife brought the coffee, Ahmet said to her, "My wife, kiss Abdullah Effendi's hand."

The woman kissed Abdullah's hand and then she stood there, waiting for further instructions. Ahmet then said, "Uncle Abdullah, look at my wife's eyes."

Abdullah Effendi said, "Son, she has beautiful eyes. Yes, she has beautiful blue-gray eyes. May Allah make you very happy!"

Ahmet then took from a drawer in the coffee table a small sack of gold which he had hidden there. He said, "Uncle Abdullah, I once asked Allah for a sack of gold and a beautiful girl with blue-gray eyes. Even though you slapped me for asking Allah for those things, Allah granted them to me."

Abdullah Effendi now felt greatly relieved. "Oh, Ahmet, at last I am certain that it is really you that I see. May your father rest in peace. I have suffered much in seeking you. I have even had to sell my shoe store. But finally I have found you!"

"Uncle," said Ahmet, "if you hadn't slapped me, I wouldn't be here today. May Allah be pleased with you!"

Abdullah Effendi then said, "Oh, my son, your mother is greatly upset by your absence. She has even complained to the police about me."

"Do not worry, uncle. We shall attend to that matter. Here. Take this sack of gold for yourself. If you need more than that to recover your shoe store and to make yourself comfortable, just ask for it. I am so happy and so grateful to you. It was you who made me a real man and a businessman. Give my greetings to my mother. I cannot return to my hometown at this time, but I shall have my mother brought here."

Surprised by all this, Abdullah Effendi said, "Thank you. Thank you! May Allah bless you and your family. And now, with your permission, I must leave." And so he went.

They had their wishes fulfilled, and may we have ours fulfilled too. This is where our story ends.

The Faithful Son of the Lâla

O nce there was and twice there wasn't a padishah. This man, the padishah of Yemen, had everything that any ruler in this world could want except for one thing, and that was an heir. He had prayed daily to Allah for a son, but Allah had not answered his pleas. He offered sacrifices, he fed the hungry, he clothed the poor, but still he had no child. Finally one day he said to his *lâla*, "*Lâla*, let us go on a journey together." They packed their clothes and food and departed on their travels. Perhaps somewhere in their journey they would find someone who could solve the padishah's problem.

After they had traveled for some distance, they sat down in a field to rest. While they were resting there, they saw an old man with white hair and a long white beard coming toward them. When he reached them, he said, "*Selâmünaleyküm.*"

"*Aleykümselâm,*" they answered.

To the padishah he said then, "Friend, a cushion. My padishah, is there not a cushion for me as well as for you?"

"Oh, father! How did you know that I was a padishah? Since you know this much about me, you may very well know also what it is that is troubling my spirit. But come, father, and share our meat and drink."

They ate and drank together, and when they had finished their meal, they arose. The old man gave each of them an apple. He said, "My padishah, I know that both you and your *lâla* are childless. Take one of these apples, and your *lâla* should take the other. Tonight, each of you should share the apple with your wife; furthermore, each should give the peeling to his best mare. You will each have a son, but do not name your sons until I return to name them myself." After saying this, he disappeared, and the winds blew in his place.

The padishah and his *lâla* turned their horses back in the direction from which they had come, and returned home. That night, the padishah took the apple from his sash and said to his wife, "My dear, today I was given this apple by Hızır. Perhaps it holds the answer to our prayers. Go now and get a knife." With the knife he peeled the apple and cut the flesh in half. Taking one half for himself and handing the other half to his wife, he said, "We have been ordered by Hızır to eat this apple." After they had finished the flesh, the padishah took the peeling of the apple and fed it to the best mare in his stable. Meanwhile, in his own quarters, the *lâla* did just as the padishah had

123

done: he shared the flesh of the apple with his wife and fed the peeling to his own mare. On exactly that same night, at the same hour, both the padishah's wife and the *lâla's* wife became pregnant.

Nine months, nine days, and nine hours after this time, the wife of the padishah was confined to bed with labor pains, and very soon after that, she gave birth to a son. At the same time, the wife of the *lâla* was also confined to bed, and she too bore a son. In celebration of these events, the padishah and the *lâla* both sacrificed animals every day for three or five months, giving the meat and other gifts to the poor in thanksgiving for this answer to their prayers.

As the children grew from babies to boys, the padishah kept them within the palace grounds most of the time, but occasionally they were allowed to go outside the walls. One day when they were playing with some neighborhood children, the two boys were taunted by the others. "Oh, the padishah has a son, but that son has no name. Oh, the *lâla* of the padishah also has a son, but that son is without a name."

The two boys went to the padishah and asked, "Why do we not have names like everyone else? The other children said to us, 'Oh, the padishah has a son, but that son has no name. Oh, the *lâla* of the padishah also has a son, but that son is without a name.' Why is it that we have no names?"

Hearing this, the padishah called a crier and said, "Give this news to all the people. Tell them that they should gather at the palace tonight. On this occasion we shall name my son and the son of my *lâla*."

A large group of people came and were seated in a group within the palace. All of the doors and even the chimneys were locked. Everyone who was there was known to everyone else, but suddenly an old man with white hair and a long white beard appeared in the room. He walked right up to the padishah and said, "*Selâmünaleyküm.*"

And, "*Aleykümselâm,*" the padishah answered.

"Friend, a cushion. My padishah, is there not a cushion for me as well as for you?"

The padishah, recognizing Hızır, immediately got up and gave his seat to the old man. The people laughed among themselves at this unusual behavior of the padishah. Some of them said to others, "See that! An old dervish has entered the room, and our padishah has arisen and given him his own seat!"

The old man then said, "Bring the boys to me!" When this had been done, he touched the arm of the son of the padishah and said, "Let your arm never fall! Let your name be Yusuf." Turning to the son of the *lâla*, he said, "Let your head never be without trouble. Let your name be Ali Shah." After naming the children in this way, the old man vanished. The padishah had reached into his broad sash to give gold to the old man, but he had disappeared, and the winds were blowing in his place.

124

Now that the children had been named, the padishah said to his *lâla*, "Let us hire a teacher for these boys. We shall shut them up in quarters where no sunlight enters, so that they will think only of their education and not be distracted by the outside world." A teacher was hired, and suitable quarters were prepared for the boys and their teacher, who remained with them day and night. They began to learn their lessons, but they were growing up without knowing a thing about the world outside their quarters. They saw no sun, and they knew nothing of all that the sun shines upon.

One day when their meal was brought to them, they found a bone in it. The cook had been ordered never to serve them food with bones in it, but this time one had been left in their meat. Yusuf bit into it, but he could not chew it. He threw it aside, but it struck a windowpane which had been painted to keep the sunlight out. When it struck the window, the bone broke the glass, and immediately sunshine poured through the opening. "What is this? What is this?" both boys cried, for they had not seen sunlight since they were quite young, and they had forgotten its very existence. As they were running here and there trying to catch the rays of sunlight that danced upon the wall, their teacher entered. He hurried at once to summon the padishah.

"What is the matter with you?" the padishah asked as the boys ran here and there. "What happened?"

"There was something hard in our meat, my father—this thing," said the padishah's son, picking up the bone from the floor. "When I threw it against the wall, it made a hole and let in all this strange light."

"That thing is a bone, and it is not a thing to play with, my son," said the padishah. "I shall bring you instead a golden ball that you can both play with." And so he did.

One day while they were playing with the ball, Yusuf stuck his head out through the hole in the window. He saw a crowd of people outside, and among them the women who came to the fountain to fill their water jugs. When he saw an old woman come to the fountain to fill her jug, he threw his golden ball to her. The old woman was greatly surprised, and of course she did not catch the ball. But it hit her water jug and broke it into many pieces.

The old woman looked up and said to him, "Oh, you! What can I say to you, boy? You are, after all, the only son of the padishah of our land. Still, you have broken my water jug. For that reason, I shall lay a curse on you: May you fall in love with Princess Dilefrema, the arrogant daughter of the padishah of India." At the very moment that the old woman had finished uttering her curse, Yusuf's heart began to burn with love for this princess that he had never even seen.

As the fire of love for this girl grew hotter and hotter within him, the son of the padishah said to Ali Shah, the son of the *lâla*, "Let us ride the horses that our fathers gave us. We need to get outside of this room and see what other people see." Now, these horses were the ones born from their

125

mothers' having eaten the peelings of the two apples given by Hızır to the padishah and his *lâla*, and they were fine horses indeed. The grooms helped the boys mount the horses, and Yusuf and Ali Shah rode around and around the garden.

"Ah, I like this!" said Yusuf. "Ali Shah, take this key and go to my father's treasury and fill a saddlebag with gold, for we are going to ride outside the garden and away from this place, perhaps even to India."

When Ali Shah had returned from the treasury, the two divided the gold between them, putting half in each one's saddlebag. Then they mounted their horses and rode this way and that way until they saw an opportunity to leave. There was a crowd of people watching them as they rode. Suddenly, Yusuf said, "Come! Whip your horse and ride through that gate at a gallop!" And both Yusuf and Ali Shah whipped their horses and galloped toward the gate.

"Catch them! Pull them down from their horses!" shouted their fathers and the palace guards.

But who would dare to touch the sons of the padishah and his *lâla*? They rode away and escaped without any hindrance at all. They rode all day, and when evening arrived, they stopped beside a fountain. Yusuf said, "Let us spend the night here by this fountain and then continue our journey tomorrow." So they settled themselves to rest. The son of the padishah fell

126

asleep at once, but the son of the *lâla* lay awake, listening to the sounds of the night.

Within an hour, there arose from the fountain what arose every evening at that time, a glass dome that enclosed the entire area around the fountain. A desk was placed near the center beneath the dome. A child entered the domed area, walked to the desk, and sat down at it. An old man with white hair and a long white beard then entered and said, "O padishah of the dome! Let us talk with one another for a while."

"No, no, I cannot do that. I have a guest," the child answered.

"Oh, yes. I know. I know. I know your guest."

"Grandfather, who is this guest?"

"I cannot tell you, son. Do not ask me that question."

"Please, grandfather! Who is this guest?"

"He is the son of the padishah of Yemen, my child. He has fallen in love with the daughter of the padishah of India, and he and the son of his father's *lâla* are now on their way to try to win her. But it is very difficult to reach her. If the son of the padishah is asleep and the son of the *lâla* is awake, let him heed my words. In the morning they will arise. On the shelf at the right side of this domed area there is a whip. He should take this whip and use it when they come to a sea. If he will strike the surface of the sea with this whip, the sea will become a dusty road, and they will then be able to pass along on it, but if no such road were opened for them, they would not be able to reach the girl. After they have found the girl and are leaving with her, they will be pursued by a female giant who has magical powers. This giant could kill them and take the girl back if she were not prevented from doing so. There is a special sword lying over there in that other part of the domed area. If he takes that sword along and hits the giant woman with it, all of her magical power will be destroyed and she will be unable to harm them. They will then be able to proceed a little farther with the girl. Soon after that, however, they will be attacked by a magical red horse who will neigh and charge against them. If he strikes the horse with that sword, its magical power will be destroyed. They will then be able to come back in this direction a little farther. In fact, they will be able to reach the padishah's palace. Now, if Ali Shah is still awake, let him hear this! After Yusuf and the princess have been married and have been delivered to the nuptial chamber, they will be beset by a black snake whose sting will fatally poison the bridegroom. If Ali Shah cuts the snake apart with his sword, they will be saved, and there will be no further obstacles to the marriage. But if Ali Shah should ever tell these secrets to anyone, he will be turned into stone from heel to head. If he does all these things which I have described, however, he will be invulnerable: if he is struck by any blade, no blood will flow."

In the morning when he arose, Ali Shah looked and saw that there was indeed a whip where the old man had said there would be, and there was a sword waiting at the place he had described. Ali Shah took both of these objects, and then the two young men set out again on their journey. When they came to a sea, the son of the *lâla* struck the surface with the whip, and the sea became a dusty road. They passed along this dusty road for a very great distance, going and going and going, until finally they came to an inn where they hoped to stay. Yusuf called, "O innkeeper brother, what country is this? And are you willing to accept us as guests at your inn?"

The innkeeper answered, "This is India. I am willing to be your host in this country, but do not ever look out of that window in your room."

"Why not?" asked Yusuf.

"The daughter of the padishah of this land builds castles from the skulls of men who have come seeking her hand in marriage, so do not look out of that window!"

When Ali Shah heard this, he asked the innkeeper, "Please go and bring me a goldsmith."

When the goldsmith arrived, Ali Shah said to him, "Here is a large quantity of gold. With it you are to construct a golden ram large enough for my friend Yusuf to enter. It will have a mouth with which to eat, eyes with which to see, and ears with which to hear, but the bottoms of the four hoofs will be left open. It will be able to be opened, and it will be able to be locked from within. Also, you will make four golden shoes to fit my friend."

"I shall do those things with pleasure," said the goldsmith. He took the gold and in three or five days he returned with the golden ram and the shoes that he had made. Ali Shah paid the goldsmith well for his work, and the goldsmith left.

Then the son of the *lâla* said to Yusuf, "Now, get inside the golden ram, and when you are inside the ram, I shall put on your hands and your feet the golden shoes that were made. I shall place a chain around the ram's neck and lead it to the marketplace and have it dance. Of course, *you* will be dancing, instead, on your four golden shoes, inside the ram. I shall charge one lira to those who wish to watch the golden ram dance."

Yusuf quickly got inside the golden ram and locked the door. Then he fitted his hands and his feet into the golden shoes. He walked here and there within the room while Ali Shah went out to buy a chain.

Then the son of the *lâla* and the golden ram walked to the very center of the marketplace. Ali Shah stopped, and the ram stopped. "I have here a dancing golden ram!" Ali Shah shouted. "For only one lira, you can see this golden ram dance!"

Now, this was the last day of Ramazan, and the padishah of India was out in the marketplace himself buying sweets for the *bayram*. As soon as he had heard Ali Shah shouting, he came closer to watch the dancing golden ram. Ali Shah was chanting,

128

"Dance, my pretty toy. Dance!
If you dance well, I shall treat you well.
If you dance ill, I shall beat you well.
Dance, my pretty toy. Dance!"

The padishah of India had one child, a girl, who was clever but arrogant and domineering. She was so demanding that her father feared her. He even visited her and paid his respects to her during the *bayram* instead of his daughter's coming to pay her respects to him on that holiday! Moreover, he had just been told that his daughter was especially angry with him at this time because of his failure to visit her recently. Thinking, "*İnşallah*, may my daughter not be angry at me!" he decided to take the golden ram to her as a *bayram* surprise. He said to Ali Shah, who was making the marvelous golden ram dance, "Oh, my son, let us take this ram to the palace. The princess is angry at me, but perhaps when she sees the golden ram dance, she will be distracted from her anger."

They took the golden ram to the palace, with the ram dancing and prancing. The padishah of India knocked at his daughter's door and said, "Oh, my girl, open your door and see this dancing ram which I have brought to perform for you as a *bayram* surprise." The daughter opened the door, and, oh, she was as beautiful as the fourteenth of the moon! Forgetting her anger at her father, the girl admired the golden ram, too, and she kept it dancing until evening while the son of the *lâla* watched and waited.

When evening arrived, Ali Shah asked, "May we have your permission to leave?"

"Yes," answered the princess, "but do not take the golden ram away with you. Leave it here in a corner when you go."

"Very well," he said. "But if I am going to do that, let me first take it outside, tighten its screws, and put it in its place." He took the golden ram out of that room. To Yusuf, still inside the ram, he said softly, "Listen! If she should fall in love with you, be careful! Remember the warning we have had that she builds castles of human skulls!"

"Do not worry. Nothing bad will happen," said Yusuf.

Ali Shah took the golden ram back to the room of the princess and left it standing in the corner. Later in the evening when everyone else had gone, the princess and her forty female companions ate and drank together. They then prepared to retire, and the companions piled up a mound of forty pillows for the bed of the princess. At her head they placed a large golden candelabrum, and at her feet they placed an equally large silver candelabrum. The princess climbed to the top of the pile of pillows and fell asleep there. The companions spread forty mattresses in a circle around the princess, and then they too fell asleep.

Now, the companions had put pitchers of sherbet on the table in the

130

room, and with them they had put plates of nuts. Ali Shah, inside the ram, had been observing all of this, and so after the girls were sound asleep, *mışıl mışıl*, he came forth from the golden ram, ate the nuts, and drank the sherbet. He moved the golden candlestick to the foot of the princess's bed, and the silver one to the head of her bed. He then returned to the golden ram, got inside it, and locked the door.

In the middle of the night, the princess awoke and called out, "Girls, bring me some of that sherbet!"

Her companions arose immediately and looked around. They were amazed. "Our princess, there is no sherbet. You must have drunk it all already."

"Bring me some nuts, then," she said.

"Our princess, you must have eaten them all already," they answered.

"Who changed the positions of the candelabra?"

"Our princess, we do not know," they said. And indeed they did not.

In the morning, the princess dismissed all of her forty companions as night guards in her room. "What good are you to me at such a time?" she said angrily. "Do not sleep any longer in my room."

Later that day, Ali Shah, the owner of the golden ram, came again and made the ram dance until evening. Then, as he had done the day before, he led the ram to a corner of the girl's room and left it there. He then returned to the inn.

To her forty companions, the princess said, "Of course, you are not to sleep in this room tonight, but before you leave, I want you to prepare my room for the night." She had them fill pitchers and pitchers with sherbet. She had them place plates and plates of nuts on the table. She had them put the golden candelabrum at the head of her bed and the silver candelabrum at its foot. She had them pile her forty pillows into a mound. Then she climbed up on her mound of pillows and fell asleep, *mışıl mışıl*.

Yusuf, observing all of this from inside the golden ram, watched and waited until he was sure that the princess was asleep. Then, as he had done the night before, he came forth from the ram, ate all of the nuts, drank all of the sherbet, and changed the positions of the two candelabra. In the middle of the night, the princess arose, as was her habit, to eat and drink, but again she found that there was neither food nor sherbet on the table. She noticed at once that the candelabra had been moved. "Aha!" she said. "My companions were not here tonight to do any of these things. Who could have done this? I shall watch and see."

The next evening before retiring, she cut her finger deeply and rubbed salt into the wound in order to stay awake. She had the room prepared in exactly the same way it had been on previous nights. She climbed to the top of her pile of forty pillows, but of course she was unable to sleep because of the pain in her finger. Still, she snored softly, pretending to be asleep. After a

131

while, she heard a sound, *link*, come from the golden ram as Yusuf turned the key in the lock.

The young man came out of the golden ram and went to the table. "After waiting so long, I shall now be able to fill myself with food," he said. The princess watched him closely as he ate the nuts, drank the sherbet, and changed the positions of the candelabra. As she watched, she fell deeply in love with him. After all, he was handsome. Wasn't he the son of a padishah?

When he was about to reenter the ram, the princess slid down from her mound of pillows, grabbed his wrist, and asked, "Who are you?"

"I am the son of the padishah of Yemen. I have come here for you, and I planned all of this in order to win you." As he said this, he embraced the princess, and she was glad.

"Ah, is this so?" she asked. "Then let us travel away from here tomorrow. I shall pretend that I am ill in order to get the keys to my father's treasury. We shall take from it things that are light in weight but heavy in value to aid us in our escape."

It was not long after morning arrived when news reached the padishah that his daughter was ill. He went to her immediately and asked, "My daughter, what is the matter with you?"

"Father, I am so ill that I should not care very much even if I should die, except . . . except that I have not seen your treasury even once. Knowing that I must be of such small value to you has made me very ill."

"Here, my daughter. Let the keys to my treasury be a sacrifice for your health," said the padishah, handing his keys to her.

After her father had left the room, the princess went immediately to the treasury and filled a bag with things that were light in weight but heavy in value—diamonds and rubies and fine gold. She got the bag out of the treasury by lowering it from a window to her most trustworthy servant. And all the while, the padishah knew nothing of this. How could he know?

That evening, the princess asked Ali Shah to remain after the room had been prepared for the night. When midnight had arrived, the two young men and the princess lowered themselves from the palace on ropes. They recovered the bag from the servant and hurried to the inn, where they gave the golden ram to the innkeeper. Ali Shah and Yusuf took their horses from the inn stable and mounted them, with the princess seated on Yusuf's horse with him. Then they set off at once on their long journey. Ali Shah alone knew what was going to happen, so he followed along behind the couple.

They had not gone very far when Ali Shah saw a female giant rushing at them in great rage. Raising his sword, the son of the *lâla* struck down this giant woman and destroyed her magic power. As Ali Shah was sheathing his sword, Yusuf looked around at him, and immediately he became suspicious. "Oh, is this what your friendship is like? Have you too discovered that this woman is beautiful, and are you going to kill me in order to have her?"

132

"You know that is not so. But I shall be glad to ride ahead, if you wish, and let you follow me."

But they proceeded as they had been before, with the princess seated behind Yusuf on his horse and Ali Shah riding after them. After a short distance, Ali Shah saw coming from one side the magic red horse, charging at them and neighing as he came. The son of the *lâla* struck the red horse with his sword and destroyed its magic power. A moment later the son of the padishah looked around and saw Ali Shah sheathing his sword, and he asked again, "Is this what your friendship is like?"

"If you do not trust me, then let me ride ahead of you, and you can follow," replied Ali Shah.

But they continued in the same way, riding and riding. When they arrived at last at their own country, they were greeted by many people along their route, for Yusuf was, after all, the only son of their padishah. As soon as possible, the wedding of Yusuf and the princess was celebrated. After all of the marriage ceremonies had been completed, the young couple were led to the nuptial chamber and left there. But, knowing the danger that awaited them in that room, Ali Shah had entered it secretly before they arrived there. When the snake came out of a hole in the floor, the son of the *lâla* drew his sword, struck it, and cut it into several pieces.

Yusuf did not know any of this, but when he realized that Ali Shah was

in the room, he noticed that the son of the *lâla* was sheathing his sword. He said, "Well, if this is the way things stand, it is not necessary that I have this bride. Let her be yours!" Then Yusuf went immediately to the padishah and reported, "My father, the son of your *lâla* has been plotting against me, and he considered stabbing me on three different occasions."

But the son of the *lâla* had come, too, and a number of people had gathered out of curiosity. Ali Shah said to Yusuf, "Oh, do not compel me to tell what really happened, or you will be sorry for it."

"Why should I be sorry?" said Yusuf, for he was truly angry.

"All right, then, if nothing would make you sorry, let me tell you, before everyone here, what actually did happen on our journey. After we left this place, we were guests at a domed building near a fountain. You slept deeply, but I was awake for a long time. There were two other people who appeared in the dome besides us. A white-haired, white-bearded old man was talking to his grandson about me. He said, 'There is a whip on the shelf and there is a sword lying at one side of this dome which Ali Shah should take with him because they will be useful on the journey. When they come to a sea, they will not be able to proceed, but if Ali Shah strikes the surface of the water with the whip, the sea will turn into a dusty road upon which they may travel easily.' Did you know about this?

"The old man in the dome continued, 'After they travel along that dusty road for a great distance, they will come to the land of India, and they will start back with the daughter of the padishah of India. But the three of them will be pursued by a female giant with magic powers. This giant will kill both of the young men and take the girl back to India unless Ali Shah destroys her magic power by striking her with the magic sword which he has taken from this dome.'"

Having recounted their adventures up to that point, Ali Shah was turned to stone from his feet up to his knees. When this was observed by everyone present, Yusuf cried out, "Do not tell any more! Do not tell any more!"

"No? What can I do now but continue the story from this point? It is too late to make any difference to me. Then the white-haired, white-bearded old man said to the boy, his grandson, 'After that, they will proceed for a short distance, but then they will be beset by a magic red horse that will charge at them, neighing. If Ali Shah hits the horse with his sword, the horse will be powerless.' That was the second time I had used the magic sword, and each time, O son of the padishah, you saw nothing of this except my sheathing of my sword afterward."

After he had progressed this far in the story of their adventures, Ali Shah had been turned into stone up to his chest. Yusuf pleaded with him, "Please do not tell any more!" And the *lâla* began to weep for the fate of his son.

134

"What else can I do now besides talk? So I shall tell it all. The grandfather went on, 'When they return home with the girl, and Yusuf and the princess are married, the bride and groom will be delivered to the nuptial chamber. There a black snake will come through a hole to sting Yusuf to death and then take the girl back to India. If Ali Shah cuts that snake into pieces with his magic sword, he will destroy the power of that snake, and their troubles will be at an end.' I killed that snake, but all you saw of the incident was my sheathing of my sword afterward."

At this moment, the son of the *lâla* grew stiff and silent and perfectly erect, like a stone statue. The crowd of people gathered there began to weep for him.

When the son of the padishah heard this story and saw what had happened to the faithful son of the *lâla*, his heart burned within him. At once, he mounted his horse and rode away. He rode until he reached the fountain where the two had spent the first night of their journey. He stayed there beside the fountain for the night, but he did not allow himself to fall asleep. Within an hour, he saw arising from the fountain the same glass dome that arose every evening and enclosed the entire area around the fountain. Again, there came the desk, the child who sat at the desk, and the white-haired, white-bearded old man who came and spoke to the child.

The old man greeted the child, saying, "O padishah of the dome! Come, let us talk with one another for a while."

"No, no, I cannot come. I have a guest."

"Yes, I know. I know. I know your guest."

"Grandfather, who is this guest?"

"I cannot tell you! Do not compel me to speak of him."

"Please, grandfather, who is he?"

"My boy, at an earlier time, the son of the padishah of Yemen went on a journey to bring back the daughter of the padishah of India. I told his companion, Ali Shah, all the secret information they would need to complete their dangerous mission, and I warned Ali Shah never to reveal these secrets or he would be turned into stone. When they arrived home with the girl, he was forced to tell these secrets, and he was turned into stone, as I had warned him that he would be. The present guest has come for a cure for his friend. If that guest is not sleeping, he should listen carefully to my words. There is a large vial of medicine in the corner at the right side of the shelf near him. If he takes that vial and rubs its contents on the stone statue, the stone will crack apart, and the man within will step forth. If he does not do this, then he himself will also turn into stone."

The son of the padishah waited eagerly for morning to come. When dawn came at last, he arose and started looking around. There indeed was the large vial of medicine. Taking the medicine, he returned to his father's palace, and there he found, all still weeping near the statue, the same crowd

135

of people that had been there when he had left. He rubbed the medicine on the statue, all over the stone surface. Soon the stone cracked and crumbled, and out stepped the son of the *lâla*.

A suitable bride was found for Ali Shah, and both the son of the padishah and the son of the *lâla* were married at the great wedding that was then held, a wedding that lasted forty days and forty nights. I know, for I was there to see them married.

They stayed in Yemen, and as far as I know, they are still there. As for me, I came here to tell you this tale. May it bring you joy!

Okra for Dinner

A villager moved into the city of Yozgat. One day when he was in a grocery store, he saw a man there buying 250 grams of okra. When that customer left with his okra, the villager said to the shopkeeper, "Give me a kilo of okra."

"Oh, that would be too much," the shopkeeper said.

"Haven't you put this out in order to sell it? Give me a kilo," the villager insisted. In that time, when our money had more value than it does now, he gave the grocer fifty Turkish liras and received thirty-five liras in change. "Didn't you overcharge me?" asked the villager.

"No. Okra costs fifteen liras a kilo."

When he reached home, the villager gave the packet of okra to his wife. "What is this?" she asked him.

"It is something to eat."

"What is it called?" she asked.

"Okra."

"I don't know how to cook it."

The villager thought for a minute, and then he said, "I know how we can find out. You pretend that you are sick. I'll unroll your bed, and you will lie on it. Then I shall go and call my brother's wife. She knows all about such dishes." He unrolled the bed, placed his wife on it, and covered her with two quilts. "Just lie there without moving, but pay close attention to how she cooks the okra," he said.

He then went and got his sister-in-law to cook the meal, saying that his wife was sick in bed. When the sister-in-law arrived at his house, she asked, "Where is the meat to cook with it?"

The clever villager said, "Well, I bought it, but I must have forgotten and left it at the shop. I'll go and get it right away." Of course, he had not known that okra is cooked with meat, but he went at once and bought some meat and a lemon.

As the sister-in-law was cooking the okra, she asked, "What happened to your wife? She seemed to be all right when I saw her earlier today."

"Yes, but she became ill quite suddenly just before time for dinner."

All for a Wrinkled Little Pomegranate

Once long ago, when fleas were porters and camels were barbers—well, in those days there was a padishah of India who had a beautiful daughter named Gülsün. At the same time, there was a padishah of Iran who had a handsome son named Hasan. "My friend," said the padishah of Iran, "let us marry my son to your daughter." And the padishah of India agreed, so the marriage was arranged.

Never was a wedding celebrated with such splendor. For forty days and forty nights there was great feasting and rejoicing, and thus the two were married.

On the morning of the forty-first day, Hasan gathered his bride and all her belongings, and they started with a long procession toward Iran. On the way, Hasan happened to see a wrinkled little pomegranate by the side of the road. "Stop, my princess," he said. And while Gülsün watched, he dismounted and picked up the pomegranate. He dusted it off, and, breaking it open, he offered half of it to her.

"Öf!" said Gülsün, very much offended. For indeed she was quite proud. "I would never pick up anything along the roadside! Nor can I live the rest of my life with a prince who would do such a thing." And she turned her horse's head and rode back toward India.

Well, Hasan was greatly surprised. As for the padishah of Iran, he was annoyed beyond measure. At once he arranged an engagement between his son and another princess.

But Hasan could not forget the beautiful girl he had married. He would have Gülsün for his wife, he decided. "First, however," he said to himself, "I must teach her not to be so proud."

At once, Hasan disguised himself as a peasant gardener, in a ragged pair of baggy trousers and a plain shirt and an old cap. He went to the palace of the padishah of India. "Sire," said he, "I am a fine gardener. Please let me work for you."

The padishah liked his manner and agreed to hire him. "This will be your house," said the padishah, showing him a small hut at the foot of the garden. "You have a straw mat to sleep on. And you may eat your meals in the palace kitchen."

Well, the prince went to work in earnest, and proved himself a fine gar-

138

dener indeed. His roses were lovelier, his hyacinths were sweeter, his lilies were whiter than any the padishah had ever seen.

The princess herself had been noticing the change in the garden, and she went to walk one day among the roses. The gardener was singing to himself as she came, and he took care to let her hear his song.

"If you love roses, surely a beauty you must be.
Smile, my princess, so my luck will smile at me.
If you'll not be cross with me, princess, I'll tell you
That the name of my sweetheart is Gülsün, too."

"Oh!" she thought. "So he loves a girl named Gülsün. Well, it can do no harm to speak to him." And she began talking with him pleasantly enough about the garden. Day after day, Gülsün went to the garden to talk with the gardener, and before long she had fallen in love with him. And he, of course, was already in love with her.

"My princess," he said to her one day, "this will never do. In my own country I was a simple gooseherd. Your father would never allow me to marry you."

"Then let us run off together," she said, "for I will marry no one but you."

So they ran away together on two horses that Gülsün led forth from her father's stable. As they rode along and rode along, Hasan saw a broken comb by the roadside. "Oh, a comb!" he exclaimed. "How lucky for us! Dismount and pick it up, my sweet."

"But it is broken," she said. "What do we want with a broken comb?"

"My dear," he said patiently, "I have told you I am only a gooseherd. You will be lucky to have even a broken comb. Come, pick it up so we can be on our way."

Though she was too proud to want the comb, she loved the gardener very much and she wanted to please him. She dismounted and picked up the broken comb and put it in her saddlebag. Then they went on their way again.

A little farther along, they came upon a battered bath dipper. "Oh, a bath dipper!" Hasan exclaimed. "How lucky for us! Dismount and pick it up, my sweet."

"That bent old bath dipper?" she asked. "What do we want with an old bath dipper?"

"My dear," he said gently, "I have told you I am only a gooseherd. You will be lucky to have even a bent bath dipper. Come, pick it up so that we can be on our way."

Though she was too proud to want that bath dipper, she loved the gardener very much and she wanted to please him. She dismounted and picked up the bath dipper and put it in her saddlebag. Then they went on their way again.

139

A little farther along, they came upon a tattered bath wrapper. "Oh, a *peştamal!*" he exclaimed. "How lucky for us! Dismount and pick it up, my sweet."

"But it is torn and full of holes," she said. "What do we want with a tattered *peştamal?*"

"My dear," he said cheerfully, "I have told you I am only a gooseherd. You will be lucky to have even a tattered *peştamal* to take to the public bath. Come, pick it up so that we can be on our way."

Though it was almost too much for her pride, she loved the gardener very much and she wanted to please him. She dismounted and picked up the tattered *peştamal* and put it in her saddlebag. Then they went on their way again.

As soon as they came to a village where there was a *hoca,* they were married. Oh, how happy they were! They went along and went along till they came to the palace of the padishah of Iran. "I am the gooseherd for the padishah of Iran," said Hasan. "Come. I shall show you where we shall live." And he led her to a poor little goosecoop with a patched roof and a dirt floor. Over in the corner were two straw mats to sleep on. "It is a poor place," he said, "but we shall manage. Only be patient, my dear." And because she loved him, of course she was patient. They had bread and cheese and olives to eat, and tea to drink, and they managed quite well from day to day.

One afternoon Hasan came home and said to Gülsün, "The padishah's son is soon to be married, and the cooks in the kitchen are going to be sorting rice tomorrow for the banquet. You are to go and help them, my dear."

"Of course," she agreed.

"But that is not all," he said. "Just before you leave, you must slip a few handfuls of rice into your pockets to bring home."

"What! Do you want me to become a thief?"

"Oh, my dear," he answered, "the padishah has so much rice that a few handfuls will never be missed. We can make soup with it."

Well, Gülsün went the next day to the palace kitchen to sort rice. She sorted and sorted, and it was almost too much for her pride. Still, she loved her husband and she wanted to please him, so she stayed and worked all day. Just before she was ready to leave, she slipped two handfuls of rice into each of her pockets, when nobody seemed to be watching.

But a moment later, the chief cook said, "My girl, we must search your pockets. Sometimes girls steal a bit of rice, you know." For Hasan himself had asked the cook to search the gooseherd's wife. And when they searched her pockets, they found the rice.

"For shame!" said the cook. "If you had *asked* for rice, we would have given you some. But what a thing, to steal it!"

Gülsün left, feeling very much ashamed, and hurried home to her husband. "How could you make me *do* such a thing?" she cried. "They searched

140

me and found the rice. I am so ashamed!"

"Never mind, my dear," Hasan said gently. "Remember, I am a goose-herd. Such things are not counted shameful for us." And so he soothed her wounded feelings.

Three or five days later, Hasan came home with the news that the next day, seamstresses at the palace were going to make the bride's dresses. "I want you to go there and help them tomorrow, my dear," he said. "And before you come home, slip a few meters of cloth inside your blouse and bring them along home. If we should have a baby, we should want to make dresses for it."

"I shall go," she said, "but I will not steal any cloth. You know what happened about the rice."

"Never mind, my sweet," he said. "Just do as I say. Perhaps they will not find you out this time."

So she went the next day to help with the dresses. She worked hard all day long. At last, just before she was ready to leave, she slipped a few meters of cloth into her blouse. But again Hasan had asked the palace women to search Gülsün before she left, and again they found that she had stolen something.

"Oh, my dear girl, how can you *do* such things?" they exclaimed. "If you need cloth, all you have to do is to *ask*. But to *steal* is shameful."

Gülsün hurried home to her husband. "Oh, I am so ashamed!" she cried. "They searched me again today, and they found the meters of cloth I had hidden in my blouse. I will *never* steal again."

"Do not distress yourself, my dear," he said calmly. "You know I am only a gooseherd. Such things are not counted shameful for us. After all, you were not punished, were you? You see, they *expect* such things of a goose-herd's wife." And she was somewhat comforted.

A few days later, Hasan came home with the news that the next day, seamstresses would be sewing beads and coins on the bride's dresses. "I want you to go and help, my dear. And this time, just before you leave, slip a gold coin under your tongue. No one will ever find it there."

"No," she said, "I will not steal again."

"My sweet, what is one gold coin to the padishah of Iran?"

"I cannot do it," she said.

"If you love me, you will," said he.

And, true enough, the next morning she went to the palace to help the seamstresses sew beads and coins on the bride's dresses. And just before she left, she managed to slip a gold coin under her tongue.

Now, Hasan had asked his mother, the padishah's wife, to search the gooseherd's wife. As Gülsün was leaving, therefore, the padishah's wife said, "I must search you, my dear." She searched Gülsün's pockets, and, finding nothing there, suddenly she commanded her to open her mouth. Of course,

141

the coin was found.

"Have you no pride at all?" exclaimed the padishah's wife. "Who ever heard of hiding a gold coin under the tongue?" And she sent Gülsün along to the goosecoop.

Gülsün was crying when she arrived home. "How could you do this to me?" she said. "The padishah's wife herself searched me and found the gold coin. My pride is totally broken. I have no self-respect left at all. I'll never go to the palace again—*never!*" And she wept and would not be comforted.

Two days later it was time for the wedding bath. "Look, my dear," Hasan said. "Every one of the women is going to the public bath. There will be no charge for bathing today. You, too, must go, to be clean for the wedding."

"How can I go?" she asked. "I don't have a comb or a bath dipper or even a *peştamal*. How can I go to the bath?"

"What ever happened to the comb and the dipper and the *peştamal* that we found?" Hasan asked. "Surely they are better than nothing!"

Well, Gülsün cried and protested, but at last she agreed to go to the bathhouse. She arrived well ahead of everyone else and hurried down to the farthest corner. She wrapped herself in that rag of a *peştamal*, and rinsed herself with the bent bath dipper, and combed her hair with the broken comb.

While she was washing, the bride-to-be and all her party arrived. There was great merrymaking among the bridal party and feasting on fruits and sweet drinks and dainties of all kinds. And the bride-to-be was wrapped in a gold-embroidered *peştamal*, and rinsed with a golden bath dipper, and had her hair combed with a golden comb.

While the bride-to-be was being washed, the padishah's son brought a tray to the door of the bathhouse. On the tray were a gold piece, a piece of candy, a rose, a thorn, and a wrinkled little pomegranate. "This is a riddle," he told the bathhouse keeper. "Whoever is able to guess this riddle is my true bride."

"Surely you are jesting!" exclaimed the bathhouse keeper. "Your bride-to-be is now inside the bathhouse with her bridal party."

"You heard what I said," insisted the prince. "Ask this riddle of every person in the bathhouse, beginning with the one who calls herself my bride."

So the bathhouse keeper took the tray inside. She asked first the bride-to-be and then every member of the bridal party what riddle was set by the objects on the tray, but none could guess the riddle. She took the tray back to the prince. "None could answer it, my prince," she said.

"Try again," insisted the prince. "My wife must be able to guess this riddle, or she is not truly my wife."

Again the bathhouse keeper took the tray around, first to the bride-to-be and then to the rest of the bridal party. Still, no one could guess the riddle. Once again the bathhouse keeper took the tray back to the prince.

"Are you *sure* you have asked everyone?" said the prince. "Is there no one else in the bathhouse?"

"Well, yes, there is the gooseherd's wife, washing herself in the farthest corner," admitted the bathhouse keeper.

"Then ask her," said the prince. "After all, she is a person, isn't she?"

So the bathhouse keeper carried the tray to the farthest corner of the bathhouse. "This is a riddle," she said. "Can you guess it?"

Gülsün looked at the articles on the tray. Then she said,

"Ah, once as precious as gold was I,
And as sweet as candy, too;
From the only rose in a garden of joy
To a common thorn I grew,
And all the cause for this change in guise
In a wrinkled little pomegranate lies."

The bathhouse keeper hurried back to the prince and said, "The gooseherd's wife guessed the riddle. Here is her answer:

"Ah, once as precious as gold was I,
And as sweet as candy, too;
From the only rose in a garden of joy
To a common thorn I grew,
And all the cause for this change in guise
In a wrinkled little pomegranate lies."

"Well, then," said the prince, "she is the one who will be my wife."

"How can that be?" asked the bathhouse keeper. "Your bride-to-be is already inside for the wedding bath. Besides, the gooseherd's wife is already married."

"You heard what I said," the prince insisted. "Get the gooseherd's wife bathed and dressed, and bring her to me."

So the bathhouse keeper and the bride-to-be's attendants led the gooseherd's wife from the farthest corner of the bathhouse. They wrapped her in the gold-embroidered *peştamal*, and rinsed her with the golden bath dipper, and combed her hair with the golden comb. "What *is* this? What are you doing?" Gülsün kept asking.

And, "The padishah's son is going to marry you," they answered.

"But I have my husband already. He is the gooseherd, and I love him very much. I will not marry the prince!"

Still, they kept washing her, and afterwards they dressed her in one of the bride's new dresses. All the time, she was weeping. And of course the former bride-to-be was weeping, too, but for quite a different reason.

The prince called for a carriage and had her taken to the palace, where she was given a beautiful room of her own. In the evening, the prince came. When Gülsün saw that he was Prince Hasan, she was *sure* she did not want to marry him. "I have my gooseherd," she wept. "He is the only one I want for my husband."

The prince left the room. He put on his peasant clothing—the ragged baggy trousers, the plain shirt, and the old cap. Then he came back to Gülsün. She stared at him in surprise and disbelief.

"You see, my dear," he said, "I am both the prince and the gooseherd. And you are my lovely bride Gülsün."

For pure happiness, they were married all over again, with festivities that lasted for forty days and forty nights. May we have a share of their happiness!

How the Siege of Van Was Lifted

Shah Abbas, padishah of Iran, was a proud man, a very proud man. One day he said to his court, "Consider my lands, my people, my power, my wealth. There is no padishah anywhere in the world who is greater than I am."

Now, in the padishah's court there was one vizier who had courage enough to speak his mind to the padishah. "It is true, my padishah," he said, "that you govern much land, that you have many people under your rule, that you hold great power, and that your treasury is full. But, my padishah, there are several Turkish padishahs who may well be your equals. The padishah of Van is one such ruler. Do you think that you could possibly capture his fortress at Van?"

"You will see," said Shah Abbas. "I shall take the fortress of Van, and I myself shall lead the troops. *Then* none can question the power of the padishah of Iran!"

Marshalling all of the troops available in his land, the padishah of Iran raised a mighty army in forty days. Under the leadership of Shah Abbas, the army began to march toward Van. It was a long march, but after many days they reached the city and began their attacks. Over and over, great forces were thrown against the walls of Van, and almost as quickly they were thrown back. The losses among the Iranian army mounted; still the troops were unable to conquer the city.

After some time, Shah Abbas decided to change his tactics. "No fortress in the world can stand against hunger. We shall *starve* the defenders into submission." He summoned the whole army to appear before him. "Hear me!" he announced. "Every soldier in my army must plant a garden and tend it carefully. Those within the wall will be unable to grow their own food, and they will be starved into surrendering the fortress."

Though the soldiers had no particular liking for gardening, they knew the power both of hunger and of Shah Abbas, and each one set about the business he had been given. At the same time, the battles between the attackers and the defenders were renewed. The siege continued for seven years, and by the end of that time, the defenders of the fortress were beginning to be in desperate condition. Because he detected their sense of despair, the padishah of Van called his people together and said, "Should we surrender the city? There seems to be little hope of holding the fortress much longer. What do you think?"

An old woman came forward from the crowd and said, "Please do not surrender the city yet, Your Majesty. Let me first go and visit the Iranian padishah. If I fail in my plan, then you will still have time to surrender." And the padishah of Van agreed to let her try what she could do to save the city.

That old woman had three ewes. She milked those sheep and made a pot of yogurt with the milk. Taking this yogurt with her, she went to see Shah Abbas. She said to him, "I am only an old woman and so I cannot do very much, but I brought you some fresh yogurt. You have not had any for seven years, and I thought that perhaps you had begun to miss it."

The Iranian padishah was amazed to hear this. He stared at her and at her gift, and he thought, "I supposed that I was going to defeat these people by means of starvation. But even now, after all this time, they are able to make this yogurt from cow's milk or sheep's milk. Perhaps I shall not be able to starve them out, after all."

145

Just at that moment, the people within the city dumped some lime dust down the front wall of the fortress. The Iranian padishah asked the old woman, "What are they pouring down that wall?"

"I can't see very well from this distance. I don't know," said the old woman.

"Whatever it is, it is something white," said Shah Abbas.

"Oh, that!" said the old woman. "Some of the Turkish soldiers' flour has weevils in it. I think that they must be throwing it out now."

After hearing that, the padishah of Iran decided that he could not take the city of Van. Without any delay, he lifted the siege and ordered a retreat to his own country.

The Köse and the Three Swindlers

S irs, this is a true story. It took place in a village in my own *kaza* of
Alaşehir.

In our village, then, there was a *köse* who was so shrewd that no
one could deceive him. Word of his shrewdness spread from our village and
our *kaza* even to the town of Sarıgöl, in the next *kaza*. And, "How can we
fool that *köse?*" the people of Sarıgöl asked each other.

One year there was a drought in our area, and as a result the *köse* harvested a very small crop. Though the *köse* had little money, still he wanted
very much to have his only son married. He said to his son one day, "Take
our two oxen to Sarıgöl and sell them so that we shall have enough money
for your wedding."

The *köse's* son was a naive young man, by no means as shrewd as his
father. As he approached the market, word went around that this was the son
of that *köse* from Alaşehir. "Now is the time to trick that *köse*," said a swindler, and he was the first to look the two oxen over. Pointing to one ox, the
swindler asked, "How much do you want for this ox?"

The boy named the price his father had set, and he waited for the buyer's answer. "I'd like to buy this ox," said the swindler, "but its ears are much
too long. Shorten its ears, and I'll buy it."

The boy looked at the ox and then at the swindler, but he gave no answer. Still, when the buyer started to move along, the boy called out to him,
"All right. I'll shorten its ears for you."

With a large pair of sheep shears, he trimmed the ox's ears a good bit
shorter. When the swindler examined the ears, he said, "Oh, you have cut
them too short. I don't want your ox now." And he went along, well satisfied
that he had managed to cheat that *köse* from Alaşehir.

A few minutes later, a second swindler came along. "Here's the son of
that *köse* of Alaşehir," he said to himself. "Let me trick him!" And he looked
at the second ox. "How much do you want for this ox?" he asked.

The boy named the price his father had set, and he waited for the buyer's answer. "I'd like to buy this ox," said the second swindler, "but its tail is
much too long. If you will shorten the tail of this ox, I'll buy it from you."

The boy looked at the ox and then at the buyer, and he said, "All right.
I'll shorten its tail for you." With that large pair of sheep shears, he trimmed
the ox's tail a good bit.

But the second swindler said, "Oh, you have cut off too much! The tail

147

is so short now that the ox will not even be able to brush the flies away. I don't want such an ox!" And the swindler moved on, well satisfied that he had managed to cheat that *köse* from Alaşehir.

When no one would buy his mutilated oxen, the boy did not know what to do. Just then, a third swindler came along. "Here's the son of that *köse* of Alaşehir," he said to himself. "Let me trick him!" And he said, "Those oxen are fit only for slaughtering. Why don't you kill them so that I and other butchers can buy their meat?"

The boy cut the throats of the oxen and then looked for butchers, but there were none to be found. Meanwhile, the third swindler sent a man to the boy. "Boy," he said, "if some official came along and looked at this meat, he would say that it is unfit to eat. Why don't you take those carcasses somewhere else to sell them?"

Pull and tug as he might, the boy could not move the carcasses. "Well, boy," said the man, "leave them right here, and I'll cart them away for you." And the boy agreed to this. As the boy turned to go home, the whole town of Sarıgöl rejoiced that three of its clever men had finally been able to cheat that *köse* of Alaşehir.

When the boy returned home, the *köse* asked him for the money from the sale of the oxen, but the boy had no money to show for his labor. "Father," he said, "one man promised to buy an ox if I would shorten its ears, but when I shortened them, the man refused to buy the ox. A second man wanted the second ox's tail cut shorter, and I did cut it, but then he refused to buy it. A third man said he would buy the meat if I slaughtered the oxen, but when I had cut their throats, the man had disappeared. Since the oxen were too heavy for me to bring home, another man offered to dispose of them, so I left them there and came along home."

The *köse* ground his teeth when he discovered that his son had been such a fool, but he said nothing. He resolved to do something about those swindlers himself. Going to Sarıgöl, he found out the names of the three swindlers. After all, wasn't the whole town talking about those three clever fellows? He then invited those three to dinner at his house the following day.

On the way home, the *köse* caught two rabbits and tucked them inside his shirt. When he arrived at his house, he took them out and put them into a cage. The following day, he said to his wife, "When our guests arrive, I shall be in the field working. Take one of these rabbits out and tell it to go to me and ask me to come home."

When the guests came and—*Tak! Tak! Tak!*—knocked at the door, the *köse*'s wife welcomed them and seated them comfortably. Then she said, "My husband is working in the field, but please wait here. I shall send our rabbit to him with the message that you have arrived."

"How can a rabbit carry a message?" the first swindler asked.

"Well, our rabbit has been specially trained to do that," she said, and she released one of the rabbits. The rabbit ran straight out the door and across the field. Of course, he was just running away, but how could the swindlers know that? For it was only a few minutes before the *köse* appeared to welcome them.

After greeting the three guests, the *köse* called to his wife, "Woman, prepare some food for our guests."

While his wife was preparing their meal, the *köse* and his guests talked of this and that. Finally, the second swindler asked, "Köse, would you be willing to sell us your trained rabbit?"

"It is too valuable to sell," he said.

"But we shall pay you thirty gold coins for this remarkable rabbit," said the third swindler.

The *köse* thought and thought, and each of the three swindlers counted out ten gold coins to help him make up his mind. At last the *köse* agreed to sell the rabbit for the price they named, and they paid him the thirty gold coins.

After eating dinner, the first swindler said, "Thank you for your hospitality. May we please have your permission to leave? Oh, and of course we shall want our rabbit."

"Certainly," said the *köse*, and he handed the rabbit to the third swindler. "Treat it kindly and it will serve you well, just as it has served me and

my wife. May you have joy of it!" he said, and he saw them off.

When the three swindlers reached Sarıgöl, the third swindler stroked the rabbit and said to it, "Go directly to my house and tell my wife that we are coming," he said, and released the rabbit.

Of course, when the rabbit was released, it just disappeared into the nearest clump of bushes and hid there. "*Aman!*" said the first swindler. "That *köse* cheated us! Let's go to his house tomorrow and avenge ourselves against him." And they agreed to go together the next day.

The *köse* knew that the three swindlers would be angry and would come again, so he prepared another trick for them. "My wife," he said, "when those three swindlers come tomorrow, I shall shout at you and curse you and pretend to cut your throat. Take the windpipe from our cock, fill it with blood, and tie it around your neck, and I shall cut only that. Fall to the floor as if you are dead. Then when I play a few notes on this *kaval*, you will come to life again and get up."

When the three swindlers arrived at the *köse's* house the next day, they found the *köse* and his wife quarreling bitterly. "You cursed woman!" the *köse* shouted, and, snatching up a knife, he thrust it at his wife's throat.

"*Aman!*" said the second swindler as the blood flowed from her throat. "Look! You have *killed* the poor woman." And the three swindlers bent over her as she lay on the floor.

"Oh, don't worry about that," said the *köse*. "I was only teaching her a lesson. I shall revive her now." Saying this, he played a few notes on his *kaval* and restored her to life.

The three swindlers looked at each other in amazement. Then the third swindler said, "My wife needs a lesson, too."

"And mine!" "And mine!" said the other two, almost in one voice.

"Köse, will you sell us that wonderful flute?" asked the first swindler.

"No. I might need it again," he said.

"We shall pay you a hundred gold pieces for it," said the third swindler, for he thought that they could sell it in Sarıgöl for much more than that.

At last, the *köse* agreed to sell the wonderful flute for 120 gold pieces, and each of the swindlers quickly paid him forty gold pieces and then left with the flute, greatly pleased with their purchase.

Shortly after they had returned home, the second swindler had a dinner at his house for several of his friends from Sarıgöl. Though the wives of all three swindlers worked together to prepare the meal, the food was still not ready to serve the guests. Pretending to be very angry, the three swindlers cut their wives' throats—*Slish! Slish! Slish!*

The guests were horrified at this, but the three swindlers laughed, and the first one said, "Don't worry. We shall revive them." And he played a few notes on the flute.

When his wife did not get up, he handed the flute to the second one.

"You didn't play the right notes," said that one, and he played a different tune. When the wives still did not get up, the third swindler grabbed the flute and played still another tune. Alas, the wives still lay there, dead as dead.

The guests left quickly, looking back anxiously as they went. As soon as the guests had gone, the swindlers said to one another, "That terrible *köse* has cheated us again! He made us kill our wives!"

"We must kill that *köse*," said the first swindler.

"Yes," said the second.

"And we'll kill him tomorrow," said the third.

Going to the *köse*'s house the next morning, they caught him and tied him in a tough canvas sack. After all, there were three of them and only one *köse*. How could he hope to escape?

Taking turns, they carried him to the shore of the bottomless lake. "We'll drown him in this lake, and he will play no more tricks on anyone!" said the third swindler. "Let's do it right now."

But the other two were tired and out of breath. "He's safe enough here," said the first one. "Let's leave him here in this sack and go to the coffeehouse to refresh ourselves a little."

And, "Yes," agreed the second swindler. "If we have a glass or two of tea, we can throw him farther out." So they left the *köse* tied tightly in the sack and went along to the coffeehouse to rest a bit.

Soon, from inside the bag, the *köse* heard sheep bells, and he knew that a flock of sheep was passing by. He began to shout, "No, I won't do it! I won't marry her!"

Hearing this, the shepherd went to the sack and asked, "What are you doing in that sack? And who is it that you will not marry?"

"Oh, shepherd," said the *köse*, "I have refused to marry the padishah's daughter, and now they are taking me to the palace against my will to marry her anyway."

"How lucky you are!" said the shepherd. "I wish I had a bit of your good luck. I should be very happy to marry the padishah's daughter."

"Well, friend, you can do so if you wish. Just change places with me, and they will take you to the palace."

So the shepherd untied the sack, and the *köse* came out. Then the shepherd climbed into the sack. After the *köse* had tied the sack tightly, he took the shepherd's flock and began herding it toward a pasture well away from the lake.

Meanwhile, the three swindlers had had their tea, and they returned to the shore. "There's the sack," said the first swindler, "right where we left it."

"Yes," said the second, "and now we can give that *köse* exactly what we promised him."

The third one laughed, and then he said, "It will take all three of us to

151

152

do it right." So the three swindlers took hold of the sack, and with a "One! Two! Three!" they flung it as far into the lake as they could. They watched as the sack sank, and then they started home.

Long before they had reached Sarıgöl, they saw the *köse* grazing a flock of sheep. "We drowned you!" the first swindler said. "What are you doing here with these sheep?"

"No, you didn't really drown me," said the *köse*. "Instead, you did me a great favor, for the lake along the shore is just *filled* with sheep. If you had only thrown me out farther, I might have gotten more than these forty sheep!"

"Can we also get sheep in this same way?" asked the second swindler.

"Of course," said the *köse*.

They all returned to the shore. "I want to be first!" said the first swindler. So with a "One! Two! Three!" they flung him into the lake as far as they could throw. As the first one sank, he made a *kırk, kırk, kırk* sound.

"You see," said the *köse*, "he is saying, 'Forty, forty, forty!'"

"I want *more* than forty sheep," said the second swindler. "Throw me even farther out!" (How could he know that the first one was not indeed saying "Forty!" but was gurgling as he drowned?)

So the *köse* and the third swindler threw the second one, with a "One! Two! Three!" as far as they could throw. As they heard the second one saying, "*Kırk, kırk, kırk!*" the third swindler said, "*Aman!* That wasn't far enough! He's still found only forty sheep. Köse, throw me farther out than that!"

With all his strength and a "One! Two! Three!" the *köse* flung the third swindler far out into the bottomless lake. Then, without even waiting until he heard how many sheep the third one had found, the *köse* turned and headed homeward with his sheep. After all, he needed to help with the preparations for his son's wedding.

I went to that wedding myself, and I ate and drank the whole night through. May *you* have such good fortune!

The Hoca and the Drought

One day, Nasreddin Hoca happened to be visiting in a small village which had had no rain for many weeks. The villagers, despite great care in the use of their water, had at last found themselves reduced to just a cupful or two for each family.

"Oh, Hoca," begged one of the men, "please *do* something. If this drought continues, we shall all die."

Do something about *rain*? Rain was in the hands of Allah. No one could be certain when it would rain . . . Suddenly the Hoca smiled. "Bring me a bucket of water," he said, "and, Allah willing, the rain will come."

The villagers hurried to bring their small hoards of water, a cup here, a cup there. With all their supplies, they could fill no more than a little pail.

To their astonishment, the Hoca removed his shirt and began to wash it in the precious water. "*Aman*, Hoca!" said one of the men. "How can you *do* that? We have been saving that water to preserve the very lives of our children!"

But the Hoca made no response at all, either to this protest or to the increased grumblings that followed. He scrubbed earnestly at his shirt until it had been thoroughly washed. Then, wringing it out carefully, he hung it on a bush to dry.

No sooner had the shirt been safely draped over the bush when the skies opened and a veritable *cloudburst* came. Drenched by the welcome rain, the villagers gathered around the Hoca and asked him how he had managed such a miracle. "Well, you see," said the Hoca, "I never yet have hung my clean shirt out to dry but what the heavens have sent a regular deluge!"

Charity above All

Once there was and once there was not, when Allah's people were many, when it was virtuous to love much and sinful to love but little—well, back in those days I traveled a short distance, I traveled a long distance; I crossed rivers, climbed over hills, and went across plains, but when I turned to look at how far I had come, I found that I had gone no farther than the length of a grain of barley.

Back then, there were two does who could find no grass to eat, and so they grew very hungry. They entered a nearby village, crying as they walked in the streets in search of food. When they came upon a merciful woman, they spoke to her, saying, "We are very hungry. Because the drought has been severe, there is hardly any grass anywhere. Allah has given us the ability to speak, and we now ask you for some bread."

The woman was compassionate, so she brought out bread and fed the deer until their hunger was appeased. After the deer had eaten the bread and drunk some water, they returned again to the mountains. When they had been there for a very brief time, they met three brigands who had fled into those same mountains.

Each of these brigands had killed, over many years, a total of ninety-nine people. Now they were having second thoughts about their behavior. "What will become of us?" they asked each other. "We have no place to go in either this world or the next. How could our many sins ever be forgiven?"

The deer overheard this conversation, and again they were enabled to speak by the will of Allah. One of them said to the brigands, "There is a *hoca* in such and such a village. Go and attend the Friday prayer service at his mosque, and afterward ask him what you can do to be forgiven. If you listen to him carefully, that *hoca* will explain to you whether or not there is any way for you to be able to go to heaven instead of to hell."

The brigands went on the next Friday to the village mosque that the deer had indicated and listened to the sermon. Afterward, they talked privately with the *hoca* about their problem. The *hoca* said to them, "For forty days you must not commit any brigandage or kill anyone. During that same period you must perform every *namaz* and pray to Allah. If you do that, Allah will not only forgive you but will also grant whatever you wish most."

The three brigands returned to the mountains and did as the *hoca* had directed. They worshiped at every *namaz* and prayed to Allah for forty days. After they had completed forty days of such worship, they were visited by the blessed Hızır.

"What are your wishes?" asked Hızır.

The first of the brigands said, "There is a stud farm near Konya. I should like to have that farm." Hızır gave him that stud farm.

The second former brigand said, "There is a farm near Eskişehir named Sultan Ahmet Farm. I should like to have that farm." Hızır gave him that farm.

The third former brigand said, "My wish is to have a trustworthy and dependable woman as my wife."

The blessed Hızır lifted the third man onto the back of his own horse and took him to another village. The trustworthy woman that Hızır had selected for the third man was already engaged, and her wedding was now in progress. Dressed and made up as a dervish, Hızır attended that wedding. His hair and his beard were long and tangled, and he had a very frightening appearance. Everyone was terrified by him. He said, "You will either fulfill my wish or I shall take all your lives!"

"Father, what is your wish?" they asked.

"I wish to have Ayşe *Hanım* marry my son. This is my son here with me."

"But, father, Ayşe *Hanım* is already engaged to another man, and these festivities are part of her wedding ceremony."

"I do not understand."

There was a wise man among the crowd who moved forward and said, "Let me give him three tests. If he can pass them, then he deserves to have the girl. If he cannot pass them, then we shall take him into the forest and

burn him as an impostor." When the crowd had agreed with this suggestion, the wise man went to the dervish and said, "There is a date pit planted at this spot in the ground. If you can make it sprout, grow, and provide us with its fruit as we stand here, we shall understand that you are a very special person."

The dervish only struck the ground with his staff and said, "O Allah!" and somehow the date plant broke through the surface of the ground, grew rapidly, and bore dates.

"Very well," said the wise man. "This was the first test. Now if you can make a pumpkin mature suddenly from its blossom and feed it to us, you will have passed the second test."

Again the dervish struck the earth with his staff, and a pumpkin grew from a mere pumpkin flower. The dervish cut the pumpkin into slices and distributed them among the crowd.

The wise man said, "Very well. Now the last test is to answer this question correctly: Are there more women or men in this world?"

The dervish thought for a moment and then said, "Those men who are ruled by the words of their wives are also called women. Therefore the correct answer must be that there are more women than men."

"That is correct," said the wise man, "and you are entitled to take the girl."

After Hızır had handed over the girl to the former brigand, he bade the two farewell and departed. The young couple left that place and began walking down the road. As they walked along, the former brigand said, "We have nowhere to sleep and no shelter from the weather. I wonder what we are going to do."

The trustworthy and dependable woman who believed in Allah and His Prophet said, "Let us go to the home of an *ağa* or other prominent person and tell him that we are poor. We can offer to herd his cows and sheep in return for food and housing."

Going to the home of an *ağa*, they made this proposal to him. He accepted their proposal, and gathering together all the people of that village, he said to them, "These strangers are poor, and everyone is to help them."

Everyone agreed to do this, and because the village was made up of five thousand families, they received a great amount of assistance. They were given a house to live in and many other things. Everyone in that village had a guest stone near the mosque. If a stranger came to that village and sat on a guest stone, the owner of the stone would know that he had been sent a guest for the night; the owner then would provide food and shelter for his guest. Therefore Mıstık, the third former brigand, also had a guest stone made and placed it in front of the mosque.

After another year or two had passed, Allah one day said to the blessed Hızır, "Go and see how those three brigands I forgave are now doing."

Hızır went to Konya to the stud farm which the first of the former brigands had been given. He found there a thriving and very prosperous farm where large herds of cattle and large flocks of sheep were grazing. The owner was living as if he would never die. Hızır went to one of the workers on this farm and said to him, "Go and tell your *ağa* that I am an old and exhausted man. If he will lend me a horse and a man to help me, I shall go to the next village."

The worker went to his master and said, "My *ağa*, a poor old man has come along. He asks that you lend him a horse and a man to accompany him to the next village."

The *ağa* answered, "You go and tell him to get to the next village just the same way that he got here."

When the worker reported this to Hızır, a bolt of lightning struck the farm, and a fierce storm followed. The rain fell so hard and so long that most of the farm's crops and livestock were swept away in the flood.

From there, Hızır went to the Sultan Ahmet Farm at Eskişehir which had been given to the second former brigand. This farm had also prospered, and everywhere one looked there were herds of cattle, flocks of sheep, vineyards, and villas. Hızır greeted the owner, "*Selâmünaleyküm.*"

"*Aleykümselâm.*"

"I am old and poor. I have no money at all. It has been a long time since I have eaten any meat. Give me a sheep so that I shall be able to eat some meat."

"I cannot give any animal from my flock. I shall give you some money and you can go and buy what you wish with it."

Hızır responded, "Wherever your wealth came from, may it depart in a flood." The rain that began shortly after that continued until that farm was also destroyed.

From there, Hızır went to the village of the former brigand who had married the trustworthy and dependable woman. He went to the mosque and sat upon the guest stone of the third former brigand. This man came and took Hızır from the stone to his own home. There Hızır said to him, "I want to eat forty different kinds of food."

"Very well," said the former brigand. And to his wife he said, "We have a guest who wishes to have forty different kinds of food." The woman immediately set about preparing forty different dishes.

After Hızır had eaten some of each of the forty food dishes, he said to the couple, "May Allah give you assistance in everything that you do." He then left their home satisfied.

"A Bouquet of Roses for an Eye!"

O nce there was and once there wasn't, when I was rocking my mother's cradle *tıngır mıngır*—well, in those times there lived a young peasant and his wife. They were poor, so poor they had neither bread to eat nor wood to burn, and the woman was going to have a baby.

The woman said one day, "What a pity our baby must be born in the chill heart of winter! We are so poor, and our house is so cold."

"I have been thinking about that myself," said her husband. "The bathhouse keeper is a friend of mine. When the time comes, I'll beg the keys of the bathhouse from him. It's nice and warm there, and it would be a good place to have the baby."

"Ah, but what would I do there?" his wife asked. "I'd be afraid there, with the jinns and witches that play in the *hamam*."

"What else can we do?" said the man. "You'd freeze here. We have no wood to make a good fire."

When the woman was ready to have her baby, the man ran to his friend the bathhouse keeper and said, "My wife is going to have a baby, but our house is cold. Can she have her baby here in the *hamam* tonight where it's nice and warm?" And his friend let him take the key.

Quickly he took his wife to the bathhouse and left her on one of the benches. While she was waiting there, a great big jinn with his toes on the ground and his turban almost touching the sky appeared before her. "*Selâmünaleyküm!*"

And, "*Aleykümselâm!*" answered the young woman, trembling.

"Don't be afraid," the jinn said. "I won't do you any harm; I'll help you." And she was helped and gave birth to a baby girl. The jinn brought the clothes needed for the baby, and the child was washed and wrapped and laid in a corner to sleep.

Then the Wednesday witches came, and the first one said, "May pearls and corals pour from her eyes whenever she cries." Another said, "May pink roses bloom on her cheeks whenever she laughs." A third one said, "May green grass grow on the ground wherever she treads." And a fourth witch said, "May water turn into gold whenever she is washed."

The witches washed the young mother, and then they began to dance. "Come and dance with us," they said. And the young woman got up to dance with them.

"It's Wednesday, it is; it's Wednesday! It's Thursday, it is; it's Thursday! It's Friday-y-y!" the witches sang as they danced.

And, "It's Wednesday, it is; it's Wednesday! It's Thursday, it is; it's Thursday! It's Friday-y-y!" the young woman sang, exactly as they did, and she danced and danced with them.

Just after the witches had gone, the husband came and saw that he had a beautiful little girl all nicely dressed and sleeping there happy and warm. He wrapped them both up well and put them on a cart and took them home.

As soon as they were inside the door, the woman told him everything that had happened, from first to last, and her husband listened, amazed.

"Can it be true about the gold?" he wondered. And he went here and there in the darkness and found some bits of sticks and made a tiny fire. He heated some water and poured the warm water over the baby's head, and *Cuş!* came the gold. "Oh, woman, woman, surely Allah Himself has granted us this wonderful child!" he cried.

In the morning he took the gold and bought wood and food and everything else that they needed. And in the evening they washed the child again. Day by day they became richer.

As for the child, it was just as the witches had said. When she laughed, pink roses bloomed on her cheeks. When she cried, pearls and corals poured from her eyes. And wherever she put her feet, the green grass grew. "Praise Allah!" they said, and they were very, very happy.

Now, the woman had a sister who was also expecting a baby, and she said one day, "How is it that you were once so very poor and have now become so rich?" And the happy woman told her the whole story, from first to

161

last, leaving out not a single detail. That evening her sister told the story to her own husband. Determined to have the same kind of good fortune for themselves, they decided that she, too, would go to the bathhouse to have her baby. Thus when the time came, her husband borrowed the key of the *hamam*, and she went inside.

While the woman was sitting by the water basin, there came that great big jinn, with his toes on the ground and his turban almost touching the sky. "What are you doing here?" asked the jinn.

"Get out of here, you great, ugly thing," the woman answered. "What is it to *you* whether I am here or not? And what are *you* doing here?"

Not liking this at all, the jinn went away. Later the Wednesday witches came, and they helped the woman with her baby. But when it came to saying their wishes, one said, "May the donkey's boil grow on the child's forehead," and none of the others said anything at all.

When the witches started dancing, they asked the woman to come and join them. And with them she sang, "It's Wednesday, it is; it's Wednesday!" But when they sang, "It's Thursday, it is; it's Thursday!" she cried, "Indeed! How can it be Thursday when it's Wednesday?" And when they sang, "It's Friday-y-y!" she shouted, "No! It's Wednesday, you fools; it's Wednesday!" Angry with her, they stamped off, and at once the donkey's boil began to grow on the child's brow.

Just after the witches had left, the husband came, and he saw the baby. But what was that on the baby's forehead? His wife said bitterly, "We have a daughter, too, but we had a curse instead of good wishes. Look at that donkey's boil she has on her forehead!" And they took the baby home.

Both girls grew up, and the fame of the first girl spread all over the land and to countries far beyond it. People here and there said, "There is a girl we have heard of, and *such* a girl! When she laughs, pink roses bloom on her cheeks, and when she cries, pearls and corals pour from her eyes. When she's washed, the water becomes gold, and on the ground where she treads, green grass grows." And everybody became very curious about her.

The son of the padishah of India heard about her, and since he was very fond of wonders, he wanted to marry her. "All right," agreed his father. "If she's the one you want, we shall get her for you."

They came to see the girl, and everything they had heard was true. She was as beautiful as hyacinths and angels, and as she came to kiss their hands, grass grew on the ground she trod. They asked, in the name of the Prophet and by the will of Allah, that the girl might become the bride of their son.

Well, the peasant and his wife had become so comfortable by now that they cared not at all whom their daughter married, except that she be happy. When the prince asked for her hand in marriage, therefore, her father and mother said, "All right. If you want her, you may have her. We give her to you with our blessing."

162

The padishah of India was pleased, and he said, "When everything is ready for the wedding, send the girl to our country. We shall have the festivities there." Then he and his son and their servants returned to India.

At once, wedding preparations started in both places. When it was time for the girl to go, the girl's aunt said to her sister, "Sister, how can you send her to India with *strangers?* It is only fitting that someone kin to her—like me—should take her to India."

The mother answered, "Why, of course. You are right. It is very kind of you to take her." Thus it was decided that the aunt would take the bride-to-be to India. They made ready to go, and when it was time to leave, the aunt took her own daughter along, too.

They got into the carriage and started on the way. Since it was a long journey, they had taken with them various foods to eat. After a while, the bride-to-be felt hungry, and she said, "Please, Auntie, I'm very hungry. Can you give me anything to eat?"

The aunt, evil woman that she was, had prepared some sort of pastry that was very, very salty. It was so salty that when the girl had eaten a piece no bigger than a walnut, she began burning and scorching inside. "Auntie," she said, "I'm very thirsty. Could you please find some water for me to drink?"

Her aunt said, "Don't be foolish, girl. Look around! In all this dry land, do you see a single stream? Yet I've heard," she went on craftily, "that there is a place by the foot of this mountain where they sell a cup of water for an eye. If you are willing to give one of your eyes to me, I'll fetch a cup of water for you."

"Oh, Auntie," the girl said, "I'm so thirsty I cannot resist it. You had better take one of my eyes and fetch me a cup of water." So the aunt took one of the girl's eyes out and put it in her pocket. She had some water hidden, and she took a cupful out and handed it to the girl.

They went on for a little while, but the pastry the girl had eaten was so salty that one cup of water could not quench her thirst, and she asked again, "Please, Auntie, won't you find another cup of water for me?"

The aunt said, "What can I do? I have told you that they only have water here for the price of an eye. By that hill there, I am told, they sell water in exchange for an eye. If you want another cup of water, you must give your other eye to me."

"All right," said the girl. "If I must, I shall give my other eye." So her aunt took the other eye out of its socket and put it in her pocket. Now that the girl could not see anymore, the aunt pushed her out of the carriage and into an abandoned well that was near the road. And in her place she put her own ugly daughter.

On to India the aunt took her own daughter, with the big boil on her forehead—though she had taken care to have it bandaged. When they ar-

163

rived in the city where the girl was expected, they were greeted with grandeur suitable to a prince's wedding. Soldiers, bands, and cheering crowds all met them. But some of them saw the bride close at hand, and a shocked whisper spread among them. "What's this? Why did our padishah's son choose such an ugly bride? She isn't pretty at all. She is unfit to be a prince's wife!"

After the wedding festivities, when the bridegroom went into the bridal chamber and opened the bride's veil, he found that this was not at all the girl he had been expecting. This one was so *ugly*. When he said, "What has happened to you? What has made you change so much?" she answered, "What did you expect? I have been traveling for days and days, and I am tired. I'm exhausted."

All night long in the bedchamber the prince heard a gnawing and scratching kind of noise coming from his bride's side of the bed. In the morning, he asked, "What was it you were doing all night long? What was that sound?"

"Oh," she said, "I had some crackers that were left over from the journey, and I felt hungry, so I ate them." But in truth she had been digging and scratching at the ugly boil that was on her forehead.

And the prince said, "What is that on your forehead?"

"The bandage?" she asked. "I have a dreadful headache, that's all." And for days and days after that, she complained of a headache.

One day the prince asked, "What about the pink roses that bloom on your cheeks when you laugh, and the pearls and corals that pour from your eyes when you cry?"

"Oh," she said, "everything has a time and place." And to all his questions, she gave no other answer.

As for the beautiful girl, while she was moaning in despair, hungry and thirsty in the depths of the dry well, an old shepherd happened to pass by. He heard a strange sound and, after looking all around, he finally went to the old well. As he leaned over, he saw there a beautiful girl almost at the point of death. "What are you doing there?" he asked, and without waiting for an answer he climbed down into the well and lifted her out. At once he saw that the girl had neither of her eyes. Feeling pity for her, he took her home and said to his wife, "Look. I have brought a nice girl to help you."

And the wife said, "Have you gone mad? What shall I do with a girl who has no eyes?"

"Wife, it's sinful to talk like that," said the shepherd. "She is Allah's guest. And she's so hungry and thirsty and dusty and dirty. Please, my dear, get some water heated, and let's wash her a little and get the dirt off her face and hands. Even if she dies, let her be in comfort."

They heated some water and brought it to the girl, and they started washing her face and hair. When they poured the water over her head, *Cuş!* came the gold. They poured some more water, and *Cuş!* came more gold.

165

They were so surprised that their hearts almost burst at this strange sight. They bought clothes and food and all they needed with the money they got through washing her. They fed her and dressed her, and they kept her comfortable in a sunny corner of their cottage.

As time passed, she began to feel a little better, and as she laughed, pink roses bloomed on her cheeks. As she remembered the bad days and cried, pearls and corals began to pour from her eye sockets. And as they held her hand and took her out for walks, all the land on which she stepped became covered with green grass.

After several months had gone by, the girl laughed and said to the shepherd, "Please pick some roses from my cheeks and make a nice bouquet and take it to the padishah's palace and sell it, crying, 'A bouquet of roses for an eye! A bouquet of roses for an eye!'"

And he said, "All right." How could they say no to anything she asked? So he and his wife picked the roses from the girl's cheeks and made a beautiful bouquet, and the shepherd took the roses to the palace and began walking in front of the palace, crying, "A bouquet of roses for an eye! A bouquet of roses for an eye!"

The wicked aunt and her daughter heard this cry, and the aunt said, "Oh, Daughter, let's buy some of those roses and pretend that they grew on your cheeks, and give them to the prince. I have grown tired of his demand for roses."

"All right," said the daughter. So they gave one of the girl's eyes to the shepherd and got the bouquet of roses, and they put the roses in a vase of water. In the evening when the prince came, he saw the flowers, and he was greatly pleased. "How did you get these roses?" he asked.

And his wife answered, "I told you there was a time for everything. I laughed today, and they grew on my cheeks." The prince smelled the roses, and, oh, how happy he felt!

Meanwhile, the old man took that one eye home and he said, "Now stand still, my dear, and I'll put the eye in one of your eye sockets." And he gave it a very gentle rub, and he prayed and blew on it. *Tup!* It fitted into its place, and the girl began to see as clear as a mirror.

A few weeks later they made another bouquet of roses, and the old man took them again to the palace. When he began to sell this bouquet, the wicked aunt and her daughter knew that roses in this season could only have come from the cheeks of the beautiful girl, and that she must not be dead, after all. But the aunt said, "All right. Let's give her her eye and get the roses and never mind her. What do we care?"

The old man brought the second eye home, and, as he had done before, he put the eye into its socket, and rubbed it very gently, and prayed and blew on it. *Put!* It fitted into its place, and the girl began to see as clear as a mirror.

166

Now, the prince knew that he had been given the wrong girl on his wedding day. And after he had seen the second bouquet of pink roses, he began to suspect that his real bride must not be far away. He was determined to find the girl, and he went about the matter very cleverly. Calling his grooms, he said, "Give a horse from my stables to every household in the land, and tell the householder that you will be back to get the horse at the end of the month." So they began to take a horse to every household.

When the beautiful girl heard about this, she urged the shepherd to ask for a horse, too, even if a groom did not come to bring him one. And the old man said, "Why? Do you want trouble on your head?"

But the girl said, "I love horses, Father. Please get me a horse. I want to ride on it."

So the shepherd went to the prince's stables and told the grooms, "I have a daughter, and she would like very much to have one of the horses. Can you please leave a horse with us?" And the grooms brought him the very last horse in the stables, a horse as thin as a needle, and they tied the horse in the shepherd's stable.

Every day from that time on, the girl took very good care of the horse. She fed it and she brushed it, and as she walked in front of the horse the horse ate the fresh green grass that grew under her feet. They came to love each other, and he was so well taken care of that nobody else could handle him except the girl.

When the month was over and the horses were to be collected and taken back, all the other horses were returned unchanged to the grooms. But this horse was different. When the grooms came to take him out of the shepherd's stable, he would not let them get near him. He just reared and bolted. He had become used to having only the girl around him. So the grooms went back and reported the matter to the prince. "Sire," they said, "an old man came and took a horse, the poorest one in your stables. But when we went to take it back, we could not get near the horse. He's so well fed, and, oh, he fairly prances the skies! We cannot bring him back."

So the prince said, "Well, let me try it." And he came and tried *his* hand with the horse, but he fared not one bit better than the others. The horse reared and bolted, and neighed and neighed and refused to let anyone near him. The prince asked the old man, "Have you fed this horse so well that he refuses to return to my stables?"

"Oh, no," said the shepherd. "I have a daughter, and she has fed him."

The prince said, "Well, if she is the only one who can take him out of your stable, let her come and do so, or you will have to buy the horse."

"But, sire," replied the old man, "we have no need of a horse. I have no use for it myself, and I have no one besides my daughter to ride it."

"All right, then," said the prince, "call the girl and have her lead the horse out of the stable."

When the girl came and saw them all there, she began to laugh. As she laughed, pink roses bloomed on her cheeks. And as she came nearer the horse, grass grew under her feet. When the horse saw her, he whinnied and neighed, and pranced about. She held the horse by the reins and led him out of the stable, and all the while the green grass was growing under her feet.

As the prince saw these things, he said, "Thanks be to Allah, I have found my bride." He sent the horse back with the grooms, and then he went inside the cottage and talked with the old man. "Please, sir, in the name of the Prophet and by the will of Allah, I want to marry your daughter."

And the shepherd said, "All right. If you want to marry her, let her be yours." They got the girl ready, and they held a simple wedding, and afterward the prince took the girl to the palace.

As soon as the prince had arrived at the palace, he sent for the aunt and said to her, "The tortures you have made this girl suffer you will be punished for. You will go back to your own country. Tell me. How do you want to go? Do you want to go on a horse or on a sharp saber?"

And the aunt said, "What should I want with a sharp saber? Keep it to use on the neck of your sweetheart. We shall take horses."

When they had made their choice, the prince had them tied to the tails of two horses, and the grooms whipped the horses. The horses rose up in the air and began to run. They ran so fast and dragged the woman and her daughter on the ground so roughly that piece by piece they fell apart, and every piece of their bodies was left at the foot of a different mountain.

As for the prince and the beautiful girl, they had a splendid wedding, far grander than the first, that lasted for forty days and forty nights, and they lived in happiness and joy thereafter. May we all have a share of their good fortune!

The Defendant Who Won through Discretion

There were once a rich man and a poor man who lived in the same village. The poor man was always in need of money, and one day he was so desperate that he went to the rich man and asked, "Would you please lend me some money?"

"How much do you want?"

"I need one thousand liras."

"All right," the rich man said. "I shall lend you one thousand liras, but if you do not repay the loan on the day that it is due, I shall have to cut one kilo of flesh from your body."

Agreeing to this proposal, the poor man took the money and left. But when the day came for the debt to be paid, the poor fellow had not a single lira in his pocket. When he had not come to pay his debt, the rich man decided to take him before a *kadı* and lodge a complaint against him. He found the poor man, and together they went on a journey to the nearest town to see the *kadı*.

Before reaching the town, they came to another village. In that village lived a *hacı* whom the rich man knew. The poor man waited in the courtyard while the rich man entered the *hacı's* house. The poor man decided, "While he is inside talking with his friend, I shall run away." And so he did. But in his haste to leave the courtyard, he collided with the *hacı's* pregnant wife and knocked her down. As a result of that collision, the *hacı's* wife had a miscarriage.

The *hacı* said to the poor man, "You ran into my wife and caused her to have a miscarriage. You have killed our only child. I am going to take my case to the *kadı*."

The *hacı* joined the rich man and the poor man, and all three set out on their journey. It was Friday when they finally reached the town, and all the men were inside the mosque for the noon prayer service. The poor man thought, "I'll just leave these others and go into the mosque. In all that crowd, how could they find me?"

He slipped into the mosque and joined in the prayer service. As he was leaving the mosque with the crowd, he decided to hide inside the minaret. He climbed the winding staircase inside the minaret until he reached the balcony from which the *ezan* was chanted. As he stood on the balcony and thought of his fate, he prayed, "O Allah, you have given me nothing but years of poverty, and now you have given me these big problems. I cannot endure my life any longer! There is only one thing I can do to end my suffering, and that is to throw myself from this balcony to the ground below. O Allah, have mercy on my soul!" And he jumped from the balcony.

But instead of striking the ground, he landed right on top of an old man who was seated at the base of the minaret enjoying the shade. The old man was killed instantly by the crushing blow. When the old man's son reached the scene, he shouted, "You fell upon my father and killed him! I am going to lodge a complaint against you with our *kadı*."

Hearing the shouting, the rich man and the *hacı* found the poor man, and they all went with the son of the dead man to the courtyard of the *kadı*. The rich man said, "You are the cause of all these troubles. Go in and see if the *kadı* is at home."

The poor man did not know the ways of town life, and he did not understand that he should knock before he entered the *kadı's* house. He simply

169

opened the door and walked right in. There indeed was the *kadı* having intimate relations with a woman! Too late, the poor man realized that he had invaded the *kadı's* privacy, and he went outside immediately and closed the door. Still, he kept his hand on the doorknob to prevent anyone else from entering.

"Is the *kadı* in there?" asked the *hacı*.

"Yes, the *kadı* is there, but he is praying with a lady. When they have finished their prayer service, we can go in."

In a short while, the lady left the *kadı's* house, and the group waiting in the courtyard entered. "Please come in and sit down," the *kadı* said. "What is your problem?"

The rich man was the first to make his complaint. "*Kadı* Effendi, I let this fellow borrow one thousand liras. We agreed that if he did not repay me that amount of money at the scheduled time, I was to cut a kilo of flesh from his body. He accepted these terms, but he has never paid me back."

"Very well, then," the *kadı* said. "He did not meet the requirements, and now you want to cut a kilo of flesh from his body. Is that correct?"

"Yes," the rich man replied.

The *kadı* handed him a large, sharp knife and said, "Go ahead and cut a kilo of flesh from this man's body now. If, however, the flesh that you cut off is one gram more or one gram less than one kilo, I shall cut two kilos from your body."

"*Aman!*" the rich man said to himself. "If I should cut even one gram more or one gram less than a kilo from this fellow's body, I would lose two kilos from my own body." To the *kadı* he said, "I am withdrawing my legal action. I do not have any complaint against this man. I want neither his money nor his flesh."

The *kadı* said, "All right, then. Just leave five hundred liras here for court expenses." The rich man's case was closed in this way.

Then it was the *hacı's* turn to make his complaint. He said, "Those two were my guests, and the poor man tried to run away. As he fled, he collided with my pregnant wife. She was knocked down upon the ground, and the shock caused her to lose our first baby. My sorrow is great over the loss of our only child."

"How long had your wife been pregnant with this child?"

"Six months."

"Are you saying that this man owes you a child six months old?"

"Yes," said the *hacı*.

"Here, then, is a possible solution," said the *kadı*. "We can give your wife to this man for six months. She will live with him during that time. She will almost surely become pregnant, and you will be given the child."

As the *kadı* was explaining this solution, the *hacı* said to himself, "*Aman, aman,* Allah! How can I give my wife to a stranger?" But to the *kadı* he said, "I

am withdrawing my case." He paid five hundred liras for court costs and left.

The last plaintiff was the man whose father had been crushed at the base of the minaret. He said, "*Kadı* Effendi, this man killed my father."

The *kadı* asked, "Just how did he kill him?"

"My father was sitting in the shade of the minaret; he was leaning back against the minaret wall. This fellow jumped from the balcony of the minaret and landed right exactly on top of my father, killing him instantly. Now I want to kill this fellow!"

"All right," said the *kadı*. "You may go ahead and kill him. We shall have him sit precisely where your father was sitting. Then you will go up to the balcony of the minaret and jump from there. If you land on top of the defendant, you will undoubtedly kill him."

The son said, "*Aman!* How can I jump from the balcony of a minaret?"

The *kadı* said, "Well, I do not know anything about that."

"I have decided to withdraw my complaint," the son said. "My father was very old anyway, and it is better that he did not suffer much pain before he died. Besides that, I will inherit all of his wealth." Saying this, he placed five hundred liras on the table and left.

Now that all of the plaintiffs had gone, the *kadı* said to the poor man, "Son, you know all about that prayer situation. You told them that I was inside praying with a woman and that I could not be disturbed at that time.

171

You knew very well that we were not praying, but you were willing to help me. It is for that reason that I have been willing to help you. If you had told them the truth about my business with that woman, I would have punished you, but you kept my secret well. A person who keeps such a secret to himself deserves to be rewarded. Take the money which I have collected from your accusers and spend it as you wish."

I have since then heard that this poor man is back again in his own village living happily with his wife and his children. When you see them, please give them my greetings.

The Frog Wife

Once there was and twice there wasn't, when jinns played *cirit* in the old *hamam*—well, in those times, there was a man who had three sons. When they had grown into young men, the two older sons were married, but the youngest son remained single. This so annoyed the father that he said to his youngest son, "If you do not choose a girl to marry, I shall get you a frog for your bride." The very next day, the father mounted his horse, rode to the bank of the Sakarya River, and there caught a frog to be the wife of his youngest son.

That evening while the bride awaited him in the nuptial chamber, the young man thought to himself, "What can I ever do with a *frog* as my wife? Perhaps I should just release it into the courtyard." Before he entered the room, however, he looked inside through the keyhole, and to his amazement he saw there the most beautiful girl he had ever seen—as beautiful as the fourteenth of the moon. As he entered the room, therefore, he decided that he would really marry this frog girl, and a regular wedding was arranged, with the bride in her frog form and the groom knowing all the time how beautiful she really was.

Three or five days after the wedding, the boy's father invited him and his frog wife to come to his home for dinner. Because her husband wished it, the frog wife appeared at the father's house in her human form, as beautiful as hyacinths and angels. And the father, eaten by envy, could not get enough of looking at her.

Following the meal, the bride went to the women's quarters in her frog form, and the father and the son sat to talk. After speaking of this and that, the father said to the boy, "My son, you must bring me a fresh cucumber, or I shall kill you with a knife and take your beautiful bride as my own."

The boy returned to his home worrying about this demand put upon him by his father. His wife said to him, "My bey, what are you thinking about so seriously?"

"My father has demanded that I bring to him a fresh cucumber. If I don't do so, he says that he will kill me and take you as his wife. How can I ever find a fresh cucumber at this time of the year?"

She said to him, "My dear, there is a way to meet his demand. Go to the bank of the Sakarya River and shout, 'Küçükatma! Küçükatma!' When my sisters appear, tell them that you want a fresh cucumber, and they will find one for you."

Following his wife's directions, the young man went to the bank of the Sakarya River and shouted, "Küçükatma! Küçükatma!" Then when the sisters appeared, he said, "My father wants a fresh cucumber. Please bring me one." Almost immediately the cucumber was produced, and the young man delivered this to his father.

Not long after that, the older of his brothers sent him an invitation: "Bring your wife and come to our house for dinner." Taking his wife in her frog form, the young man went to his older brother's house. While they were eating dinner, the father arrived, and they all ate together.

After the frog wife had gone to the women's quarters, the father said to the youngest son, "My late father, who is now in the other world, wore a special ring on his finger. I want you to get that ring for me. If you fail to do so, I shall have you executed and take your bride as my wife."

When they reached their own home late that evening, the frog wife said, "My bey, what is troubling you that you look so sad?"

"Well, my father has demanded that I bring him a certain ring from the hand of *his* father, but his father is dead and in the next world. How can I get the ring? But if I do not get it, he says that he will execute me and marry you himself."

"Is that what you are so worried about? That can be taken care of easily. Just go to the bank of the Sakarya River again and shout, 'Küçükatma! Küçükatma!' Tell my sisters that you need that ring from the hand of your grandfather, and they will help you to get it."

The husband went to the bank of the Sakarya River and once again he called, "Küçükatma! Küçükatma!" When he explained what he wanted, one of the sisters took him to the next world, where he began to look for his grandfather.

The first person he saw was an old woman who was sweeping out an oven with her breasts. "What are you doing, aunt?" he asked.

She said, "What but this should I be doing, son? When I was alive and well in the other world, I always used to leave my oven filled with ashes. I left it dirty. Now here in this world the demons compel me to clean ovens in this way."

The next person he encountered was a man building a bridge. "What are you doing, uncle?" asked the boy.

"What should I be doing, son? When I was alive and well in the other

174

world, I always wanted to build a bridge but never accomplished that task. Now the demons make me build bridges continuously in this world."

Leaving the bridge builder to do his work, the youngest son continued to search for his grandfather. At last he saw him and called, "Grandfather! Grandfather!"

"Hey! What are you doing here in this world?"

"My father said that you wore a certain ring on your finger. He wants that ring. I came here to get it from you, if you will give it to me, in order to take it back to him."

"All right, son. He always *did* want this ring, and he always gets what he wants. Here. You may have it." Saying this, he removed the ring from his finger and gave it to his grandson.

The boy took the ring and returned with it to the other world. Once there, he went immediately to his father and handed him the ring.

Three or five days after that, he and his frog wife were invited to dinner at the home of the younger of his two elder brothers. As usual, his father arrived at the dinner late, and they all ate together.

After the frog wife had gone to the women's quarters, the father said to his youngest son, "Within two days, I want you to bring to me a dwarf so small that he will stand no taller than my hand, but he must have a beard five handspans in length. If you cannot bring him to me in two days' time, I shall have you beheaded."

As the boy and his frog wife were returning late that evening from his brother's house, he was thinking hard, deeply worried about this task. "What are you worrying so much about, my bey?" asked his wife.

"My father has demanded that I bring to him within two days a dwarf only one handspan tall but having a beard five handspans in length. How could such a person ever be found? But if I cannot find him, I shall be beheaded."

"My dear, this task is not impossible. Go again to the bank of the Sakarya River and shout, 'Küçükatma! Küçükatma!' and ask one of my sisters to find such a dwarf for you."

Again the young man went to the riverbank and shouted, "Küçükatma! Küçükatma!" When his wife's sisters appeared, he said, "This time, my father has asked for a dwarf only one handspan tall but with a beard five handspans in length. If you can, will you please bring me such a dwarf?"

With scarcely a moment's delay, one of the sisters brought a dwarf of exactly the kind the boy's father had demanded, and she gave the dwarf to him. On his way home with the dwarf, the young man became so tired that he sat down to rest, but sitting led to lying, and he soon fell asleep. When he awoke, the dwarf was nowhere to be seen. "*Aman, aman*, Allah!" the young man exclaimed. "I have lost the dwarf! Now if my father wishes to behead me, that will be my fate. What can I do to prevent it?"

175

When he arrived home, his wife asked, "Well, did you get the dwarf?"

"Yes, I did, but I fell asleep on the way home and thus lost him."

"Have you looked *everywhere*? Shake out your jacket."

When he did as she directed, the dwarf fell out of the jacket to the floor. The youngest son then picked up the dwarf and took him to his father.

There the dwarf began talking. He said to the father, "You wanted a fresh cucumber, and it was brought to you. You wanted a ring from the hand of a dead man in the other world, and this was also brought to you. Then you demanded a dwarf whose height was only one handspan but whose beard was five handspans long. This, too, was found for you. Why have you committed such offenses against these people? May you petrify from your feet to your waist for your first offense!"

As soon as these words were spoken, the legs of the father turned to stone. The dwarf then spoke again: "For your second offense, may you petrify up to your neck!"

No sooner had he said this than the father's body began to stiffen until it was stone from his feet to his neck. The dwarf then said, "And for your third offense, may you petrify up to the top of your head and become one solid piece of rock so that man and beast can walk upon you!"

This is exactly what happened, and after that, the young man and his frog wife lived happily with no further troubles passing over their heads.

The Donkey That Climbed the Minaret

S irs, once long ago there was a man who was married, but he and his wife had no children. He prayed over and over, "O Allah! Please give us a child." But still no child came. At last, desperate, he begged, "O Allah! Please give us a child. If you do so, I shall mount him on a donkey and take him to the top of the minaret."

That day, the ears of heaven were open, and Allah answered his prayer. In due time, the wife bore a child, and the child gave them much joy. Still, there was that matter of the vow to Allah, and one night the man dreamed he heard Allah say, "You forgot about your promise. Fulfill it!"

The man got up the next morning and said to his wife, "My dear, dress our child nicely and get him ready to go out. I am going to buy a donkey. Then I shall be back to get the child."

After her husband had left, the wife got the boy ready. When the man came home with a donkey, he mounted the boy on its back. Then he took them to town. When he had led them to the door of the minaret, he said, "*Hödey!* It is time to climb the minaret."

The donkey just stood there, not answering, not moving. No matter how much the man insisted, the donkey would not climb the winding stairs of the minaret.

Well, the man had made a promise to Allah, and that promise he must keep. Somehow, he must get the child to the top of the minaret on the back of a donkey. Perhaps the *kadı* could suggest a way . . . So he went to the *kadı* and told him about the problem.

Finally he said, "I made that promise, and I must fulfill it. What can I do? Please give me some advice!"

The *kadı* thought for a while and then he said, "I cannot solve your problem. But there is a stream at the edge of this town, and on the bank of that stream there is a small house where a *Bektaşi* lives. Perhaps he can settle your problem."

The man got up and left. He and the child and the donkey went to the *Bektaşi*'s house. He noticed that the *Bektaşi* was drinking wine from a bottle and smoking a *çubuk*. The man said, "*Selâmünaleyküm.*"

"*Aleykümselâm,*" the *Bektaşi* answered.

"I have a problem. I vowed to Allah that if He granted us a child, I would mount the child on a donkey and take the donkey and the child to the top of the minaret. I have the child and the donkey, but I cannot make the donkey climb the minaret. Please settle my problem for me."

"All right. Here. Have a drink of this wine while I am thinking about your problem."

"No. I don't drink wine," the man answered.

"Why not?"

"Praise Allah, I am a Muslim."

"So be it. Do you smoke?'

"No. I don't smoke."

"Do you drink *rakı?*"

"No. I don't drink *rakı.*"

"Have you ever gone to bed with a woman other than your wife?"

"Allah forbid!"

"So you don't smoke, and you don't ever drink wine or *rakı*, and you don't sport about with women. What a fine donkey you are! Take that boy on your back and climb up the minaret, as you promised. And may both you and Allah Himself be satisfied that you have kept your vow."

So it was that a donkey climbed the minaret . . .

The Shoemaker and the Snake

Once there was a poor shoemaker. As he was walking along the street from his shop one day, he saw a man striking a snake, trying to kill it. The shoemaker said, "I shall give you five kuruş if you will let that snake go without further harm." The man accepted this offer, and the shoemaker gave him the five kuruş. Thus the shoemaker saved the life of the snake.

Many years later, the padishah ordered a pair of shoes made by this same shoemaker. He gave the measurements and the description for the elegant shoes he wanted, and he said to the shoemaker, "If you do not make my shoes exactly as I want them, I shall have you strangled by the snake which is my executioner."

Try as he would, the poor shoemaker could not satisfy the padishah. As a result, he was thrown into the pit with the executioner snake. When the snake saw the man, it refused to touch him, for this was the same snake that had been saved by the shoemaker many years earlier.

In this way, a kind deed was rewarded. Indeed, a kind deed is never forgotten.

Four Purchased Pieces of Advice

O nce there was and once there wasn't, when the creatures of Allah were many, and it was a sin to talk too much—well, in those times there was a poor laborer. Day come, day go, he worked, but there was little in his purse to show for his labors.

Now, the padishah had been watching this laborer, and one day he called to him and said, "Come and work for me for an hour or so."

"And what kind of work could a poor laborer like me do for a man as great as a padishah?" the man asked.

"Never mind," said the padishah. "Just come, and I shall show you." And the padishah took him down some winding stairs to the treasury. "You can use this shovel," he said. "What I want you to do is to separate the gold from the pearls. Put the gold on the left and the pearls on the right. When you have finished, come back up the stairs and I shall pay you for your work."

"Well, that doesn't seem too hard," said the laborer, and he began to shovel. "The gold on the left; the pearls on the right; the gold on the left; the pearls on the right," he chanted as the shovel went *fıç, fıç* on the floor. In three or five hours, he had separated the gold from the pearls, so he stood the shovel against the wall, and, *patur kitur, patur kitur,* he hurried up the stairs to find the padishah.

"Sir," he said, "I have finished the work. Come and see."

Indeed, the padishah came along down, and he was pleased with the laborer's work. "Well done, my man. You have earned a good wage," he said. "Dip the shovel into the pile of gold. You may have all the gold coins you can dip up with the shovel."

Fıç, fıç, fıç! The shovel scraped, but all that would stick to the shovel was four small gold coins. "*Aman!*" said the laborer. "Surely my work is worth more than those four coins!"

"All right," the padishah agreed. "Dip once again. Perhaps this time, you will dip more."

Fıç, fıç, fıç, fıç! The shovel scraped, but all that would stick to the shovel this time was four even smaller gold coins.

"You see," said the padishah, "this is a special shovel. No matter how many times you dip, you will never get more than four gold coins." As the disappointed laborer was tucking the little gold coins into his sash, the padishah said, "For one of those gold coins, I shall sell you a piece of advice. Will you buy it?"

"I'll buy it," said the laborer, and he handed the padishah one of the four coins.

"This is the advice I give you in exchange," said the padishah. "Never step into water unless you can clearly see the bottom."

"Is that all?" asked the laborer, even more disappointed with the advice than with the small coin it had cost.

"No. I can sell you another piece of advice for a second gold coin," answered the padishah.

"Very well. Here is the second coin." And the laborer handed him another gold coin.

"Here, then, is my advice," said the padishah. "Never be a guest in a household that has no male member."

"Is there no more than that?" asked the laborer as he watched the padishah put the coin into his purse.

"For a third gold coin, I can sell you another piece of advice," said the padishah.

The laborer thought and thought, fingering those last two gold coins. "All right," he said. "Here is the third gold coin. What is your third piece of advice?"

The padishah looked at him closely. "Heed this one well: When someone serves you or tries to accommodate you, let him give you as many services as he wishes. Never interrupt him by saying, 'That's enough, thank you.'"

"And that is all you can tell me?" asked the laborer. "That scarcely seems worth a gold coin."

"Perhaps you will like the fourth piece of advice better," said the padishah. "It will cost you your last gold coin."

"Here it is, then," said the laborer, handing the padishah the last of the four gold coins. "What is the piece of advice I have bought this time?"

"My fourth piece of advice is this: When someone asks you, 'What do you need?' do not state what you really need. Merely say, 'I need everything. Give me whatever you wish.' Now, for your labor today, you have earned four important pieces of advice. Put them in your pocket, and may your way be open," said the padishah.

The laborer left the palace with his purse empty and with his mind busy turning over those four pieces of advice to see what use he could make of them. On his way toward a nearby village, there was a swift-running river he had to cross. Peering into the river, he could see no sign of the bottom. He remembered the padishah's first piece of advice, and walked along the riverbank to find a safe place to cross the torrent. Just then, a horseman happened to pass by. "What is the matter with you?" asked the stranger. "Are you afraid to cross?"

"Not exactly," answered the laborer. "I am looking for the bridge. Surely there is a bridge somewhere across this torrent."

"Ah! You *are* afraid!" taunted the horseman. "Get on the back of my horse, then. It will carry us both across the river."

"No. I will not do it," the laborer said. "Come. Let us find a bridge."

But the horseman just laughed, and plunged into the torrent on his horse. He had not gone far when the current swept him off the horse's back, and he disappeared beneath the water. Relieved of his rider, the horse managed to swim back to the shore. When the laborer approached the drenched animal, he found that the horse had a sackful of gold in its saddlebag. The laborer mounted the horse, crossed the river safely on a bridge some distance upstream, and headed toward the village.

As he reached the edge of the village, the *bekçi* called, "Stranger, would you like to spend the night in our village?"

"Yes, I would."

"I know a certain woman who would be glad to give you food and shelter for the night," said the *bekçi*.

Remembering the padishah's second piece of advice, the laborer refused the offer, saying, "I cannot be a guest in a household that does not have a male member." Instead, he spent the night at a shepherd's cottage.

In the middle of the night, he was awakened by the sound of people fighting. He discovered the next morning that another man who had stayed as a guest of that woman had been robbed and thrown out into the street. The laborer was thankful once again that he had heeded the padishah's advice. "I paid dearly," he said to himself, "but I have certainly received my money's worth."

That morning, he left the village and journeyed onward, coming after a full day's travel to another village. In this village, he stayed as a guest at the home of an *ağa* known for his hospitality. To make his guest comfortable, the *ağa* ordered the servants to bring cushions and more cushions, and then more cushions and *still* more cushions, until the laborer was almost smothered by them. Remembering the padishah's third piece of advice, the guest said nothing at all about the mountain of cushions. Later, when the host had ordered food for his guest, as soon as the food was finished, the servants filled his plate again. The laborer ate and drank until the walls of his stomach were about to burst, but he never once said, "That's enough, thank you."

His visitor's willing acceptance of this overhospitality amazed the *ağa*. Finally, he said to himself, "I cannot force this man to say 'Enough!'" And he left the guest at peace throughout the night. In the morning, as the laborer was ready to leave, the host said, "Please come with me. I want to show you something." He and the laborer walked together through thirty-nine rooms of the house. When they reached the fortieth room, the laborer was astounded to find it almost *filled* with heads.

"*Aman!* What are all of these heads doing here?" he asked.

"I was going to add your head to the pile if you had refused any of my hospitality," said the *ağa.* "But you proved yourself the perfect guest. Go now with Allah, and may your way be open."

Mounting the horse, the laborer went on his way. He traveled and traveled and traveled, until finally he came to a large town. At the edge of the town, there was an elegant house with a pool and a beautiful garden. "Surely no harm should come to me from the owners of such a magnificent house," he thought, and—*Tak! Tak! Tak!*—he knocked at the door. He asked the servant who answered the door, "Is there a master in this house?"

"Certainly there is," said the servant. "This is the summer home of the padishah of India." And the servant took the visitor directly to the padishah.

The padishah of India was very hospitable to the laborer. After a fine meal and a comfortable night and a generous breakfast, the laborer went to his host to ask his permission to leave. "Son," said the padishah, "I shall grant whatever you wish. I have been honored by your visit. Though I have spent many days of each summer in this house, nobody else has come to me as my guest. Who sent you here?"

"No one," the laborer answered. "I came by choice."

"Aha!" said the padishah. "Then I shall give you anything you may need. Tell me, now. What do you need?"

Remembering his own padishah's fourth piece of advice, the laborer was

182

direct in his answer. "I need everything. Give me whatever you wish."

Hearing this, the padishah of India took the laborer to a room in which there were forty maidens, each one more beautiful than the next. Then he said, "Choose one of these lovely girls as your wife."

The laborer chose the one he considered as beautiful as the fourteenth of the moon, and the padishah of India gave them a splendid wedding lasting forty days and forty nights. Amid all this splendor, the laborer thought, "I owe my happiness and my wealth to those four pieces of advice I bought from my padishah. After all, how can the worth of good advice be measured by four gold coins?"

Let's leave him there with his bride and return to our own lives. And may we put such good advice in our own pockets!

The Stepdaughter and the Black Serpent

Once there was and once there wasn't, when Allah's creatures were many and it was a sin to talk too much—well, in those times there was a padishah who ruled over a great kingdom. But, alas, this ruler had no son.

"Someday," he thought, "I am going to die, and my kingdom will be broken up. The winds will sigh through my abandoned palace." He made vows, offered sacrifices, watched entire nights in prayer. But the heavens remained mute. Then one day the padishah could restrain himself no longer. "O Allah all-powerful, if indeed You exist, prove Your existence; give me a son, if it be only a serpent."

Now, this was the hour when the gates of heaven were open, and the wish reached the divine ear. In nine months, nine days, and nine hours the padishah's wife bore a son, a black serpent. Nurses were called to care for him, but he bit everyone who approached him, and he thus killed one after another all the nurses who tried to rear him. Terror reigned in the country because the padishah's servants sought unceasingly the wives and daughters of the peasants to serve as nurses of the monster.

But there was a poor young girl, beautiful and wise, who lived in a cottage with her stepmother. The stepmother hated her and had long wished to be rid of her. When the padishah's soldiers passed through her village, even though all the other women of the village had hidden in the forest, the stepmother opened her door and pointed out her stepdaughter. "Come, my girl," she said. "It is an honor to serve as nurse to the prince. Go, now, and follow the soldiers."

The poor girl left without a word, but she knew that the road she would walk led straight to death. As they went, they passed by a small graveyard. "Oh, soldiers," begged the girl, "we are passing by the cemetery where my mother is buried, at the foot of those tall cypress trees. Please let me kneel at her grave."

The soldiers stopped, and the young girl threw herself down on her mother's grave. "Oh, Mother, I have come to you," she cried. "In whom else can I confide my grief? Do you hear me, Mother? Do you hear me? My stepmother is sending me as nurse to the serpent prince!"

And her mother answered her from the depths of the earth: "Oh, my daughter, do not fear the black serpent. As soon as you arrive at the palace, ask for a golden box, held by two handles, and having the cover pierced by seven holes. Through these seven holes pour the milk of seven cows and present it to the black serpent. He will come and plunge himself into the creamy milk. Immediately close the lid and put the box into a diamond cradle. If other dangers threaten you, come again to me."

The young girl took comfort from her mother's words. She kissed the grave, and then she returned to the soldiers. They hastened to the palace, where the stepdaughter, following her mother's directions, tempted the black serpent with the milk. He entered the golden box and she placed it, tightly sealed, in a diamond cradle. The serpent prince grew and grew. When he was hungry, he found a new golden box full of milk, and, satisfied, slept again. Soon peace returned to the country, and the girl was taken back to her stepmother's cottage.

But the prince had grown large. In seven months he was the size of a seven-year-old. One day he said to his mother, who sat by him daily, "Mother, Mother, ask the padishah my father to find me teachers and books so that I may learn to read and write."

The padishah's wife went to find her husband. "My lord, our prince the black serpent wants to learn to read. He wishes teachers and books. What do you say?"

"My wife, there is no lack—Allah be praised!—of scholars in this kingdom." And the very next day a *hoca* of ample turban and white beard was summoned to the palace. But scarcely had the black serpent left the box when he threw himself upon the old man and killed him with a crushing bite. One after another, scholars came to teach the prince, and one after another they met the same fate. Soon there was not a scholar left in the court, and the palace soldiers were sent out in search of the most humble village teachers. They came at last to the cottage where the young girl lived out her hard life with her stepmother.

The stepmother opened the door at once. "Ah, don't you know you have found here what you have been seeking? She who nursed the serpent is surely able to teach him to read." And she thrust the young girl toward the soldiers.

"You are right," said an officer. "No one at the palace had thought of that. Come, my girl, and teach our prince to read."

Again, as they went, they passed by the small graveyard. "Oh, please, sirs," she begged. "May I stop for a moment to kneel at my mother's grave?"

The soldiers, pitying the young girl, stopped their march, and the girl ran and threw herself down on her mother's grave. "Oh, Mother," she cried, "I have come to you again. To whom else can I confide my grief? This time my stepmother has sent me to teach the serpent prince to read."

From beneath the earth came the mother's voice: "My dear daughter, the serpent prince will do you no harm. Cut from my tomb a branch of the rosebush and a branch of holly. If he will not obey, or if he does not read to suit you, strike him four times with the branch of the rosebush and once with the branch of holly. At the end of forty days, he will read. Go, my daughter, and if other dangers threaten you, come again to me."

The young girl did as her mother had directed. When the black serpent came out of his box, he recognized his nurse, but as he was raising his head, hissing, the stepdaughter struck him four times with the branch from the rosebush and once with the branch of holly. Then the serpent stopped before the open book and read on the first page the first letter of the alphabet: "Aaaaaa."

"Aaaaaa," heard the padishah, listening at the door.

"Aaaaaa," repeated his wife.

"Aaaaaa," repeated all their servants.

"Aaaaaa," repeated the soldiers of the guard.

"Aaaaaa," repeated the entire city. "Our prince is learning to read. Again this time we are saved."

The black serpent took good advantage of his lessons, and the young girl was again returned to her stepmother's cottage. "Back again, you worthless creature?" said the stepmother as her only greeting, and the same life began for the girl, full of abuse and misery.

Meanwhile, the serpent grew from day to day, and he sent a message to his father the padishah. "My father, I wish now to take a wife."

"My son, young girls are not lacking in my kingdom. Choose whomever you please."

And indeed this was done. There was brought to the young prince the first girl who pleased him. But in the morning they found her dead and drained of blood. Another met the same fate. In forty nights he caused forty brides to perish.

Again the guards of the palace went in quest, knocking at all the doors, ransacking all the villages. It was necessary, said the serpent prince, to have a bride each night. At last they arrived at the cottage where the young girl lived.

"Ah, my good sirs!" said the stepmother as soon as she saw the soldiers. "You know well that what you seek can be found here. She who has nursed and taught the black serpent is surely able to become his wife. Come, my girl; be on your way." And the woman was satisfied that at last she had rid herself of the young girl.

Again, as they went, they passed by the small graveyard. "Oh, please, sirs," she begged. "May I stop for a moment to kneel at my mother's tomb?" And the soldiers, knowing well the fate to which the girl was going, halted their march.

The young girl ran and threw herself down on her mother's grave. "My mother," she cried, "I am here again. This time they are taking me as a wife to the black serpent, whom I nursed and taught, and I shall die just as did the other girls whom he has killed all the other nights."

But from the depths of the tomb came her mother's voice: "My daughter, do not fear. This time you will become a queen. Before entering the chamber of the black serpent, put on, one after the other, forty hedgehog skins. When the serpent approaches you, he will prick himself on the quills. 'Remove those skins,' he will say. 'Oh, my prince, remove your own skin yourself,' you must answer. When he has cast his own skin, you shed one skin yourself. When he has cast his fortieth skin, order him to throw them all into the fire, and do the same with yours. Then you will become a queen."

The young girl kissed her mother's grave and left with the soldiers for the palace. The servants there wanted to dress her beautifully for her wedding with the serpent prince, but she refused all the jewels and all the ornaments. "I wish only," she said, "forty hedgehog skins."

When she had dressed, they led her to the bridal chamber. The black serpent threw himself upon her, but he stopped short. "Bride, take off that skin full of quills."

"Prince, take off your own skin and I shall remove mine."

And for each snakeskin which fell, the girl in her turn removed one hedgehog skin. Finally came the fortieth skin.

"Now gather up your skins and throw them into the fire," she said. The fire leaped up and a great light filled the room. The black serpent had been transformed into a young prince as handsome as the fourteenth of the moon. Then the girl threw into the flames the forty hedgehog skins and she became more beautiful than the moon itself.

When the young couple went out of the bridal chamber, the padishah nearly fainted with joy. And as he was very old, he at once gave his throne to his son and to his son's wife. The realm from that time on dwelt in peace.

Only the stepmother of the young queen did not get her just reward. In spite, she threw herself into the densest underbrush of the forest, and all that could be seen was a yellow serpent gliding among the dead leaves.

The Farmer and
the Padishah of Fairies

Once there was and twice there wasn't, long ago, when the flea was a porter and the rooster a barber—well, in those times there were a farmer and his wife who were forever at odds with one another. If the man asked his wife to come *this* way, she would always go the *other* way. Finally the farmer had had enough of his quarrelsome wife.

One day as he was plowing his fields, his wife brought him his lunch. Before she had come, he had covered a very deep dry well so that it could not be seen. "I shall stand here," he decided, "in the direction opposite from the well. I shall call her to come over *this* way. Since she always does exactly the opposite of what I ask, she will walk the other way instead and will thus fall into the well."

As his wife came across the field, her husband called, "Greetings, my dear! Walk *this* way."

But his wife, as determined as ever, tossed her head and started in the opposite direction. "Oh, oh!" he shouted. "Don't go *that* way, or you will fall into the old well!"

Still, she walked ahead, and of course she fell into the well. *Then* how she bellowed! As for the farmer, he just went on plowing.

But that evening his children were so hungry and noisy and quarrelsome that he decided to recover his wife from the well and let her deal with them. Shortly after sunup the next day, he took a long, stout rope and hurried to the old well. Carefully he lowered the rope into the well, and when he felt a strong tug at it, he began to pull it up. To his surprise, an old man with white hair and a white beard appeared at the end of the rope. Just as the farmer was about to lower the rope into the well again, the old man said, "Please let me out of here!"

"Who are you?" asked the farmer as he pulled the old man out.

"I am the padishah of fairies," replied the old man. "But—*aman, aman,* Allah!—I am weary!"

"Well, what have you been doing down there?" asked the farmer.

"This well was my dwelling place. I am actually much younger than I look. Until yesterday I did not have a single white hair. But yesterday a woman fell into my well, and she is such a *witch* of a woman that she caused my hair and my beard to turn white.

"In return for your kindness in saving me from her, I shall teach you something very useful. I shall tell you how to cure those who are sick and at the point of death. You will go about as a doctor, and you will pretend to pray over the patients, using magic incantations. I shall then appear and

cure the patient, and you can collect your fee and depart."

The farmer readily agreed to this plan, and, dressed as a doctor, he went about with his big book of magic cures. In this way, he treated several rich people successfully and earned a great amount of money as a result. He and his children lived comfortably and at peace with one another.

One day, however, as he was treating a particularly wealthy patient, the padishah of fairies appeared. "This is the last patient you will be allowed to treat. After this patient, I forbid you to treat any others."

Nevertheless, a few days later, the doctor was summoned to treat the son of the padishah of the land, and of course he went to the palace immediately. When he arrived there, the padishah of fairies was waiting for him at the bedside.

"Have you forgotten so quickly?" asked the padishah of fairies. "I warned you not to treat any more patients!"

"I came here not simply to treat the patient," said the farmer, "but to find you, since I knew that you would come. I must warn you that that witch of a woman has escaped from the well and is searching for you!"

"In that case," said the padishah of fairies, "you may not only *treat* patients, but *cure* them, as well. I am leaving!"

Indeed, he *did* leave, and as far as I know, that farmer is still prospering as a doctor.

Long life for him and a tale for us.

The Shepherd and His Secret

Once there was and twice there wasn't a poor shepherd who was watching his master's sheep when he heard a fire crackling. He hurried toward the sound. In the flames, he found a young snake, hissing, "Save me! Save me!"

Pitying the snake, the shepherd held out his staff. Quickly the snake slithered along it to the shepherd's shoulder. "Fear not," he said. "I shall not harm you. But take me to my father, the king of snakes. He will richly reward you for saving me."

"I need no reward," said the shepherd. "I did only what a human being should do. Besides, I must stay here and watch my master's sheep."

"The sheep are resting," said the snake. "You will be gone only a short while. Please carry me to my father."

The shepherd left his sheep in the care of his two huge sheep dogs and set off toward the forest with the snake. "My father will offer you gold and

silver and precious stones," said the snake. "Take none of these rewards, but ask instead to understand the language of birds and beasts. He will not want to give this to you, but you must ask for it until he does."

"I have no need to know the language of birds and beasts," the shepherd replied.

But, "Do as I say," insisted the snake. "You will find this gift valuable indeed."

The shepherd finally agreed to do as the young snake advised. At that moment, he found himself at the door of the snake king's home. The snakes guarding the door darted at him, but the young snake hissed a command, and the door was opened.

The snake king greeted his son with cries of joy. "We had thought you were lost forever!" he exclaimed.

At once, the snake son told the king of his rescue by the shepherd. "If it were not for this young man," he said, "I should never have returned to you."

The snake king turned his glittering eyes toward the shepherd. "What can I give you as a fitting reward?" he asked. "In my treasury, I have much gold. Will you have gold?"

"Sire, I wish only your good health," said the shepherd.

"But for yourself, will you take silver?" asked the king.

"No, sire. I ask only that you have good health," answered the shepherd.

"My health is for myself," said the king. "What, then, for *you?* Will you take precious stones as your reward?"

"No, thank you, sire," the shepherd said. "I seek no reward at all, unless . . ."

"Yes? Yes? What is it you would like?" asked the king.

"I am out all day in the fields with the sheep," said the shepherd, "and the days are long. I *would* like to understand the language of birds and beasts, so that my days would pass more quickly. If such a gift lies within your power, I should like that; otherwise, I seek no reward at all."

The snake king stared at him. Slowly he shook his head. "You are unwise to ask for such a thing," he said. "If you had that gift and told any living soul about it, you would immediately die. Come. Ask for something else."

The shepherd stood silent a moment. Then he said, "No, sire. If I cannot have that gift, I want nothing at all. May Allah be with you." And he turned to go.

"Wait!" called the snake king. "I will give it to you. But, I pray you, tell no one of it, or you will surely die. Open your mouth, for I must blow into it."

The shepherd opened his mouth, and, "*Hffff!*" the snake king blew into it. Then, "Now you must blow into *my* mouth," the king commanded. He opened his mouth wide.

"*Hffff!*" The shepherd blew into the king's mouth.

Twice more the blowing was repeated. "Now," said the snake king, "you will be able to understand the language of birds and beasts. But guard your secret well."

"I shall remember," said the shepherd, and, leaving the snake king's home, he returned to his master's sheep.

True enough, as he walked along, he could understand what the birds and the beasts were saying to each other.

Finding the sheep safe, he lay down to rest. He had barely closed his eyes when three crows alighted on a branch above him. "See that poor shepherd lying there," said one.

"Yes," said the second. "If he only knew it, he lies just a few feet away from a treasure which could make him rich."

"You are right," said the third, "for just beneath the spot where the black ram lies, there is a cave filled with silver and gold."

The shepherd could scarcely believe what he had heard. Nevertheless, he arose and, going where the black ram lay, he made a small pile of stones to mark the spot.

That evening when he took the sheep home, he said to his master, "Sire, there seems to be a hollow place beneath the pasture where the sheep fed today. I have marked the place. Could there be a cave beneath it?"

"There may well be," said his master. "Tomorrow we shall look and see."

The next day, the two removed the pile of stones and began to dig. As Allah would have it, there *was* a large cave beneath the pasture, containing more silver and gold than the master had ever seen. He and the shepherd carried the treasure home. "My son," said the master, who was above all an honorable man, "the treasure is rightfully yours, since you were the one who found the cave."

"But the land, my master, is yours," said the shepherd, "and all that is on it or in it belongs to you."

"Nonsense, my son," said the master. "Use the treasure to build yourself a house. Marry, have children, and enjoy a rich, full life." Thus the matter was decided.

In time, the shepherd found a wife who suited him, and they settled down to lead a prosperous life—so prosperous, in fact, that his wife became quite the largest lady in the country 'round. Since he loved her, the former shepherd resolved not to bother her about it. Still, she *was* very fat, in truth.

One day, the two went out to view their lands. The former shepherd rode his best stallion, while his wife rode a fine mare. As they trotted along, the mare fell somewhat behind. The former shepherd jogged along comfortably enough, not noticing. Suddenly, "Come along, why don't you?" said the stallion to the mare.

"It's all very well for *you* to talk!" answered the mare crossly. "*You're* only carrying the master, while I have to lug his wife, who weighs three times as much as *he* does!"

Hearing this, the former shepherd burst into laughter.

"Are you laughing at me?" his wife demanded.

193

"No, no, not at all!" exclaimed her husband, and he *tried* not to laugh any more, but, truly, what the mare had said was so funny that he had to laugh again.

"You *are* laughing at me!" his wife said angrily.

"Indeed *not,*" said her husband, and the prospect of a quarrel drove all thought of laughter from his head.

"Then what *were* you laughing at?" she demanded.

"I cannot tell you," said he. "Believe me, it was nothing important at all."

"Tell me!" she insisted.

"I cannot," he replied.

But it is more difficult to make a stubborn person listen to reason than it is to make a camel jump a ditch, and she insisted so strongly that he knew he must tell her *why* he could not tell her. "My wife," said he, "if I were to tell you my secret, I would die immediately."

Still, she heard only his refusal. "Then it *was* important!" she said triumphantly, and she nagged and nagged at him so to tell her that he decided he must tell her, after all. And at such a price . . . The snake king had been right in his warning.

"Before I tell you, I must have my coffin made," said he, and immediately he ordered the village carpenter to make him a coffin. Oh, how his wife fussed and fumed all the while he was overseeing the making of the coffin!

"Now I must wash myself and prepare for burial," he said sadly, and so he did. When he was ready, he climbed into the coffin. "My wife," he said, "after I have been buried, you will please take this new coffin to the mosque yard so that it can be used by others in our village. Meanwhile, I have need of it myself."

But while he was settling himself down in the coffin, he chanced to overhear the rooster talking to the sheep dog. "He may be rich, but he knows nothing about wives!" said the rooster.

"He's a good man," answered the dog, "and the best master I ever had." And he laid a stout stick in the coffin as a gift for the master he loved.

"Still, he's a fool," the rooster retorted. "Here I manage a hundred hens, with not a one getting the upper hand of me, and he cannot rule even one wife!"

"Why, the rooster is right!" thought the former shepherd. "And what is the use of knowing the language of birds and of beasts if I cannot profit from their wisdom?" Grasping the stick that the dog had given him, he stood up in the coffin.

At a glance, the wife read the message of the stick. "Oh, my husband," she said, "now I recall what I should have remembered before: 'Part with your head, but not with your secret.' In the name of Allah, let us be at peace."

Thus it was that the former shepherd kept both his comfortable life and the gift the snake king had given him. Would that we could *all* share in his good fortune!

194

Akıllı, Taşkafalı, and the Three Gifts

O nce there was and twice there wasn't, when Allah had many creatures, and it was a sin to talk too much—well, in those days there
was a wealthy widow who lived in a village with her two sons,
Akıllı and Taşkafalı. Time come, time go—at last the widow died. Akıllı and
Taşkafalı decided to live apart from one another on the family's land. They
therefore built a second house and a new barn not too far from the first one.

Now, the mother had had much livestock, including oxen and water
buffaloes, and these had to be divided fairly between the two sons. Akıllı, the
clever one, said, "Look here, Brother. There is no need to count, 'One for me,
one for you, one for me, one for you.' Let's just let the animals choose the
barn in which they wish to live."

"All right," said Taşkafalı, with scarcely wit enough to salt one dolma.

That day when the herds were brought in from the pasture, the animals
were turned loose to choose where they would live. Akıllı, that clever fellow,
had kept his mother's house and her old barns, and had given the new house
and barn to Taşkafalı. Of course, the cattle went to the barns where they had
always stayed—except for one newborn calf who lost its way and stumbled
into the new barn owned by Taşkafalı.

The next day, Taşkafalı said to his wife, "What can we do with one
small calf? I'll take it to market and sell it." Since the calf was too young to
walk far, Taşkafalı tied its two front legs together and its two hind legs together, hoisted it onto his shoulders, and began to walk toward the marketplace.

On his way, Taşkafalı came to a forest, and the trees were rustling and
whispering in the breeze. Taşkafalı, who was really rather stupid, thought he
heard a beech tree say to him, "I'll buy it! I'll buy it!"

Tying the calf to this tree, Taşkafalı said, "All right. How much will you
pay for my calf?"

Listening closely, he was sure that he heard, "Forty-five! Forty-five!"

"Well, forty-five liras is a fair price," said Taşkafalı. "I'll be back for the
money tomorrow." And leaving the calf with its new owner, Taşkafalı turned
away and went back home. He told his wife, "Well, I didn't even need to go
all the way to the market! I sold it for forty-five liras, and I'll go there tomorrow to get the money."

The following morning when he returned for the money, Taşkafalı saw

195

that the calf was gone, rope and all. "Where is my money?" he asked the beech tree, but the beech tree gave no answer. How could it? There was no wind blowing at all.

"See here!" said Taşkafalı. "I'll have either my calf or my forty-five liras!" When the beech tree just stood there, mute, Taşkafalı shouted, "You'll see what will happen to thieves like you!" And he went home to fetch a pickax.

Back he came, and, "I'll give you one more chance!" he said. "Either forty-five liras or my calf!" When the beech tree still gave no reply, Taşkafalı swung his pickax with full force against the earth around the roots of the tree.

Suddenly out of the hole the pickax had made, there came a huge *Arap*, with one lip in the sky and the other touching the ground. "What do you want?" the *Arap* asked.

"Either my money or my calf!" said Taşkafalı, too angry to be afraid.

"I know nothing about either your money or your calf," said the *Arap*. "Take this little *sofra* instead. Just say to it, 'Open, my table! Open, my table!'" Then the *Arap* disappeared.

On the way home, Taşkafalı felt hungry. Setting the table down on the ground, he said, "Open, my table! Open, my table!" To his amazement, the top of the table unfolded, and all kinds of good foods were spread out on it. He ate and he ate, until at last he was satisfied. Then, "Close, my table! Close, my table!" he said. At once, the rest of the foods vanished, and the table folded itself.

A few days later, Taşkafalı said to his wife, "Tomorrow will mark the fortieth day since my mother's death, and I want to have a Mevlüt service for her. We'll have a large feast after the service, and we'll invite everybody, even the padishah!" And so it was arranged.

After the service, the feast began. Taşkafalı said, "Open, my table! Open, my table!" and he and his wife carried all of the foods out to the guests. By opening and closing the *sofra* several times, he produced a great quantity of delicious foods.

Now, the padishah had been watching all this, and he marveled at the unusual little table. Wanting it for himself, he had a cabinetmaker build a table that looked exactly like the magic one. Several days later, one of the padishah's men stole Taşkafalı's magic table and left the new one in its place.

The next day, Taşkafalı and his wife wanted to eat. He said, "Open, my table! Open, my table!" But the table just sat there like any ordinary table. "Open, my table! Open, my table!" he said, again and again, but the table still sat there.

Taking the table and his pickax to the forest, Taşkafalı began digging dirt away from the beech tree's roots. Suddenly, there came that huge *Arap*, with one lip in the sky and the other touching the ground. "What do you want now?" asked the *Arap*.

"I want either my money or my calf!" said Taşkafalı.

196

"I don't know anything about either your money or your calf, but here is a special donkey for you," said the *Arap*. Then the *Arap* disappeared. Taşkafalı looked and, indeed, there was a donkey.

Taşkafalı mounted the donkey and began riding homeward on it. Along the way, there was a pit in the road, and Taşkafalı said "*Çüş!*" to the donkey. As he spoke, he heard something hit the ground, *putt*. Looking behind the donkey, he saw a shiny gold piece that the donkey had dropped. Dismounting, Taşkafalı picked up the gold piece and tucked it into his sash. Then, remounting, he rode straight home and into his stable and dismounted. "*Çüş! Çüş! Çüş! Çüş!*" he said, over and over and over. And over and over and over, the donkey dropped gold, until he had given a whole saddlebag full of gold coins. In this way, Taşkafalı and his wife gained enough to lead a rich, comfortable life.

One day, Taşkafalı said to himself, "The padishah rides on *his* donkey to the public bath. Why shouldn't I go on *my* donkey?" He rode to the *hamam* and hitched his gold-dropping donkey to a rail where other donkeys were tied. But when he was ready to pay his entrance fee to the bath, he realized that he had no money in his pocket. "One moment," he said to the bath attendant. "Let me go and get some money from my donkey."

In the meantime, the padishah had arrived at the *hamam*. The hitching rail was already crowded. To make room for his own donkey, the padishah moved Taşkafalı's donkey a little to one side and then said, "*Çüş!*" When the donkey heard this sound, it dropped a gold coin. Amazed to see this, the padishah hitched his own donkey to the rail and immediately mounted Taşkafalı's donkey and rode it straight to the palace.

Taşkafalı came to his donkey to get some money for his entrance fee. "*Çüş!*" he said. But no gold fell from the donkey. He said "*Çüş! Çüş! Çüş!*" but the donkey did not drop a single gold coin.

Returning on foot to his home, he got his pickax and went to the forest. Once more, he began to dig out the earth at the roots of the beech tree. Again, the *Arap* arose from the hole, that huge *Arap* with one lip in the sky and the other lip touching the ground. "What do you want *this* time?" he asked.

"I want either my money or my calf!" said Taşkafalı.

"I know nothing about either your money or your calf," said the *Arap*. "Take this pumpkin." Then he whispered, "Don't you *dare* to say, 'Open, my pumpkin! Open, my pumpkin!' And don't you *ever* dare to ask anything of me again!" *Hfff!* The *Arap* disappeared.

Taşkafalı took his pickax and the pumpkin and started home with them. Although he had been told not to open the pumpkin, he was curious, so he stopped halfway home and said, "Open, my pumpkin! Open, my pumpkin!" Immediately, two wooden hammers came forth from the pumpkin and began to beat him on the head, *Putt-a-kitt-a! Putt-a-kitt-a!* They beat him and beat him until he finally remembered to say, "Close, my pumpkin!

197

Close, my pumpkin!" The moment he had said this, the two mallets returned to the pumpkin, and—*Chunk!*—they went inside.

When Taşkafalı came home, he immediately whispered softly into his wife's ear, "Don't you *ever* dare to say, 'Open, my pumpkin! Open, my pumpkin!'" His wife heard him say this, but still she was curious. Perhaps this pumpkin was as wonderful as the magic table and the gold-dropping donkey . . . Finally, she said, "Open, my pumpkin! Open, my pumpkin!" As soon as the words were out of her mouth, those wooden hammers were out of the pumpkin, beating *Putt-a-kitt-a! Putt-a-kitt-a!* on her head. As Allah would have it, her husband was there, and he quickly said, "Close, my pumpkin! Close, my pumpkin!" At once—*Chunk!*—the mallets disappeared inside the pumpkin.

At last, by asking here and looking there, Taşkafalı learned that it was the padishah himself who now had the magic table and the gold-dropping donkey. He went to the padishah with that pumpkin and said, "You have *taken* both my magic table and my gold-dropping donkey, but I'm going to *give* you this pumpkin as a present. Be sure, though, never to say, 'Open, my pumpkin! Open, my pumpkin!'" he whispered very, very softly.

The padishah, knowing well the benefits of the magic table and the gold-dropping donkey, was sure that the pumpkin also had special powers. To find out, he said loudly, "Open, my pumpkin! Open, my pumpkin!" The wooden hammers came out immediately and, *Putt-a-kitt-a! Putt-a-kitt-a!* they began to beat the padishah on the head. The padishah shouted, "I'll give you back your magic table and your gold-dropping donkey if only you will stop these hammers!"

As soon as he was quite sure that the padishah meant to keep his promise, Taşkafalı said, "Close, my pumpkin! Close, my pumpkin!" and the mallets disappeared inside the pumpkin. Thus when he left the palace, Taşkafalı had all three of the gifts provided by the *Arap* in exchange for his calf: his magic table, his gold-dropping donkey, and that wonderful pumpkin—worth much more, indeed, than the cattle clever Akıllı had denied him through that trick about the barns.

Taşkafalı had all of his wishes fulfilled. Let's go up and sit in his seat!

199

The Woodcutter's Heroic Wife

O nce there was and once there wasn't, when the flea was a porter and the camel a barber, there was a padishah who was very, very quick tempered. Since his word was law in that region, all his subjects lived in fear of the padishah's anger.

Alas, irritated one day because one of his wives had displeased him, the padishah summoned every woman in the whole region to a certain bathhouse. They were to be shut up inside, and then the bathhouse was to be flooded. "I say that's what women deserve!" he shouted. "They *all* have long hair and short brains!"

The women were gathered, as the padishah had ordered, and the padishah rubbed his hands with satisfaction to hear them weeping. "Now, are they all inside?" he asked his grand vizier.

"All of them except one, my padishah," the grand vizier answered. "Mehmet the woodcutter refused to order his wife to be taken to the bathhouse."

"Bring that Mehmet the woodcutter to me at once," demanded the ruler. And Mehmet the woodcutter was very quickly delivered to the furious padishah.

"So you defied my order to send your wife to the bathhouse!" exclaimed the ruler. "I am the padishah, and you are my subject, a weak and lowly woodcutter. How dare you defy my order?"

"It is true that I refused to obey you, my padishah, but I have a sound reason for my refusal. Please listen to my story. Then, if you still insist, I shall not prevent your soldiers from going to my house for my wife.

"I have not always been a woodcutter. Earlier in my life, I had fought with many strong men and had never been defeated by any of them. One day as I was sitting outside the coffeehouse, I saw a horseman approaching at such great speed that he was raising a cloud of dust and smoke as he came. The rider was a handsome young man, and I liked him at first sight. He rode straight to the blacksmith shop and ordered the blacksmith to shoe his horse at once.

"'I shall shoe your horse,' said the blacksmith, 'as soon as I finish shoeing the horse of Mehmet *Ağa*, one of the finest fighters in our region.'

"'I care nothing about your Mehmet *Ağa*,' said the horseman. 'You will shoe my horse at once.' And he struck the blacksmith a mighty blow.

"I was watching all this, and I liked the young man's spirit. I happened

200

201

to own that blacksmith shop, and the blacksmith was my servant, so I shouted, 'Shoe his horse and let him go!'

"While his horse was being shod, the stranger went to a restaurant and ordered a meal. When his food was served on an ordinary plate, he said, 'I am not a child. Bring my food to me in large pans.'

"When he had finished eating, he refused to pay the bill the restaurant manager brought. Instead, he struck the manager a mighty blow. I happened to own that restaurant, too, and as I watched all this, I said to myself, 'What sort of fellow is this? Acting in such a way in this town, he will destroy my reputation as a fighter.'

"The young stranger then came to the coffeehouse where I was sitting and drank coffee. Again, instead of paying the bill for his coffee, he struck the coffeehouse manager a mighty blow. From there he went back to the blacksmith shop, where his horse had by then been shod. Mounting his horse, he rode away without any further word to anyone.

"After he had gone, every man in town came by to stare at me. Finally, one of them said, 'How could anyone as brave and strong and gallant as you are behave in this meek way in the presence of a young stranger? All the shops in the town belong to you, but you did nothing while your servants were struck. Why didn't you do something to defend your people and your reputation as a fighter?'

"Realizing that I had indeed made a mistake in the matter, I armed myself and mounted my horse and pursued the young man. When I had caught up with him, I called, 'Oh, young man, stop! You have ruined my reputation. Didn't you know that I was Mehmet *Ağa*?'

"Since the young man made no response to my question, I dealt him a tremendous blow with my mace. But the young man did not even look at me. When I raised my arm to strike again, the stranger grabbed my arm and pulled me from my horse. He then dismounted and jumped on top of me as I lay on the ground. 'Why did you chase me and then hit me with your mace?' he asked. 'Why?'

"'Because you came to our town, abused my people, and robbed me of my good name. I had to do something to recapture my reputation as a fighter and an *ağa*. Now, however, I realize that you are much stronger than I am, and so I beg your pardon. Please do not take my life.'

"'Very well. I shall not kill you, but in return for this you must follow me wherever I go, and you must obey my orders.'

"'All right. Since you have spared my life, I shall go wherever you say.'

"We rode a little, we rode far, and at last we came to the mouth of a huge cave into which a large stream flowed. Were we going into the cave? I dared not ask.

"'Mehmet *Ağa*,' said the stranger, 'you must remain right here. I once had six brothers. All six of my brothers were killed by the giant who lives in this cave, and I have now come to take my revenge against him. I shall enter this cave, and in about half an hour I shall shout. When you hear my first shout, you will know that I have started fighting. When you hear my second shout, you will know that I am about to win. And when you hear my third shout, you must also enter the cave, for by that time I shall have torn the giant to pieces. If you do *not* hear any shouts from me and you have to flee, ride on my horse instead of on your own. The saddlebags on my horse are filled with emeralds and rubies and diamonds that will provide enough for you for the rest of your life. But hear this: if you run away before I end my fight, I shall pursue you and bring you back, even if you should fly on the wings of a bird.'

"The young man entered the cave, and I listened closely. Then, one after another, I heard the shouts. At the third shout, I drew my sword and entered the cave. When I looked around inside, the stream was filled with blood, and bits of the giant floated in it. The giant had indeed been torn to pieces. We emerged from the cave and washed ourselves.

"Then the young man said, 'If you will come with me, I shall serve as your slave. I will sacrifice my life for you. If you do not wish to come with me, that is your choice. In that case, I shall give you one of the saddlebags filled with jewels.'

"How could I know what to say? On one hand, I feared that if I refused to come with him, he would beat me, perhaps destroy me. On the other hand, who could know where he might take me next—into what dangers? Still, there was certain to be adventure, wherever he went. So I said, 'Please, I do not want you to be my slave. Let me be your slave and go with you.'

"'All right, then. Come along!'

"This young man was a truly great warrior who could fight as many as fifty men like me at one time. We rode together for thirty or forty days, talking as we went along, and still I had not learned his name, but we were companions. One day he suggested that I be married in the next town we would come to, a town where there were people that he knew. I agreed to this, and after we had arrived in that town, he found a bride suitable for me, and a wedding was arranged. On the wedding night, I waited and waited in my room for the bride, but she did not come. The young stranger then came to me and asked, 'Has your bride come yet?'

"'No.'

"'Very well! I shall soon present your bride to you, but first close all the chimney openings and the windows and doors.' He then removed his mask and revealed—not a man, but a woman as beautiful as the full moon. 'I am to be your bride,' she said, 'and we shall be married. I shall be yours and you will be mine from this time onward.'

"My padishah, that young warrior whom I told you about is still my wife today. Surely you must realize now why I did not send her to the bathhouse with the other women. If you must take her, send soldiers to my home and let them try to do so, but I shall have no part in it."

The padishah sat in silence. No longer angry at Mehmet *Ağa* the wood-cutter or even at the wife who had displeased him, he said, "Well, not *all* women have long hair and short brains! Release those women from the bathhouse and send them along home. As for you, Mehmet *Ağa* the woodcutter, may your way be open. Go back to your wife with a clean heart, and live long."

Thus it was that the heroic wife of Mehmet *Ağa* the woodcutter saved the women of a whole region. May there continue to be such noble women in our land!

Good to the Good and Damnation to the Evil

One day in times long gone by, a padishah said to his grand vizier, "Go out and find me a poor man who will give me good advice every day and for this earn some money."

The grand vizier went out and found such a man. The man came to the padishah and said, "Yes, Your Majesty? You sent for me?"

"Well, now, my man, I want you to come to me three times every day, and each time you come, you are to repeat this piece of advice: 'Good to the good and damnation to the evil.' You will come once in the morning, once at noon, and once in the evening. For this service, I shall pay you three gold coins each day."

The next morning the man appeared in the presence of the padishah, standing there with his head tilted to one side and his hands clasped before him, and said, "Your Majesty, 'Good to the good and damnation to the evil.'" He received his pay of one golden lira and left. This went on three times daily for some time, and the man became quite wealthy, for he collected many golden liras on this job.

One day as he was about to go into the presence of the padishah, the man was stopped by the grand vizier. As they were talking, the grand vizier detected from the strong smell of the man's breath that he had been eating garlic. The grand vizier warned the man, "The padishah does not like the smell of either garlic or onions. If he learns that you have eaten one of these foods before appearing in his presence, he will have you beheaded."

"Your Honor, it just happened that there was some garlic in the salad I had today."

"If that is the case," said the grand vizier, "go into the padishah's presence with your face wrapped in a cloth, and do not stand close to him, lest he smell your breath."

The man wrapped his face in a length of cloth and then went before the padishah, greeting him respectfully. Then he repeated, "'Good to the good and damnation to the evil,'" after which he received his gold coin and went away.

After the man had gone, the grand vizier entered the padishah's presence and asked him, "Your Majesty, did you notice how that man looked when he came to you today?"

"Well, I noticed that his head and face were wrapped in cloth, and I thought that perhaps he was ill."

"He is not ill at all," said the grand vizier. "Do you know what he told me outside? He said, 'Our padishah's breath smells terrible. I have wrapped my face so that I will not smell it. It is, in fact, so bad that I would not come to visit him if I were not afraid of his great power.'"

"So that was what he said? Very well."

When the man appeared the next day, he had nothing wrapped about his face, for he had been careful not to eat any foods that were strong-smelling. As usual, he said, "Your Majesty, 'Good to the good and damnation to the evil.'" He received his reward and was leaving when the padishah stopped him.

"Wait a moment, my good man," said the padishah. He then handed the man a sealed envelope. "Take this letter to such and such a place, where you have a reward awaiting you. Take the wealth accumulated there for you, and then go your way, visiting me no more."

Quite unaware of what was going on, the man took the envelope, thanked the padishah, and left. As he was leaving, he met the grand vizier, who said to him, "What do you have in your hand?"

"Sir," said the man, "I have been told not to return. I am taking this letter to such and such a place, where I am to collect a reward that has been accumulating there for me. I shall collect it and depart."

"Give me that letter," said the grand vizier. "I shall go and draw the money for you."

After the man had handed him the letter, the grand vizier went to the place to which the padishah had directed the man to deliver it. The secretary of that place took the letter and examined it, and then he checked among the records. "I find no one by that name listed among our creditors," he said. In fact, the contents of the letter were quite different from what the grand vizier had supposed: the letter read simply, "The one who brings this letter is to be executed at once."

The secretary summoned the executioners, and one of them said to the grand vizier, "Bow your neck."

"Look here," he said. "I am the grand vizier. How can you do such a thing to me?"

The secretary showed him the letter. "Here is the padishah's *firman*, which says, 'The one who brings this letter is to be executed at once.' You will therefore be executed."

"Just a minute," said the grand vizier. "I am sure this message was intended for someone else. Let me ask the padishah."

"There is no need for that," they said. "We have the instructions in the padishah's *firman*." With no further delay, the grand vizier was executed.

The padishah knew nothing of all this. One day while he was out riding in his carriage, he saw on the street the man whom he had ordered executed. "I sent that man to such and such a place. Why did he not go there? Call him here!" When the man was brought into the padishah's presence, the padishah asked him, "Where did I send you with that letter the other day? Why did you not go there?"

The man said, "Your Majesty, I took the letter to go with it to the place you directed. But your grand vizier stopped me and told me to give the letter to him, saying that he wanted to get my accumulated wealth for me. I gave him the letter, and he went there."

The padishah sent word to that place, saying that he wanted to know what had become of his grand vizier. The answer came back that, according to his *firman*'s order, the bearer of the letter had been put to death. The padi-

206

shah then called the man to him and asked him, "Why was it that a few days ago you came into my presence with your head and face covered?"

"Your Majesty, on that day I had eaten some garlic in my food. Your grand vizier warned me that you disliked the smell of garlic and onions. I therefore wrapped my face so that you would not be offended by my breath."

The padishah said, "That is a very different explanation from the one given to me by my grand vizier. He reported that you said, 'The padishah has such foul breath that I am wrapping my face in order not to have to smell it.' Now I realize my wisdom in paying you those fees each day. Good will indeed find good, and the evil will indeed find damnation. From now on, you yourself will be my grand vizier. You are good, and you have found goodness. He was evil, and he has found damnation."

Thus it was that the man became the padishah's grand vizier. May we have a share both of his goodness and of his reward.

Cihanşah and Şemsi Bâni

O nce there was and once there wasn't, long ago, when the flea was a porter and the camel a barber—well, in those times Rüstem, the padishah of Georgia, had a son named Cihanşah. After Cihanşah had grown to manhood, he ordered his men to prepare a ship for a long voyage, and the ship was made ready.

Then he went to his padishah father. "My father," he said, "I want to travel around the entire world to see what is there. Please give me your blessing before I go."

"Oh, my son," said Rüstem Pasha, "do not leave this land of ours. One day, you will become padishah in my place, and I want you here with me."

But Cihanşah's heart was set on going, and he said as much to his padishah father. "Aman, aman, Allah!" his father exclaimed. Then, "If you must go, then go with Allah's blessing as well as mine, and may your way be open!"

Cihanşah went aboard ship with his crew and his squadron of soldiers, and the ship set sail. They went along and went along, visiting one country after another with no difficulties at all.

One day, however, when the ship was so far at sea that no land was in sight, a severe storm struck. The ship pitched and wallowed in the huge waves, and finally it sank, carrying all the crew and the soldiers to their deaths. Allah be praised, Cihanşah himself survived because he clung with all his strength to a stout board that had washed from the deck and was floating in the raging sea.

After being tossed on the sea for several days, Cihanşah finally sighted land, and gradually he came close enough so that he could swim ashore. Glad to have his feet on solid ground once more, he walked here and there in a land that he had never visited. In the distance, he heard the bells of a camel caravan. Closer and closer it came, until Cihanşah could call out to its leader, "Where are you going?"

"We are going to the city of Kaf, at the foot of Kabur Mountain," the leader answered.

"Will you take me with you?" Cihanşah asked. "I would be happy to work just to earn my bread and cheese."

"Yes. Come along." And they made him welcome.

After many days' travel, the camel caravan reached the city of Kaf. "This is the end of our journey," said the leader. "In a city this large, surely you can find some work to do."

Just then, a harsh-voiced man cried out, "Whoever works for us for one hour will receive a sword, a horse, and some gold liras!" Without money and in a strange land, Cihanşah decided to take this job, whatever it was. He hurried to the agent.

"I'll take that job," he said, "whatever it is. Where do I go?"

The agent led him to a mule caravan, and Cihanşah was hired. "Mount a mule and come with us," said the leader. And Cihanşah rode with them to a brush-covered area where they slaughtered a horse. After they had cleaned out the entrails of the horse, the leader said to Cihanşah, "This is your job. You are to get inside this carcass, and we shall sew it up again. Sleep inside the horse's belly for an hour and then tell us what you dreamed while you were sleeping. You will be paid after you have told us your dream."

Cihanşah crawled inside the belly of the horse, and the opening was sewed closed. As he listened, he could hear the mule caravan move on. After the caravan had left, Cihanşah heard the flapping of huge wings, and then he felt himself being carried through the air. In a short while, the carcass was set down, and the great *Anka* birds who had carried it began tearing at the horse's flesh with their strong beaks and their sharp claws. As soon as an opening had been made in the skin, Cihanşah slipped out and hurried to the shelter of a pile of rocks. From his hiding place, he watched the enormous *Anka* birds feast on the horse until nothing but the bones and the mane were left. Then they flew away.

Cihanşah came out then and looked around. He found himself on a rocky peak of Kabur Mountain, with the city of Kaf far, far below him. The men from his mule caravan gathered at the foot of the mountain and shouted up to Cihanşah, "If you will throw down to us some of the stones lying there on that peak, we shall tell you how to get down from there."

Cihanşah looked then at the stones, which sparkled with gems. He threw down several stones, but the caravan leader and his men just gathered

208

them up and carried them away without helping him at all.

Poor Cihanşah! He went this way; he went that way. But there seemed no safe way down from that peak. Finally he found a faint path that was a little less steep, and he decided to try it. Picking up a long horse bone to use as a walking stick, he began working his way down very slowly. When he had gone about halfway down to a small plateau, a pebble slipped beneath his walking stick, and he tumbled the rest of the rocky way down the precipice.

By the time he reached the bottom, he was covered with blood, and he ached in every bone. Seeing a fountain nearby, he dragged himself to the fountain and began to wash in its waters. Almost at once, his wounds were healed, and his bones no longer ached.

Refreshed, he stood up and began walking very slowly along a path that led from the fountain. After a short time, he came to a seven-story palace surrounded by a large garden filled with rosebushes and hundreds of flowers. He knocked—*Tak! Tak! Tak!*—at the palace door, but no one came. He tried the door and it was unlocked, so he entered and walked along the hall, opening door after door after door. Thirty-nine doors he opened, and he still saw no living creature at all.

Finally he opened the fortieth door, and there he found something which was indeed alive. But what a strange creature it was! It had a human head and the body of a bird. Yes, it was the padishah of birds, and his name was Murguşah.

Murguşah looked up as he heard the door open. "Oh, my son," he said to Cihanşah, "how did you get here? Did you come up out of the earth or drop from the sky? Or did one of my birds carry you here on his wings?"

"Oh, father, please do not ask me! My story is both long and strange," said Cihanşah. "Please, just send me back to my own country."

Murguşah answered, "I shall do as you ask. İnşallah, it will be possible for me to send you back to your own country, but only Allah knows how long it may take—one year, three years, five years. I have a great many birds which come here once a year. I put forth King Solomon's scepter, and when the birds see that, they come here, they eat, they drink, and then they go. I shall ask my birds if any of them knows your country. If there is one who does know it, I shall put you on his wings and send you back to your own country."

Unable to do anything else, Cihanşah had to accept these conditions. He therefore began to watch for the birds. After two or three months had passed, Murguşah said to Cihanşah, "My son, I am one hundred years old. I have a brother who is twice as old as I am, and I am going to visit him. While I am away, you may enter any room in my palace except this one. Never, under any circumstances, enter this room while I am gone." After saying this, Murguşah departed.

Curious about the palace, Cihanşah explored all of the rooms, all the way up to the seventh story. But, like the first thirty-nine rooms he had opened, he found no living creatures in any room in the entire palace. Finally, tempted beyond his strength to resist, he went to the door of the forbidden room. He had found Murguşah there. Perhaps he could find someone else.

Very, very slowly he opened the door of that room. But what was this? This time, he found a beautiful garden filled with multicolored flowers and great clumps of rosebushes and several fine stands of trees. In the center of the garden there was a large pool.

As Cihanşah sat to rest beneath a large plane tree in this beautiful garden, three pigeons flew in and alighted on a branch of the very tree under which he was resting. After a few minutes, two of the pigeons flew down to the edge of the pool, took off their feathered skins, and jumped into the pool. As they did so, they became beautiful girls.

The third pigeon, the youngest of them, remained perched in the tree. "I shall not go into the pool today," she said. "I smell a human being here."

Her older sisters said, "What silly talk! How could any human being get here? No son of man could reach this place. Come down, Şemsi Bâni!"

Hearing how her sisters mocked her, the youngest pigeon flew down, took off her feathered skin, and plunged into the pool. When Cihanşah saw the youngest sister become a girl as beautiful as the fourteenth of the moon, his heart burned with love for her, and he sank senseless beneath the tree.

It seems that these three girls were the daughters of the padishah of fairies. When they had finished bathing in the pool, they dressed again in their feathered skins and flew away as pigeons.

211

Not long after that, Murguşah returned from visiting his older brother. He looked here and there for Cihanşah but could find him nowhere. He called, "Cihanşah! Cihanşah! Where are you?" but there was no answer. At last he found the young prince in the forbidden room, still senseless. Murguşah lifted him from the ground and placed him on a couch.

When Cihanşah had come to his senses again, he told Murguşah what had happened. Then he said, "I have fallen in love with the youngest of those girls, and I want to marry her."

"Cihanşah, my son," the old man said, "those three pigeons come here only once a year. If you want this girl, you will have to wait for another year. You will then have to hide yourself well in the plane tree. After the three pigeons have landed on a branch of that tree to rest, two of them will fly down, take off their feathered skins, and jump into the pool. As they do so, they will become girls. The third pigeon, the youngest, will stay on the branch of the plane tree, saying, 'I shall not go into the pool today. I smell a human being here.'

"But the two older sisters will say, 'What silly talk! How could any human being get here? No son of man could reach this place. Come down, Şemsi Bâni!'

"Just as soon as the third one is in the pool, climb out of the plane tree and sit on the youngest girl's feathered skin. Be sure that you do not give that feathered skin back to Şemsi Bâni, no matter how much she begs you to do so. Do not ever let her have it again, or you will lose her. To be certain that she will not recover her feathered skin, you yourself should wear it under your own shirt at all times."

Cihanşah smiled to himself at such a thought. Surely Murguşah was jesting about the importance of that skin . . . To *wear* it would be nonsense for him. But he would never return it to his beautiful Şemsi Bâni.

He and Murguşah waited an entire year for the return of the pigeons. Then Murguşah said, "My son, the pigeons will come today. And may Allah grant you success!"

Cihanşah hid himself well in the plane tree. Soon afterwards, the three pigeons arrived and perched on a branch of that tree to rest. Then the two older ones flew down to the edge of the pool, removed their feathered skins, and jumped into the pool, becoming beautiful girls once more. The oldest called to the youngest, "Come down, Sister! Come down and join us in the pool!"

But the youngest pigeon still sat on the branch. "I shall not go into the pool today," she said. "I smell a human being here."

"What silly talk! How could any human being get here?" said the second sister. "No son of man could reach this place. Come down, Şemsi Bâni!"

So the youngest pigeon flew down to the edge of the pool. She removed her feathered skin and plunged into the pool, once more becoming a girl as beautiful as the fourteenth of the moon.

As soon as Şemsi Bâni was well away from the edge of the pool, Cihanşah left his hiding place in the tree, went to the pool, and sat on the feathered skin of the youngest girl. When the two older girls saw a human being in the garden, they quickly left the pool, put on their feathered skins, and flew away as pigeons. But since Cihanşah was sitting on the feathered skin of the youngest, she could not follow her sisters.

Murguşah entered the garden then. "I see that you have gained your sweetheart," he said to Cihanşah. "Remember, my son, the warning that I gave you about her feathered skin: wear it yourself at all times, or you will lose what you have gained. Now both of you must wait a year for the coming of my birds. When they arrive, surely one of them will be able to take you to your own country."

Meanwhile, what had become of Cihanşah's father? Rüstem Pasha had sought everywhere for his only son, but he was nowhere to be found. Nor did any of his squadron of soldiers return. Indeed, how could they? They had all perished in the storm. Still, Rüstem Pasha kept the small bird of hope alive in his breast. Daily, he stationed guards to watch for the coming of Cihanşah.

As for Cihanşah, the year of waiting passed quickly, with his beloved Şemsi Bâni and the company of Murguşah and the ever-changing beauties of the garden. Then came the day of the birds' return. After the birds had eaten and drunk their fill, Murguşah said to them, "Tell me. Which one of you knows where the land of this young man can be found? He is the prince of Georgia."

Among the group there was a very old bird, more than three hundred sixty years old. That old one said, "I know where that young man's country lies."

Murguşah said, "If you know where it is, then with the aid of Allah you will take this young man and his sweetheart there." The prince and his beloved thus rode on the old bird's broad back to Cihanşah's land, where they were left in the middle of a road not far from Rüstem Pasha's palace.

Several of the padishah's guards had rubbed their eyes, amazed, as Cihanşah and Şemsi Bâni stepped down from the back of the old bird. As soon as the bird had flown away, the guards rushed toward the young prince and his beloved and took them at once to the palace.

Rüstem Pasha wept with joy at the return of Cihanşah, and Cihanşah, too, wept as father and son embraced each other. Then, "Father," said Cihanşah, "this is my beloved, Şemsi Bâni. Please arrange a wedding for us, with festivities for all our people."

At once, Rüstem Pasha sent servants scurrying here and there, preparing a splendid wedding with a celebration that would last for forty days and forty nights. While these preparations were going on, Cihanşah ordered that a fine new palace be built. He said to the builders, "I have a precious something that must be buried deep inside a marble stone beneath the foundation of my palace. Cut into that marble stone a small, deep hole." As Cihanşah watched, the workmen prepared the hole. Then Cihanşah took from its safe place inside his shirt the feathered skin of Şemsi Bâni and stuffed that skin deep inside the hole. "Seal the hole now," he ordered, "so that none can ever take out that valuable something. It must never be removed." So the builders sealed the hole in the marble stone and then began to lay the foundations for Cihanşah's palace. By the time all of the wedding celebrations had been completed, the new palace was ready.

On the nuptial night, Şemsi Bâni asked to be allowed to enter the palace first, and Cihanşah, certain that his secret was safe, had the bride's attendants go with her to her new home. As soon as they had passed through the gates of the palace, Şemsi Bâni said, "Please wait here for me. I wish to go into the nuptial chamber to pray." And the attendants waited there.

As for Şemsi Bâni, she went here and there through the palace, sniffing for her feathered skin. Certainly it was hidden somewhere in the new palace! As a daughter of the padishah of fairies, she was able to find the place where her feathered skin had been buried. She struck her fist against the foundation stone and split the stone apart. Beneath it lay the marble stone. She broke open the marble stone, also, and recovered her feathered skin. As soon as she had put it on, she became a pigeon. She then flew to a piece of the marble stone and perched on it to wait for Cihanşah.

When Cihanşah entered the palace and found the attendants just inside the gates, his blood froze in his veins. Where, then, was Şemsi Bâni? And had she found her feathered skin, after all? Searching here and there, he found the smashed foundation stone. And close by, perched on a piece of the marble stone, was Şemsi Bâni, once again a pigeon.

"O Cihanşah, my beloved," said the pigeon, "you did not heed Murgu-şah's warning. Now if you want me, you must seek until you find me!" And she flew away.

Poor Cihanşah! As he watched his beloved Şemsi Bâni fly away, he was so grieved that he sank senseless to the floor. It was there that the padishah's servants found him the following morning. But where was the bride? They had searched the nuptial chamber, and she was not there.

Slowly, Cihanşah came to his senses, and at the sight of the broken marble stone he remembered only too clearly what had happened. "I must seek her! I must seek her!" he exclaimed. "My beloved has gone, and I cannot live in peace until I find her."

Immediately, he ordered another ship prepared. When it was ready, he and the crew went aboard, and just behind them came a squadron of soldiers. "We shall seek until we find Şemsi Bâni," he declared, and the ship set sail.

214

Again, they visited one country after another, this time looking for
Şemsi Bâni, but with no success at all. Again, a severe storm came upon
them, and the crew and the soldiers worked as one man to save the ship.
Still, the ship sank, and again everyone aboard except Cihanşah was drowned.
After many days of floating on a stout plank, Cihanşah was washed ashore,
to find himself in the same country where he had landed before. As he walked
away from the shore, he met the same camel caravan he had met before, and
again he joined it as it traveled to the mountains of Kaf.

When they had arrived at the city of Kaf, at the foot of Kabur Mountain,
he heard again that harsh-voiced man crying, "Whoever works for us for one
hour will receive a sword, a horse, and some gold liras!"

Cihanşah hurried to the agent. "I'll take that job," he said, "whatever it
is. Where do I go?"

The agent led him to that same mule caravan, and Cihanşah was hired.
"Mount a mule and come with us," said the leader. And Cihanşah rode with
them to a brush-covered area where they slaughtered a horse. After they had
cleaned out the entrails of the horse, the leader said to Cihanşah, "This is
your job. You are to get inside this carcass, and we shall sew it up again.
Sleep inside the horse's belly for an hour and then tell us what you dreamed
while you were sleeping. You will be paid after you have told us your dream."

Cihanşah crawled inside the belly of the horse, and the opening was
sewed closed. As he listened, he could hear the mule caravan move on.
Again, after the caravan had gone, Cihanşah heard the flapping of huge
wings, and then again he felt himself being carried through the air. In a short
while, the carcass was set down, and the great *Anka* birds who had carried
it began tearing at the horse's flesh with their strong beaks and their sharp
claws.

Again, as soon as an opening had been made in the skin, Cihanşah
slipped out and hurried to the shelter of that same pile of rocks. From his
hiding place, he watched the *Anka* birds feast on the horse until nothing
but the bones and the mane were left. Then they flew away.

When Cihanşah walked to the edge of the peak, again he saw those
same men from the mule caravan far, far below. Again they were shouting,
"If you will throw down to us some of the stones lying there on that peak,
we shall tell you how to get down from there!"

But this time, Cihanşah shouted back, "No, no!" He knew that they
were just lying to him, and he did not throw down a single stone. Instead, he
looked around until he had found another long horse bone to use as a walking stick, and he started picking his way down the precipice. At the same
spot where he had slipped before, he again lost his footing and tumbled
down the last half of the rocky peak to the small plateau below. Bleeding
and badly bruised, he dragged himself to the fountain of curative waters
and washed, and he was healed.

215

Again, he found the path that led from the fountain and followed that path until he came to the seven-story palace of the padishah of birds. He knocked—*Tak! Tak! Tak!*—at the palace door, and this time Murguşah came to answer the knock. "Ah, Cihanşah, you have come again! What has passed over your head since you and your beloved left my garden?"

After Cihanşah had told his story from first to last, Murguşah said, "*Aman, aman*, Allah! I tried to warn you, but you would not put my words in your pocket. You should have worn Şemsi Bâni's feathered skin yourself the whole time. My son, fairies are very strong creatures, far stronger than any man. They can break rocks; they can smash stone walls. Those three pigeons have not been here since you left, and they will never come here again. Your only hope now is to find the land of the padishah of fairies.

"When my birds return the next time, I shall ask them whether any one of them knows where the land of the padishah of fairies lies. If none of them knows, then perhaps the birds of my next-older brother will know. He is two hundred years old, and his birds are older than mine, and so they know much more than my birds do."

Cihanşah waited there a whole year with Murguşah, and then the birds returned. After the birds had eaten and drunk their fill, Murguşah said to them, "Tell me. Which one of you knows where the land of the padishah of fairies can be found?"

Not a single bird knew that place, so Murguşah ordered one of them to carry Cihanşah to the palace of Murguşah's next-older brother. They arrived there just as the last of the older brother's birds had flown away, so Cihanşah had to wait for still another year to pass.

At the end of that year, the older brother's birds returned. After the birds had eaten and drunk their fill, Murguşah's older brother said to them, "Tell me. Which one of you knows where the land of the padishah of fairies can be found?"

Not a single one of the birds knew. "Cihanşah," said the older brother, "we may still be able to help you. Murguşah and I have a brother who is older than either of us. He is three hundred years old. His birds are much older than mine and are therefore much wiser than mine. *İnşallah*, one of his birds will be able to find for you the land of the padishah of fairies." Turning to a large, strong bird, Murguşah's older brother said, "Carry Cihanşah to the palace of our oldest brother."

Cihanşah and the bird arrived at the palace of the oldest brother just as the last bird of that brother was flying away, so Cihanşah waited with the oldest of the brothers until still another year had passed. When that year had gone by, the birds of the oldest brother again returned. After the birds had eaten and drunk their fill, the oldest brother said to them, "Tell me. Which one of you knows where the land of the padishah of fairies can be found?"

A bird so extremely old that it had only three feathers left on its body

216

said, "I know that land. I tried to hatch some chicks there during three different springtimes, but the fairies gave my offspring no chance to survive. Each time, they stole my eggs just before they were ready to hatch. I can carry Cihanşah to the border of that land, but I cannot enter it. I shall leave him right on the border," the old bird said.

Meanwhile, what had become of Şemsi Bâni? In truth, she loved Cihanşah very much, and her heart ached to see him again. For that reason, as soon as she had returned to her father's kingdom, she ordered her soldiers to watch for strangers and to bring to her any that they captured. As soon as the old bird had left Cihanşah at the border of the land of the padishah of fairies, three of the soldiers saw him. Capturing him, they took him directly to Şemsi Bâni.

Of course, Şemsi Bâni recognized Cihanşah at once, and they embraced one another. Within a few days, a splendid wedding had been arranged, and the sweethearts were married. They lived together in the land of the padishah of fairies for some time, and then they decided to go to visit Cihanşah's father, for they had been away from Rüstem Pasha for several years. They were carried to Georgia once more on the back of a giant bird.

Now, it so happened that just at that very time, the enemies of Rüstem Pasha had declared war on him. These enemies had invaded the land and had dealt several serious losses to its army. When Cihanşah and Şemsi Bâni arrived, they saw at once what the situation was. Şemsi Bâni called her soldiers from the land of the padishah of fairies, and with their help the troops of Rüstem Pasha were able to drive off the invaders in total defeat.

Cihanşah and Şemsi Bâni lived very happily together after that time for several years, part of the time in her land and part in his. Then one day as they were leaving her country on the way to Georgia, they pitched their golden tent beside a fountain. While Cihanşah rested, Şemsi Bâni went to the fountain for some water. As she bent to dip the water, a jealous fairy monster arose from the fountain and attacked her. Although Cihanşah rushed to help her, he was too late to save her from the savage attack, and the monster killed her.

With his heart numb with grief, Cihanşah had a double tomb built beside the fountain for Şemsi Bâni and himself. He buried his beloved wife in that tomb, and inscribed this message on the portal of the tomb: "When I die, I, Cihanşah, will be buried here beside Şemsi Bâni." When the time came, he, too, was buried there.

I and many others have seen that tomb ourselves. And it is said that the account of Cihanşah and Şemsi Bâni was told by Şahmeran, padishah of snakes, to Camesap during those seven long years that Camesap spent in the otherworld. May it live long!

217

Camesap and Şahmeran

Once there was and once there wasn't a young hunter named Camesap. As Camesap was hunting near the shore of a lake one day, along came a mule caravan. "Where are you going?" Camesap called.

"Why are you asking such a question?" asked the Gypsy caravan leader.

"For no reason at all, effendi," answered Camesap. "I was just curious—that's all."

But the Gypsy mule drivers and others in the caravan discussed this matter among themselves. "What is his real intention?" asked one. "He may be planning to do something harmful to us."

"And what business is it of his, asking us where we are going?" said a second man. "Does he mean to report us to the padishah?"

"We can prevent him from harming us," said the leader. "We'll take him along with us." And he called to Camesap, "Hey, son, come along with us."

Still curious, Camesap joined the caravan, and the group moved on. But the Gypsy caravan leader had a plan for taking care of Camesap. "We'll throw that young hunter into the first dry well we can find," he told his men. And so indeed they did.

This well was so deep that Camesap fell for three days and three nights before he came to the bottom. And he landed with such a sound THUMP that he lay there for a whole day without moving.

When he finally opened his eyes, Camesap saw a light gleaming in one corner of the base of the well. He got up and walked slowly toward the light. As he came nearer, he saw Şahmeran, padishah of snakes, lying there on his golden throne.

"Why are you here?" asked Şahmeran. "And how did you get here?"

"As I was hunting," the young man answered, "I saw a Gypsy mule caravan passing by. When I asked where they were going, they seemed troubled by my question, but they invited me to come along with them. I joined them, but as soon as they came to this well, they threw me into it. It must be a very deep well, for it took me three days and three nights to reach the bottom. I lay there senseless for a whole day, and when I finally awoke, I saw a light over here, so I walked toward it. I am at your mercy, O padishah."

"My son, good fortune has sent you here to be my guest. Let us become friends. Remain with me, and eat and drink and enjoy yourself. And to entertain you, I shall tell you tales of wonder—such tales! What more could you possibly want?"

Camesap accepted Şahmeran's invitation and remained there with him for seven years. True, with whatever he wished to eat and drink and with a new tale of wonder every day, he had everything that a man could want. But still one day Şahmeran saw the young man weeping, with his eyes flowing like two fountains.

"Camesap, why are you weeping?" Şahmeran asked. "Has anything happened to upset you or hurt you?"

"No. Oh, no, Şahmeran! Nothing has happened. But just now I remembered my parents, and I long to see them again. That is why I was weeping."

"If you are lonely without your father and your mother," said Şahmeran, "I shall show you a secret passage out of the well so that you can return to them. My heart aches for you in your loneliness. But, my son, I ask you to promise me one thing: You must never tell anyone where you found me. That will be a secret between us forever."

"Ah, Şahmeran," said Camesap, "you have been both father and mother to me all these seven years. Nothing this side of heaven could cause me to betray your secret. I promise that with my whole heart."

Şahmeran then led Camesap along a corridor at the base of the well and up a winding path to the surface of the earth. "May Allah be with you, my son," he said. "Go now, but remember your promise." And he slipped away before Camesap could see that Şahmeran himself was weeping.

After one long look behind him at the well—that well in which he had lived for seven wonder-filled years—Camesap hurried homeward. There he and his parents were reunited, and great was the joy of all three. To every question asked about where he had spent those seven years, Camesap wove a tale that would satisfy his parents. But he never once spoke of Şahmeran.

Not long after Camesap had returned home, word began to spread that the padishah of that country had become very ill. Doctors were called from here and there, but none could find a remedy for the padishah's strange illness. At last, as the padishah lay grieving, despairing, a new doctor came from India. When he had examined the padishah, he said, "There is only one cure for this kind of illness. My padishah, if you wish to recover, you must drink broth made from the middle portion of the body of Şahmeran. Without this broth, you will die."

"A cure! A cure!" The people rejoiced. But there was still the problem of finding Şahmeran and of capturing him.

"How can anyone find this Şahmeran?" asked the padishah. "After all, he is the padishah of snakes, and who knows where he might be?"

"Ah," said the Indian doctor, "there must be someone in your vast kingdom who has seen Şahmeran and can tell you where he lives. You will know such a person by the skin on his back. No matter how long he lives, that skin will always be scaly."

Then, "Let every man from seven to seventy come tomorrow to the Sultan Ahmet *hamam*," said the padishah. "My soldiers will examine each one. *İnşallah*, they will find one who has scaly skin on his back, and that one will lead us to Şahmeran."

The following day, every man in the land came to the Sultan Ahmet bathhouse, and each one was examined closely for the sign the Indian doctor had described. But no matter how earnestly they searched, the soldiers were unable to find even one man with scaly skin on his back.

"Has *every* man come to be examined?" the grand vizier asked. After much questioning, one old man said that there was a young hunter that he had not seen that day at the *hamam*.

"His name is Camesap. He and his parents live on the mountainside. Perhaps they did not know about the padishah's order," said the old man.

At once, the grand vizier sent a messenger to fetch Camesap, and Camesap was taken into the *hamam* to be examined by the padishah's soldiers. True enough, the skin on the young hunter's back was scaly. "You know where Şahmeran lives!" said the soldiers. "You must tell us where that place is. Our padishah's life depends on it!"

"Şahmeran?" asked Camesap. "How should I know where Şahmeran lives? I hunt animals, not snakes. How should I know anything at all about Şahmeran?"

Still, that scaly skin was the sign they had been looking for, and it had been found on Camesap. So the young hunter was taken before the padishah. "You say you do not know Şahmeran," said the padishah, "but your scaly skin tells more truth than your tongue. If you do not tell us where Şahmeran can be found, you will die by hanging."

What was Camesap to do? The executioners were already setting up the gallows and oiling the rope. "But how can I break my promise to Şahmeran, who helped me and who then set my feet toward home? On the other hand, there are the executioners . . ." Turning to the padishah, Camesap said, "Wait! Do not send me to the gallows! I shall tell you where Şahmeran is to be found. And may Allah Himself forgive me for breaking my promise!" Then Camesap described the well that was the home of Şahmeran.

Ah, but those men who served the padishah were clever! Instead of descending into the well, they constructed a strong wooden box with a tight-fitting lid. They carried this box to the mouth of the well, opened the lid so that it could not be seen from the well, and carefully filled the box with fresh milk. Then they stood aside to watch.

As soon as Şahmeran smelled that milk, he rose to the surface of the well, plunged into the box, and began drinking the milk. At that moment, the padishah's men covered the box with the lid and fastened it tightly. Thus they captured Şahmeran. Then they took the captive to the padishah's palace.

Camesap stood by as the box was opened, his face wet with tears. When Şahmeran saw Camesap, he said, "What happened to the promise that you

221

made before you left me?"

At this reproach, Camesap wept afresh. "Please, Şahmeran, forgive me! I would never have told them if they had not made the gallows ready for me and oiled the rope. I *had* to tell them then."

"I understand, Camesap, and I do forgive you," said Şahmeran. "You really had no choice. But choose now to stay by me until the moment of my own death."

Thus Camesap remained by the box while the padishah's men left to order the kettles for the broths. As soon as they had gone, Şahmeran said, "My son, I shall now do one last favor for you. They will cut me open and then divide my body into three parts. The head part and the tail part are poisonous, but the middle part is not. They will boil the three parts of my body in three separate kettles of water, and they will give the broth to you and to the padishah. The first container of broth will be from my head, and the third container of broth will be from my tail. The second container will hold the broth from my middle part. They will give you the first container and order you to drink that broth, and then they will give the second container of broth to the grand vizier to test before they offer it to the padishah. You must switch the first and the second containers while the padishah is entering the room and the rest are watching him. If you should fail in this task, you will be poisoned, and I do not wish that fate for you, my son.

"There is one other thing that you must know: If you succeed in switching the two containers and thus drink the broth from my middle part, you will not only be safe from poisoning, but you will be able from that time onward to understand the language of plants. Each plant knows the illnesses that it can cure. With that knowledge, you yourself can provide the cure for the padishah's illness. As for the grand vizier, he will die immediately from the poison in the first container of broth, so that broth will not be offered to the padishah. He will still need a cure, and you will be able to provide that cure."

As Şahmeran finished speaking, the padishah's men came to get him. True enough, they cut him open and then separated his body into three parts. Each part was boiled in a separate kettle of water. When the broth was ready, it was poured very carefully, from the first kettle into the first container, from the second kettle into the second container . . . Just as the broth from the third kettle was to be poured, the padishah was brought into the room on a litter, and all except Camesap paid their respects to their ruler. Taking advantage of this moment, Camesap switched the first and the second containers. Then he bowed to the ailing padishah.

The padishah's men gave the first container of broth to Camesap. "Drink!" said one. And they all watched as Camesap drank the contents of that container. To their surprise, the young hunter seemed unchanged by the poisoned potion. Perhaps the poison was slow to act . . .

222

Then, picking up the second container, the grand vizier said, "My padishah, I shall test this potion before you drink it, just as I test every food that you eat." The grand vizier bowed to the padishah and then he took a small sip of the broth and set the container down again on the table. His hand had no sooner left the container when he fell dead at the padishah's feet.

"Where is that Indian doctor?" demanded the padishah. "He will pay with his life for the loss of my grand vizier!" And the gallows and the oiled rope, prepared for Camesap, were used instead for the doctor, who had clearly been wrong in his prescription—perhaps had even intended the death of the padishah himself.

Still, the padishah was ill, and who now would dare to suggest a cure for him? Suddenly the padishah turned to Camesap, still well despite the broth that the doctor had said would be poisoned. "Camesap," ordered the padishah, "I shall give you forty days in which to find a cure for my illness. Perhaps as a hunter you know things that are not known by the men of my court. Go forth and search, and may Allah attend you in your mission."

Camesap left the padishah's palace, his heart heavy with the task that he had been given. If not even the wisest doctors could find a cure, how was a poor hunter to find one?

But as he walked back toward his home on the mountainside, Camesap began to notice strange sounds, voices that he had never heard before. He stared about him, and then he knew what he was hearing. It was just as Şahmeran had promised: he could now understand the language of plants!

Days and days passed over his head, with Camesap listening here and there to what the plants were saying, each with its own voice telling what cures it could provide. At last, on the thirty-ninth day, Camesap found the plant he had been seeking. Digging it up carefully, roots and all, he carried it to his parents' home and prepared the potion that the plant had directed. Guarding it carefully, Camesap took it down, down the mountainside and straight to the padishah's palace.

"My padishah," he said, "İnşallah, this is the cure that we have all wanted for your illness. I shall test it first, so that you may know it is safe for you to take." And Camesap took a small sip of the potion. Since Camesap had not been poisoned by the potion, the padishah accepted the rest of the potion and drank it. In little more than an hour, he was feeling much better, and by the end of the fortieth day he was entirely well.

On the forty-first day, the padishah summoned Camesap to the palace. "Camesap," he said, "you have done what none of my wisest doctors could do. You have saved my life. Tell me. What do you wish as your reward? Do you wish to become my grand vizier?"

"Ah, no, my padishah," the young hunter answered. "I desire no such high post. I ask only to be allowed to return to my parents and to my simple life as a hunter. Know that I shall be willing to serve you if you should need

223

me. But what I have now is quite enough for me."

"Go, then," said the padishah, "and may your way be open."

Thus it was that Camesap returned to his home on the mountainside. I left him there and came here to tell you this tale.

Sheepskin Girl and the Promise

Once there was and once there wasn't, when I was rocking my father's cradle *tıngır mıngır*—well, in those times there were a wealthy, loving couple and their small daughter, Perihan.

Of a sudden, the beautiful wife became very ill. As she lay dying, she gave her husband her two gold bracelets. "Promise me this, my dear: You will seek and marry the woman whom these bracelets will fit."

How can a husband deny his beloved wife's last request? "My dear," he said, "*if* I ever marry again, it will be a woman sought and whom your bracelets will fit."

Within moments, she was dead. As for the bracelets, he laid them aside

224

in his grief. Years passed, and he refused to marry again, though his friends urged him to find another wife. Meanwhile, Perihan grew, and she was curious about her mother. One day, while trying on some of her mother's clothing, she found the bracelets. "See, Father!" she called. "These beautiful bracelets fit me *exactly*. Were they my mother's?"

Her father stared in horror and distress, remembering the promise he had made to his dying wife. And Perihan was speechless when her father told her of that promise. Then suddenly she smiled. "Don't worry, Father," she said. "You have not *sought* me. And of course the bracelets fit me. I am a young girl, barely fifteen, and my hands are small and slim. You can keep your promise if you let me seek for you a woman whose arms will fit the bracelets. Give me just forty days and forty nights, and we shall see . . ."

To disguise herself as a poor servant, Perihan made a sheepskin dress, long-sleeved and full-skirted, large enough to cover two of her loveliest dresses, one on top of the other. "I shall call myself Sheepskin Girl," Perihan told her father. Then, carrying a small packet containing an elegant pair of shoes, one of her mother's gold bracelets, a bit of bread and cheese, and a handful of gold liras, she kissed her father's hands and then set out on foot for the big town beyond the mountain.

Two days of walking, walking, walking brought her to the end of her journey and the last of her bread and cheese. *Tak! Tak! Tak!* She knocked at the door of the largest house she could find. To the servant who answered the knock, Perihan said, "I am Sheepskin Girl, all alone in the world. Is there work in this house that I can do to earn my bread and cheese?"

The rich widow who owned the house hurried to the door when she heard the girl's voice. "My dear," she said, "come in. We can surely find work for you. And you can sleep in the little room next to the stable. The cook will use your help in the kitchen."

Sheepskin Girl was taken to her room at once. Quickly she removed her sheepskin dress, took off both of her beautiful gowns, and put on her sheepskin dress again. She folded her gowns and put those and her elegant shoes and her mother's gold bracelet in the large wooden chest beside her bed. Then she went upstairs to the kitchen.

The others made fun of her sheepskin dress—except for the widow, whose love for Allah's creatures was warm. "Let her wear it, if she wishes," said the widow. And she, too, began to call her Sheepskin Girl. "Sheepskin Girl, do this!" "Sheepskin Girl, go there!" "Sheepskin Girl, fetch that ladle!" One servant after another ordered her about, but she worked so cheerfully and so well that they soon were glad of her coming.

Now, the widow's only child, a son, had not married, and his mother was eager to find him a bride. Soon after Sheepskin Girl arrived, all the women of the household were invited to a wedding party at the house of a wealthy bride-to-be. "It may be that one of the guests would be a suitable bride for

225

my son," said the widow. "We'll *all* go. There will be dancing and feasting. Come, Sheepskin Girl! You will enjoy the party. Let me give you a pretty dress to wear instead of that sheepskin. And you can help me seek a bride for Beyoğlu!"

But Sheepskin Girl refused. "What would a poor girl like me do at such a merrymaking? I'll stay here, and you can tell me all about it in the morning."

So the rest went off without her. As soon as they had turned the corner, Sheepskin Girl hurried to her room. Off came the sheepskin dress, and on went the plainer of her two gowns. With her hair brushed and her eyes shining, she went in her elegant shoes to the wedding party. And how they all marveled when she came in! Even the bride could not match her for beauty.

With eating and dancing and merrymaking, the evening passed quickly. Before the party was half over, everyone had been told that the beautiful girl was the daughter of a caravan owner from another country and that she was eager to know their customs. The hour grew late, and Sheepskin Girl left. But, "Promise me you'll come again tomorrow night," begged the bride-to-be. And Sheepskin Girl agreed to come.

She ran back quickly to her room, folded her dress and put it with the elegant shoes into the wooden chest, and slipped into bed before the rest came home. The next morning, all the talk was of the beautiful stranger. "Daughter of a caravan owner or not," said the widow, "she would make a fine bride for my son. *Do* come with us tonight, Sheepskin Girl, and tell me what you think of her as a wife for Beyoğlu!"

But again, Sheepskin Girl said, "What would a poor girl like me know of such matters? *You* go, and tell me all about it in the morning." Again, she would stay behind while the rest went to the house of the bride-to-be.

That afternoon, Sheepskin Girl heard the rich widow and Beyoğlu planning a way for Beyoğlu to see the beautiful stranger. The parents of the bride-to-be agreed to allow Beyoğlu to open a hole in the roof of the house so that he could watch the women at their merrymaking. That stranger might indeed please him as a bride.

After the rest of the women had left for the party, with Beyoğlu going there by another way, Sheepskin Girl hurried to her room. She dressed in her more beautiful gown, the *fışır-fışır* one, brushed her hair till it shone, slipped on her mother's gold bracelet and her elegant shoes, and went along to join the merrymaking.

The bride-to-be and her guests welcomed the stranger with joy. As for Beyoğlu, watching through the opening in the roof, he fell in love with the beautiful stranger at first glance. And his mother, the rich widow, *knew* this was the right bride for her son.

After they had eaten and several of the guests had danced, the bride-to-be begged the beautiful stranger to show them one of the dances from her own land. "I might dance a few steps," agreed Sheepskin Girl, and then—

how she danced! She whirled and snapped her fingers with such grace that Beyoğlu, watching through the hole in the roof, dropped his gold ring at her feet. Swooping quick as thought, she scooped up the ring and tucked it into her blouse, missing not a single step.

Though they urged her, she would not dance again. Instead, she said, "Tomorrow morning very early my father's caravan will be moving on, and I have promised to go to him earlier this evening to make ready to leave. But I have a game we could play. Here is my gold bracelet. It will belong to the one whose wrist it fits."

Eagerly, one after another, they tried the bracelet, beginning with the bride-to-be, but none of them could get it over her hand. Sheepskin Girl looked around, disappointed. "Can *no* one wear it, then?" she exclaimed. "Has *everyone* tried it?"

"My dear," said the rich widow, "*I* haven't tried it. Shall I?" And Beyoğlu's mother reached for the gold bracelet. *Slsh!* It slipped over her hand and nestled on her wrist as if it had been made for her alone.

"It fits!" they all cried and crowded around to admire it. As for Sheepskin Girl, her heart was overflowing with joy as she kissed the hand of that kind mistress.

"Now I must go," she said, and in spite of their pleas, she left. Hurrying to the widow's house, she reached her own room, put away her *fışır-fışır* dress and her elegant shoes and Beyoğlu's ring, and slipped into bed before the rest had returned. Not even Beyoğlu had been quick enough to see which way she had gone.

And *how* the women all talked the next morning about the beautiful stranger! "Sheepskin Girl," said the widow, "what a pity you did not see her dance. So graceful she was, and so gracious! She must surely be my Beyoğlu's bride."

As for Beyoğlu, he, too, was determined to wed the beautiful stranger. That very day, he made preparations to find the caravan belonging to the girl's father. While he and two of his friends readied their horses and their saddlebags, all of the widow's servants baked breads and sweets for the widow's son and his companions to eat along the way. Sheepskin Girl found a bit of leftover dough, slipped Beyoğlu's ring inside it, and baked it with the rest.

"Oh, Sheepskin Girl!" the others said. "You *can't* send such a small, ugly loaf with our young master!" And they were ready to throw it into the trash.

But Beyoğlu heard the fuss, and said, "Never mind. Let her put it with the rest. You never know—we may need it along the way." And Sheepskin Girl's odd little loaf was packed at the very bottom of Beyoğlu's saddlebag.

The three companions rode here and there, asking along every road leading from the town about a caravan that had left the town at such and such a time. But no one had seen the caravan, no matter how many people the companions asked. At last, they had tried everything they could think

227

of, and they stopped once more by a fountain to refresh themselves and to eat a bit.

When they searched their saddlebags, the only food left was that odd little loaf that Sheepskin Girl had made. "We can moisten this with a bit of water from the fountain and share it. At least it's *something*," said Beyoğlu. But his friends laughed at such a notion and rode off toward the next village to seek something better to eat.

Beyoğlu, determined to eat the loaf, sprinkled a little water on it and bit into it. Suddenly he bit down on something hard. It was a ring—*his* ring.

"Come back! Come back!" he called to his friends, and they came to him, curious about his excitement. "We have been seeking the stranger here and there, but all the time she has been in my own house," he said. And he told them about the dancing stranger and the ring. Then he sent them home at full speed to ask his mother to start the wedding preparations, for he had found the bride he was seeking.

When he arrived home, riding at a leisurely pace, his mother met him at the door. "We are making ready for your wedding, my son," she said happily. "But where is your bride?" And she looked in vain for the beautiful stranger.

"Mother, you will see her soon enough," said Beyoğlu. "But now I'd like a cup of coffee and a bit of rest. The coffee must be brought to me only by Sheepskin Girl."

His mother was surprised, but she hurried to the kitchen to order the coffee. Every other servant asked to take the coffee to the young master, for he was a great favorite, but Beyoğlu's mother insisted that Sheepskin Girl alone must go—after she had tidied her hair a bit.

Sheepskin Girl hurried to her room and put on her *fışır-fışır* dress under her sheepskin dress. After brushing her hair until it shone, she went to the kitchen for the coffee and carried it directly to Beyoğlu's room.

Beyoğlu met her at the door, and as soon as she had entered the room, he shut the door and locked it. "So, my dear, we shall see what a treasure has been in this house, and none of us knew it at all." And, taking a large pair of shears, he cut the sheepskin dress here and there, until it lay in pieces at Sheepskin Girl's feet. And there stood the beautiful stranger in her *fışır-fışır* dress.

"Mother!" Beyoğlu called. "Come and see!" And he unlocked the door and invited his mother inside.

The widow saw the bits of sheepskin on the floor, and cried, "What have you done, my son? Have you *killed* the poor girl?"

"No, no, indeed, Mother!" laughed Beyoğlu. "Only look at my bride, the beauty that was all the time hiding under that sheepskin!"

And the widow stared in amazement at the lovely stranger, soon to be her son's wife. As for Perihan, no longer Sheepskin Girl, she kissed the wid-

ow's hand and touched it to her forehead. And there on the widow's wrist was the gold bracelet . . .

"May I ask one special thing of you?" Perihan said. "I *do* have a father—not a caravan owner, but a fine man who lives on the other side of the mountain. I'd like very much to send for him so that he could be here for our wedding."

"Of course, my dear," said Beyoğlu and his mother, almost in one voice. A messenger was sent at once to Perihan's father, and in good time her father came, bringing the second gold bracelet.

On the fortieth day of Perihan's quest, she and Beyoğlu were married, in a wedding that lasted forty days and forty nights. When *their* wishes were fulfilled, Perihan's father slipped the second gold bracelet on the wrist of Beyoğlu's mother, and they, too, had a wedding that lasted forty days and forty nights.

Long life for them, and a story for us.

The Quest for a Nightingale

Once there was and once there wasn't, long ago, when Allah had many creatures, and to speak too much was a sin—well, in those times there was a padishah who had a splendid mosque built, the largest and most beautiful mosque in all the land. As the wise men of the kingdom were feasting their eyes on this mosque, along came an old man with white hair and a long white beard. After looking at the mosque this way and that way, he said to the padishah, "The mosque itself is beautiful, but it lacks something."

"Oh?" said the padishah.

"Yes," said the old man. "If you could only bring to this mosque the Hazaran nightingale, its singing would make this mosque a perfect tribute to Allah." As soon as he had finished speaking, the old man disappeared, and the winds blew in his place.

"Hızır! That must have been Hızır!" the wise men said.

When the padishah realized that it had indeed been Hızır who had spoken, he called his three sons to him and said, "You must each take a saddlebag full of gold and mount your horses and go in search of the Hazaran nightingale. Where it is to be found I do not know, but it must be found and brought back so that we can complete this work to the glory of Allah."

The three sons immediately prepared themselves and their horses for what must certainly be a long and difficult quest. Then they kissed their father's and mother's hands, mounted their horses, and rode away together.

230

Along their way, they came to a triple fork in the road. Each chose a road to take, and the youngest, choosing last, had only one road to choose, one marked "The Road of No Return." Let us now leave the two older brothers and follow the youngest brother on his journey along the road of no return.

Soon after he had entered this road, the youngest son met that same old man, with white hair and a long white beard. The man said to him, "I know where you are going. You are seeking the Hazaran nightingale. You will be able to find the nightingale, all right, but you must follow my advice. You must ride for two more days, and then you will see a large house without a door. Shout there for somebody to come, and when someone appears, you will ask that person to accept you in the house for the night as a guest. If you are accepted, go on in. If you are not accepted, take this sword I am giving you and defend yourself with it." And the old man gave him a sword with a blade as sharp as a razor. Then he disappeared, and the winds blew in his place.

The youngest son rode for two more days. True enough, there was a large house with no door. He shouted for someone to come. When a beautiful girl looked out of a window, he said, "Please, lady, I am hungry and thirsty. Will you give me food and lodging for the night?"

The girl answered, "I should be glad to let you in, but I am the prisoner of a giant here. If he comes home and finds you here, he will eat you."

"Give me something to eat, and I shall take care of the giant," the young man answered.

"Very well," said the girl, and she let him in and then fed him plentifully.

A short while later, a seven-headed giant approached the house, *gurul, gurul,* with his footsteps making a sound like thunder. The young man drew the sword given to him by Hızır, charged at the seven-headed giant, and killed him. Then he returned to the large house.

The girl, grateful for being saved from the giant, asked the young man to remain with her in that house. The young man said, "I cannot stay, for I must seek the Hazaran nightingale."

"Very well. Some distance ahead of you, however, there is an eight-headed giant with whom you will have to fight. I am afraid that you cannot survive against him."

"*İnşallah,* I shall be safe. You remain here, and I shall come for you on my return." To himself, the young man said, "She is somewhat older than I am. She would make a good bride for my first brother."

He left the girl, and after three or five days, he reached the land of the eight-headed giant. When he came to the home of the giant, he shouted for someone to come, and again a girl looked out of a window. He said, "Please, lady, I am hungry and thirsty. Will you give me food and lodging for the night?"

232

The girl said, "I am sorry that I cannot give you bread or anything else that you could eat. The giant who keeps me imprisoned here brings home nothing but raw meat. We eat that, but you could not eat it until you had become as accustomed to it as I have."

Shortly after that, the eight-headed giant arrived, and as soon as he saw the young man, the two of them began to fight. Following a very long struggle, the young man finally managed to cut off all eight heads of the giant. Then he entered the house where the girl lived and said to her, "I had not taken time to notice it before, but you are a very beautiful girl. You will make a splendid bride for my second-oldest brother. As for me, I must leave immediately for the land of the Hazaran nightingale. I must capture that nightingale and take it to my father."

"Very well, but along your way you will have to meet and fight the nine-headed female giant. She is so powerful that no one has been able to defeat her. And what is worse, she has nine sons, each as powerful as she is. I have some advice for you: Approach her secretly, grab one of her breasts, and nurse from it. You will thus become her milk son, and she will not do you any harm. She will also then protect you from her nine powerful sons."

After riding for a week, the young man reached the house of the nine-headed giant. He saw from a distance that she was sound asleep, so he approached her very, very quietly, grabbed one of her huge breasts, and began to nurse from it. The giant awoke at once and said, "*Aman, aman!* Who told you to suck my breast? You are now my milk son, and I must protect you." She hid him in a split in the sole of her foot.

Shortly after this, her nine sons, each slightly larger than all the others, arrived. Each of them had nine heads, like their mother. They said in one voice, "Mother, we smell human flesh."

"No, you are mistaken, my sons," she said.

"But we smell a human being, and we shall search for it," the oldest replied, and they did search. But they could find nothing.

She then said to them, "Suppose a human being should come here and nurse from my breast. What would you call him?"

"We would call him our brother," they answered.

The mother then let the young man come out of the split in the sole of her foot. "This little man is your brother, then," she said.

"Very well. We shall accept him as our brother," said the oldest one. And the rest agreed.

The giant mother then asked the young man, "Who are you, and where are you going?"

"I am the son of a padishah, and I am going to find the Hazaran nightingale and take it back to sing in the mosque which my father built."

"Well, the land of the Hazaran nightingale is very far away from here, but my giant sons can accompany you as far as the boundary of my territory. From there on, you will have to go alone. The nightingale you seek is in the palace of the padishah of fairies. It will take a true hero to capture that bird and get it home safely."

His giant brothers took the young man as far as the river which marked the boundary of their territory. "We cannot take you farther," said the oldest, "for we cannot cross running water. But I can give you some useful advice. If you heed this advice, you may well succeed in capturing the Hazaran nightingale.

"On this side of the river," he said, "there is a white rock beneath which lies a bridle. Take the bridle from under the rock, strike it on the surface of the water, and wait for a river horse to rise to the surface. Mount this horse, which will carry you across to the opposite shore. There you will see a forest. Break a branch from a tree in this forest and then continue on your journey. You will come to a lion and a horse; in front of the lion there will be a heap of grass, and in front of the horse there will be a heap of meat. Give the grass to the horse and the meat to the lion, and then go on. Along the way you will come to two gates; one will be standing open and the other one will be closed. Hit the closed gate with the branch, and it will open. Pass through the gate, and you will come to a fountain through the spout of which runs muddy water. Take a drink from this fountain, and praise the fountain by saying, 'What fine water!' You will then pass through a bushy area where you will break a branch from a thornbush and say, 'How beautiful it smells!' All of these things will assist you in your quest. You will then reach the garden of the padishah of fairies, where you will see many fairies. If they are asleep, their eyes will be shining; if their eyes are not shining, then the fairies will be awake. If they are awake, be careful not to go near them. The nightingale which you seek is in a golden cage in this garden, and a thousand fairies guard it."

The young man thanked his giant brothers, and they turned toward home. As for the young man, he found the white rock on the riverbank and took from beneath it the bridle that he saw there. When he struck this bridle on the surface of the river, a river horse arose and came to him. He mounted this river horse and was carried to the opposite bank. There he saw a huge forest, which he entered and where he broke a branch from one of the trees. He then came to a place where there stood a lion and a horse. Before the lion there was a heap of grass, and before the horse there was a heap of meat. He stopped and switched this food so that the meat was in front of the lion and the grass was in front of the horse. Then he continued on his way. Soon he came to the two gates, one open and the other closed. When he struck the closed door with the branch, it swung open. Passing through this gate, he soon came to a fountain through the spout of which ran muddy water. He took a drink from this fountain and said, "What fine water!" Next he came to a bushy area. He broke a branch from a thornbush and smelled it, saying, "How beautiful it smells!" Finally he reached the garden of the padishah of fairies.

All of the fairies were asleep, with their eyes shining like tinned kettles. He found the golden cage, grasped it, and started running from the garden with it. But the fairies, who heard the nightingale begin to sing, awoke and shouted to the thornbush, "Catch that man! He has our padishah's Hazaran nightingale!"

The thornbush answered, "You called me prickly bush and did not praise me, but that young man admired my scent. *I* will not catch him!"

The fairies then called to the fountain, "Catch that man! He has our padishah's Hazaran nightingale!"

The fountain answered, "You have always mocked me and refused to drink from me, but that young man drank from my spout and said, 'What fine water!' *I* will not catch him!"

Then the fairies shouted, "Gate, catch that man! He has our padishah's Hazaran nightingale!"

The gate answered, "I remained closed for seven years, but that young man opened me. *I* will not catch him!"

The fairies then shouted, "Lion, catch that man! He has our padishah's Hazaran nightingale!"

The lion answered, "I had been eating nothing but grass for seven years until that man gave me meat to eat. *I* will not catch him!"

The young man came running to the river, where the river horse still waited for him, and the horse carried him to the opposite shore. When he

235

finally got back to the home of the nine-headed giants, he found a beautiful girl whom he had not seen there before. The nine-headed mother suggested that the young man marry the beautiful girl. He took this girl with him and returned to the land of the eight-headed giant. There he took the girl from the dead giant's house and went on to the house of the seven-headed giant. He also took the girl awaiting him in that dead giant's house. Then he started home with the three girls.

Before he had reached the triple forking of the road, he met the white-haired, white-bearded old man again. This man, Hızır, said, "Your brothers have not yet returned."

Leaving the three girls and the nightingale with Hızır, the young man now went in search of his brothers. He finally found them, with none of their money left and in miserable condition. He bought horses for them, and all three rode together toward the place where they had separated.

After they had reached that place and had started toward home again, however, the two older brothers became very jealous of the youngest one. The second-oldest said, "He found the nightingale, and he also chose the most beautiful of the three girls for himself."

"Furthermore," said the oldest one, "he is our father's favorite son, and our father will probably make him the next padishah. We must do something to get rid of him."

Along the way, they came to a well. "Ah!" said the oldest son. "Here is our chance to put an end to our brother." So they lowered him on a rope to get water for all of them, but when he had reached the bottom, they let the rope drop into the well. When his chosen fiancée saw this, she cried out in protest, but the older brothers ordered that both she and the other two girls remain silent about the whole matter.

Taking the nightingale and the three girls with them, the two older brothers returned to their father's palace, and with great ceremony the nightingale was placed in the mosque. But the nightingale would not sing at all. They waited and waited, but the bird refused to sing. Fifteen days passed like that, and many scholars tried to discover why the Hazaran nightingale would not sing.

In the meantime, the padishah of fairies had grown very angry about the loss of her nightingale. She came and built a palace right opposite the palace of the padishah who had had the mosque built. She sent this message to the padishah: "I want the person who killed the giants and took my nightingale. Otherwise, I shall destroy your entire land!"

The oldest son of the padishah was sent to her at once, and he said, "I am the man who killed the giants and took the Hazaran nightingale."

"What did you see along the way?" she asked.

"Well, I found your palace and stole the nightingale."

"No, you were not the man," said the padishah of fairies. "Go back and tell the person who really took the nightingale to come and tell me his story."

He returned to his father's palace and sent the second-oldest son. "I am the man," this one said.

"Tell me what you did along the way," said the padishah of fairies.

"I went, I stole, and I returned," he said.

"No, you were not the man, either," said the padishah of fairies. "Send me the man who really did these things."

Meanwhile, it happened that a caravan passing along the road came to the well where the young man had been left. When the camel drivers lowered a bucket into the well for water, the young man grabbed it and was thus pulled up to the surface. He went with that caravan to the next village, where he found a job as a servant.

Since the youngest son had not been at the palace—and who knows where he might be?—the padishah of fairies announced that everyone in the kingdom between the ages of seven and seventy must march past her palace to the mosque. When the one who had stolen the nightingale passed, surely the Hazaran nightingale would begin to sing. In that way, the one who had stolen the nightingale would be discovered.

Everyone between the ages of seven and seventy—slim, fat, tall, short, handsome, ugly, married, single, brave, cowardly—walked past the palace of the padishah of fairies to the mosque, but the Hazaran nightingale still did not sing. A second announcement was made by the criers: "Who has not walked past the palace? Bring the names of all those who have not walked past the palace of the padishah of fairies to the mosque!"

Then the man who had employed the youngest son came to the padishah of that land. "Your Majesty, there is a young man who is part of my household who has not walked past the palace."

"Tell him to come at once, then, and walk past the front of the palace to the mosque," ordered the padishah.

When the youngest son had walked past the palace and was approaching the mosque, the Hazaran nightingale began to sing, with a voice so heartbreakingly beautiful that all who heard it began to weep for joy. But, "Catch that young man!" called the padishah of fairies, and the youngest son was caught. As she looked at the young man, the padishah of fairies was certain that this was indeed the one who had stolen the nightingale. But she must make sure that this was so. "Tell me, young man, how you managed to capture my Hazaran nightingale," she asked.

"When my brothers and I set out to capture the nightingale," he began, "I took the road marked 'The Road of No Return.' I killed a seven-headed giant and took from his house a girl whom he had imprisoned there. Then I killed an eight-headed giant and also took a girl whom he had held captive. When I arrived at the home of a nine-headed female giant, I nursed from her breast and thus became her milk son. Her nine nine-headed giant sons then

237

accepted me as their brother and helped me to enter your land. I took a bridle from beneath a white rock on the bank of a river. When I struck the surface of the river with this bridle, a river horse arose and carried me across the river. I entered a forest, where I broke a branch from a tree, and I took the branch with me. Along the way I came to a lion with grass before him and a horse with meat before him, so I switched the food so that the meat was before the lion and the grass was before the horse. When I came to two gates, I struck the closed gate with the branch, and it opened. Beyond the gate I found a fountain from whose spout ran muddy water. Drinking from this fountain, I said, 'What fine water!' When I reached a bushy area, I broke a branch from a thornbush, smelled it, and said, 'What a beautiful scent!' Then I came to the garden of your palace, where I saw many fairies asleep with their eyes shining like tinned kettles.

"Then I grabbed the golden cage of the Hazaran nightingale and started to run from the garden. But when the nightingale began to sing, it awakened the fairies, and they called to the thornbush, 'Catch that man! He has our padishah's Hazaran nightingale!' The thornbush answered, 'You called me prickly bush and did not praise me, but that young man admired my scent. *I* will not catch him!' The fairies then called to the fountain, 'Catch that man! He has our padishah's Hazaran nightingale!' But the fountain answered, 'You have always mocked me and refused to drink from me, but that young man drank from my spout and said, "What fine water!" *I* will not catch him!' Then the fairies shouted to the gate, 'Gate, catch that man! He has our padishah's Hazaran nightingale!' The gate answered, 'I had remained closed for seven years, but that young man opened me. *I* will not catch him!' The fairies then shouted to the lion, 'Lion, catch that man! He has our padishah's Hazaran nightingale!' The lion answered. 'I had been eating nothing but grass for seven years until that man gave me meat to eat. *I* will not catch him!'

"When I reached the river, the river horse was waiting to carry me to the other side. At the home of the nine-headed giants there was a beautiful girl whom I had not seen before. My giant mother suggested that I marry this girl. I got from the house of the eight-headed giant the girl I had left there for my second-oldest brother, and from the house of the seven-headed giant the girl I had left there for my oldest brother.

"When I met my brothers on the way home, they left me in a well and returned home with the nightingale and the three girls. Camel drivers in a caravan pulled me from the well, and I got a job in the next village. Today I was brought here by order of the padishah."

"You have told the truth," said the padishah of fairies, "and the Hazaran nightingale is now yours. I shall also be yours, if you will accept me as your wife. I once made a vow that I should offer myself in marriage to the young man who proved my superior."

When the padishah of that land had heard the news, he ordered the

238

oldest and second-oldest sons put to death. The youngest son was then made padishah. He married both the youngest girl he had brought back and the padishah of fairies.

Three apples fell from the sky, the first for the teller of this tale, the second for the listener, and the third for the one who says, "I'll tell it, too!"

Guide to Pronunciation of the Turkish Alphabet

Turkish Alphabet: *a, â, b, c, ç, d, e, f, g, ğ, h, ı, i, j, k, l, m, n, o, ö, p, r, s, ş, t, u, ü, v, y, z*

Sounded as in English: *b, d, f, l, m, n, p, t, v, z*

Not used at all: *q, w, x*

Difficult sound to make: *ğ*. Suggestion: Lengthen the sound of the vowel that immediately precedes it (example: **a**ğa) and give the *ğ* no sound at all.

Character Pronunciation	Example
a as *o* in *lobby*	**hamam** (Turkish bathhouse)
â as *ya* in *kayak*	*lâla* (tutor for boy; often lifelong companion)
c as *j* in *judge*	*hoca* (Muslim preacher/teacher)
ç as *ch* in *chess*	*bekçi* (night watchman)
e as *e* in *get*	*ezan* (Muslim call to prayer)
g as *g* in *go*	*Gülistan* (girl's name)
h as *h* in *happen*	*hacı* (Muslim who has completed the pilgrimage to Mecca)
ı as *u* in *run*	*kadı* (Muslim judge in pre-Republican Turkey)
i as *i* in *rich*	*imam* (Muslim prayer leader)
j as *s* in *pleasure*	*ejder* (dragon)
k as *k* in *kitchen*	*rakı* (Turkish alcoholic liquor)
o as *o* in *coat*	*Bolu* (a province in Turkey)
ö as *ir* in *skirt*	*köse* (beardless man)
r as *r* in *rabbit*	*Ramazan* (Muslim fasting period)
s as *s* in *sacrifice*	*sofra* (low dining table)
ş as *sh* in *shipwreck*	*mışıl mışıl* (sound of soft snoring)
u as *u* in *pull*	*Murad* (boy's name)
ü as *ew* in *pew*	*üh-üh-üh-üh-üh-h-h* (sound of a rooster crowing)
y as *y* in *yesterday*	*yayla* (high plateau, used for summer pasture)

Glossary of Turkish Terms and Folk Elements

Turkish words or words derived from the Turkish are rendered in the Turkish alphabet.

ABLUTIONS Required ritual washing by Muslims preparatory to prayer; subsequent to various other acts

AĞA Rural landholder, not aristocratic, but often wealthy and sometimes powerful; by extension, used as term of respect following a person's name, as Mehmet *Ağa*

ALEYKÜMSELÂM! Response of Muslim to another Muslim's greeting *Selâmünaleyküm!*; meaning: "And peace to you, too!"

ALLAH The Muslim term for God

AMAN! Expression used when surprised, distressed, or dismayed; stronger forms: *Aman, aman!* and *Aman, aman,* Allah!

ANKA BIRD A gigantic bird similar to Roc of *The Arabian Nights*; thought to be long-lived, fearsome, able to carry large animals or people in its talons

APPLE OF CONCEPTION Apple given by Hızır or some unidentified dervish to childless man; apple to be peeled, each partner to eat half of flesh of apple, and peelings of apple to be fed to best mare in stable; pregnancy immediate; child and colt to be named by giver of apple

ARAP Peasant version of "Arab"; an enormously large supernatural jinnlike creature with somewhat Negroid features; assumed by most peasant narrators to be black, though Arabs not in fact black; performs tasks ordered by one summoning him

BAGGY TROUSERS (Turkish: *şalvar*) Traditional rural dress, warm in winter and cool in summer; trousers baggy in seat, low in crotch, gathered at waist, and narrow at ankles; men's *şalvar* wool, solid-colored black, gray, or brown

BATH CLOG (Turkish: *nalın*) 3- or 4-inch-thick wooden clog worn in Turkish bath; usually beautifully decorated; keeps bather's feet above water splashed from basins

BATH DIPPER (Turkish: *hamam tası*) A round metal handleless bowl with a centered indentation on the lower side of the bottom; used to pour water over oneself after soaping at Turkish bath

BAYRAM Feast day or days, especially those following end of Ramazan; sweet treats exchanged, and respects paid by children and young people to their elders, especially parents; includes both religious and government holidays

241

BEAT THE KNEES Traditional way for both men and women to express deep grief

BEKÇİ Night watchman in town or city

BEKTAŞİ Member of a freethinking order of Muslim dervishes often blasphemous and given to drinking and to moral looseness

BEY Formerly a title inferior to "pasha" and superior to "*ağa*"; used as term of respect following a name (as Ahmet Bey) or as term signifying "gentleman" or "chief"

BEYOĞLU Meaning: "son of the bey"; used instead of personal name

BİSMİLLÂH! Meaning: "in the name of Allah"; used by Muslims when beginning any task or undertaking

BLOODY SHIRT Evidence required by one who has ordered the killing of someone and wants proof of completion of the deed

BREAD AND CHEESE Expression used to suggest "daily food"

BREASTS OF FEMALE GIANT In Turkish tales, breasts flung over shoulders when kneading bread; nursing undetected from breast important to afford hero status as milk child and thus protected

CHANCES OF A TURK ARE THREE, THE. Turkish proverb

CHIMNEY LOCKED Expression indicating all available means of access to house or room closed, preventing entry or listening by others

CHOICE BY ARROW-SHOOTING Method used to determine which candidate will win prize by being first to recover arrow or which bride (or groom) will be selected by arrow's landing on her house (his house)

CHOICE BY BALL-THROWING Method used to determine which groom chosen by being the one hit by the ball thrown by the princess

CİRİT A game played by men on horseback armed with sharp-pointed sticks (similar to javelins)

COFFEEHOUSE Place restricted to men for drinking of tea and coffee (usually tea) and socializing; part of coffeehouse often extends outdoors; forerunner of European sidewalk cafés

COFFIN In villages, a wooden box with four handles, one at each corner, for carrying deceased to graveyard; returned to mosque yard after burial of corpse wrapped in shroud; used as needed by members of Muslim community

CRIER Messenger sent out to announce loudly through the streets an order or an important piece of news; in many areas, criers still being used in twentieth century where other media unavailable

CUŞ! Onomatopoeia for water being poured

ÇUBUK A kind of water pipe for smoking

ÇÜŞ! Turkish equivalent for "Whoa!"

DERVİSH A member of any of various Muslim religious orders dedicated to a life of poverty and chastity

EFFENDİ Term of respect added to a personal name (as Ahmet Effendi) or, more recently debased, used in addressing children and servants

EYVAH! Turkish expression of distress; meaning: "alas!"

EZAN The five-times-daily call to prayer from the minaret

FATHER Term of respect used by younger person to older male not member of family; other similar terms of address to unrelated individuals: aunt, daughter, grandfather, grandmother, uncle, son

FIRMAN Official order or directive issued by or in the name of a ruler such as a sultan or a padishah; obedience to the order required

FIŞIR-FIŞIR Onomatopoeia for rustling sound made by taffeta or similar fabric in its movement

FORTIETH ROOM In many Turkish tales, the forbidden room, one not to be opened

FORTY DAYS AND FORTY NIGHTS Formulaic period of time for wedding festivities or for completing an assigned task or quest

FORTY SWORDS OR FORTY MULES? (Turkish: *Kırk satırmı? Kırk katırmı?*) Choice often offered to villain after villainy revealed; if forty mules chosen, villain tied part by part to forty mules then whipped to a gallop, thus tearing villain apart

FORTY THIEVES Traditional number of members of *any* given group, whether of thieves or female servants or pilgrims or hunting companions

FOUNTAIN Any public source of water, most often supplied through a faucet or faucets; sometimes enclosed to provide a round trough for watering animals

FRIDAY NOON SERVICE The holiest of the Muslim prayer services in the entire week, since Friday the traditional Muslim Sabbath; a sermon usually preached at this service

GENDARME Officer assigned to maintain order in village, neighborhood, or area of countryside; now, member of army forces designated to serve Ministry of Interior

GIANTS AND WATER Giants, witches, and other supernatural creatures still believed unable to cross running water

HACI One who has completed the pilgrimage to Mecca, one of five basic tenets of Islamic faith

HAMAM Public bathhouse to which people go not only to bathe but to enjoy social gathering; certain sections for men and others for women, or certain days for men and others for women; no mixing of sexes at *hamam*

HANIM Title of respect, meaning "lady," used when addressing a woman; example: Ayşe *Hanım*

HAREM The women's quarters in any residence or complex; most often associated with those quarters in the sultan's palace, but not limited to that site; viewed by Muslims as protective of women from encounters with males outside nuclear family

HAZARAN A place in Iran reputed to be source of special breed of nightingale

HELVA A dessert or candy made from sesame oil, farina or flour, and syrup; occasionally, nuts and spices added

HERROP! Turkish for "Hurrah!"

HIZIR Most frequently mentioned Muslim saint; guardian of the virtuous and deserving; last-minute rescuer in time of danger; usually represented as an old man with white hair and long white beard; disappears as soon as mission accomplished

HIS BONES ARE MINE, BUT HIS FLESH IS YOURS. Statement made by parent to master of new apprentice or to teacher of new student; permission thus given for physical punishment as needed, short of outright abuse

HOCA Muslim preacher or teacher, with hoca teaching either in mosque or in school

HOLLY A shrub believed since Roman times (cited in Pliny) capable of reducing even the wildest and fiercest animal to obedience

İMAM Prayer leader in mosque; also a religious leader in Islamic faith

İNŞALLAH! Term meaning "if Allah wills"; said when one states a plan or expresses a desire for something

IRON SHOES AND AN IRON STAFF Traditional equipment provided to hero or heroine for use in quest of lost sweetheart or spouse

JINN A supernatural being appearing or able to be summoned to perform unusual tasks; usually large and fearsome

KADI Judge of Muslim canonical law in pre-Republican Turkey; in folktales, any judge, religious or secular, past or contemporary

KAF Location of the Mountains of Kaf, part of Muslim mythology, and thought to form the rim of the world around the edges of the Circumambient Ocean

KAVAL Wooden shepherd's pipe, or flute, similar to the modern-day recorder, and used by shepherds to calm and direct their sheep and to entertain themselves

KAZA Equivalent of "county" in the States; political subdivision of a province in Turkey

KELOĞLAN A boy or man bald from a scalp disease; in folktales, degraded but clever and lucky; next to Nasreddin Hoca, the most popular folk hero

KIRK Turkish word for the number 40; "kırk gün kırk gece," Turkish for "forty days and forty nights," found in many Turkish folktales to complete the plot just prior to the formulaic ending

KİSMET Fate, or fortune

KÖSE A man with little or no beard, bowed legs, a heart-shaped face, and a high voice; in folktales, a villain, treacherous and highly untrustworthy

KURUŞ A small copper coin; in earlier times, 100 kuruş equal to one lira; with lira now severely devalued, kuruş worthless

LANGUAGE OF ANIMALS Understanding of this language, held traditionally

244

by the Biblical Solomon, given as reward in tales for extraordinary service; agent of gift often snake

LANGUAGE OF PLANTS This language, important in healing, understood by some in folktales either as reward for rescue or aid or as evidence of generosity of giver

LÂLA Tutor for a boy; often becomes his lifelong advisor

LIGHT IN WEIGHT BUT HEAVY IN VALUE Traditional description for items taken from home or treasury when leaving on a journey

MACE A heavy club, often with a spiked metal head

MANGAL Metal charcoal-fueled, portable one-burner stove used now in rural and marginal homes as both space heater and cookstove

MEVLÜT SERVICE Memorial service at which famous cantata on birth and life of Mohammed, the Prophet, performed; audience participation at certain points; candy, rose water, and sherbet normally served to guests

MIŞIL MIŞIL Onomatopoeia for the softest kind of sleeping sound, no louder than that made by a sleeping baby

MILITARY SERVICE Mandatory in Turkey for all males between 18 and 40, with average service two years; preceding Republic, males expected to serve in the military as needed; failure to meet today's military obligation cause for shame to entire family

MILK SIBLINGS In everyday life as in folktales, babies occasionally nursed by other than own mothers to cement relationships among families; milk siblings expected to help and protect one another

MİMBER Staircase, enclosed and usually rather ornate, leading up to the pulpit in the mosque

MINARET A tall, slender tower attached to a mosque and encircled with one or more balconies, from one of which the *ezan* chanted five times daily to call faithful Muslims to prayer; encloses a narrow, steep, winding staircase usually without handrail

MONSTROUS OFFSPRING Traditionally, result of rash request made by childless person in appealing for a child; request for "even a serpent" honored

NAMAZ Turkish term for Muslim religious service; five held daily

NASREDDİN HOCA Best-known Turkish folk character; believed to have lived in time of Tamerlane, but Hoca anecdotes universally appropriate; sometimes wise, sometimes foolish, but always entirely human; subject of thousands of anecdotes; served as preacher, teacher, and occasionally village judge

NINE MONTHS, NINE DAYS, AND NINE HOURS Traditional gestation period for child conceived as result of apple of conception

ONE IS AS WISE AS ONE'S HEAD, NOT ONE'S YEARS. Turkish proverb

ÖF! Turkish equivalent of "Ugh!"

PADİSHAH Ruler or king of a country or of a class of subjects (padishah of

245

birds, padishah of fairies, padishah of snakes); has power of life and death over his subjects

PART WITH YOUR HEAD, BUT NOT WITH YOUR SECRET. Turkish proverb

PASHA A high military or civil official; title sometimes added to a name as mark of respect or flattery: Murad Pasha

PASSED OVER YOUR HEAD Traditional equivalent for "happened"

PATUR KİTUR Onomatopoeia for running upstairs or hurrying somewhere

PERMISSION TO LEAVE Custom of a guest's asking his host's permission to leave still strong in Turkey and in tales; a mark of courtesy and good breeding

PEŞTAMAL Large, colorful, decorative cloth used by woman as bath wrapper when bathing at Turkish bath

PETITION WRITERS Sidewalk secretaries, long familiar sights in Turkish towns and cities, as service to clients unable to read or write and needing to have letters written; nowadays, equipped with typewriters, but earlier confined to pen and ink for their work

PİLAV A rice dish, often including pine nuts and dried currants, and sometimes bits of meat such as chicken; a staple item in Turkish diet

PILGRIMAGE For Muslims, a journey at a specified time to the holy city of Mecca to perform certain rituals and prayers; the pilgrimage one of the five basic tenets of Islamic faith; on return, pilgrim titled *hacı*; both men and women included on pilgrimage

PRAYER BEADS A string of 99 beads, each representing one of the "names," or attributes, of Allah; beads told one by one, named as moved along string, to be sure to please Allah with name preferred most by Him that day; similar to rosary

PRRRT! Onomatopoeia for birds' wings in flight

PUT MY WORDS IN YOUR POCKET. Expression meaning "remember them"

PUTT-A-KİTT-A! PUTT-A-KİTT-A! Sound made by sticks or mallets striking a board or a head

RAKI A strong alcoholic beverage made from rice, molasses, or grain and having an anise flavor; when mixed with water, becomes milky in appearance, thus often called lion's milk

RAMAZAN The 30-day fasting period observed each year by faithful Muslims; during daylight periods of this month, absolutely nothing eaten or drunk; exempted from fasting: children, invalids, pregnant women, and travelers; nighttime hours spent in eating and socializing and storytelling

RIVER HORSE Horse arising from river to mate with land mare or to provide special service for hero in folktale; has magic powers

SALT IN A CUT Device used by hero or heroine to keep self awake to detect a dragon, an intruder, or one performing services secretly

SASH A cummerbund; a long, wide strip of cloth wound several times around the waist of a man or woman, both to carry valuables such as money and to provide abdominal support while doing heavy work

SEA STALLION Horse arising from sea to mate with mare on land; colt born of mating equipped with special traits and powers

SEAT Seat of honor in village home the one exactly opposite the door; presumptuous of someone not being honored to take that seat; humiliating to be asked to move down (toward the door); hero in folktale considered worthy of seat of honor

SELÂMÜNALEYKÜM! Greeting given by one Muslim to another when meeting as strangers; meaning: "Peace to you!"; designed to show intention to be cordial

SHERBET In Turkey, a cold sweet fruit drink served at festivals, used to announce a birth or some other happy event, and enjoyed during outings at Turkish bath

SHROUD A white piece of cloth 30 feet long and 5 feet wide wrapped around the corpse of a Muslim after the body ritually washed for burial; body buried without material possessions and without coffin

SOFRA Dining table with legs only 4 or 5 inches long; diners sit on floor around table to eat

SOLOMON (Biblical figure) Found in many tales in Turkish oral tradition; sometimes confused by narrators with Süleyman the Magnificent (sixteenth-century Turkish sultan); understands language of birds and animals

STATE BIRD Upon death of childless padishah, padishah's dove (the state bird) set free to fly over gathered crowd to select new padishah; one on whose head the dove alights named new padishah

STREET CRIES Used by sellers of produce and other goods, both along streets and in marketplace, to call attention to worth of product being sold; also used in seeking workers to fill certain jobs

SULTAN A Muslim ruler having the power of life and death over his subjects; in tales tends to govern more territory than a padishah

TEA SELLER One carrying on his back concentrated tea and an urn of hot water to serve hot tea to customers along the street; common drinking container used; cold water likewise sold along street

TEKERLEME Nonsensical rhymed beginning formula of a folktale catching listeners' attention and preparing them to hear a tale; unlikely and impossible situations described; removes listeners from everyday life, ready to enter world of the tale; sometimes used as separate tale when plot complete and conflict resolved

THREE OR FIVE Expression indicating *a few* of anything: months, coins, people, pomegranates

TINGIR MINGIR Onomatopoeia for rocking of cradle

TUKKIR, TUKKIR Onomatopoeia for cantering of a horse

UNROLL YOUR BED Refers to rural and small-town practice of using sleeping mats that can be rolled up and stored during daytime, saving space in small house for other activities; when bed needed, mat unrolled and put on sofa frame for sleeping

VİZİER A high officer during the Ottoman Empire, serving as advisor to a sultan or a padishah; safeguarded the ruler by first tasting the foods and drinks himself; not always loyal

WEDNESDAY WITCHES Small folk with tousled hair, visitors to *hamam* only on Wednesday nights, when *hamam* normally unoccupied; have power to grant wishes, to endow people with certain traits, and to punish; tend to dance and sing a nonsense song during visit; Turkish children with tousled hair called "Wednesday witches"

WITCH Person in folktales who may or may not have supernatural powers; in many narratives, simply a meddling or malicious old woman serving as an accomplice of the villain; huge pottery urn (Turkish: *küp*) used as transportation through air by witch

YAYLA High plateau, used as summer pasture

ZURNA A simple double-reed instrument usually played along with a drum in folk music, especially for weddings and festivals

Index of Tales by Title